Praise for
Hearts Among Ourselves

"Umwagarwa's prose, as narrated by Karabo, pops with inventive turns of phrase … a complex and empathetic perspective on [the Rwanda genocide's] difficult aftermath … Karabo's story provides readers with an illuminating investigation into the ways that people can dehumanize one another." *Kirkus Reviews*

"*Hearts Among Ourselves* tells both a specific history of Rwanda and its deathly conflict as well as a universal tale of disaffection. … echoes of pure beauty … a powerfully emotional tale." *BlueInk Review*

"A. Happy Umwagarwa has created a profound novel that is a love story, a coming of age story, but also a deep look into the effects of war and genocide on a population, and how ethnicity designations, hatred, and confusion don't just go away because the massacres and/or wars are over." *Jades Hughes, Writer and Editor*

"Umwagarwa uses Karabo's story to explore questions of ethnicity and identity in a deep and interesting way. I think everyone knows that the 1994 genocide was Rwandans of Hutu ethnicity massacring Rwandans of Tutsi ethnicity. … has a unique voice which truly allowed this story to come to life for me." *Stephanie Jane, Book Blogger*

"Beautifully written. Completely drew me in as a reader, to the point where I lost track of what was going on around me and became totally involved in the story. Heart-rending and real. It was a privilege to read Hearts Among Ourselves and A. Happy Umwagarwa has done a stunning job delivering a book that once you read it will stick with you for a very long time." *Holly Senecal, Book Reviewer*

"Totally intriguing, thought-stretching insights into the life of a typical young distressed girl after the 1994 Genocide against the Tutsi. Happy brings out a powerful and practical primer of the harmony and social cohesion of the societies after such brutal bloodshed, but also points out one communal approach to healing such a society and minimizing transgenerational trauma" *Dr. Joseph Ryarasa Nkurunziza, Executive Director, Never Again Rwanda*

"In 'Hearts Among Ourselves', A. Happy Umwagarwa has masterfully recreated the intricacies and complexities of the post-genocide Rwanda and the difficulties for Rwandans to grapple with the meaning and implications of their own individual and family stories in a society where the stigma attached to the 'Hutu' and 'Tutsi' groups have for long left little room for any other stories." *Um'Khonde Patrick Habamenshi, Author, Rwanda Where Souls Turn to Dust*

Hearts Among Ourselves

A Novel

A. Happy Umwagarwa

To Vivens K.,
You'll always be there,
in my best days, in my worst days.

Acknowledgments

To my editor Ms. Reba Hilbert, Dog Ear Publishing team, Wheatmark team and everybody who contributed to the editing and the publishing process of this book.

To Bliss and Crissy, my daughters, for their smiles that warm my heart, despite the thorns of life.

To Vivens, my husband, for thrilling my life with his love and support.

To the memory of my mother Thérèse and my father Canisius, for their love beyond a lifetime.

To my brothers and sisters, John, Peace, Queen, and Strong, for the bond we share.

To the memory of my brothers Touring JP and Lucky JC, for the souls that claim the dignity of their names.

To my special friends whose names are not omitted but kept a secret, for making my name a reality.

To those who are pushed back by the past and worry for the future of Rwanda, for their courage to keep moving.

To the reader who shall love me, hate me, look for me, talk to me, and end it all with a hug of impore.

To you, I mean you, now and here, reading this page.

One

The city reeked like a stinky jungle. Dogs, crows, and black kites had all sucked the blood of our innocent people. There were soldiers everywhere. The Kinyarwanda language had lost its convincing power. If you did speak it correctly, you would appear to be a born-in-Rwanda, if not a Hutu guilty party; you could be a Tutsi survivor of the killings. *"Wewe ni mtu wa aina gani?"*—which translated as *"What kind of a person are you?"*—was the question asked by the soldiers on Kigali streets with guns on their shoulders. I would move my lips and pretend not to understand Swahili. I spoke Biryogo Swahili, or a mixture of different versions of Swahili, even though my non-Swahili parents never allowed that language at the dinner table. I couldn't respond to the soldiers' question, for I did not know the kind of a person I was. I had no family. I had nobody else but Devota, a woman who used to be just a neighbor and had become the elder sister I had never had.

Living with Devota was equivalent to living with a sentence. She could not stop weeping; she carried in her womb a baby of her Hutu rapist Abdullah. I had to give my ears to Devota as she narrated how Abdullah used to force his dirty, hard-agitated organ in her soft and virgin body during the three months she had spent in his house when he and other Hutu militants hunted the Tutsis. Maybe it would also have been my fate if, after surviving the shootings of my family, Devota had not taken me out of the river of the blood of my father and sisters. To persuade Devota, Abdullah had rushed me to Kigali General Hospital, where I spent the months of April, May, and June 1994.

In January 1995, I left Biryogo. My paternal uncle Kamanzi was a colonel in the new army. He took me to live with him in Kiyovu, known as Kiyovu, of the rich people. It used to be the elite neighborhood of the previous government officials and Kigali tycoons, but after the war, it had become like a military camp. High-ranking army officers who could not live there had settled their families in relatively modern houses. Those Rwandans had returned to the country from Uganda, Burundi, Zaire, and other countries where they had lived for many years as refugees. They spoke different languages, with a not-so-perfect Kinyarwanda. Uncle Kamanzi's compound was full of dark-skinned *Kadogo* teen soldiers who proved respect to him with "yes, Afande" salutes. Being the only girl in that compound, my only companions were the ghosts of my father and sisters, who visited me in both my daytime dreams and my nightmares. I had to live. I had to survive. I had to adjust to my new life if it was life at all.

One Sunday, to get out of the boredom that smelled in the compound, I asked Uncle Kamanzi for permission to go to the Sunday Mass.

"Shema should accompany you," he said, rushing through the door.

Shema was one of the *Kadogo* soldiers, a favorite of Uncle Kamanzi, my designated caregiver and protector since the first day I entered that compound. Shema's eyes had something that prevented me from making him a companion with whom I would converse. That Sunday, Colonel Kamanzi had left me with the task to convey his instructions to that tall, dark-skinned *Kadogo* with long white teeth and a chocolate gum.

"Shema, Uncle Kamanzi said you should accompany me to St Michael Cathedral." I shyly slipped the words out.

Shema raised his hand and hit the fingertips to the forehead as if he was giving me the same salute he used to pay to Colonel Kamanzi.

I did not get what he meant by that; he had to obey Colonel Kamanzi's instructions.

After putting on my red dress, I came out and said, "Let's go." He followed me and quickly caught my steps.

We were so silent. The only sounds that played music to our ears were of the birds that decorated the tall trees of Kiyovu.

After about a hundred steps, Shema pretended to cough.

"Would you do me a favor, please?" he asked.

Walking the streets with Shema made me bite my nails, and talking to him gave me sweaty palms. Something crossed my heart, but I had to pretend I had everything under control.

"Hmm?" I asked.

"Since the day you came to live with us, I have never seen your teeth," Shema said as he played his eyes left and right. "Would you please smile? I beg you."

"Okay, here are my teeth."

"Thank you," he smiled back. "Will you also accept that whenever I am with you, we can have a conversation and smile at life?"

"A conversation? Yes. But smiling at life? No. There is nothing cheery about life."

"Indeed. But I smile so that life may be afraid of me."

"Life has never been afraid of me," I argued back. "It attacked and hurt me."

"It has done the same to me, but I chose to smile to prove to it I am still okay."

"Life hurt you too?" I asked.

"It took away my mother. I call her name, but she never responds. Hutus killed her together with all my five siblings."

"Oh, sorry, how about your father?"

"My father was killed in 1990. He had spent six months in prison undergoing torture. He was so seriously injured when he came out and succumbed to death a few days after."

Behind Shema's appearance, there was sorrow. But it was bolstering to learn that we had something in common. We were both survivors of the massacres that had targeted the Tutsi.

"I share your pain," I said.

"Now you understand why I smile, don't you? I want to show my teeth. The inner smile shall be real only when there are no more Hutus or their lookalikes in this world."

"Do you mean when there will be no Hutus in the world?" I asked. "Where will they go?"

"I wish my world shall never cross theirs."

"Hmm, unfortunately," I responded, "Hutus are there to stay."

"Karabo, they did the unspeakable to us. Look at you— if they hadn't killed your mother and father, would you be living with Colonel Kamanzi?"

His words pushed the bone from my stomach to move

to the chest. I did not want him to read the controversy from my eyes.

"Let's not talk about that. Tell me instead about how we should smile at life."

"Yeah. We should smile and show our teeth to the Hutus."

He told me more about his family, and I loved how he could throw in some jokes and make me laugh. It was the first time to have a friendly conversation with him, but not the last. From that day, he ceased to be my uncle's *Kadogo* escort, but a friend I shared much in common. Only one thing remained a puzzle: What if I had told him everything about my family? I mused.

→

On Tuesday of the following week, I was seated in the living room, listening to the radio. Shema asked if he could bring a cassette of French love songs. I accepted. That day, I had a terrible headache. Shema put in the recording and invited me to lay my head on his lap. He put one hand in my hair while the other stretched my eyebrows. It wasn't only medicine for the headache, but bemusing drugs for the whole body.

A throaty voice accompanied the radio.

"O Shema, how God loves you,
Right from the jungle battle,
And as you were still mourning your loved ones,
God sent you a red rose flower.
Let me spoil you, my Karabo.
I will protect you from the bees that rush to taste your beauty.

I will protect you from the sharp sunshine of the afternoon.
I will make sure the darkness of the night does not scare
you,
And that the sunshine of the morning does not burn your
cocoa-brown skin…"

"Shema, what are you singing?" I asked.

"I was singing that song. I was not talking to you." His big smile tickled my chest.

"But you were singing in English. Is that song in English?"

"No, it's in French. I translated. Oh, don't tell me you don't know French!"

"Okay, I don't. Please continue to translate for me. I bet your words are far better than those of Frederic Francois."

Electrical chemistry bounced in my heart. It punctured my stomach and the upper level of my legs. I wondered if that was what they called love. I had no strength to get up from his lap and run away. I closed my eyes and listened to those French love songs, as Shema stroked my hair and eyebrows. I pretended we were in some secret love corner of Paris. I forgave myself for being easygoing. Without Shema in that boring home of Uncle Kamanzi, full of men in military uniforms, I would run mad. Shema moved his hands all over my face as if he checked whether I met the *Bwiza Bwa Mashira* beauty standards. He slowly advanced to my neck. I had no strength to stop him from exploring the chest.

Suddenly, I don't know if I can say, unfortunately, the sound of Uncle's car interrupted us. Shema stood up, removed the cassette, and went outside to give some salutes to his colonel. I got up from the couch and rushed to my room. I had done something that tasted like a honeyed secret. The whole night I was with Shema in my dreams.

I dreamt about the interrupted moment, which could have led to our first kiss. I longed to lay my head on his chest and forget whether the earth turned around itself or the sun.

⟶

In the morning, the boredom in the compound of Uncle Kamanzi's house reappeared. Shema was not talking to me, and even when our eyes crossed, he would turn his head. I had to hold myself from making the first step and talking to him. He was the man. He had to make the first step, but he did not. I could not spend the whole day without talking to Shema. If he did not want to caress my hair, that was okay. But he had to know I needed him either as a friend or a brother I never had. Shema was the only person who could add some spice in my life. I came up with a plan that worked. I asked Uncle Kamanzi for permission to pay a visit to Devota, and as usual, he called Shema and instructed him to accompany me.

"Why haven't you talked to me today?" I asked after we got out of the compound.

"I had much work," Shema responded.

"Or... Is it because of yesterday?"

"Yesterday? What happened yesterday?" Shema asked, his eyes facing the sky.

"Nothing."

Shema could not keep his mouth muffled for long. On our way to Gikondo at Devota's, he told me funny stories, some real and others unreal.

Devota had given birth to a baby girl. She had named her Mbabazi. Because of the visitors, I did not find time to talk to Devota in private. She could pretend to others, but not to me. She was not as happy as a new mother should be.

The baby could cry for many minutes, and Devota would breastfeed her only for a few seconds and put her back to bed before she was satisfied. I could not say anything in front of all those strangers, including Shema, but I could not help but recall her story, which she had narrated to me after she got me out of Kigali General Hospital in July 1994. Devota read on the face of the little angel the movie of the days she had spent with the Hutu killer and rapist Abdullah. She recalled not only the pain of carrying his body as he pushed his dirty organ inside her, but also the slaps and insults. Maybe it could have been good if Devota had opted for abortion, but it was against her religious faith.

At around 6:00 p.m., we said good-bye to Devota and left. When we were a hundred meters from Uncle Kaman-zi's house, Shema stopped.

"Karabo, would you please allow me to say good-bye to you properly and wish you good night? If we go inside, I may not be able to do so."

"Hmm? Yes."

Shema crossed his arms around my body, and with hands caressing my hair, he laid his head on my shoulders, and I put mine on his chest. We spent about five minutes in that hug. I could listen to the music of Shema's heartbeat and smell the perfume of his body. He put his hands on my cheeks, stared at me for some minutes, and like how birds do it, pushed out his lips to mine.

"*Je t' aime.*" When I tried to figure out what to say, he held my hand and said, "Let's go home."

It was not a question but a statement that did not call for an answer.

We did not say any other word to each other till we arrived home and I rushed to the big house. He went to the boys' quarters, where he stayed with other soldiers.

Uncle Kamanzi was with his mother in the living room. I greeted them and rushed to my room. I had a lot to think about. What was going on between Shema and me? Why was I that easygoing? Maybe I was in love, but deep at the bottom of my conscience, I knew we could not build our relationship on a lie. Perhaps Shema had been attracted by the fact that we were both Tutsi survivors. I was puzzled. What if I had told him that the Hutu militants had only killed my father and my sisters? What would I have said about the whereabouts of my mother? I cried. I pulled my red pillow and went to sleep.

In my nightmares, I replayed the day the killers came calling the name of my father. Kalisa, Kalisa, where is that *Inyenzi* with a nose as long as a trunk of an elephant? Among them, there were many of our Biryogo neighbors. They had machetes, others with wooden clubs, and a few of them had guns. Many of them were in the *Interahamwe* militia uniforms, tailored from African loincloth of green, red, yellow, and black colors. They did not look like human beings. Their eyes were like those of roaring lions that scared the whole jungle and pushed impala and zebra out of it. I replayed the movie of how they killed us. I was lying in so much blood with so much pain in my chest, not far from the armpit. I screamed. After some hours, I woke up. Uncle Kamanzi and my step-grandma were in my room. They narrated to me everything I had said and the names I had called in the night. I had called Mama in vain. I had called Papa. I had called my sisters. I had called Devota.

Step-grandma left on Saturday. During all the three days of her visit, I had not gotten a chance to speak to Shema, due to the spying eyes of an older woman. That day, I had my menstrual period, with a terrible pain in both my abdomen and my back. Uncle Kamanzi, who had no idea what I was suffering from, instructed Shema to take care of me. I lay down on the bed in my room. At around noon, someone knocked on the door. He announced himself as Shema. He was bringing to me some soup made of spinach and fish.

"Shema, I am sorry," I said. "I don't feel like eating."

"You'll have to eat. Listen, if you taste the soup, I will put in for you the French love songs and sing for you. A deal?" His eyes twinkled. "And if you refuse, I will get out."

I couldn't say no to Shema. He put in the cassette of French songs, took a spoon, and fed me like a baby. We both smiled whenever our eyes shot at each other. I didn't finish the soup. He took back the bowl to the kitchen.

"Make sure you come back as promised," I said.

"No, Princess. May we postpone the business of singing to tomorrow?"

"No. If you don't come back, I won't be happy with you. There is something I want to tell you."

"Yes, Princess."

He came back, locked the door, and sat on my bed. I laid my head on his lap as we listened to the French love songs. He caressed my hair and my eyebrows as he sang for me *"Laisse-moi t'aimer"* by Mike Brant. He moved his hands from my hair down to my neck. After a few minutes, he raised his legs to the bed and lay by my side. His cuddles killed the pain in my body. I could not get a more effective medicine. His hands reached to my breasts to stroke the nipples. The electrical fire crossed my whole body, but the brain kept its reservations. I could not stop him. Our lips found each other. His saliva was as sweet as vanilla honey. He went down to my belly button. I gently moved his hands up to restart the journey. I was not ready between my legs. With a tongue stuck in his mouth, eyes that had turned red, and a strong body scent, he placed his warm-cool hands on my face.

"Karabo, I love you. I love you so much," he said.

He asked me if I would be his girlfriend. My eyes and body conveyed better the message of my heart. Shema resided already in my secret love corners.

In the night, at around 9:00, Uncle Kamanzi entered the house. He called my name. He knocked on the door of my room. I did not say a word. He tried to open it, but it was locked. He left for some minutes and came back. I did not respond. He did not come back. Shema stayed on my bed as we waited for Uncle Kamanzi to go to sleep. We could not talk with fear that he would hear us. That moment of silence gave enough space to our hearts to connect more. At around 11.30 p.m., we asked, through the window, one of the other soldiers to check for us if Uncle had gone to sleep. He told us that he was in his bedroom. I got out as if I was going to drink some water from the kitchen. When I noticed there was nobody, I coughed, and Shema got the message. He came out and kissed me on the cheeks and went to the boys' quarters. The flame of my love for Shema continued to burn in my heart, but my head bothered me about the secret I had kept from him. A little voice whispered to the ears of my soul that sometimes it is best to go with the flow, and that is what I did. There was no way I could cut off the electrical wires of the love that tickled my heart.

After a few weeks, schools reopened, and Uncle Kamanzi secured me a place at Mother Teresa's school. My life was taking some shape little by little. I had promised my father that I would pursue studies up to the highest level of the university. But sometimes, I would get to school and feel absentminded. My former classmate Sugira had also come to the same school. I was not particularly eager to talk to him because I did not trust him. In primary school, whenever the teacher asked us to stand up according to our ethnicity, Sugira stood among Hutus. What if his family had participated in the killings? There was no way I could befriend a child of killers. He greeted me every morning, but as for me, I said hello to him only when I wanted him to help me with the subjects I found hard to grasp. We called him Mr. Genius. His strength was in math and science.

It didn't take long before my ancestral curse came hunting me. One day, in class, I searched for my math book but could not find it. My friend Kazuba told me Kayitesi had taken it. I asked Kayitesi to give me back my book.

"Me?" she shouted. "Where did my ways cross those of your book?"

"I have been told you took it," I responded.

"Okay. So, do you mean I am a thief? You people never have shame."

"Let me search in your bag, please."

Kayitesi turned to the class and shouted, "Look at this *Interahamwe*, who calls herself Karabo. She is calling me a thief. When will you people get tired of persecuting us?"

Before I could respond, Sugira stood up for my defense. "What the hell are you saying? How dare you call Karabo *Interahamwe*?"

Kazuba and Mutoni joined Sugira to confront Kayitesi.

"If you didn't know," Kazuba said, "Karabo, whom you call *Interahamwe*, is a Tutsi whose whole family was exterminated during the killings that targeted the Tutsi."

Kayitesi, as if she was in a courtroom, argued, "I know

what I am talking about. It would help if you asked Karabo whether Mugabo and Ngabire aren't her cousins. Their father was the leader of killers in Nyamirambo and Nyakabanda zones. Karabo is from a family of Hutu killers. She has fooled everybody by calling herself a Tutsi and a survivor. We sometimes keep quiet, but that doesn't mean we don't know the truth about some people like Karabo."

All those who were defending me muted. There were only some hullabaloos in class.

"Tell us, Kayitesi, please tell us. Who pretends to be who she is not?"

Kayitesi did not know me well, but I had lost the argument. Would I have lied that I had no idea which cousins she was talking about? Perhaps I would argue and shout out that I was indeed a Tutsi. So, what? Would I have added that I was also related somehow to Hutus that had made me an orphan? I was no longer sure of what side of the camp I belonged to. Tutsi or Hutu? Maybe neither of the two or none of the two, but not one or the other. I laid my head on the table and failed to respond to the noises. I felt so visible for every wrong reason on earth.

Sugira came and held my hand. "Come, let's go."

"Where?" I asked.

"Please accompany me somewhere... I will show you."

Perhaps he wants to hide me from the bullying eyes of my classmates.

We went to sit on the small greenly pacifying garden, not far from our classroom. Sugira took from his pocket his hankie and gently wiped my tears. I looked at all those flowers of many shapes and shades which dressed that garden. I was amazed by how they shared the waters from the sky and the soil, and when satisfied, pushed each other to breathe the air without hurting each other. Maybe Mr. and Mrs. Human should also learn the meaning of the word harmony. Sugira's voice woke me up from my quandaries.

"Don't give Kayitesi the pleasure of according importance to what she said. It's wicked of her to confuse you with those who killed your family."

Sugira did not know the whole truth. He knew me as a Tutsi. In primary school, when the teacher counted students per their ethnicity, I always stood up among Tutsis. In Rwanda, children take the identity of the father. It was discomfiting that among all my friends, the Hutu guy that I did not have much empathy for was the one who had stretched his hands to wipe my tears.

When it was time to go home, Sugira escorted me to my uncle's car. I appreciatively waved good-bye to him.

"Karabo, what has happened to you?" Uncle Kamanzi asked.

"Nothing."

"Nothing? And how about those red eyes?"

"It's okay. I have nothing."

He insisted, but I could not find words to tell him my heart was more bloodshot than my eyes.

At home, I rushed to hide in my room, laid my head on the bed, and pretended to close my eyes. I wanted the darkness and the emptiness of life.

I spent three days with no words getting out of my mouth. The only person at school who would come to say hello to me was Sugira. Sometimes Kazuba and Mutoni would move their lips to give me a deceitful smile. They did not find time to hang out with me as usual. Maybe they had believed what Kayitesi had said about me. My classmates' gossip smothered my ears every time I passed.

Two

On Sunday, I had no plan to go to church. Shema found me seated on the sofa in the living room.

"Jesus has sent for you. He wants you today."

"Shema, please don't start again with your jokes. Where did you meet Jesus?"

"He has appeared in my dream. He said that all those who are burdened should go to him for the rest of their souls. And looking at you, I figured Jesus referred to you. Don't you think so?"

"That's somehow right," I responded. "I don't only have one burden but a mountain."

We headed to St. Michael Cathedral. A priest in a white gown stood like a Lucifer-angel in front of a bunch of Rwandan hypocrites pretending to be saints heading to heavens. Maybe converting back to the Rwandan religion would resuscitate the embittered memories of their ancestors. Rwandans had found it more convenient to talk to St. Peter or St. Paul, who knew nothing about the blood-filled rivers and the wounded hearts.

After sharing the bread, the priest said, "May peace be with you."

On our way back home, when we were about to enter the compound of our home, before giving Shema a good-bye kiss on the cheek, I said, "Thank you."

"For what?" he asked.

"For having encouraged me to go to church."

"How about the burdens? Oh, you forgot to give them to Jesus? Look, you still have them."

"Shema, please. Didn't you hear the priest saying, may peace be with me? I must go. Good-bye."

"Hmm? Okay. 'Bye."

I rushed inside. I wanted to go talk to Uncle Kamanzi. I had made a decision that would hurt Shema. I was not sure Uncle would accept, but I had to tell him anyway.

"Hello, Uncle, there is something I would like to discuss with you."

"What is it, my dear? I have noticed the sorrow in your eyes for the last few days."

I did not want to tell him how I had been bullied at school. I was scared that he would worsen my wounds by repeating to me that I should come to terms with the fact my mother and her Hutu relatives were considered evil by many. I had no choice but to tell him the whole truth of what I had endured at school. He was the only person who could grant me what I wanted.

"A child at your school bullied you?" he asked. "That's not acceptable. What did your school leaders say? Don't worry, tomorrow, we will go to your school together."

Uncle Kamanzi was furious. He did not want others to say to me what he always said to me. To him, I was his brother's daughter but unfortunately born from a Hutu mother. I was not sure how he would handle the situation. A few days had elapsed, and I did not want to hit the already shaking box.

"I suggest you don't go to school," I said. "I am all right, but I don't want to go back to that school."

"Darling, I understand. Hutus did the unspeakable. The hearts of many people are wounded. They cannot stand anything that reminds them of Hutus."

That was typical of Uncle Kamanzi. Those were his own feelings toward Hutus.

"How I wish I could hate Hutus for the pain they caused to my life," I said. "They didn't only kill my father and siblings, they also separated me from my mother's chest. Those who call me a Hutu make it difficult for me. I cannot hate them when I am constantly reminded that their blood runs in my veins. I want to leave this country."

I told him I wanted to go to live in Kenya with my other uncle, Rutayisire. In Kenya, I would neither meet the faces of the Hutu extremists who made me an orphan, nor those of the Tutsi extremists who blamed me for the actions of my Hutu relatives.

Uncle Kamanzi refuted the idea, but I insisted.

"Okay," he finally said. "I will discuss it with Rutayisire."

My second request was permission to pay a visit to Devota the following day. He granted it to me but added Shema should accompany me. I refused and begged him to allow me to go alone.

"Alone? Do you want to go to Gikondo alone?"

"It's okay, Uncle, I will take the bus through Rugunga."

He asked me to wait for the following weekend when he would get some time to drop me off there. I rejected the offer. I needed to have a private conversation with Devota. She was the only one who could understand me.

In the morning, at school, Kazuba and Mutoni spoke to me. They advised I should not be concerned with what Kayitesi had said because they had learned the truth. I did not respond to them. They had just avowed that they had doubted me. I only wondered how they would react the day they learned that there was some truth in what Kayitesi had said. Sugira, who was earning a good friend's place, found me in the basketball playground, standing as a player with no playmates.

After greeting me, he threw his hand in the big blue school bag and handed me a candy. "Suck this bonbon," he said. "Let it sweeten your life."

With a smile, I said, "Thank you." I had neither the courage nor the time to reflect on the meaning of that gesture.

After school, in the late afternoon, I made my way to Devota's house in Gikondo. I was lucky to find her alone. Her brother Muhire was not around. Devota's baby was growing well. She could follow the movement of my finger with her eyes, and sometimes pretend to give a smile with no teeth.

"Her name is Mbabazi," Devota said.

"Eh? Why did you give her an old name?"

"I wanted her name to remind me that I should forgive her father, Abdullah. By calling her name, I will be reminded that the word 'forgiveness' exists in the Kinyarwanda dictionary."

"Devota, what's wrong? When will you dry your tears?"

"Karabo, I will cry till there are no more tears in my cranium. I can't raise this child. I mothered her but can never be her mother. I wish I could give her to someone for adoption. I don't want her. I don't want to raise a child fathered by a Hutu killer. No. I don't."

"Devota, don't say that. Mbabazi is your child."

"Yes, she is, because I gave birth to her. But she is unwanted. I wouldn't have this child if I wasn't raped by

Abdullah. She is the fruit of the ordeal I went through. Besides, I can't endure any longer the insults of my brother Muhire. Whenever he comes home, he asks why this small Hutu is not sleeping. Whenever she cries, Muhire threatens to kill her if I don't manage to make her stop crying."

As I listened to Devota, looking at the baby who was already carrying the burden of the sins of her father as well as the pain of her mother, I lost control of my own emotions.

"Devota, stop it, please. What's Mbabazi's sin? Did you not carry her in your womb? Are you not the one who gave birth to her? Tell me, what percentage of Abdullah's blood does she have? What gives you the right to conclude she is more Hutu than Tutsi? You call her the child of a Hutu; why can't she be the child of her Tutsi mother?"

"Karabo. Karabo, listen."

"No, Devota, Mbabazi wasn't among those who committed the killings. Why do you want her to carry the cross of her father's sins?"

"Karabo, please. What has come over you? Why are you raising your voice at me? I don't understand."

"Devota, sorry for shouting at you. You have no idea what happened to me at school. One of my classmates announced to the whole class that I am a Hutu and that my family is of killers. When I endeavored to argue, she defended her case by saying that she knows well my uncle Rwasibo. Now tell me... Hutu militants killed my family. They shot me. And today...today, someone stands on her both feet and calls me a Hutu. Do you understand it?"

Devota approached me and invited me to lay my head on her chest. "Stop crying, Karabo," she said. "Those who call you a Hutu don't know you well."

"Devota, you are older than me, and I owe you respect, but I must tell you what I think. You have no reason to hate Mbabazi. She is also a victim of her father's evil acts. She wasn't conceived out of love like other children. She was conceived by a body of a sad and weeping mother, who was fighting for her own life. Every experience you went through with Mbabazi in your womb, she felt your fears and sorrow when she didn't even have the faculty to comprehend what was happening. She didn't help her father to kill your sister or rape you. She was on your side, sharing your pain. Do you understand? Please love her the same way she loves you. Share her pain. Let her know she will be okay in this world. Help her overcome her fears. Mbabazi should neither carry the burden of your pain nor the guilt of her father."

"Karabo, you may be right. But please listen. I don't want to hate Mbabazi, but I hate the nightmares she resuscitates in me. I can never forget what her father did to me. When I look at Mbabazi, I replay the movie of Abdullah raping me. I am neither a girl nor a woman. Some give birth to bastards because they have had sex with their lovers before marriage. They do it in the name of love and are prepared to bear the consequences. But look at me, why me? Why?"

I took a tissue and wiped Devota's tears. I told her about the conversation I had had with Uncle Kamanzi and that I was going to live in Kenya, a land with neither Hutus nor Tutsis.

"Hmm, Karabo. Why do you want to leave me alone and lonely in this dark Rwanda?"

"Please, Devota. Don't make it difficult for me. I can't go without your blessings."

"My dear, you want to run away from your own shadow. Today, they are talking about your uncle. Tomorrow, your mother shall come back—shall you disclaim her?"

"Why not? Who knows why she hasn't yet come back to fetch me?"

"Don't say that. You don't even know if your mother is still alive or not."

It was getting late. I said good-bye to Devota and left.

Toward the bus stop, a woman shouted my name. I crossed to the other side of the road. She was Mukamana, a former Biryogo neighbor, a wife to a Hutu militiaman Gakiga. Both anger and fear choked me. The woman shouted my name again.

People standing by the road said, "Eh, girl, that lady is calling you."

"What do you want from me?" I asked Mukamana.

She crossed the road to approach me.

"Oh, Karabo. I am glad you are alive. I was told you all died."

"You were told? Or you wished all of us had died? Sorry, I am alive. Now, get lost from my sight. Let me go."

"Don't say that. I just wanted to tell you that I was with your mother in Zaire. We had agreed to return to Rwanda together. But on the day of our departure, I went to her place but couldn't find her. I didn't insist because her brother could have killed me. Your mother was convinced that you were all dead. Her brother Rwasibo told her that he saw your dead bodies with his naked eyes."

I was mute. There was no way I could share my pain with Mukamana. My head was massive on my neck. My heart wanted to jump out of my chest. I said good-bye to Mukamana and ran.

She shouted, "How about your sisters? Are they also alive?"

I did not respond.

Shema was standing by the gates of our home.

"Where are you coming from this late?"

"From Devota's."

"Eh, why are you not greeting me?"

"Shema, please. I am tired. I want to go to sleep."

"Why are you doing this to me? What did I do wrong?"

"No, Shema, don't worry. You didn't do anything wrong."

I couldn't share with Shema the reasons for my sadness. I couldn't imagine being reviled by him. As I begged him to let me go, he pulled me to his chest and hugged me so tightly.

"Even though I don't know what led to your pain, I just want you to know I am with you in all your troubles."

His words called for my tears. I laid my head on his chest for almost twenty minutes. After placing all my burdens on his shoulders, I ran to my room but noticed tears in Shema's eyes. That night I did not share dinner with Uncle Kamanzi. I told him I had a headache. He begged me to tell him why I was crying, but I refused.

In the morning, I joined Uncle Kamanzi in the living room.

"I won't go to Kenya. I don't want to run away from my own shadow. I am Karabo, a daughter to a Tutsi Kalisa and a Hutu Musanabera. That's a fact I will never change."

"My daughter, you have us all your family."

Three

Uncle Kamanzi had sponsored Shema's tuition at Rwamagana High School as more of an adopted child than an escort. Forty-six years old already, I wondered whether the idea of getting married ever entered my uncle's mind. He had many female friends but apparently no girl-friend. He was consumed more by his work than other pillars of his life, or maybe he did not want me to have details of his private life.

On the 7th of April 1998, Uncle Kamanzi organized the commemoration of our loved ones whose lives had been turned into ashes during the Tutsi genocide. I had a severe headache. My chest was about to crack. Heavy stones were upsetting my back. I had nightmares again of the day the Hutu militants stormed our house, shouting my father's name. When some people asked me to narrate what happened that day, I said, "I remember the day they killed us—" And someone would remind me that I was still alive. The truth was that from the 7th of April 1994, I had signed a pact with death. My father and sisters had been buried by Hutu militants in a mass grave, with around two hundred other victims of the genocide. It was difficult for us to exhume them for burial and meritorious funeral. As Uncle Kamanzi had planned, after a requiem mass at the St. Michael Cathedral, we headed to Biryogo to lay wreaths of white roses on the ground that accommodated our loved ones. Speeches were reserved for the evening of remembrance at Uncle Kamanzi's house in Kiyovu.

When it was time for speeches, Uncle Kamanzi took the floor. He narrated the story of my paternal family. Papa had told me about it before his death. With a voice stuck in the throat, Uncle recalled the day my grandfather was murdered in 1963 and how the family took refuge in Uganda. Only two people, Papa and Uncle Rutayisire, had decided to stay in Rwanda. In 1973 when there was unrest at the University of Rwanda, Uncle Rutayisire left the country. Uncle Kamanzi stopped for a while as if he wanted to count his words, before he said, "Kalisa's heart was so pure that he could never accept that some people are full of hatred. Now see what happened to him…" He pointed fingers at me. "Look at his daughter —where is her mother?"

I ran to my room. It was as if everything was about Papa. Everything was about their family. Nobody had an idea they were talking about my own family. I recalled the story of Rukundo that Papa had told me about. He was one of my grandfather's servants, and after Grandfather was killed, Rukundo, a Hutu, helped my paternal family to cross into Uganda. He never returned to Rwanda. He lived with Tutsi refugees in Nyakivale camps in Uganda, and two of his sons, Muhizi and Mugisha, joined the Patriotic rebels. Why did Uncle Kamanzi think that all Hutus were evil people? What about Rukundo's family? I wished I could return to the living room, to remind Uncle Kamanzi of Rukundo and tell him that he was wrong about Mama. But I could not engage my uncle in that discussion.

In the evening, normalcy resumed. After dark, visitors and many of our family members had already left. But one woman seemed to have no plan of leaving our house. She was Jane Birungi, one of the mysterious female friends of Uncle Kamanzi. Outside, under the shadows of the moonlight, I was with Shema. We had our particular ways of wiping tears from each other's cheeks. I was afraid Uncle Kamanzi would come out only to find our lips glued, and our bodies bonded. Maybe he was also warming up his own body to bond with his consoler. At around 11:00 p.m., I said good-bye to Shema and went to bed.

I woke up in the morning with an empty stomach. But I had to wait for Uncle Kamanzi so that we might share breakfast as usual. Step-Grandmother and other family members had gone to Nyanza with Uncle Rutayisire to lay wreaths on the earth that hosted our many relatives killed in the genocide against the Tutsi. Uncle Kamanzi had excused himself. At around 9:30, I forgot about Uncle and poured some Rwanda tea in my small white cup. Uncle Kamanzi and Birungi came out from his bedroom. Birungi was in a transparent white nightdress, covering her legs with *ikanga* wrap. They both said good morning to me with shy smiles. I hid my eyes. The usual seriousness on Uncle's face had disappeared.

"Karabo, dear, please go ahead," Uncle said. "We are joining you later."

"Oh, okay."

They went to shower together. It looked like some romance. Birungi and Uncle Kamanzi spent the whole day together like birds playing the beak fight games. She left in the late evening.

I spent two days expecting Uncle Kamanzi to explain something to me. *But who am I to demand explanations? I mused. Have I told him about my love relationship with Shema?*

On Saturday evening, Uncle called me to join him in the living room for a conversation.

"Karabo, I am soon getting married. You know her. Birungi. She was here a few days ago."

"Oh, wow, I am so happy. I have waited for the day you shall get married."

"In the future, you will have a second mother. You didn't like being the only lady in the house. Did you?"

Uncle was right. The fact that Shema had gone to study in Rwamagana had made my loneliness even more bitter. Birungi was splendid, tall, and with a smile adorned by a gap between her teeth.

The wedding was celebrated in August 1998. It assembled all our family members. Women were in colorful *imishanana* and men in European suits, except for a few Nyanza older men who had opted to wear black and white *imikenyero*, not to disappoint our Rwandan culture. I was in a long pink dress, with a chignon hairstyle. The religious wedding was celebrated at St. Michael Cathedral. The bride and groom walked along the corridor formed by the soldiers who raised their swords above Uncle Kamanzi and Auntie Birungi, making a metaphor for a military protection cap. A specially composed fanfare accompanied their steps. The big smile on Uncle's face confirmed to my heart it was the biggest day of his life.

The next morning, Uncle Kamanzi and Auntie Birungi left for their honeymoon in Ruhengeri. I stayed in Kigali without worries. Shema was on vacation; maybe we could also resume our sweet love game.

One day, while we chatted about Uncle Kamanzi and Aunt Birungi, Shema told me something that raised more doubts in my mind about the sustainability of our dating relationship.

"Have you noticed how stunning Birungi is?" he said. "Her beauty represents the elegance of a Tutsi woman. It looks like the way we describe those of the *Abahindiro* clan. Every time I look at her face, I imagine the beauty of your mother."

My heart leaped, but I had to hold my breath with the fear that Shema would notice his words had activated a certain premonition in me. My mother was nice-looking, but she did not look like Birungi or me. Birungi was dark-skinned; my mother had fair skin. Besides, my mother was a Hutu, and people said Hutu women were less attractive.

"Why do you think Birungi looks like Mama? She was not dark-skinned."

"All I know is that she had an amazing beauty. I can only guess where your loveliness comes from. But what am I saying? She is no longer of this world. The ruthless Hutus killed her."

Disconcerted, my eyes faced the ground as I removed imaginary dirt from my nails. Nervousness was destroying my chest's bones.

"Hmm?"

"Karabo, I hate Hutus with all my heart. I will never forgive them despite the chants of reconciliation recited by the government. I can't even shake the hand of a Hutu or someone related to them in any way."

"Even those related to them?" The words accidentally slipped from my tongue.

"Yes, even those linked to Hutus in the eighth generation. They are all spiteful."

"Shema, may we postpone this conversation on Hutus for another day? Please."

"Karabo, please, forgive me. My whole body is broken every time the word Hutu crosses my mind."

Shema clenched his teeth and slammed his chest hard.

"Sorry, I have to go," I said. "I am going to bring something. I'll be back in a moment."

I ran to my room, locked the door, and lay on the bed, holding my red pillow. I could not agree more with Shema. Hutu extremists had done the unspeakable to our families. I hated the fact that my father had married a Hutu woman. *Why did he mix our Tutsi blood with that of Hutus? I mused. How the hell would I get the strength to reveal to Shema that even though we shared the genocide cross, I had a Hutu mother, who could still be alive?*

On Friday, when Uncle Kamanzi and his wife Birungi were supposed to return from their honeymoon, the porter called my name. I had a visitor. Sugira, my classmate, had come as he had promised. He looked nervous and shy. I greeted him and offered him a cold drink. My conversation with Sugira was limited to school life and about our classmates. He always had a book in his hand, and he could talk to me about what he was reading, either a story from the First World War, the philosophies of Jean-Paul Sartre or the history of Rwanda, according to Alexis Kagame. While I chatted with Sugira, Shema entered the living room. He moved his eyebrows to say hello to Sugira but did not say a word. He went out before I could introduce the visitor. I received the message of his indignant gaze, but I pretended not to have noticed his attitude. I did not want Sugira to realize he was not welcome. After a few minutes, Sugira ended his visit.

"When will you pay me a visit?" he asked as he walked toward the door.

"I don't know. When may I come?" I was curious to go to Sugira's house. I wanted to nose out the person he was and the family that raised him.

"You can come Sunday if you don't mind."

"I will come Saturday of next week."

"Perfect. No problem."

I said good-bye and went back inside. Shema was waiting for me with a thunder face.

"Who is that guy?" he asked.

"Sugira, my classmate," I replied. "He is the smart guy I told you about. He explains math to me when I have difficulty grasping theories and formulas."

"I understand. Math is better learned on the couch in your uncle's living room. True? Karabo, what do you have to do with that Hutu? Is he my rival?"

"What? Do you take me for a cheater? If you want to know, Sugira's ethnic identity doesn't change the fact he is my classmate."

Distraught by Shema's words, I rushed to my room. I did not want to engage in the Hutu-Tutsi conversation with him. After a few hours, he found me on the living room couch, drinking tea, and watching TV. He apologized for what he had said. Peace reigned again.

A week passed and fell on Saturday, the day of the visit to Sugira. I told Uncle Kamanzi a lie that I was going to Devota's house. He would not have given me permission to visit a boy whose family he did not know. I boarded the bus for Kicukiro. Sugira's house was not far from the market. When I arrived, I knocked on the door. A doorman asked me who I was looking for. I replied I wanted to see Sugira.

He asked me to wait. Sugira's father's Mercedes-Benz was parked in the compound. After a few minutes, Sugira came out, shook my hand, and invited me to enter the house. His parents were sitting in the living room. They rose.

"Welcome," said Sugira's father. "We were looking forward to meeting you. Sugira had told us he expected a special visitor today."

I stepped forward to greet Sugira's mother.

"Welcome to our house, Karabo," she said. "Glory to Jesus."

"Glory to him for eternity," I replied, looking at the beautiful zebra rug that decorated their living room.

She turned to Sugira and asked him to give me a drink. He offered me pineapple juice. His parents continued to have a conversation with me. They asked me how my parents were doing. I told them I lived with my uncle, and that he was fine. After a few minutes, Sugira's parents left the living room one after the other. I stayed alone with Sugira.

"You have cheerful parents," I said.

"Thank you," Sugira replied. He did not say another word.

As usual, we conversed about school and classmates. After an hour, I told him I wanted to go home before it was dark.

"Let me call Mom and Dad."

Sugira's father offered to drop me at my home in Kiyovu. But, after starting the car, he recalled something.

"Karabo, do you mind if we first go to the airport before dropping you off at home? We are going to welcome Sugira's godfather, who is returning to Rwanda after many years abroad."

I accepted, and we took the way to Kigali International Airport. We waited for fifteen minutes before Sugira's godfather appeared. I could not believe my eyes. I looked for a way to disappear from the space, but my legs would not move. Sugira's godfather was my mother's brother, Gasana. I would never have guessed. Gasana was in Russia for studies when Rwanda was on fire during the genocide against the Tutsi.

"Kamana, before I greet you, tell me, where did you find the daughter of Musanabera?" Gasana said.

"Musanabera, who?" asked Sugira's father. "Who are you talking about? I don't understand."

"Musanabera, my sister, the one who was married to Kalisa. I was told none of their children survived. Am I dreaming? Please tell me."

"I don't know what you're talking about. This girl is Sugira's friend. They go to the same school. To be honest, I didn't know she is your niece."

"Oh, my God. It's a miracle. Jesus made my children's paths cross each other."

He hugged me. Although no tears ran down his cheeks, there were drums of sadness in his chest. I could not understand what was happening. It was some sort of a movie.

"Aren't you going to greet us?" Sugira's mother asked my uncle Gasana. "Please hug your godson too."

He turned to greet Kamana's family. I welcomed his wife and children. It was one of those times when my heart and head gave me different messages. The heart was delighted, but the head was bewildered by the past and the future. The past whispered to my ears that I should not trust anyone in my maternal family. The present visualized the eyes of my cousins and felt the warmth of Uncle's hugs. The future frightened me. Mr. Kamana asked me if I wanted to go back to his house for a few minutes of conversation with Uncle Gasana. I said no and begged him to take me home. I promised I would come back another day. We entered the car and headed to Kiyovu. Uncle Gasana asked where I lived, and I told him I stayed with my paternal uncle Kamanzi.

"Ah, yes. I had heard some brothers to Kalisa lived in Uganda. I will come to visit you soon."

Uncle Gasana appeared to be different from his elder brother, Rwasibo, who had led massacres that targeted Tutsis in Nyamirambo. He looked calm. I wanted to ask him if he had any news about my mother, but I could not, because of all those people we were with. When we arrived home, he asked if he could go in with me to greet Uncle Kamanzi. I said he could not, because Uncle Kamanzi was not at home. It was a lie. I did not know how Uncle Kamanzi would react to that visit. After Mr. Kamana parked the car, we remained seated for another few minutes.

"Your father Kalisa was a noble person," said Uncle Gasana. "He was courteous to everyone without any discrimination. His death so saddened me."

I did not comment. I had a bag full of questions for uncle Gasana, but it was not the moment.

"When will you pay us a visit?" I asked.

"Maybe next week. I have seen the house."

I said good-bye to everyone and got out of the car.

Uncle Kamanzi and his wife, Birungi were in the living room.

"Where are you coming from at this hour? What kind of habit have you developed?"

"I am sorry. Devota's child is sick." Another lie.

"Are you now her new nurse?" Uncle Kamanzi asked.

He told me he did not approve of my habit of coming home late. Birungi's eyes agreed with her husband.

When I turned back, I noticed Shema was listening to

my conversation with Uncle Kamanzi. Instead of going to my room, I went out to talk to him. Although I did not want to give him any details of my day, I wanted to be with the only person who knew best how to restore peace in my heart.

"Are you coming to lie to me too?" Shema asked.

"Please listen—"

"Go back inside. You must be tired after spending an afternoon with your Hutu boyfriend, aka Sugira."

Shema turned his back against me and left. One of the house helpers gawped at us. I hurried to my room, squeezed my red pillow, and breathed out all the fatigue of my soul. Everything my eyes and ears had fed my head felt too heavy to chew. I had many unanswered questions. I wondered if Uncle Gasana had any news about my mother. I wondered how I would keep in touch with my two uncles, the paternal uncle Kamanzi and the maternal uncle Gasana. I doubted if Uncle Kamanzi would recognize that even though the members of my maternal family were Hutus, they were also my relatives. My brain could not think of what could happen when Shema learned that I had family ties with Hutus. All these questions danced *sakanyosa* in my head, and my brain moved with them.

The following day smelled of acrimony. There were several lines of anger on Shema's face. He was jealous of Sugira. Around two o'clock, I decided to take the first steps toward reconciliation. I went into his room, which was in the annex house. He was not in. *Maybe he will not chase me if he finds me in,* I thought. *He might have to sit down and talk.* It did not take long before he came in.

"Karabo, what are you doing here? Please get out of my room."

I stayed imperturbable. I raised my legs, lay down on the bed, and covered myself with Shema's blue sheets, which felt like serenity. I had come for peace, not for fighting.

"I won't go anywhere until you sit down and listen to what I have to say to you."

"Okay, stay there if that's what you want," he said, rushing to the door.

I jumped up, grabbed the key, and closed the door before saying, "Shema, please, forgive me. Stop breaking my heart. I cannot take another second longer without talking to you. You know how much I love you—"

"You love me? Or you don't know what love is? What would you say to the other guy? How much do you love him?"

"Shema, I... I love you... I—"

Sadness strangled my throat. Before I finished my sentence, Shema pulled me fiercely to his chest and put his lips on mine as his hands tried to unbutton my shirt.

"Shema, stop. What are you doing?"

He was silent. His arms were resistant. He did not look like the Shema I knew. It did not feel like the romance we were used to. He was tense as if he was carried away by fury. He unbuttoned my shirt and threw it on the floor. He removed his metal-organ from his pants. It was not how I had imagined our first sex. I tried to resist him, but my arms were not as rock-hard as his. I did not want to shout for fear of drawing the attention of other people in the compound.

"Don't worry," I said. "You will have what you want. Let me help you take off your pants."

I got up a little and lowered his pants to the knee level. I pulled his cojones. He stepped back to teach me how to cuddle his sensitive balls. I grabbed my shirt from the floor and ran away to the door. I bumped into Birungi outside near the door as I buttoned up my shirt.

"Karabo, where were you?" she asked. "What were you doing in the boys' house?"

I ran to my room and closed the door. I was so ashamed of myself. Instead of reconciling with Shema, I had hurt him more.

When I got out of my room the next morning, Uncle Kamanzi had already left. Birungi and I spent the whole day playing hide-and-seek. But one thing bamboozled me: I did not smell the perfume of Shema in that house. Perhaps I would have asked other escorts, but I was ashamed of what had happened the day before.

In the evening, on his return from work, Uncle Kamanzi called my name.

"Are you a prostitute?" he asked, capturing my arm. "Don't you have shame? What is that bastard to you?"

His words ran through the bones of my chest like sharp spears. Birungi had told him I had had sex with Shema. She had also said to him that it was not our first time. A house-helper had confirmed I had been Shema's girlfriend for a long time. A violent blow hit my heart when Uncle Kamanzi told me he had driven Shema out of his house.

"Uncle, Shema is innocent," I said. "He didn't do anything."

"Stop," Uncle yelled. "You are not special, either. If you don't change your habits, you will be the next to leave this house. I cannot live under the same roof with a prostitute."

I ran to my room. I may have misbehaved, but I was not a prostitute. A prostitute sells her body to different men. I was in love with Shema. I did not sell myself to him. I regretted not having agreed to do it with him. Birungi would not have caught me buttoning my shirt. Memories of the moments we had shared, and the idea that it was the end of our love story, made me feel as if all the earth had turned against me. No other man would ever see my nakedness.

The following Sunday, at about 2 p.m., a soldier entered the house to tell Uncle Kamanzi there were two visitors named Kamana and Gasana.

"I don't know them."

The soldier turned to tell the men that they were not welcome.

Uncle stopped him and said, "It's okay. Let them in."

Uncle Gasana had kept his promise, but I was terrified. I wondered how Uncle Kamanzi would react after learning that he was the brother to my Hutu mother.

"Excuse me, have we met before?" Uncle Kamanzi asked after welcoming the two men.

"I don't think so. My name is Gasana. My friend's name is Kamana. I am the brother-in-law of the late Kalisa, your brother."

"Okay. I have never met the in-laws of Kalisa. Who directed you to my house?"

"I was in Europe for studies. I wasn't in Rwanda during the war. I came back a week ago. To my surprise, my friend Kamana welcomed me at the airport with Kalisa's daughter."

"What? Do you mean Karabo came to pick you up at the airport?"

"She didn't know who we were going to welcome," replied Mr. Kamana.

Uncle Gasana told Uncle Kamanzi how we met at Kigali

International Airport. After a few minutes, Uncle Kamanzi called me to greet the visitors.

"Do you know these people?"

"Yes."

"Who are they?"

I told him who they were and how I had met them. He asked me if I could serve them drinks. I gave beer to the visitors, but Uncle Kamanzi asked for water instead. I guessed he did not want to share the beer with strangers.

"Do you have news of your sister?" asked Uncle Kamanzi.

"No, I was told she went to Congo with my elder brother."

Uncle Gasana's words jumped into my ears. He had no news of my mother. Their conversation continued. It was about the rain and the season.

"I was happy to meet Kalisa's daughter," said Uncle Gasana. "I had been told none of his children had survived."

"No one can ever slay an entire community," said Uncle Kamanzi.

"Those who killed Tutsis claimed Rwanda belonged only to them, but they were defeated. Look at Karabo, their daughter; they killed her father and her sisters."

Uncle Gasana remained silent. He was one of those whom Kamanzi was talking about. He had called me their daughter. Although I was Tutsi by my father, for Uncle Kamanzi, I was also a granddaughter of Hutus.

After accompanying the visitors to the door, Uncle Kamanzi came back, shouting my name.

"Karabo, come here. How dare you invite your Hutu relatives to my home?"

"Uncle..."

I was shaken by that question. Why had Uncle Kamanzi welcomed Uncle Gasana and Mr. Kamana if he did not want them?

"Listen and listen well," he added. "Your Hutu relatives are not welcome in my house. The next time they come back here, you shall take your things and go live with them."

As usual, I ran to my room, held my red pillow, and sprinkled it with tears. Uncle Kamanzi hated Hutus, but he had absolutely no right to say that my Hutu relatives were not welcome in his house. He had warned me he would chase me away from his home the same way he had sent Shema away.

Four

Ihad finished high school and sat for the national exam before going on vacation. One day, in January 2000, Uncle Kamanzi came home from work with a forty-tooth smile.

"Karabo, I have excellent news for you," he said.

"Hey, what is it?" I asked.

"The government has sent you to study at the University of Kigali City. You will do political science. Come on, come, and give me a hug."

I jumped for joy and made some noise, falling on his chest. I had made my uncle so proud of me, and I was going to pursue the study program of my choice. I asked Uncle Kamanzi for permission to go and tell the good news to Devota the following day.

"You have my permission," he said. "But for now, please, go put on your best dress. I want to take you somewhere."

I ran to my room, joy bouncing my heart. I put on the long black dress Uncle Kamanzi had bought for me from Kampala. When I came out, the splendor of Birungi in her long blue evening dress hit my eyes.

In the four-by-four, we headed to the Africa Luna restaurant. We took place by the pool, adorned with affable-leaf palm trees. I craved Italian food and chose lasagna as my main dish. Birungi, more African than Africa itself, ordered banana steamed with boiled chicken and green vegetables. Uncle Kamanzi ordered the same plate as his wife; he did not have time to study the menu. His main concern was to give me some life lessons.

"My daughter, you are now an adult. You must understand this world better. You must protect yourself from the wicked people and maintain friendship with the noble ones. You have to get away from boys who have no other goal but to distract you from the real purpose of your life. You have to focus on your studies. Do you understand me?"

"Yes."

I was glad Uncle Kamanzi had taken the time to give me some hints of life. After dinner, before leaving the restaurant, Birungi threw her hands in her bag and pulled out something, then she handed it to Uncle Kamanzi.

"My daughter, please, accept this gift from us."

It was a black cell phone with an antenna like that of the radiophone of Uncle's lead escort. I gave a big hug to Uncle Kamanzi and his wife, Birungi. We left the restaurant and went home.

At home, I rushed to my room and fell on the bed to sleep like a little baby.

In the morning, after sharing breakfast with Uncle Kamanzi and Birungi, I went to Gikondo at Devota's. I knocked on the door, but nobody answered. Nobody was home. In distress, I decided to go and ask the neighbors.

"Are you not aware Devota has fallen ill?" one of Devota's neighbors asked.

"No. Since when? Where is she?"

"She has been at Kigali General Hospital for two weeks. Do you know her brother Muhire is in prison?"

"How? Why has he been put in jail?" I asked.

"He assaulted someone. It must have been because of the drugs he had taken."

"And Mbabazi, Devota's daughter? Where is she?"

"Mbabazi is with Kabibi, our neighbor."

Mbabazi lived with strangers. I could not imagine the depth of Devota's sadness, alone in the hospital, and her only brother in prison. My memory brought out the film of all that Devota had gone through in her life. If Hutu militants had not killed her family, Devota would not be alone in the hospital with nobody to look after her. Muhire, Devota's brother, was a calm person before he started to ruin himself with drugs. He used to say drugs helped him cope with life despite its bitterness. What sin did the survivors of the genocide commit? I wondered. The world never saves her people.

I boarded a bus to the city center. At the hospital, the heart jumped from my chest. What kind of illness had eaten up Devota in just two weeks? She seemed to have spent a whole year on that bed.

With a tongue stuck in her mouth, she moved her lips to talk to me.

"Karabo, I'm about to leave you. Please take good care of yourself. You are now an adult."

"Devota, what are you saying? You are not going anywhere. Doctors are doing everything they can for you to get better."

"My sweetheart, they cannot do much. My illness is incurable." She turned to the other side of the bed to hide her face.

"An incurable disease?" I asked.

"No, I only have tuberculosis," she said, tears forming in her eyes.

Devota is hiding something from me, I mused.

"Will you do me a favor?" she asked. "Go to the orphanage of Nyamirambo Catholic nuns to ask them if they can take Mbabazi."

"Why would they take Mbabazi? To do what? Do you want her to be raised in an orphanage?"

"Mbabazi is a miserable girl," said Devota. "I was unable to give her all my love when she was a baby. And now that she's able to smile and call me mommy, I'm about to leave her alone in this world. Do you understand?"

The nurses reminded me the visiting hours were over. I begged them to give me a minute to say something to Devota.

"Devota, you didn't leave me the day I was lying on the ground, surrounded by the corpses of my family. I will also make sure Mbabazi never stays alone. And besides, you're not going anywhere."

I gave her a kiss before going out.

When I arrived at home, I rushed into my room, squeezed my red pillow against my chest, and cried all my sorrow.

In the evening, after Uncle Kamanzi had returned from work, I joined him in the living room for a conversation.

"Devota is not well," I said. "She is at Kigali General Hospital. Her brother Muhire is in prison. Her daughter, Mbabazi, lives with strangers."

"What is Devota suffering from?" asked Uncle. "What offense did Muhire commit?"

I gave him all the details of Muhire's case before I described the sorrow I had read from Devota's face.

"I'm sure the Hutus infected her with HIV," said Uncle Kamanzi.

"Hmm? No. No, don't say that. Devota doesn't have AIDS. God cannot allow that to happen to her."

"Let's hope so. Don't worry, everything will be fine."

Devota had told me she had an incurable disease. I picked at my nails and nodded before telling my uncle that Devota had asked me to take his daughter Mbabazi to the Nyamirambo Catholic Sisters' Orphanage. I added that I would never dare do that to Devota's child.

"What shall be her fate if you don't take her to the orphanage?" Uncle Kamanzi asked.

"Devota didn't take me to an orphanage when she found me alone in this world without a parent. She took me to live with her despite the fact she didn't have a house. I will never take Devota's daughter to an orphanage."

"What will you do then?"

"What would you recommend? I would be grateful if you could help Mbabazi."

"How?" he asked. "Don't tell me you are suggesting bringing a Hutu bastard to my house?"

"A Hutu bastard?" I asked. "Mbabazi is the daughter of Devota. I don't care who her father is."

I got up to run to my room. Uncle called my name. I obeyed.

He gaped at me for minutes, before saying, "Get out of my sight. Go away."

I told him that the next morning I would go back to the hospital. He did not answer. I rushed to my room and let my eyes do what they could do best.

After two weeks, Devota was released from the hospital. Uncle Kamanzi gave me permission to accompany her for a full recovery. I wanted to make sure she regained her puffy black hair and her cocoa-brown skin tone. I stayed with Devota for about three weeks until the Sunday before my first day at the university.

On my first day of university, with my afro hair, I was in black pants and a white top. We received several forms to complete. We gathered in a large room to follow orientation presentations. There were so many new students. Some guys entered the room. One of the faces was familiar. *Sugira again? From primary school to university?* I mused. It was as if our destinies had been drawn in parallel. The day was so overloaded that it was hard to find a second to greet each other. The campus was cool with a lot of back-and-forth students and employees. Everyone and everything moved fast. Sugira was lost in that organized chaos. After a long search, I saw him from a distance and ran toward him.

"Oh, Sugira, it has been a long time. How are you?"

"Good. And you?"

I waited for a few seconds before asking him if he had any news about my uncle Gasana. I wondered why he had not come back to visit us. Sugira answered my question with another one.

"And you? Why did you have to wait for him? You could have taken the initiative to visit him."

"Yes, I could, but I don't know where he stays."

Sugira gave me directions to Uncle Gasana's house. I decided that after school hours, I would go to Kacyiru at my maternal uncle's place

After the Dominican Priests' Centre, I turned left, counted ten gates, and stopped at the green gates. I knocked on the door, and the doorman came out. I told him who I was and who I was looking for. He told me to wait. Their house was large and modern, with a garden decorated with roses, lilies, chrysanthemums, daisies, and other beautiful flowering plants. After a while, Uncle Gasana's wife came out and invited me in. My eyes traveled to every corner of the house. To my left, there were glass shelves that contained a lot of glasses, a combination that looked like a fountain of pure water. I imagined that was how western living rooms were decorated.

"Your uncle is not yet back from the office," said Mrs. Gasana.

"From the office?" I asked. "Does he have a job already? He didn't search for long."

"No, he didn't. Didn't you know? Maybe you never watch national television. He has been appointed the permanent secretary of the Ministry of Water and Forests."

I was so happy to learn that my uncle had been offered that high-level position in the new government. I wondered how the people of the regime knew him to entrust him with those critical responsibilities. I said to my heart, *Maybe he is indeed a reliable person.* We watched television. It was a show about the Olympics, and I was struck by Asian women's athletic talents. After a few minutes, we heard a car horn.

"Here he is, your uncle," said Mrs. Gasana.

Uncle Gasana had changed so much. He undoubtedly looked like an official of an African government.

"Hey Karabo, it's been a long time," said Uncle Gasana, untying his tie and handing over the briefcase to his wife. "How are you? Did your uncle Kamanzi tell you how he chased me out of his house?" He gave me a hug. "Glory to Jesus."

"Glory to him for all eternity," I replied. "What did Uncle Kamanzi do? Did he chase you out of his house?"

"I came to visit you. The guard asked me to identify myself. He told me to wait at the door. After five minutes, another soldier came out to tell me words I will never forget."

"What did he say?" I asked.

"He called me a *muginga* and ordered me to do a U-turn and to never set foot near Colonel Kamanzi's house. He said if I ever dared to return, I would be turned into a coffin heading towards the cemetery."

"How?"

"My daughter, those words hit my eardrums and pushed me to question my decision to have returned to Rwanda."

Uncle Kamanzi had dropped the milk gourd. Maybe he did not like my maternal family, maybe he hated Hutus, but he could not in any way ignore my maternal uncle Gasana, who was not even in Rwanda during the genocide against the Tutsi.

"Please, forgive Uncle Kamanzi," I said. "He isn't a bad person. I don't know what had come over him."

Uncle Gasana's wife stood up as if she were going to make a statement in court.

"Listen to this, child," She said. "You can only speak for yourself. Our country has been invaded by wicked people."

Uncle Gasana gave her a warning look as if he wanted her to remain silent.

"Fortunately, when I was trying to digest what Kamanzi had done to me, I received a phone call telling me the Cabinet of Ministers had appointed me the permanent secretary of the Ministry of Water and Forests. I had never thought I would work for this government. Maybe all the people in this regime are not that bad."

"Indeed. I'm glad you were not discouraged by Uncle Kamanzi's behavior."

"I have been working for a month now. We have some

real patriots. But of course, we also have some Tutsi extremists like your uncle Kamanzi."

"Don't be fooled easily," argued Mrs. Gasana, with a sickly laugh. "When did the Tutsis do any good to anyone? You only have to do the work as their loyal Hutu servant, but never fall into their trap."

Uncle Gasana did not give his wife a slap for putting forward those mean words, full of hatred against Tutsis. How could she dare to open her dirty mouth with those words, when she knew I was Tutsi?

Instead of scolding her, Uncle Gasana looked at her warningly and said, "Please, don't say that."

I wanted to snatch the vase of flowers from the table and hit the so-called wife to my uncle Gasana in the head. I did not find the patience to keep quiet.

"It's pitiful," I said. "So, until now, you have the same hatred against Tutsis. I cannot believe it."

"No. Karabo," said Uncle Gasana. "Please don't take it the wrong way. She meant that there are Tutsis who are mean. You are still young. There are truths of our history that you don't understand."

"What don't I comprehend? Have I forgotten my family was killed because they were Tutsi? Don't I recall that the murderers of my family sang that the world belonged only to Hutus? What else do I need to know?"

"Karabo, please, let's end this conversation. Maybe you should know Hutus were also offended and killed by Tutsis."

"When? Where? By who? That's not true."

"I don't want to talk about it," said Uncle Gasana.

The fact that he did not want to explain what he meant made me more furious. I decided to leave their house; otherwise, I could insult my uncle or go crazy.

On the way, I wondered about the demons who owned the hearts of Rwandans.

"Miss, why are you not getting off the bus?" shouted the bus conductor. "We have arrived downtown."

"Are we there?" I asked. "Oh, let me get out."

"And the payment?"

"Oh, sorry. Take, please."

After the bus was gone, I realized I had paid him more than the trip fare. I looked left and right as if I did not know where to go. In that wandering, I saw a familiar face on the other side of the road.

"Shema, Shema, hold on, look," I called his name out loud.

He turned around, raised his hand to greet me, and walked away. He was wearing old, dirty blue jeans that had not known laundry for several months. His eyes were as red as those of a person who had not slept for ten years, and his hair did not know the meaning of a comb. As I tried to cross the road to catch him, a car horn interrupted me.

"Miss, are you looking for death?" asked the driver, pointing at me as if he wanted to pull me for a slap.

I ran after Shema and pulled his blue T-shirt.

"What do you want from me?" he asked.

"Shema, please. I want to talk to you. Where do you stay? How did you leave Uncle Kamanzi's house?"

"Where do I stay? The same place where true orphans spend nights and days. I live in the streets. Don't you now have the answer to your question? Please, let me go now. Stop pulling my T-shirt before people conclude I have done something wrong to you."

He grasped my arm as if he wanted to take it off at the armpit.

"Shema, I beg you. What happened to you? Don't make me sadder than I already am. You are the only person I have in this world. I don't care about Uncle Kamanzi."

Many people rubbernecked at us.

"Please, wipe those tears," said Shema. "No one on this street cares."

Clenching his teeth, Shema held my hands and invited me to take the stairs to the third floor of the Rukiriza building. We sat on the balcony in front of the cafe.

"Karabo, wipe away your tears and go back to your uncle Kamanzi's house," he said. "You must forget me. It's over between us."

"I cannot forget you. Please don't ask me to. I cannot."

Shema swallowed a little saliva, scratched his forehead, and looked left and right.

"Karabo, I loved you beyond comprehension. Your love had covered all the wounds of my heart. Every time you laid your head on my chest, I forgot I was alone in this world without parents, brothers, or sisters. I accompanied you to school and to church. It wasn't because Colonel Kamanzi had asked me to. It was because I had sworn to protect your body and your soul. Karabo, I am a man. It wasn't only my heart that was in love with you, but my whole person. My body was hungry and thirsty for you. Look at me now, look at what our love has done to me."

He held back his tears but could not stop his eyes from turning bloodshot. I put my hand on his. I had never doubted Shema's love for me. I was convinced what he had done was because of jealousy. My heart, my chest, my stomach, my lips, my brain, my whole person, my body, and my soul were in love with Shema. If Shema had told me to leave everything and follow him, I would have seized the opportunity without hesitation. I had lost Shema once and did not want to lose him for the second time.

"Shema, please forgive me for everything that happened to you."

"Karabo, I needed you. My body was thirsty for you. Even though we didn't sleep in the same room, in my dreams of each night, you were my companion. I caressed your lips and your body, to realize, the following morning, that my body had reached its extreme joy. I am really ashamed of my behavior that day. I shouldn't have forced you to do what you weren't ready for, but I was so afraid another guy would give you his chest. Please, forgive me."

"I'm sorry for what happened."

"Karabo, get up. You must leave. It's over. I'm no longer the same Shema you fell in love with. I am now a true orphan. I am neither a soldier nor a civilian, but a demobilized soldier. I am neither a student nor a worker but a street boy. I don't have a house. I spend my days wandering the streets of Kigali. The world turns, and I turn too, without going from one state to another. This is where I meet the ghosts of my father, my mother, my brothers, and my sisters."

"Wait a minute, what are you saying? Have you been demobilized from the army? Have you dropped out of school? Why?"

"Yes, I have been demobilized from the army. Don't ask me about the school. What did you expect? I was financially supported by Colonel Kamanzi. How would I have continued with studies?"

"Oh, sorry, everything was my fault. But you shouldn't have stopped studying. You would have been supported by the government, either as a demobilized soldier or as a survivor. Why didn't you go to the Fund for Assistance to Genocide Survivors?"

"The Fund pays tuition fees. Would they also have given me shelter and food? Please, stop being a little naive."

I had so much to say to Shema, but I did not know where to start. Would I have told him I was already in university? Would I have told him I also wanted to get out of Uncle Kamanzi's house? I could not. He could ask me questions I could not find answers to. It was getting dark. I said good-bye to him. He accompanied me to the bus stop. I informed him of Devota's state of health and that Muhire was in prison.

"Tss, they are real orphans like me," he said. "When shall this country understand the grief of the survivors?"

"The government has programs in place to support them. Don't you think so?"

"Does the government know where I live or how I live? Or, I'm probably not one of those they should support?"

I did not find the courage to answer him. The government would probably have paid the tuition fees, but it could never replace parents and siblings. To have a good life and receive one's blessings, one must be rooted in a family. Without a family, a person doesn't see the sun or the moon; everything seems dark. I did not think about our love anymore. I just wanted to be there for him. I wanted to be the sister he had lost, and I wanted him to be the brother I never had.

"Shema, I neither have parents nor siblings. I beg you, please, don't leave me. I want to be there for you. I want you to be there for me. Be my brother, I will be your sister."

I removed a piece of paper and a pen from my bag, wrote my phone number, and asked him how I could contact him too.

"I don't have a telephone. Don't worry. I'll call you. I stay in Cyahafi in a studio with one of my friends. We only have a small mattress that we share, and sometimes, when one of us doesn't pay enough attention, he slips to lie on the floor. Never try to visit me. I'll call you every time I get some coins."

At the bus station, I threw myself into Shema's chest and squeezed him tightly. I entered the bus. Shema stayed there to wait for the bus to leave. I could read the sadness from his face, but when my eyes met his, he smiled at me, pretending everything was fine. The bus was started, and I waved good-bye to Shema.

At home, Uncle Kamanzi was waiting for me. I was afraid to scream that I was mad at him. Maybe I was less worried about how he had chased Uncle Gasana out of his house, but I hated him for having sent Shema to the streets.

"Karabo, is this the time when other students come back from school?" he asked.

"I'm sorry. I have gone to visit Devota."

"That Devota is starting to become a big concern in this family. Will you take care of her until she dies?"

I did not have the strength to shed more tears. My conclusion was made about Uncle Kamanzi. He had no empathy for anyone. Maybe he has taken care of me because he considers me his daughter, but not because he cares about humanity, I thought.

"I am sorry."

"Hey, where are you going to like that?"

"Excuse me. I am so tired. I'm going to bed."

"Go away. You are becoming impossible."

I hurried to my room and took my red pillow to ask it many questions.

Five

The next morning, I went to school. Sadness was my toe-to-hair dress. At lunchtime, I went to sit under an acacia tree. Someone covered my eyes with his hands.

"Who are you? Tell me, please."

"Guess who I am."

"You're Sugira. How are you?"

"Good. And you? What's wrong? It's as if the world has become too big for you, and you don't know how to navigate it."

He insisted I should tell him what tormented me. I told him I had visited Uncle Gasana and that he had told me how Uncle Kamanzi had driven him out of his house as if he were a criminal. Sugira told me he had heard his parents talk about it.

"So, you knew it, and you didn't find it important to tell me?" I asked.

"After what happened to your uncle Gasana, my parents warned me to never return to Colonel Kamanzi's house."

"Sugira, it broke my heart. Uncle Kamanzi has no regard for the fact Gasana is my maternal uncle."

"Don't take it to heart. Maybe your uncle has his reasons. Come on, let's go somewhere."

Sugira did not want to continue that conversation. He took me to the campus restaurant. We shared lunch before returning to our different classrooms.

The following Saturday, I woke up with the decision to stay home to prove to Uncle Kamanzi I could be a good girl. While we were having lunch, my phone rang. My heart jumped for joy, thinking it was Shema's call. I apologized to Uncle and his wife and went to my room to take the call.

"It's Kabibi, I wanted to inform you Devota has been readmitted at Kigali General Hospital."

A sharp fear hit my heart. My brain reminded me Uncle Kamanzi believed Devota was infected with HIV. I went back to the dining room with a miserable face.

"What's the matter? Why that sadness?" asked Uncle Kamanzi.

"It was Devota's neighbor. She has been readmitted."

I added I needed to rush to the hospital. Uncle Kamanzi glanced at his wife, then raised his eyebrows, indicating I had permission.

Devota's condition had worsened. She had developed a dreadful fever. Her skin was covered with many fear-provoking eruptions. Although her tongue could not move to allow her to say a word, she asked me to approach and showed me her back. My chest creaked as my eyes stared at that cryptic wound with a disgusting hole inside. A doctor entered.

"Doctor, is it because of this wound Devota has developed a fever?"

"These are shingles, otherwise known as zona. Yes, it causes fever. But there could be other reasons too. Devota has also caught malaria."

Devota was alone. She was taken care of by sympathizers. I went to the small shops at the hospital entrance and bought her milk and fruit juice before going to see Mbabazi in Gikondo.

Mbabazi had lost a lot of weight, but that was not her concern.

"Have you visited Mom at the hospital?" she asked.

"Yes. She's getting better," I said.

"My friends told me that Mom will die soon."

"No Mbabazi, that's not true. The doctors are treating your mom. She will recover very soon."

I gave her the biscuits I had brought for her and offered to Kabibi some money I was left with. I headed for Nyamirambo. I had no choice but to reconsider Devota's idea of taking Mbabazi to an orphanage.

The orphanage was home to many babies and children who behaved like adults. With depressed faces, the children had neither the enthusiasm nor the urge to jump and play. I told the principal about Devota and her daughter Mbabazi. The orphanage received children whose parents had died. They would only accept Mbabazi if her mother had died or if the doctors confirmed Devota was suffering from an incurable disease. My little brain could not stomach either of those two possibilities. I left the orphanage and promised the principal I would come back.

Dreams of sadness and distress accompanied me all night.

In the morning, I returned to the hospital to talk to Devota about my visit to the orphanage. Her condition had improved, but her eyes were projecting riddles of life. She hid her face as if she was following some kind of tunnel. In the evening, I said good-bye. My brain replayed the time Devota had found me at Kigali General Hospital after the 1994 genocide. *Why couldn't I stay with her in that hospital room?*

At home, Uncle Kamanzi and his wife Birungi were not

yet back from work. I ran to my room and threw myself on the bed with all my sorrow.

The next morning, I went to school. I wondered if I would not fail. I had attended elementary and secondary school in French, but at the university, all subjects were taught in English. I followed diligently, but sometimes the bitterness of my life stole my mind and soul and made me lose the sense of what the teachers talked about.

At lunchtime, as usual, Sugira came to ask me to accompany him to the restaurant. I was hungry, but I had to refuse. I wanted to go to the hospital. I told Sugira I had to visit a friend admitted to Kigali General Hospital. I told him how Devota had saved my life in 1994 despite the fact and that she was also an orphan with no one to look after her.

"Oh, that's sad. Why didn't you tell me before?" Sugira asked.

"My mother would do everything she could to help people in similar situations."

"No, Sugira, please, don't bother your mother with Devota's problems."

"I know my mother. She wouldn't be bothered. Mom has suffered a lot in her life. Her entire family was killed during the genocide against the Tutsi. She will be happy to help another survivor of the genocide."

The discovery of the fact Sugira was also of mixed ethnicity warmed my heart. I wanted to give him a big hug, but I had to restrain myself. He accompanied me to the hospital to visit Devota. Her condition had worsened. My hope for Devota's recovery was diminishing.

In the evening, we went to Kicukiro to talk to Gatarina, Sugira's mother. Knowing that she was a survivor, I told her how the Hutu militants killed my father and my sisters, and how Devota found me in a river of blood. I did not miss any details, including the fact I did not know the whereabouts of my Hutu mother. Sugira's mother was married to a Hutu. Maybe she did not label all Hutus as killers, I thought. She invited me to lie on her chest and hugged me tightly.

"*Impore*," she said.

Nobody had ever told me that magical Rwandan word that could never be translated into other languages. It meant more than I share your pain. It could perhaps be explained as May your heart find its peace and sweetness. My paternal family had helped me a lot, but they had never wiped the tears of my soul.

Sugira knelt down, raised his hands, and said, "Mom, you're the only person who could help Devota and her daughter Mbabazi. Please, accept to be her mother during these days that could be her last."

I had considered Sugira a Hutu guy, calm and intelligent, but that day he revealed another face of the person he was. Gatarina agreed to accompany us to the hospital the next day.

That evening I had a calm conversation with Uncle Kamanzi. We talked about the rain, the seasons, and the news of the world. I did not share with him my challenges of life. I did not tell him anything about Uncle Gasana, or about Shema, or about Devota's health. There was no need to bother him with anything. After a moment, Birungi invited us to the table.

"It's been a long time since we shared dinner with you. Who's the guy who takes up all your time?" Uncle Kamanzi teased me, as he added more vegetables to my plate.

"No one, but Devota."

"Yes, of course. Is she getting better?"

"No."

"Sorry to tell you again. Hutus infected her with AIDS. You must count Devota among the dead."

"No, my darling, don't say that," Birungi told Uncle Kamanzi, putting her hands on his shoulders.

"Devota is still alive," I said. "My duty is to take care of her, and the rest I leave to God. We should rather think about her daughter, Mbabazi."

"No, Karabo, I told you I could never accept a daughter of a Hutu killer in my house." He paused for a few seconds before adding, "Devota is ours, but not Mbabazi."

"Excuse me. I am going to sleep," I said.

Uncle Kamanzi's hatred against Hutus had robbed him of the melting salt of a human heart. He needed to learn nobility begins with the purity of the soul before it is read on the lips and eyes.

In the morning, I went to school as usual. At noon, Sugira came to tell me his mother had come for us. We entered her car and went to the hospital.

After greeting Devota, Gatarina removed the food container and served food on a plate. She sat down on the bed, invited Devota to lean on her shoulder, and fed her. Devota looked at me as if she was surprised by how Gatarina treated her. I told her she was Sugira's mother. After giving Devota food, we did not stay there for long because we had to go back to school.

On the way, I talked to Gatarina about Mbabazi and the conditions she lived in at Kabibi's house. I also told her Devota had asked me to take Mbabazi to an orphanage, and that I was not comfortable with that idea.

"Do you think Devota would accept if I volunteered to help Mbabazi?" she asked after a moment of silence.

"Perhaps," I replied.

"Please have a conversation with her and let me know if she would agree."

After two days, I told Devota that Gatarina would like to take care of Mbabazi. She nodded. I informed Gatarina. The following Saturday, she took Mbabazi to her place.

Devota's state of health grew bitter every day. One illness called for another. When she had no fever, she had diarrhea. Every morning, Gatarina went to the hospital to shower and feed Devota. Mbabazi was already enrolled in elementary school. She was fit, happy, and cheerful. Gatarina was like the grandmother she never had.

On January 15, 2001, when I went to bed, my phone rang. It was already 10:00 p.m., and I was not used to receiving phone calls so late. I was afraid the call would announce the death of Devota. It was a male voice, maybe someone drunk. His tongue was stuck somewhere between his teeth.

"Who are you?" I asked.

"Babe...I miss you," he replied.

"Who are you? Shema? Are you okay?"

"Sweetheart...I miss you... Please come. I want you. I need you—"

"Where are you? Shema, Shema—"

The phone went silent.

My heart jumped at Shema's call, but we could not talk. He was drunk. *Maybe he is in danger,* I thought. I called back the number he had used to call me, but it was off. I walked around every corner of my room, wondering what I could do. Shema did not have anyone in the world. The call was for me to go to his rescue. All night long, I could not sleep thinking he might call again.

Around 5 a.m., my phone rang again.

"Shema, where are you?" I said. "Are you okay?"

"Karabo, it's me, Kabibi," the lady on the line replied. "I wanted to tell you Devota has passed."

"Who? Devota? Noooo. No, that's not true."

A heavy feeling smashed my spine, and something choked my throat and prevented me from making noise. I put my head down on my arms and tried to cry, but my tears were stubborn for the first time.

"Karabo, did you hear what I have said?"

"Yes. I am coming to the hospital."

I dialed Sugira's phone number and told him Devota had passed.

Uncle Kamanzi pushed the door to my room, and asked, "What has happened?"

"It's over," I said. "Devota has left me. No, why did God allow it? Devota was my family. She was my mother and my sister. She cannot leave me alone in this world."

Uncle Kamanzi put his hand on his cheek as if he wondered how to console me, then said, "Dry your tears, darling. You have us. We are your family."

"No, you can never replace Devota. How can she leave me? And Mbabazi, her daughter? How can she leave her in this wicked world? And her brother Muhire? This is neither the day nor the time. Devota cannot die."

I ran outside to take a bus to the city center. When I got out, I found I was still in my nightgown. I went into the house, put on black pants and a black T-shirt.

"Karabo, wait for me," said Uncle Kamanzi. "Let me take you by car."

I jumped in his car, and we left. We did not speak to each other. I was weeping.

Devota's body was covered with blue sheets. I removed the coverings to look at her dry, calm face. I put my hands on her cold cheeks, rounded to kiss her forehead, and whispered in her ear, "Now I understand. Devota, rest in peace. Never again, the worries of life. Never again, the pain. Never again, the sorrow. All is finished."

Sugira and his parents, Kamana and Gatarina, were already there. They had come with Mbabazi. Gatarina's head was covered with a white scarf. She held in her hands a rosary and a book of Christian prayers. She approached Devota. Mr. Kamana stood beside Uncle Kamanzi, but their eyes avoided each other. After a while, the nurses told us they wanted to take the body to the morgue.

"Please, give us a few minutes for some prayers before taking her away," said Gatarina.

"You'll excuse me, I have to go to work," said Uncle Kamanzi.

Gatarina led us in a prayer that she launched with the song in Kinyarwanda known as *"Nyir'ibambe ndaje unyakire,"* translated as, "My Lord, I am coming to your house, please, welcome me. I've been away from you for a long time, and now I'm coming home."

The nurses came back and asked if we were Devota's only family. We said yes. They gave us the death certificate and took Devota's body to the morgue. Mbabazi scrutinized everything that was happening. Although she seemed petrified, she did not weep. After accompanying Devota to the morgue, Mr. Kamana invited us to his home to discuss the funeral arrangements.

"Maybe some of us have to go to the prison to tell Muhire," I said.

"Yes, Muhire must be informed his only sister has passed away," said Mr. Kamana. "But we must not bother him about funeral funding.

Devota is Mbabazi's mother. We are his family. We will organize a dignified and decent burial for her."

The nobleness that characterized Sugira's parents was beyond comprehension. They asked Sugira to accompany me to the prison to inform Muhire. It was a complicated mission.

At the prison, we told the supervisors we were looking for Muhire. One of them went to call him.

"Karabo, it's been a long time," Muhire said, "How are you?"

"It's okay."

I introduced Sugira to Muhire, and they greeted each other. Muhire winked at me, asking if Sugira was my boyfriend. I said no.

"Karabo, why the sadness in your eyes? Don't worry. Everything is fine here. I am used to prison life."

"No. We… We wanted… We came to…to tell you that…Devota has passed."

"How? What did Devota do?" Muhire asked.

"She has gone to live with the Lord," I replied.

"Hmm, that's what I expected," said Muhire with a treacherous smile. "She, too, is gone like the others. Tell her to say hello to our parents and siblings."

Sugira and I stared at him with muted mouths.

"We were wondering if you could get permission to come with us for the funeral," I said.

"To do what? To bring her back to life? I won't ask for permission," he said before asking, "Where is Mbabazi?"

"Don't worry, Mbabazi is with me." I could not tell him Mbabazi lived with people he did not know.

"Thank you for having come to inform me. Now I can go back to my sorrowful solitude. Do you have a piece of paper and a pen?"

"Yes, here you are."

He gave me a phone number of his friend Karega and asked me to inform him. He added that if we needed support, Karega could help us. We went back to Mr. Kamana's place to report on our conversation with Muhire.

Mr. Kamana and his wife organized the funeral of Devota. Gatarina asked Kabibi to inform Devota's neighbors. I also told some survivors of the genocide against the Tutsi. Gatarina compiled a list of everything we needed, and I accompanied her for shopping.

On the day of the burial, my little brain could not imagine Devota was the one in that coffin, surrounded by many white flowers. The women, including myself, were in traditional white *imishanana*, and men in black suits and white shirts. Uncle Kamanzi did not come to the funeral. Shema was there. He had received the text I had sent to the mysterious number that had called me. We went to church before going to the Gatenga cemetery. Mr. Kamana asked me to say something. I told them how Devota had saved my life, but a lump in the throat prevented me from saying more about her own ordeal. It was no longer a secret Devota had died of AIDS. The idea that survivors of the genocide against the Tutsi would continue to die for many years afterward gave me a severe stomachache. When the coffin was lowered into the grave, Mbabazi screamed and ran into the bush to hide her eyes. I followed her. We sat down on a stone, and I invited her to lay her head on my chest. We cried rivers asking God why he had taken our Devota. Gatarina approached us and invited us to enter her car. From the cemetery, we went to Gikondo in Devota's house. It was there that we spent the week of mourning before the house was handed over to the owner.

———➤

The day I went back to school, I had one principal goal: to go to the Dean of Student Affairs and ask him to give me a room on campus. Fortunately, the rooms occupied by the postgraduate students who were writing their theses were released. He showed me a room with two small beds, one for me and another for Karigirwa. I was so happy. I ran to inform Sugira.

"Why do you want to leave your uncle's house for a room on campus?" he asked.

"Sugira, I'm mature enough to live alone. It's time for me to leave Uncle Kamanzi's house."

I loved Uncle Kamanzi. He had given me everything— shelter, food, clothes, school… I could perhaps understand his resentment towards Hutus, but I would never forgive him for not having supported Devota when she needed it the most. He had told me the reason he had not come to the funeral was that I had involved all my Hutu friends, referring to Sugira's parents, who had proved to be nobler than he was.

At home at night, I joined Uncle Kamanzi for a conversation in the living room.

"I have been offered a room on campus," I said.

"Why did you ask for a room on campus while you have a house?"

"It will be best for me. I will devote more time to my studies and participate in study groups with my classmates."

"Do you need to spend nights on campus?" asked

Birungi. "Can you not participate in those study groups during the day?"

"Uncle, Auntie, I'm really grateful for everything you have done for me. But the time has come for me to run on my feet."

"Do you mean you are now grown enough to take care of yourself?" asked Uncle Kamanzi. "My dear, a parent is always a parent. It never changes. Maybe you have other reasons."

I did not want to lie to him, but I could not tell him the whole truth.

"I am now an adult. My outlook on life may be different from yours. I have my own friends, including those you may not approve of. There is a kind of freedom I need, which you may not be able to provide."

Uncle Kamanzi stared at me, and his lips danced as if he wanted to say something. He scratched his head and said, "I have understood. Go live on campus, but keep in mind your room in this house will always be waiting for you."

In the morning, I packed my bags and went to live on campus. I had to copy notes about what the others had covered during the time I was away. Sugira offered me an hour a day to help me catch up.

Six

Two weeks later, I called Shema on the number he had called me with.

"Hello."

"Hello, my name is Karabo. May I talk to Shema?"

"Oh, how are you, Karabo? My name is Murenzi. Shema told me about you. He isn't well. He had an accident."

"An accident? How? Where is he? May I talk to him?"

"No. I'm not with him. I will be home around 5 p.m."

Shema was alone in the tiny room he had described to me with no one to look after him. Whether he wanted it or not, I had to be by his side. I told Murenzi that I would call him after work hours.

Late in the afternoon, I begged Murenzi to take me to Shema. He refused. I insisted.

My heart broke into pieces as we descended the road from Gakinjiro to Cyahafi. Children dressed in unclean and torn clothes played in the muddy and stinking pathways between the timeworn small houses. Their mothers were in African loincloths that covered their bodies only to the level of the chest. Charcoal stoves with cassava ugali pots blocked our way.

When we arrived at their place, Murenzi opened a small door made of iron sheets. We entered a complex that had many studios. They looked like walls reinforced with concrete, but over time they had turned into mud-covered ramparts. Murenzi pushed a small door that had been recycled from a metal barrel and invited me into their studio room.

Shema lay on the little mattress in that room of about two by two meters. He had a lot of injuries, the biggest of all on his face above the eyebrow.

He turned his face to the wall to hide his face from me before asking, "What are you doing here?"

I bowed to kiss him on the cheek. Tears stung my eyes, but I had to hold back my emotions. Murenzi told me Shema had fallen down. I did not believe it. Maybe he had engaged in a fight with people. Looking at his swollen eye, I understood his opponents might have pushed him to fall on rocky ground.

"Did you go to the hospital?" I asked.

It was apparent they had not gone there.

"Listen to this rich kid," said Murenzi. "No need to go to the hospital because of simple wounds. These heal with time."

In the corner of the room, there was only a dirty jerrycan and a pot as black as the charcoal stove. There were no plates, no forks or knives.

"These injuries can attract tetanus, which can turn into a more serious situation," I said. "Please, let's go to the hospital."

"If Shema agrees with that, you can accompany him," replied Murenzi. "I work day and night. I'm going to my night watchman job."

"Okay, I will call a taxi to take us. But you'll have to help Shema walk to the road."

"I'm not going anywhere," said Shema. "Karabo, who gave you the right to give us orders?"

"Shema, please, do it for your own good," I said.

He kept silent for a few seconds before saying, "Wipe those tears. Okay. Let's go. Maybe you have a lot of money to waste."

I called a taxi driver, and Murenzi helped Shema walk to the road.

When we arrived at the hospital, they treated the cuts, applied the medications, and plastered the bleeding wounds. They prescribed anti-inflammatory and antibiotic tablets. I did not want to take Shema back to his dirty studio in Cyahafi, but I had no choice. Reluctantly, I called the same taxi driver to take us back to Cyahafi. I asked him to pass by the campus; I needed to pick up something to calm Shema so that he would accept to give me more minutes with him.

From campus, I took my little radio cassette and the cassette of French love songs. I put in my bag sheets, detergent, and one or two other things. I went to the canteen and bought juice and snacks before getting back into the car.

In Cyahafi, the taxi driver helped Shema walk to his studio. I begged Shema to allow me to clean their room.

"We are back from the hospital," he said. "Isn't that what you wanted? Now you can go. Please, at the exit, lock and slide the key under the door."

"Yes. I will leave in a moment. But I won't go until you allow me to help you shower and eat something."

I removed the radio and the cassette from my bag, then played the French love songs.

"If you don't sing these songs for me, I won't go anywhere."

"Karabo, you don't change," Shema said with a smile. "Do you want Colonel Kamanzi to kick me out of Rwanda?"

I could only imagine his heart was begging him to go with the flow. I helped him go outside to the small bathroom. I carried with me a basin full of water and a torch. In that bathroom of four corners without a shower or a bathtub, I took the gloves and bathed my boyfriend. There was nothing to hide from each other. After the bath, we went back into the room.

"Don't worry," he said. "I don't need to put on clothes."

"I understand. Let me wash these clothes so you can put them on tomorrow."

"Karabo, please. I'm not the poorest person in the world. Look up there, I have a bag full of clean clothes that I never wear. But I don't want to wear anything now. Please, approach. Let me tell you something."

I sat on his mattress. He invited me to lie down beside him.

"You are still far from me," he said. "My voice can't reach there."

Accompanying the radio cassette, he sang, *"Est-ce que tu es seule ce soir ?"* by Frédéric François, up to the point where he said: *"Même si la vie nous sépare."* In a few minutes, his hands were in my hair and down to the neck and chest. I could not stop him. It could cost me many more months of loneliness. That night, I could not go back to campus. Murenzi had left for his job as a night watchman, and Shema and I watched our love for the whole night. I was already twenty-two and at the university. Nobody would reprimand me if I lost my hymen at that age. I stroked Shema's manly chest and admired his masculine shape.

"Karabo, I want you," he said. "I'm thrilled, but my body is suffering."

I pulled my lips away from his and went down all the way to his neck and chest. I did not stop at his belly button. I continued to the middle of his legs to find the little Shema who wanted me. I sucked it until it was bigger-heavy in my mouth. Shema shouted, calling me all the sweet names, my darling, my cocoon, my beloved, my sweetheart, and Karabo. I tasted his bottom juice and swallowed it to seal the pact of our love.

To conclude the action, I took a towel and cleaned my boyfriend, before closing our eyes, lying on the bed, one close to the other, at zero distance.

Around 2 a.m. Shema asked where I had put the torch.

"What are you looking for at this hour of the night?" I asked.

"I can't catch sleep. Please bring me a small package that is in the back pocket of my bag."

I got up to get the package.

"Shema, what is this?"

"Give it to me. I'll tell you what it is."

"No, tell me. What is it?"

"It's marijuana. It helps me sleep well."

"Shema, do you take drugs?"

I could not believe my eyes and ears.

"Marijuana is light. It's not bad."

Shema could not sleep without taking marijuana, and I thought that was a sign of dependency. I refused to give it to him. He tried to get up to get it himself, but he was hurting too much because of the injuries.

"Let me help you sleep," I said. "My own marijuana is more magical."

I caressed his face, stretched his eyebrows, and told him the story of Nyashya and her brother Baba, who lived alone in a forest without parents. Baba would go hunting, and whenever he came up, to announce his arrival to his sister, he sang:

"Nyashya of Baba, open for me,
I have killed a gazelle, it's for you and me,
I have killed an antelope, it's for you and me,
And the biggest of all, we will share."

Shema fell asleep. I put my arms on his body and laid my head on his chest.

The next morning, after taking a bath and putting on clothes, I gave him the tablets and kept the rest with me so that I may come back at night to give him another dose. I was afraid he would replace the medicine with his marijuana.

At the campus, I rushed to my room, changed clothes, and went to class. At lunchtime, Sugira, as usual, invited me to the campus restaurant. I could not face him. I had the impression he could read from my face that I had spent a night in bed with a guy.

"Have you slept well? Are you getting used to campus life?" he asked.

"Yes, I have slept well. Thanks."

I did not want him to ask me more questions about the unforgettable night. I had spent several months without feeling the magic in my body, and laying my head on Shema's chest was the sedative I needed after Devota's death.

In the evening, I went back to Shema's house to give him medicine. He begged me to stay again for the night, but I refused. I had to go to school to read because we were preparing for exams.

A few days before 7 April 2001, we were preparing to

commemorate the genocide against the Tutsi. At the university, the preparations were led by the association of student-survivors of the genocide, of which I was a member. One week before the commemoration period, we invited professional advisers from Ruhuka Centre. They guided us on how to deal with flashbacks resurrected by the commemoration period. They said, "The symptoms of depression include feelings of hopelessness and pessimism. A depressed person gives up on life and avoids decisions that can lead to a better life. Some depressed people turn to drugs and alcohol to distract themselves from the challenges of life." There were two names in my mind, Muhire, and Shema. I approached Doctor Baziga, one of the counselors, and asked him for advice. He advised me to persuade my two friends to go to the Ruhuka Centre for professional help. That was a challenging mission.

In the evening, Uncle Kamanzi invited me to discuss the commemoration of our family members killed during the genocide against the Tutsi. Birungi greeted me with a big hug. Her face and figure had changed. She was pregnant. Uncle Kamanzi joined us in the living room.

"How is it going with studies?" he asked, inviting me for a hug.

"Great."

"It must be. You don't even find the time to visit us."

"I am sorry. I'll catch up."

I had not paid them a visit for a long time. The little time I would leave the campus, I would go to Shema's house, or visit Mbabazi at Kamana's.

"Karabo, this year, we will all go to Nyanza to commemorate our family members who were killed by Hutus. We will only pass by Biryogo to lay wreaths of flowers on the land that hosts your father and sisters, before heading to Nyanza."

"I understand. I wondered when we would exhume the remains of Papa and my sisters and offer them a dignified and decent funeral."

"I really don't know. Do you think I would organize the exhumation of more than two hundred bodies in the same mass grave with your father? And even if I wanted to, I couldn't do it before consulting all the families involved."

"I know. It's not easy."

Uncle Kamanzi asked me to help him compile a list of people with whom we would go to Nyanza. He listed some names of family members and friends and asked me if I had any other names to add.

"Yes. You can write down Kazuba, Mutoni, Sugira, and his parents, Kamana and Gatarina, and Uncle Gasana and his family."

I avoided mentioning Shema, lest Uncle Kamanzi ask me how I was aware of his whereabouts.

"Karabo, what's your problem? Your uncle Gasana cannot be bothered by the commemoration of Tutsis! And the same applies to those other people you just mentioned. I hope you aren't referring to those Hutus you had gathered on the day of Devota's death."

I was voiceless because I could not speak back to my uncle. I let him compile his list. Every time he asked for my opinion, I only nodded. He could decide who would go to Nyanza, but he would not dictate who would go to Biryogo to lay wreaths of flowers on the land that hosted my own family.

From Uncle Kamanzi's house, I went to inform my maternal uncle Gasana and Sugira's parents. They all promised they would be with me on April 7th.

The whole night of the sixth to the seventh, I could not sleep. In the morning, the radio played Nyiranyamibwa songs, and my mind replayed the moments of the death of my father and sisters.

At 10:00 a.m., after I had put on my black dress and combed my hair, someone knocked on the door. It was Sugira. He gave me a card on which it was written: "Do not cry alone, I am with you. I will give you my shoulders to lean on. Let me carry the burden of your sorrow." Those words relieved my heart. The physical appearance of Sugira, with a big, flat nose and a round face, had nothing to do with his inner beauty. He was dressed in a gray suit and a purple shirt, holding a bouquet of white roses in his hands.

"Take heart, let's go," he said. "I have come with a taxi-car to take us to Biryogo."

"Thank you. Wait a minute, I'll be right back."

I went back inside, slipped a purple scarf over my long black dress, and wore sunglasses.

We were the first to arrive at Biryogo, where the bodies of Papa and my two sisters rested in peace. Many people joined us later. Among them were our old neighbors; the sons of Muvunyi; Zurufati and her sons; and many others. Many friends of Uncle Kamanzi and a few of those who were friends of Papa and Mama were also there. We were with Tutsis and Hutus, but a Hutu I had expected to see, my maternal uncle Gasana, was not there. It was not the first time he had dodged the moments of honoring the lives of the genocide victims. Mr. Kamana and his wife Gatarina were there. Sugira's mom had honored my family's memory with the traditional *imishanana*. After a few minutes, Shema and Murenzi arrived in their dirty, old-fashioned jeans. They stood apart from other people as if they did not want to mingle with those upper-middle-class people. I waved at them, thinking I would have time to talk to them later. Uncle Kamanzi delivered his welcome and thank-you speech before giving the floor to Fidele, a former work buddy of Papa. He spoke a lot about Papa's kindness, nobility, and loyalty, as well as how Papa loved his wife and children so dearly. The members of the choir concluded by leading us in prayer. It was time to go to Nyanza.

"Who are these people you are inviting to accompany us to Nyanza?" Uncle Kamanzi asked.

"I—"

"Karabo, please, I don't want that. Whoever is not a Tutsi should not come. They must let us mourn our own. Do you get it?"

When I was about to raise my voice and reply to Uncle Kamanzi, I noticed Gatarina had heard everything my uncle had said.

"Karabo darling, please don't argue with your uncle," she whispered in my ear. "Don't add to his distress. We are going home, and we will keep you in our prayers."

In Nyanza, we celebrated a requiem mass before laying wreaths of flowers on our family members' graves, starting with the grave for Grandmother, Papa's mother. Many people took the time to talk about the nobility of our family and their horrible experience.

⟶

On the campus, the night of Kwibuka was on the ninth of April 2001. Sugira, even though he was not a member of the association of the student-survivors of the genocide against the Tutsi, he joined us. After candle lighting, accompanied by mourning songs, the ceremony's master led us into Kwibuka moments. Each of us took a turn to talk about loved ones killed during the genocide against the Tutsi.

When it was my turn, I said: "In memory of my father,

Kalisa, whose blood runs in my veins, as I wished you had come back to resume the conversation we had before your death. The woman to whom you gave your heart and life did not come back. Even her brother, who came back, is only interested in the milk and honey of Rwanda, but with no regard to the link, you had sworn to strengthen. I met your brothers. They protected me from hunger and thirst, but not from the heaviness of my heart. Papa, I'm going to have to end our conversation here so that my brothers and sisters, with whom I share sadness and pain, may have time to talk to their loved ones."

Other students took turns to honor their loved ones. I caught sight of Sugira wiping tears in his eyes. Of all those present, he was the only one who knew that I was of mixed ethnicity. Was he hurt by what I had said? I wondered. After the Kwibuka evening, I accompanied him to the campus doors.

"Sugira, I hope you're not hurt by what was said there."

"Why?"

"Don't take it badly. You are from a noble family. But those who killed our families sang that the world belonged only to Hutus. Don't take it to heart when people talk about Hutus."

"Karabo, don't worry," he said, putting his hands on my cheeks. "I am a Hutu. Some people emphasize I am. Some want me to bow my head and share the shame of those who killed the Tutsis. But that's not the reason I shed tears."

"Hmm?"

"What you have said pushed tears to fall from my eyes. When I was younger, I used to curse the day my father married a Tutsi woman. But today, I hate the fact my mother married a Hutu."

"Why?"

I had always considered Sugira a Hutu, despite the fact his mother was a Tutsi. In Rwanda, children take the ethnicity of their fathers. He continued his testimony.

"Every time we visited our paternal grandparents, some of our family members said, 'They behave like their mother; they are not ours.' And another person would say, 'Don't care about these children of the Tutsi woman; she raised them the Tutsi way.' We were not accepted one hundred percent by our Hutu family. We were always brought back to our Tutsi identity."

"Oh, Sugira, I am touched. You and I have a lot in common."

"I haven't told you everything. When Hutus were killing Tutsis, my mother was hidden in the ceiling of our kitchen. Every night, Dad would join her in the ceiling and spend nights fighting with rats. During the day, whenever Hutu militants came looking for her, Papa told them she had gone to visit her family and that she might already be dead. One day, a Hutu militant, who suspected Papa was lying, hit him with a machete. He lives with a scar on his left leg."

I wanted to hug Sugira, but chose to simply say, "Take heart."

"Karabo, today, when it is apparently shameful to be a Hutu, I am called a Hutu like my father, and nobody cares that my mother is a Tutsi. One day, a cousin of my mother, whom I consider my real aunt, told me I shouldn't walk around exposing my big flat nose. She thought she was simply frank. She didn't realize she hurt my heart."

"I'm sorry for what you experienced, Sugira."

"I hope someday people will call me Sugira. I am tired of being a Hutu, but not at a hundred percent. I'm tired of being a Tutsi, but not at a hundred percent. I am neither Hutu nor Tutsi. I am a human being with only one blood type. I don't have two blood types fighting in one body."

I could relate to what Sugira was telling me. We were both entangled in the Hutu-Tutsi conflict. Maybe a guy like him would understand me better, but my heart had already fallen for Shema, who was bound to one of the extremes of our history. It was already dark. Sugira kissed me good-bye and left.

Three days later, I paid a visit to Shema. I knocked on the door, but he did not answer. Murenzi had told me he had left Shema at home. I knocked again, and with more strength.

"Who is it? Do you want to break my door? Go away. I don't want to open."

"Shema, it's me. It's me, Karabo."

He kept silent. I begged him once more to open for me.

"Karabo, please. We'll talk another day."

I waited for about thirty minutes until I shouted, "Shema, who are you with, in that room? Why don't you want to open?"

"Eh? Are you still there? I'm not with anyone," he replied before opening the door for me.

He was in red shorts. His bare chest exposed ribs that resembled those of the victims of malnutrition. His face was bitten, his eyes were as red as blood, and his hair had become dirtier. Shema had spent the entire week of commemoration in that small room without eating anything.

"Karabo, I don't want to see those tears," he said. "Wipe them, please."

He gave me a handshake and went back to lie on the mattress. I did not interrupt his grinding of teeth. I took a mop and a piece of a used chemise, borrowed from one of their neighbors, and cleaned the dirty, already smelly room. When I finished, I went to bed by his side. He did neither touch me nor speak to me.

"Shema, do you love me as much as I love you?"

"Why are you asking me that question?"

"Don't reply with another question. Tell me, do you love me?"

"If I had told you I loved you, what would we do with our love?"

Shema's words stabbed my heart like a very sharp spear. I did not understand what he meant.

"Shema, don't you love me?" I asked again.

"Karabo, the truth is that I always try to erase you in the memory of my heart, but I'm unable to. I wish I could run away from you and forget your smile, but our paths are perhaps destined to cross forever. Karabo, I love you with all my heart, with all my soul, and with all my spirit. I want to love you, love you again, and love you more, but..."

A lump in the throat interrupted him. His eyes were ready to cry, but his tears had been dry for a long time.

"But what?" I asked.

"Please, understand me," he said. "Hutus killed our parents; we are orphans. Life hasn't offered me the same opportunities it gave you. I am alone and lonely in this world. I exist, but I don't live. I have no future. If anyone had asked me what my vision was, I would say I am looking forward to the day when death shall knock on my door."

Shema had given up on life. Maybe it was a good time to talk to him about the professionals of Ruhuka Centre, but I did not know how.

"You're alive," I said, placing my hands on his shoulders. "If you don't want to live for yourself, please live for me. I will fight with this world that brings sorrow into your life. I will win the battle and put a smile back on your face."

Shema smiled, inviting me to lay my head on his chest.

"Your problem is more serious than mine," he said. "How can you, a university student, date a street boy like me?"

"You will also go back to school. I promise you."

"Please, not again. Who is that false Samaritan who will support me for one term, only to drop me during the second?"

"Leave that to me. Do you want to go back to school? I'll show you how."

"I don't want to. Let's stop talking about that nonsense."

"Nonsense?"

"Yes. If you love me, let me swing into this life of poverty. It's my destiny."

We spent the whole day together. I cooked for him, and we shared lunch and took a nap together. Late in the afternoon, I returned to campus.

The next morning, I called Doctor Baziga, the professional counselor, to talk about my previous day's conversation with Shema.

"Don't push him to act. Just encourage him to talk about his feelings. Little by little, he will open up and tell you his true wishes. When that moment arrives, don't rush him to a professional counselor. Let him think more about what he could do to make his dreams come true. Please, don't offer your advice or solutions to his problems."

"How? Shema has a pessimistic view of the world. He will never find solutions to his problems if we don't help him."

"The exercise of asking questions about his life, and trying to find answers, will enable him to listen to his inner voice. He will try, and sometimes he will fail because of his depression. And that's when he will understand that he may need to talk to someone."

I had a mission, and I swore to fulfill it. Living on campus had given me the freedom I would not have enjoyed if I was still living with Uncle Kamanzi, who was already celebrating his first daughter, Neza. I had more time and space to be with Shema and help him overcome some life challenges. I spent days with him. I spent nights with him. And I allowed the only guy in my life to break my hymen and seal the pact of our love with the blood of my virginity. As time passed, Shema made some progress, little things like bathing and teeth-brushing each morning. Everything was as much for our love as for the salvation of my man's soul.

Seven

On the morning of September 03, 2003, at the campus, Sugira ran to me with much enthusiasm.

"Congratulations, you are now a niece of a minister," he said.

"Which minister?" I asked.

"Your uncle Gasana. He has been appointed Minister of Water and Forests."

"You should rather congratulate him, not me."

I was not thrilled with the news. Uncle Gasana owed that appointment to his hypocrisy. His speech in public reflected neither his actual behavior nor what he said in his living room. I had already concluded he was just an opportunist who worked for a regime that promoted values and practices he did not agree with.

"Aren't you happy for him?"

"Sugira, please, let's talk about something else."

"Okay. I wanted to ask you for a favor. What are you planning for Friday night? May I take you somewhere?"

"Do you want us to pay a visit to your mother on Friday night?"

"No, please, it has nothing to do with Mom. Let's say I would like to take you out."

"A date?"

"Why not?"

"Where will we go?"

"I'll tell you. It is a surprise."

Friday nights were reserved for love games with Shema. But I was curious about what Sugira had in mind. Where did he want to take me?

"Okay, I'll be all yours."

The idea that Sugira might want to take our friendship to another level puzzled me. The choice between Sugira and Shema would be a declaration of war between the heart and the head. Shema was the prince charming whom my heart longed for. On the other hand, Sugira had convinced my head that he had all the attributes of a good guy. Shema was my lover, Sugira was my best friend, and I needed both. With Sugira, I was comfortable talking about my worries and my joys. With Shema, I liberated my sensuality and my sexuality. With Sugira, I felt right and rational. With Shema, I felt naive and innocent. It reminded me of the singer who had sung, "The most beautiful is called Fanta, and the kindest is called Amina," and like him, my heart wavered.

The week went quickly. Three dresses were placed on my bed at around six o'clock. I did not know which to wear for the occasion. The short red dress, the long black dress with a bare chest, or the long black dress with white stripes. I wore them one after the other and looked at myself in the mirror. I struggled to give a definition to my date with Sugira. The long black dress that showed the elegance of the gazelle-neck won the competition. I liked the fact that it looked like the night itself. I wanted to hide in that darkness to discover the other side of Sugira, different from an intelligent Hutu kid from a wealthy family. The demon of my love for Shema did not miss the opportunity to remind me that I was not allowed to think about any other boy than Shema. I felt like a little cheater.

At exactly seven o'clock someone knocked on the door. Sugira had a bouquet of red roses in his hands. Looking at his face, I could tell he had been delayed by the hairdresser. I suspected he had put some powder on his face, and I was slightly more curious about the brand of his perfume. Sugira was tall, but not thin. His face was wildly virile, in such a way that sometimes it repulsed me and urged me to back off. But that day, in his black pants and a black polo T-shirt topped with a black coat, he looked more welcoming. He kissed me on both cheeks and gave me the flowers. I put on my high heels. He had come with his father's Mercedes-Benz. He opened the door for me, and we took off.

"Where are we going?" I asked.

"It's not far, be patient, you'll see," he replied.

"Why are you killing me with curiosity?"

After a few meters, I began to guess. I could not imagine why Sugira had chosen that place. After a few minutes, we arrived. He parked the car and opened the door. Joy and timidity were juggling in my heart. I had never imagined myself at Corners of Lovers with a guy, and more precisely with Sugira. It was a bar-restaurant decorated with different corners of tables for two so that no one could go there alone or with more than one person.

All the guests were in couples. Sugira held my hand and invited me forward. I was feeling uncomfortable. I wanted to ask him to change the place, and probably go where there would be more noise with a DJ playing African music. I could not imagine the topics that would characterize our conversation. Math and physics could not be part of the conversation at Corners of Lovers. We were not going to Corners of Lovers to discuss Rwanda's history and how we suffered because of our so-called ethnicity. Nobody puts on a beautiful evening dress and goes to Corners of Lovers with a guy to discuss how the guy's mother is a kind person. The waiter suggested a table in the corner next to the water fountain. He brought us the drinks menu. I did not know what to take. I wanted to follow Karigirwa's advice and order sweet white wine, but my lips were too shy to say those words.

"Have you made your choice?" Sugira asked.

"Yes."

I could not pretend to be a real city girl. I had to be myself. I did not want to be like those girls who wore high heels, which they were not used to, to fall at their first steps.

"What are you taking?" the waiter asked.

"Lemon tea."

"Are you sure?" Sugira asked, before ordering red wine.

The waiter brought us drinks, and when it was time to order food, like a born-in-Rwanda girl, I ordered grilled chicken, but I tried to add a little bit of elegance; instead of French fries, I ordered an assortment of vegetables. Sugira ordered a dish he called sizzling beef or pork. That was settled, but the subject of our conversation seemed to be more problematic.

"How do you like this place?" he asked.

"It's wonderful."

We spent a few minutes in silence before resuming the conversation.

"I'll take you to other nice places in Kigali," Sugira said.

"Thanks," I replied.

"Do you like going to the cinema?"

"I've never been there, but I guess I'd love to."

"I'll take you there."

The evening was so long. Sugira stared at me, and after eating, he further complicated the situation by rubbing my hands. I pushed him fiercely. My heart jumped at the sight of any tall, dark-skinned guy, and my head reminded me that Shema would not come to such a luxurious place. Even though I tried to hide my eyes, Sugira had already read from my face that I was not in my best state. After a moment of silence, Sugira paid the bill, held my hand, and invited me to the car.

At the campus, he parked the car and locked it to accompany me to my room.

"Why are you in a hurry?" he asked.

"I am tired. I am going to bed, cover myself, and sleep instantly."

"When will we go to the movies?"

"This weekend, I will be busy reading," I replied. "Maybe next week."

The truth was that I did not know what was happening to me. I had left the campus happy and ready to discover Sugira, but instead of enjoying the moment, my heart and head were fighting to remind me of Shema. I missed him.

"I'm sorry," I said. "Please, let me go to sleep. We'll see each other Monday."

"Okay. Good night."

He did not leave. Maybe he was waiting for a good-bye kiss. He approached me, pulled my chin, and kissed me. Nauseated by the taste of his saliva, I ran to my room. What game was Sugira playing? I wondered. He had won the seat of a special friend. What else did he want? Maybe my mind could say yes to his big heart and smart brain, but my heart was not attracted to his charm.

At 11:00 the next morning, the phone rang. Karega told me the good news. Muhire had been released from prison. I put on my blue jeans and a T-shirt and took a taxi-car to go to the general prison of Kigali city. We waited for a few minutes before Muhire came out. He carried a black bag on his back, and in his hands a large black Bible. He gave me a hug. His face seemed calm.

"Let's go," said Karega. "Karabo, you are also welcome to my place."

He lived in Muhima in a small two-bedroom apartment in the same compound with other doors, or apartments. The living room was furnished with armchairs known in Kigali as '*Je commence la vie*' of black, beige, and brown. On the other side of the room, there was a small dinner table surrounded by four simple chairs. The walls were decorated with papers, including one on which it was written: "The Lord is my shepherd; I shall not want. He makes me lie down in green pastures, He leads me beside the still waters…" Karega offered us milk and the famous Rwandan meal of *Imvange*, a mixture of potatoes, beans, and several sorts of vegetables.

"Karabo, I am now a changed person," said Muhire. "I learned a lot from prison."

"How? What could you learn from prison?" I asked.

"I went to jail with a lot of anger. I couldn't comprehend how I would be put behind bars simply because I had hit a Hutu idiot. When I arrived at the prison, the first person who greeted me was a former secretary of my commune of birth. During the genocide against the Tutsi, Habiyakare was the leader of the killers in Kibuye. He asked me what I was doing in prison, and when I raised my hand to punch him on the face, other prisoners stopped me. Although it took me many weeks to trust Habiyakare, I can confirm that he is now one of my best friends."

"What do you mean? How dare you befriend a genocide perpetrator?" I asked.

"Karabo, many horrible things go on in prison; some I can tell you, but others, I won't tell you much. Much as I insulted and rebuffed him, Habiyakare protected me from other prisoners who wanted to rape me. Let me spare you details. Other than that, I didn't have anyone in the world, nobody visited me, and in prison, we weren't provided with everything. Habiyakare shared with me the little his wife brought him. I didn't lack anything, from soap to tooth-paste. He even gave me money to buy what I needed from the prison canteen."

"But that doesn't change the fact he's an assassin," I said.

"Yes. Habiyakare indeed killed a lot of Tutsis, and he recognizes that. But I can testify he repented. He trembled, and tears streamed down his cheeks every time he replayed what he had done during the genocide against the Tutsi."

"Most former Hutu militants claim they regret what they did," I said. "Did Habiyakare turn you into a *murokore*, I mean a born-again Christian?"

"Yes, he has also contributed. Karega had preached to me, but I was too stubborn to listen. Life in prison was like a tunnel with a light at the end."

"Have you also stopped smoking weed?"

"Yes, of course. Look where the drugs took me. If the person I hit were dead, I would be in jail for the rest of my life. I would be called a murderer like those at whom I was angry."

It was reassuring to know Muhire had stopped smoking weed. But I was not sure about the soundness of the mind of that Muhire who had come out of the prison, with a Bible in his hands, claiming to have forgiven Hutus.

"Karabo, tell me about Mbabazi. Where is she?" Muhire asked.

"She is fine."

"Where is she?"

I told him how Sugira's parents had helped us when Devota was sick and how they had taken Mbabazi to live with them.

"Who is Sugira?"

"The guy with whom I came to the prison to announce the death of Devota."

"That reminds me of someone. How is Shema? I'm talking about the young soldier who stayed at your uncle's."

"He is fine," I replied. "He has been demobilized from the army. Maybe he'll be interested in listening to you. You have to talk to him about the risks associated with drug addiction."

"Does he smoke weed? It's sad. Is he still at Colonel Kamanzi's?"

"No. Shema stays in Cyahafi with a friend."

"I have to talk to him. We, the survivors of the genocide, must strengthen our fraternity, and rebuild the family ties. Seniors must become like parents to the youngest, we must be brothers and sisters to the survivors who are alone and lonely, and we must be the children to parents who have lost their sons and daughters."

"Indeed. I will encourage Shema to pay you a visit."

He kept telling me about life in prison. I also gave him

details of the endurance his sister Devota had gone through before her death.

In the late afternoon, I said good-bye to Muhire and decided to go to Shema's so that I could dedicate the following Sunday to reading.

Admiring the beauty of the blue skies of Rwanda, Shema was sitting on a small stool at the doors of his studio. In khaki pants and a blue shirt, he looked relaxed. I took advantage of that big smile to suggest him a walk.

"Where do you want to take me?" he asked.

"It is a surprise," I said.

I wanted to catch him at his best moment and show him there was still sweetness in life.

"Okay. Let's go," Shema said.

We climbed the road from Gakinjiro to Gitega. I had never been to the Mayaka Cinema Centre before, apart from reading the signposts and posters.

We arrived a few minutes before the screening of the movie Titanic. Many people had told me about that movie, and I was happy to watch it with my own Jack.

"I had no idea you knew places like this," said Shema. "You are a city girl, indeed."

"Hey, remember I grew up in Biryogo."

My answer seemed convincing, but although I grew up in Biryogo, our father did not allow us to go to places like Mayaka Centre.

"I know it. You aren't like me who grew up in neighborhoods with entrances on which it was written *chiens méchants*, but don't forget today I am freer than the Biryogos."

"I hope you'll like the movie Titanic. I hear it's a breath-taking movie. It's a love story."

He smiled and gave me a kiss on the cheek. We bought our tickets and entered the room. The lights were immediately extinguished. While Jack and Rose engaged in their love fights, Shema and I also boarded our own ship that would take us to another planet where even a needle tick would not interrupt our dreams. Our eyes were fixed on the screen, while our souls had incarnated Jack and Rose. Why did God not give Africans the ability to build ships like the Titanic? I wished I could take Shema away in the middle of an ocean. I would be better than Rose. I would not let my Shema die. I would die with him or survive with him.

"Now it's my turn, I invite you to the *Kimansuro* party," Shema said after the movie.

I accepted. We went to the *Kimansuro* party in a small motel with a name I could not remember.

Shema ordered some beer. I ordered a Coke. The almost naked girls danced as if their goal was to invite their clients to erotic games. Shema begged me to put my leg on his knee. To applaud the dance, he grabbed me and kissed me with passion. After a bottle of beer, he ordered another, and another, until I stopped counting. Each sip was followed by a kiss.

In the corner near Muchoma's bar, a giant guy gawked at us. "Hey, dudes, look, this one is the best," he said, pointing fingers to Shema. "He has come with his own slut."

"What are you talking about? Who have you just called a slut?" Shema got up to teach a lesson to the ill-mannered giant.

"I mean that *'fille-de-joie'* you are with."

Shema gave him a big punch in the face before saying

"You bastard. What shall we do with these people? They will never understand their time is over."

"Shema, please," I said. "Stop fighting. Let's go."

The other guy was very drunk. He was more muscular than Shema. One insult led to another, punches from left to right, and from right to left. In a few minutes, Shema was on the ground, blood running down his face. The police appeared and took the giant. Shema was transported to the hospital in an ambulance without paying for the beer he had consumed. He shouted that a Hutu was about to kill him. According to Shema, any evil person could only be a Hutu.

We spent the night in the hospital. They treated his wounds and gave him painkillers.

We returned to Cyahafi the next morning. Shema could not tell me more lies about the cause of his recurring injuries. Although I was not a prayer girl, I had to talk to God. I asked the Creator if he knew Shema. I begged the Lord to take care of an orphan. Shema was a cool person. He simply struggled to come to terms with what had happened to his life, and to make matters worse, he had turned to drugs that made him even more confused.

One day I told Shema about Muhire's experience in prison and how he had changed.

"It is good Muhire has finally been released," said Shema. "He shouldn't have been imprisoned for teaching a good lesson to a Hutu."

"Because the law doesn't permit people to assault others for whatever reason," I responded. "He recognizes and regrets his crime. I think he won't do it again."

"Does he have a choice? Those who killed our families walk freely in this country. When we touch one of them, the police throw us in jail. I wonder if this government is of Tutsis, as some people believe, or if it has been invaded by Hutus."

"Shema, what you are saying isn't true. Tutsis, Hutus, and Twas must live in harmony in this country. Moreover, those who killed our people are arrested and brought to justice."

"Hmm, when did you start talking like lying politicians? Wherever I go, I meet on the road the Hutu killers who roam freely as if nothing happened."

"What tells you they're killers? Is it written on their forehead?"

"Karabo, please stop asking me those questions. Is it you who is speaking or another person? How can you defend Hutus after everything they did to your family? Wouldn't you recognize a Hutu if you had met one on your way? And you ask me how I know they are killers? Do you know a single Hutu who is not a murderer?"

"I don't defend them," I said. "Let's end this conversation."

I had to stop it there. It was not a good time for me to tell Shema that I, too, wanted to hate Hutus with all my heart, soul, and mind, but also to say to him that hating Hutus would be like hating a part of the person I was. Whenever Shema spoke of Hutus, the Tutsi in me agreed with him, but the Hutu in me was offended and ashamed. I understood better than anyone the sense of unity and reconciliation. To me, it was not about the reconciliation of Hutus and Tutsis, but the integration of my two conflicting identities.

After a few days, Shema and I went to pay a visit to Muhire. I was delighted to hear that Muhire had accompanied Karega to his carpentry shop in Gakinjiro. He was learning from Karega how to work for a living.

We arrived a few minutes after they returned from work. They were still in their carpenter's aprons. They welcomed us, invited us to take a seat, and offered us drinks.

"Sorry, my friend," said Shema to Muhire. "It wasn't fair to send you to jail."

"Shema, I learned a lot from that experience. What we go through in life makes us better or worse. What I have to do is making sure I draw from that experience lessons that will make me a better person."

I appreciated those words of wisdom from Muhire and waited for Shema's reaction.

"Hmm, has the prison life made you better or worse?"

"I don't know. All I know is that I came out with the decision to aim for what is good and avoid all that is bad."

"Weren't you a good person before being put in prison?"

"My friend, I was put in prison because I had hit a person."

"No, Muhire. You had hit a Hutu bastard."

"A bastard or a Hutu, it makes no difference. I had hit a human being."

"Muhire, what happened to you? Maybe you weren't in prison but a chapel. As for me, whoever shall want to preach to me that I should not hate Hutus should let me go to hell if that's the punishment for hating them."

"I get why you think so. It is because of the pain caused by Hutu militants who killed your family. I also went through those moments. One day, you will realize a Hutu and an assassin are two different words that have nothing in common. But for now, let's pack this conversation for another day. Okay?"

"Yes, stop talking about it now," I said.

According to what Doctor Baziga had told me, if they had continued to argue, Shema and Muhire would have lost the opportunity to build their friendship, which would allow Muhire to gradually influence Shema's opinions and behaviors.

To change the subject, I asked Muhire about his new adventure.

"Are you a carpenter now?"

"Yes, there is no point in living in this world like a walking dead."

"That is true. Are you now able to make furniture?"

"Yes, but I still have a lot to learn. There is nothing more rewarding than changing a piece of wood into a well-formed piece of furniture. It's like creating. Besides, the little money I earn helps me support myself. If I continue to be a good boy and follow the lessons of my coach Karega, tomorrow I could be counted among the magnates of the city of Kigali."

Shema was silent until the minute I said good-bye to Muhire and his friend Karega.

From Muhima, Shema went to his studio in Cyahafi, and I returned to the campus.

In my room, I called Karega's phone and asked to speak to Muhire. I begged him to take responsibility for helping Shema. I asked him to become Shema's friend and, from time to time, encourage him to change some of his perspectives. As I spoke, Muhire interrupted me.

"Tell me the truth. I smell a love relationship between you and Shema. Am I right?"

"Muhire, I cannot hide it from you. I love Shema so much, and he loves me. But it concerns me that the bitterness of his life has closed all his doors of blessing. Shema lives miserably. In fact, he survives instead of living."

"I understand. I'll take the time to call Shema, and pay him a visit him. We'll talk like a man to another man."

"You'll have to be careful. He shouldn't feel as if you are pushing him to change."

Eight

On the second Saturday of February 2004, I woke up with discomfort and a severe headache. As I headed to the nearby pharmacy to buy painkillers, cars on the other side of the road slowed down. I wondered what was going on. A police motorcycle passed by with horns that hit my eardrums. Maybe I was walking in the middle of the road. When I noticed it was a presidential procession, I jumped and fell into a furrow. I felt a great pain in my head as if someone had hit me with a cudgel.

"Mama," I shouted.

The street boys who were sniffing some glue laughed.

"Listen to this young lady," one of the boys said. "She is calling her mama. She isn't like us who have forgotten the meaning of that word."

How did the word "Mama" slip from my lips? I wondered. A mother whom I could not run to, and who could not wipe my tears in moments of sorrow. I wanted to tell the street boys they were wrong. I did not have a mother to call. Someone interrupted my thoughts and pulled my shirt; my heart leaped to my head.

"Hello, Karabo, do you remember me?" he asked.

"No, I don't."

"I'm Mugabo, your cousin."

"Okay, how are you?"

"I'm fine. How are you?"

"Good."

I knew who he was. He had not changed much, except for the misery that appeared on his face. I turned back to go to the pharmacy. I did not have the energy to talk to him.

"Karabo, don't walk away. Let's talk for a moment."

"I am sorry, I have to go," I replied.

"I have a message from your mother," he said.

When he mentioned my mother, I stopped and turned to him. I was afraid to hear what he had to say.

"Do you have a message from Mama? Where is she?"

"We cannot speak in the middle of the road. Please, let's find a quieter place."

"Please, tell me. Is Mama still alive? Where is she? Is she back in Rwanda?"

"Karabo, I will answer all your questions. We can't talk here. Let's find a quiet place where we can sit. I will tell you everything and give you her message."

I did not want to sit down with that cousin whom I considered the son of a Hutu murderer, my maternal uncle Rwasibo. I was afraid of what he wanted to tell me about Mama. I was not sure if I wanted her alive or dead. We sat on a bench at the bus stop.

"Please, tell me now."

"Karabo, we have gone through horrifying experiences in refugee camps in Congo. My mother and sister, Ngabire, have been killed. Dad had joined the soldiers. The only person to whom I owe my life is your mother."

"Killed? How? And your father, what kind of army did he join?" I asked.

"They were killed during the war in Congo. It was said that the rockets that killed them were thrown by the new Rwandan soldiers who had pursued us in Congo. Dad joined the soldiers of the old army."

"Please, I beg you," I said. "Don't tell me about your experiences in Congo. I'm not at all interested. Where is my mother? What message did she give to you?"

He bent his head as if he avoided tears, then said, "Your mother lives in Malawi with her husband and children."

"Her husband? Children? What are you talking about?"

"Your mother has remarried. She lives in Malawi. But—"

"Okay. That's enough," I interrupted him. "Thank you for the news. Good-bye. Please, send my regards when you meet her again."

I got up and ran.

"Karabo, please, take this letter she wrote to you," Mugabo said.

He ran after me and threw the letter to my back. I took it and went on. I forgot I was going to the pharmacy. I rushed to return to campus. I could hear the sounds of cars and people running in my little head. My back gave me a sharp pain, and all the organs of my stomach fought against each other. Maybe I was going crazy. When I reached the street boys who had made fun of me because I had shouted Mama, I stopped.

"Guys, I don't have a mother," I told them.

"Hey, are you also a trash eater like us?" asked one of the boys. "You look like a child of those whose needs have all been satisfied."

I threw the letter to them. There was nothing to read in it. My heart was bulkier than the whole planet Earth. The world had become vast, but I could not fit in. My brain could not digest the information Mugabo had given me.

How could Mama forget so easily? How could she marry one of the Hutus she had run with? I wanted to call Papa and tell him he had made a big mistake in marrying a Hutu woman. She did not deserve to be my mother. She was as good as dead to me. The puzzle that had been difficult for me had been made easier. I had nothing to do with Hutus. I reached the campus, went to bed, took my red pillow, and cried for my family.

On Sunday, my phone rang, I did not recognize the number. I took the call.

"Karabo, how are you? It's been long. You've forgotten us."

"No. I didn't forget you."

"Karabo, something is stuck in your throat," said Uncle Kamanzi.

"What's the matter? Why don't you come to pay us a visit?"

Maybe I should have run to him and cried on his chest, but I judged it would not be a good idea. He would remind me I should not have expected better from my Hutu mother.

"Today, I'll have to read my notes," I replied. "I am preparing for an exam."

He insisted, and I finally agreed.

I had missed the beautiful smell of Kiyovu's big trees. I knocked on the door, and the doorkeeper opened. Neza smiled at me. Birungi greeted me with a kiss on the cheek. After a few minutes, Uncle Kamanzi entered.

"How are you, darling?" he said to Birungi, with a kiss. He turned to me and said, "We missed you. I guess studies have become more demanding."

"Yeah, it's not easy. I am writing my dissertation."

"Oh, it's going fast. You are already on the verge of completing the first-degree program. What are you writing on?"

"I am writing about the impact of political and social integration of all ethnic groups on conflict prevention in Rwanda."

"It looks like a big subject. Why did you choose it?"

"As a political scientist, I am interested in studying the relationship between ethnic integration and conflict prevention. But many of my professors discourage me. They say it could be a thesis for a postgraduate degree. But I want to do it. Maybe I can start with a simple dissertation and develop it further at the postgraduate level."

"You're as smart as your father Kalisa," said Uncle Kamanzi.

Birungi gave us drinks and snacks.

"Recently, someone called me to inform me that those whose loved ones are in the same mass grave with your father and sisters want to organize a decent burial for them," said Uncle Kamanzi.

"Oh, how did they manage to identify everyone whose relatives are in that mass grave?"

"Local authorities have launched announcements to find all the families. They are planning the exhumation and burial in April of this year. We will have to participate in the planning meetings."

I was happy to hear that my father and sisters were finally going to receive the decent burial they deserved. I had no reason to wait. Mama had another Hutu family. My father and sisters counted on me only. I hesitated to talk to Uncle Kamanzi about my mother, but I thought he had proven to be better than the woman who had fed me milk from her breasts.

"I...I have bad news."

"What is it, Karabo?"

"It's... It's about...about Mama."

"What happened to her?"

"Nothing. She is fine. She lives in Malawi."

"In Malawi? How did she get there?" he asked, before adding with a laugh, "Those Hutus toured Africa."

"I don't know how she got there. All I know is that she's fine. She has… She has another husband and children."

Uncle Kamanzi approached me, invited me to lay my head on his chest, and said, "Stop crying. Please, wipe your tears."

I wanted to tell him everything about the pain of my heart, but I did not have words to describe my immense sorrow. Would I have said to him I was sad my mother was still alive? Was I unhappy that she had married another man? Maybe neither one nor the other. Mama had forgotten the love pact she had signed with Papa. Mugabo had not told me the kind of man Mama had picked, but I could guess she was with one of the Hutus she had met in the Congo refugee camps. *What if she married one of the Hutu militants who killed her husband and children?* I mused. Uncle Kamanzi wiped my tears, but the eyes poured more.

"Who gave you the news?" he asked.

"My cousin Mugabo who was with her in Congo."

"Karabo, you have to stop talking to those Hutus you call your relatives," said Uncle. "Their goal is to hurt you even more."

I nodded. Maybe Uncle Kamanzi was right.

We concluded on the exhumation and burial of Papa and my two sisters Fifi and Dudu. I said good-bye to him, and to his wife and daughter, and went back to the campus.

In my nightmares, I replayed the memories of the past, our family tea parties with Mama and Papa smiling. I turned to the page of the present, which showed Mama with another unclean Hutu man, in dirty clothes. I shouted and asked

Mama to leave that man and go saving Papa from the Hutu killers' hands.

The following Monday, Sugira searched for me from every corner of the campus. He noticed my heart had been broken into pieces. With insistence, he asked me why I was sad. I finally told him about my meeting with my cousin Mugabo.

"What did she write in that letter?" Sugira asked, referring to the letter Mama had written to me. "Why doesn't she come back to Rwanda?"

"I don't know. I didn't read the letter. I threw it away."

He cut a leaf from the acacia tree and said, "If you don't mind, I have a suggestion."

"Tell me."

"I share your pain. But you should know why your mother did what she did."

"What else do I need to know, and why?" I asked. "Do you want me to know how she takes care of her new children? Or how much she loves her new husband?"

"No, that's not what I mean. Maybe there are other reasons why she didn't return to Rwanda. You have to think of other possibilities. What if your uncle Rwasibo forced her to that marriage?"

"It's a possibility, but it doesn't change the fact that…"

I could not understand how Mama had followed the Hutu-killers of her children in bushes in Congo, and later in Malawi. I could not fathom how she had decided to marry that Hutu before, at least, returning to Rwanda to pay her last respects to Papa.

"I don't care about all the reasons that made her remarry and why she never returned to Rwanda. She's as good as dead to me."

"Why don't you talk to your uncle Gasana? Maybe he has more details about why your mother did what she did."

"Who? Did you say Uncle Gasana? What's the difference between him and Mama, or their entire family?"

"Perhaps your uncle has not found an opportunity to share with you all the information he may have about your mother and your maternal family."

"I don't want to listen to what he has to say."

"How about Mugabo, your cousin? Where does he stay?"

"Maybe he stays with Uncle Gasana. The truth is, I don't want to meet any member of my maternal family. They are all the same."

"Karabo, if you don't mind, I will accompany you," said Sugira. "I'm sure it will be good for you to have more details. Don't worry, if it breaks your heart, I'll give you my shoulder to lean on."

"Sugira, stop that. This is serious. Don't joke about it."

We returned to our classrooms. My brain advised me to consider Sugira's advice. If having more details would not give me a chance to understand why Mama did what she did, at least it would confirm my judgment about her.

After two days, I asked Sugira to accompany me to Uncle Gasana's house. He accepted as he had promised.

Uncle Gasana had moved from Kacyiru to the new neighborhood of Nyarutarama and lived in a modern, large two-story house. We rang the bell, and the porter opened for us. Every time I went to his house, I was always amazed by my uncle's wealth. But that day, the second I entered the compound, antagonism broke my heart. How could Uncle Gasana milk Rwanda without encouraging his own family members to return to the country?

"Welcome, my children," said Uncle Gasana. "It's been a long time."

Luckily, his wife was not there.

"Hello, Mr. Gasana," Sugira replied.

"And the studies? How is it going?"

"Good," replied Sugira.

He asked us what we wanted to drink, and we chose mango juice.

Only Mugabo could save me from that boring conversation about weather, seasons, and studies. He came downstairs and greeted me with a big smile.

"Oh, Karabo, I'm glad you came to visit us."

"Thank you."

"Hey, are you okay?" Mugabo asked.

"Yes. I'm fine."

Mugabo reminded Uncle Gasana he had told him about the day we had met, and how saddened I was by what he had told me. Uncle Gasana asked me why I was sad to hear about Mama. I did not answer.

"Did you read the letter she sent you?" he asked.

"No. I didn't," I replied. "Mugabo had told me everything I would read in that letter."

"No. That's not true," Mugabo said. "I didn't know what was written in the letter."

"Uncle, what I understood is that Mama is still alive. She lives in Malawi and has a new husband and children. She is fine."

"Karabo, it's not easy for your mother," said Uncle Gasana. "She's a refugee. I believe you know what that means."

"Eh? A refugee? Why? What's she running away from?" I asked.

Uncle Gasana told me about the harsh conditions in which Rwandan refugees lived and that Mama could not abandon her new children. I maintained she had chosen her children over me. Mugabo did not agree with me. He told me about their experiences in Congo before Mama met her Hutu husband.

"Perhaps we would have died in Congo if Hagira had not made your mother his wife," Mugabo said, with wet eyes.

"How? Please, explain that to me."

"Hagira was one of the influential people in the refugee camps. Everyone feared him. But when the camps were attacked, he also had to save his own life. He found us on the way, fleeing the shooting. Your mother had difficulty crossing a bridge made of thin sticks. Hagira helped us cross the bridge, and from that moment, we continued the journey together."

"And how did he become my mother's husband?"

My back ached while my eyes fought with tears. What broke my heart more was not that they suffered in Congo, but the fact that Mama had to share the fate of the Hutu militants who killed her husband and her children.

"Karabo, let me stop here," said Mugabo. "I cannot talk about everything we experienced in Congo. No, there are details I can't tell you."

"Please, tell me. Don't worry about my tears."

"I...I also hated Hagira a lot. I hated the fact he did... He gave your mother the same ordeal she was running away from."

"What do you mean? What did he do to Mama?"

"Karabo, please, don't make me say it. What don't you understand?

He... He forced her to..."

Mugabo could not finish the sentence.

"Did he rape her?" I asked.

"Yes. Please, don't ask me how. Anyway, now they live together, with their three children."

I ran to the garden, sat in the grass, and let my skull unload all the tears that remained in it. *Is that why Mama has not come back to Rwanda?* I wondered. I could not digest the idea Mama could have gone through the same rape experience Devota had gone through during the genocide against the Tutsi. *Why is she still living with that cruel rapist?* My brain could not advise me. My heart was broken. My legs shook, and my hands shuddered. If the heavens were not far, I could hit the clouds with my head. The trees in that small garden of Nyarutarama looked at me with rage, but the grass shared my pain. Uncle Gasana came out of the house.

"Karabo, stop crying," he said. "Wipe your tears. Your mother is fine."

"How?"

"They are now a family. They only suffer from their poor refugee lives, but they are fine. We should thank God she didn't lose her life in Congo."

"Maybe it would have been better," I said. "Do you think she is alive? No. My mother is dead, even though she still wears her human body."

"Don't say that. I hope one day they will come back to Rwanda."

"When? What's stopping her from coming today if she wanted to? I don't understand."

"Her husband is afraid to return to Rwanda. He thinks he will be put in jail."

"Of course. He must return to Rwanda and face justice. He must be punished for the Tutsis he killed, and for having raped my mother. But why wouldn't Mama leave him?"

"She wouldn't want to leave her children?"

"Those children are fruits of the wickedness of the man who made Mama his captive."

Sugira came out and sat by my side. He told Uncle he must understand his sister was held a captive by Hagira, and he added that Uncle Gasana should do everything possible to bring Mama back to Rwanda.

"Sugira, I can't separate Musanabera from her family. I mean her husband and children. Karabo, you must understand your mother is now married to another man."

"No, she is not married," said Sugira. "Mugabo has said the man raped her. Please, help Karabo's mother."

"You are both still young," said Uncle Gasana with a sickly smile.

"There are many things you don't understand."

"Like what, for example?" I asked.

"I wish you could visit those Hutu refugees. You would be able to understand their pain."

"Uncle, I'm sorry, I never get you," I said. "Why do you always talk about the sufferings of Hutu refugees, when you never care about what Tutsis went through? Look at me, those you defend killed my father and sisters, and as if that wasn't enough, they held my mother a captive—do you ever understand that?"

"Karabo, do not talk to me with that tone," said Uncle. "Please, don't disrespect me. I don't owe you any explanation."

"I am sorry. I didn't mean to disrespect you," I replied. "I wanted to remind you there are Rwandans who should be judged for what they did to our country. Please don't defend them. I would also like you to sympathize with those whose parents or relatives were killed simply because they were called Tutsis."

"Please, let's end this conversation," said Uncle Gasana.

"Thank you, Uncle," I said before turning to Sugira.

"Let's go. We have got everything we wanted from this place."

Nobody accompanied us to the door.

On the way back to campus, Sugira and I did not talk to each other. The story about what Mama went through had not convinced my heart to forgive her. She was no longer the mother who had taught me what it meant to be a woman of character. Mama had surrendered herself to Hutus. She had allowed those who had killed her husband to make her their captive. She had cheated on Papa. My mother had abandoned me.

Arrived at the campus, I rushed to my room, took a warm shower, put on a nightgown, and lay on the bed.

Before I closed my eyes to sleep, the phone rang.

"Hey, honey, kiss to you," said Shema. "How are you?"

"I am all right."

"Are you sure? What's wrong?"

"Nothing. Maybe it's because I'm already in bed."

"No, that's not true."

"I am tired."

"I'm tired too, but my voice is not as overshadowed as yours."

"Are you tired too? Why?" I asked.

"Tell me if you want me to come and tell you what made me tired. I'll be there in less than five minutes."

"Do you want to come to the campus? Hmm? Maybe tomorrow. I want to sleep. But I am curious. Please tell me what made you tired?"

"I have good news."

"Hey, tell me, please."

"Not on the phone. Don't worry. Go to bed. I will come tomorrow."

"No. I will come to your house tomorrow afternoon. Okay?"

"Very good. Have a nice sleep, darling."

What does Shema want to tell me? I wondered. My ears were not ready to listen to him. They were busy with the sound of Mama whining and screaming as she pushed more wooden sticks into the fire to minimize the smoke that gave her a cold nose. Her children cried as if they were starving. On the other side of the house, a dark-blue-skinned man with red eyes was drinking banana wine *urwagwa*, calling Mama all the names of ill-mannered *abatindi*. Tears stung Mama's eyes, and she blamed it on the smoke. To distract herself from all that, she sang praises to God, begging him to save her from that misery. On the other picture of my conscious or my subconscious mind, Papa and my sisters were shining in white robes, resting near their Creator. Papa begged me to go save Mama from the devil's hands. I refused and said that Mama had chosen that misery and that she had to bear the consequences. All night, I was in dreams or nightmares that made me travel from Rwanda to all corners of the world, before returning to Rwanda. I could see Hutu militants with rifles and machetes calling Papa's name loudly. I could see Mama running away with the Hutus, and one of them ripping off her clothes to shame her womanliness. *Why did she run away with them? Why didn't she abandon herself to death to accompany Papa into the invisible universe where pain did not reside?* When I woke up from the nightmare, the sun was already waving at me through the window.

Nine

At 2 p.m., I went to Shema's house as promised. I was so curious to know what he wanted to talk to me about. I knocked on the door, and Shema opened. I jumped at the way the decor of his studio had changed. The mattress was no longer on the floor but on the bed, covered with blue sheets and a red bedspread. In the corner, they had hidden a jerry can, a bucket, pots, and other household tools under a small table. The table was covered with a white tablecloth.

"Wow, everything changed here. It looks like a total makeover."

"Thanks, my dear, we are learning to be more organized."

"When did you buy all these?"

"I took them from Muhire and Karega's workshop."

"Oh, did they give them to you?"

"No, we made them."

"You made what? Are you also a carpenter?"

"I try. Please, go slowly. I will tell you more. Something to drink?"

"Thank you. Tell me, what did you want to talk to me about yesterday?"

He pulled a bucket from under the little table. In the bucket, there was a bottle of pineapple juice. My head whispered to me that perhaps Shema had finally been convinced he had to start living instead of just surviving. His face looked clean and serene. He spoke to me and smiled at me, not rushing to jump on me for our usual bed games.

"Here you are," said Shema, giving me a glass of juice.

"Thank you. Shema, don't kill me with curiosity. What did you want to talk to me about yesterday?"

"Don't be too curious. It's not that important. I wanted to tell you I am back in school."

"Shema, do you go to school? Let me give you a hug."

"Please, add a kiss too."

"At school, do you learn carpentry?"

"No, I chose a different vocation. I study tailoring and fashion design at a Japanese school in Kacyiru. I went to the Fund for Assistance to Genocide Survivors, and I was captivated by how they welcomed me. They agreed to pay the tuition fees. I now have something to praise this government for."

"Oh my God, Shema, I must kiss you again. What can I say? I hope you also stopped smoking marijuana."

"Hey, I have no problem with marijuana. I haven't swallowed the whole gospel of Muhire. Don't ask me if I forgave the Hutus too. I must live well to complete their defeat."

"That's true. But if you don't stop smoking weed, it will prevent you from pursuing the good life you deserve."

"One day, I will stop but not today. Besides, I don't do much. It's only marijuana, except for one or two days when I tried stronger drugs."

I did not insist. The most important thing was that at least Shema had made a step toward a better life. His plans were more important than becoming a tailor. He was aiming to be a renowned fashion designer. As usual, our lips celebrated the good news. His eyes explored my face and led my heart to dance in my chest. His smile, with a chocolate gum and long white teeth, made me silly. I flung into Shema's chest and let him suck my lips and caress my body's erogenous zones.

As he traveled all over my skin with his hands, he said, "Karabo, there is something else I want to tell you."

"Hmm?"

"I have not been the best boyfriend, but now I want us to become two birds in our own nest. We will admire both the blue of the sky and the blue of the waters. Would you allow me to love you from toe to hair?"

"Shema, you know my answer. If we find it difficult to become birds and fly in the sky, we will become fish and swim in the waters, and descend to the deepest to survive with seaweed."

"My love, let's have a pact that we will always be together. Let's take an oath nothing, and no one shall ever separate us. You have neither a father nor a mother. I have nobody. You have neither a brother nor a sister. I have no one. There are only two of us in this world. I have you, you have me. Please, tell me you will always be by my side."

"Yes," I said with a voice stuck in my throat.

"Your eyes don't agree with you," said Shema, rubbing his nose.

"I am sorry. I have to go. I have an appointment with my supervisor. I have to work on my dissertation."

"Hmm? Do you want to leave? Karabo, tell me the truth... What is it?"

"Nothing. I just want to go. Please, see me off to the door."

"Please, Karabo, don't do this to me. Look at me, I want you… Please."

He pushed me back to the bed. I was not in the mood anymore. Shema deserved to know the truth about Mama. I could not tell him the truth. Maybe the best decision would be to end our relationship. Perhaps since he had vowed to change his life, he would survive our separation. I became like a tree trunk. His caresses could not take me high anymore. He gave up suddenly, put on his shirt, got up from the bed, and sat on the chair.

"Shema, please forgive me. Yes. I have a lot rocking in my head. Please don't get upset with me."

"It's okay. No worries."

"Will you see me off to the door?"

"Yes, when you're ready."

Shema's eyes had turned red like blood, and his body was sweating. He washed his face, opened the door, and suggested to accompany me up to the campus.

As we climbed Gakinjiro, I showed him cars and people wearing funny clothes and he would nod and mumble.

At the campus, I promised him a visit the following weekend. He murmured a shy "yes," rubbing his eyes. I waited for a good-bye kiss, but he only gave me a peck on the cheek. I rushed to my room and squeezed my red pillow. I had to cry for Shema. I cried for our love. Everything was by love. Everything was for love. The world had put bitterness on Shema's plate. He could not bear treason on the part of the person he trusted the most. Life without Shema was going to be like death without a coffin.

In the morning, when I woke up, there were eight missed calls on my phone. My heart wanted to call back Shema, but my head was bewildered. I had to stick to my decision.

Shema needed time for his own life. I picked my books and went to class.

At noon, Sugira invited me to lunch at the campus restaurant. He did not ask me why I was sad. He knew half the story. He had no idea my biggest concern was not Mama's plight but my love for Shema.

"Karabo, I would like to give you a piece of advice," Sugira said after a moment of silence.

"Go ahead," I said.

"It would help you if you could talk to someone."

"Speak to whom? What do you mean by that?"

"Sadness is written everywhere on your face. You have to get it out of your system."

"Sugira, it's okay. I'm fine."

"No, it's not all right. You have nothing to hide. I have my opinions, but I don't know if you would listen to me."

"My friend, for the moment, I only want to listen to my heart."

"I understand you. But keep one truth in mind; your mother will always be your mother. Good or bad, she is your mother."

"Sugira, I don't want to talk about Mama. Not now."

He kept silent, and we went back to classes.

In the evening, I could not sleep. My heart was pompous; my head was perplexed. I was going crazy. Maybe I could talk to other survivors of the genocide. Perhaps I could talk to Uncle Kamanzi. Nobody would be delighted to hear the story of a Hutu woman whom I called my mother. A woman who had left her Tutsi husband and children to be killed by Hutu militants. A woman who had followed the same Hutu militants in the bushes of Congo. A woman who had agreed to be captive to a Hutu militant whom she called her husband. Why was I interested in that woman? Why did I want to share her pain and sorrow? The same woman who had separated me from her breasts was going to separate me from Shema's chest.

———➤

The next day, I did not have the strength to go to class. After taking a shower, I sat down on the bed to mourn the ill-fated novel of my life.

After a few seconds, an idea clicked in my head. I looked for the business card of Doctor Baziga from Ruhuka Centre; it was not on the desk. I removed all the things from my purse; the card was not there. I invoked Saint Anthony of Padua before rummaging again and found it in my purse's back pocket. I called Doctor Baziga. He invited me to his office in Kinyinya. I was not taking Shema to a therapist, but myself.

The doors of the Ruhuka Centre looked like heaven for the weary. The flowers in the garden were decorated with peace and serenity. The birds hummed in the trees. Doctor Baziga came out with a big smile. He welcomed me and led me to a small empty room. The walls were painted white, and apart from a table and two chairs, there was nothing else in the room, not even paintings or pictures on the wall.

"Do you want some tea?" asked Doctor Baziga. He was in no hurry to listen to what I had to say.

"Yes."

He brought a cup of tea and a bottle of water.

"How is it going at school? Are you now in your last year?"

"Yes. I am writing a dissertation."

"Very good. You wanted to talk to me... Go ahead."

"Yes, but I don't know where to start."

"Don't worry. It doesn't have to be structured. Tell me what you can communicate."

"Doctor, you know I am a survivor of the genocide against the Tutsi, right?"

"Yes, I know."

"Maybe you don't know my mother is still alive. I am one of those called *imvange*. My mother is a Hutu."

I told him all about the misfortune that the Hutus caused my family. I told him that even though part of me loved Mama and sympathized for what she had gone through, I cursed the day she had left us. I narrated to Doctor Baziga how the Hutu militants killed my Papa and sisters and how I did not belong entirely to any ethnic group in Rwanda. The Tutsis with whom I shared the suffering did not accept me 100 percent, and the Hutus, including those to whom I was related, showed no sympathy for the pain caused to my Tutsi family. I told him about my impossible love relationship with Shema. I could not continue. He gave me a handkerchief to wipe my tears and encouraged me to tell him more.

Doctor Baziga gave me all his attention. He gave me all the time I needed to weep all my sadness.

"That's what upsets me," I said. "I belong nowhere. I share the suffering of the Tutsis, but also the remorse of the Hutus."

"From what you've told me, you were disappointed by different people in your life, including your mother. Yes?"

"Yes, Mama didn't only disappoint me. She betrayed my father. She followed the Hutus whom she considered her relatives, and married one of them when my father and my sisters were still calling for the recognition of their dignity."

"You've told me she was dragged to Congo by her own

brother, and that the husband with whom she lives raped her before marrying her. Isn't that what happened?"

"Yes, but that doesn't change the fact she failed. She didn't fight for Papa's family as their daughter or sister-in-law. Had she escaped from the Congo refugee camps, she wouldn't be in Malawi. And today? Why doesn't she come back to Rwanda? Why doesn't she come back at least to offer to Papa and my sisters the funeral they deserve? Imagine all the questions Papa's family has about the lives and deaths of their relatives in Rwanda. Wouldn't she come at least to cry with them? She has abandoned all of us. All that interests her is her new Hutu family."

"I understand you. You said your mother was a good person and full of life."

"Yes."

"Karabo, I'd like to suggest to you an exercise," said Doctor Baziga. "For our next conversation, you will tell me what you have learned from the exercise. That day, we will talk about other details of your concerns. Don't worry. It's not complicated. You will take some time to remember everything about your mother before the day she left. For example, the conversations you had with her when you were still small, the stories she told you, and all she did for you and how you felt about them. Describe the mother she was before she left. Don't think about anything that happened after she left. Go and do the exercise. Write everything on a piece of paper. We will meet next Tuesday, if possible."

"Next Tuesday would be difficult for me. Maybe Friday of next week."

"No problem. See you on Friday at four."

I drank more water and got out of there. Although Doctor Baziga had not answered any of my questions, telling my story without leaving any details was so comforting. He had given me an exercise to do, say a prescription.

On my way to campus, I thought about the exercise. My head replayed Mama's memories, our family nights that ended with prayers, Papa calling Mama to join him in their bedroom, and she would delay telling us bedtime stories.

In my campus room, I took a blank notebook to write everything down. We were a happy family.

During the whole week, I kept my meeting with Doctor Baziga, a secret. Maybe people would think I was going insane to talk to a therapist. Sugira begged me to speak with his mother. He thought I was troubled by Mama's suffering. I promised him I would find time to talk to Gatarina. She was a wise woman with a big heart. Maybe she could tell me something about Mama, but she wouldn't find a formula for solving the equation of my love for Shema.

On the Friday of my appointment with Doctor Baziga, I returned to the Ruhuka Centre. He welcomed me, gave me water to drink.

"How are you?" he asked.

"I'm fine. I did the exercise. Here you arc."

I gave him the notebook on which I had written all my memories of Mama.

"How did you feel when you were doing the exercise?"

"I don't know. I laughed. I cried. I miss Mama. I miss my family."

"If you could gather what's left of your family, where would you start?"

"What do you mean?" I asked.

"You have written down interesting memories of your family. You may not be able to restore everything, but there are one or two things you could save."

"I have nothing left, Doctor. I don't have a family. Mama, who could join me to form our little family, chose her new family, over me."

"If you had the opportunity to meet your mother, what would be your request to her?" Doctor Baziga asked again.

"Nothing. Anyway, I don't know if she would be able to give me what I would ask for."

"Would you tell me what you would request for?" the doctor insisted.

"As I told you last time, Mama betrayed the love pact she had signed with Papa. She married another man and gave birth to other children. She could at least have come back to Rwanda to honor Papa with a decent funeral."

"You told me she may have been forced to do what she did, but you don't understand why she didn't try to escape and return to Rwanda like many other Rwandans."

"Exactly."

"Maybe she wants to come back with her children. Do you ever think of them? What if they also need the warmth of the same mother you are claiming?"

"No. Never. It gives me a headache. I cannot stomach the fact Mama chose them over me. You don't understand me, Doctor, do you?"

"Yes, you, too, are her daughter. You need your mother, present both in time and space. Maybe there could be a chance to have her without separating her from her other children, whom she also carried in her womb for nine months."

"No. That won't be possible. But, Doctor, may I ask why you are focusing on Mama? I don't care about her. Maybe it would be better if she was dead. To have her alive is a shame for me."

Doctor Baziga gave me a handkerchief to wipe away

my tears. They wouldn't dry. I got up and said good-bye to Doctor Baziga.

"Karabo, I understand your pain. I'm not asking you to make decisions. I ask questions so that you can try to find your own answers."

"Yes. But I'm tired. This conversation is taking us nowhere."

"Take some time to think about it. Next time we'll talk about your other concerns, including your relationship with Shema."

"Yes."

We made another appointment for Friday of the following week. *Are the sessions with Doctor Baziga worth it? I wondered.* I did not have answers to his questions. To reconnect with Mama was as far as the moon. My heart was saturated with the sadness of what the Hutu militants had done to my family. I could not combine the identity of a survivor of the genocide against the Tutsi and a girl born to a Hutu woman who was touring Africa in Hutu refugee camps. Having Hutu blood in me had caused so much misery in my life, but separating me from Shema would be the worst of all.

On my way back to campus, my phone rang. I did not take it for fear that it could be a call from Shema. After a few seconds, it rang again. It was a call from Uncle Kamanzi.

"Karabo, why don't you answer my calls?" he asked.

"I am sorry. I was too busy with my studies."

"Not true. I hope you are not kept busy by those Hutus who are defiling you with news of your mother."

I did not answer. The resentment Uncle Kamanzi felt

for Hutus sometimes made him say to me words as sharp as a spear that devoured my chest and pulled out a piece of my organ. After a few seconds, he asked why I was not answering.

"Because I don't agree with what you've just said."

"Okay, I should give you other news, maybe good but sad."

"What is it? What happened?"

"Yesterday, I went to the meeting to plan the exhumation of the remains of your father and sisters. The funeral is scheduled for April seventh, the first day of the commemoration week. But the exhumation will start on April first."

"Hey? Is the burial planned on the first?"

"Karabo, did you hear what I've just said? Are you sure you're okay? I've said the burial is scheduled for April seventh."

"Okay, I get it."

My back and belly gave me contractions as if I was going to give birth. My eyes wanted to cry, but tears refused to come out.

"Please come home next Sunday so we can plan this important event."

"Yes, Uncle, I will come Sunday in the afternoon."

In fact, not all the ten missed calls were from Uncle Kamanzi. Eight of them had come from Shema. His text message tore my heart. "Karabo, all I have to tell you is that love liberates and heals, but it can also destroy and kill. If you want my love for you to liberate me, it will. If you want it to destroy me, it will."

I looked to the right and to the left, but I could not run from myself. I slipped about to fall down in front of a motorcycle.

"Hey, miss, what's wrong?" asked the outrider.

"I am sorry."

"What's bothering an adorable lady like you? Did he break up with you?"

"No. I am not feeling well."

"Go ask for forgiveness, he will listen to you. If he doesn't, I am also a man. I wouldn't mind holding that beauty in my arms."

Maybe neither Mama nor Shema should be blamed for the tragedy that Rwanda had gone through, I mused. Mama had been forced to follow the Hutus, with whom she shared the name but not the shame. Shema's innocence had been wiped out by the shed blood of his loved ones, which demanded justice. *Maybe Shema is right, love was the only remedy they both needed*. I was making a fool of myself. *Who am I to give them a diagnosis?* Myself, I was coming from Doctor Baziga for my therapy dose.

Am I strong enough to help Mama and Shema? I calmed the madness of my head and rushed to the campus.

When I arrived near my room, I caught sight of Shema sitting in front of the door, but I could not run away.

"What's wrong?" he asked, shaking my hand. "Your eyes are red."

"Nothing. What are you doing here?" I asked.

"I have called you many times but in vain. Have you read my text?"

"Yes."

"Karabo, why that sadness?"

"I'm fine. You can come in."

"Thank you."

I served him orange juice. I did not have the strength to drive Shema out of my room. My whole body wanted to jump on him and lie on his chest. I wished I could respond to his message. I wanted to tell him the fate of our love was in his hands. He should tell me if our love was leading us to our liberation or destruction. I was so afraid that our love's flames would burn our hearts already hurt by our life experiences. Its smoke would leave an eternal cold in our organs. I sat on the bed like a shy teenager next to a boy she secretly loved.

"Thanks for the juice, it's delicious," Shema said to break the silence. "But you didn't tell me why you look like a chick that has caught cold."

"You know, we are approaching the week of commemoration."

"Yeah. That's true. But you are weaker than usual."

"We are planning the exhumation and the funeral of Papa and my sisters on April seventh."

"And your mother? Isn't she in the same mass grave with them?"

"Eh? Mama?" Yes, she is with them too," I said, adding more juice to Shema's glass.

"Take heart, darling. I'm glad we will give to them the decent funeral they deserve. Maybe one day, I will also find the remains of my family."

"Indeed. The dignity of our families should be restored. But I am afraid of the day I will see them in skeletons with torn flesh. I recall the day I left them lying dead in a river of blood."

Telling Shema Mama was dead was not a hundred percent lie. I wanted to bury her, not because I did not love her, but because she was as good as dead to me. Our worlds were too far apart, and our reunion was almost impossible.

I leaned on Shema's chest. He lifted my legs to help me lie on the bed. He lay down by my side. My brain did not want to, but my heart was pleased. His hands brushed my hair, but they did not move to my neck and chest. Soothing songs and poems accompanied my sleep. Shema told me how much he loved me and that he would do everything to make me the happiest in the world.

After a few hours, I woke up from my dreams, Shema was not by my side.

"Shema," I shouted.

"Yes, darling, I'm here. Have you slept well?"

"What have you done to me? You have lulled me to sleep."

"How?"

"With your songs and poems, you."

"Me? How? I haven't sung for you."

"Weren't you singing for me? Weren't you lying next to me?" I asked.

"No. I guess you were dreaming. But if you want me to sing for you, I'd do it enthusiastically. You laid your head on my chest and closed your eyes. I helped you lie down on your bed before I came back to sit on my chair, admiring the sleeping beauty."

I remembered I had broken up with Shema. It was a shame I had fallen into his arms.

"Thanks, Shema. But now I have to wash my face and go to the library."

"If you want me to leave, I'll go. But may I know the reason for that sudden decision to go to the library on Friday night? Can't you go there tomorrow?"

"I told you I am writing my dissertation. I have to spend more time at the library."

"Okay. Wash your face and see me off to the gates."

Shema's eyes did not agree with me, but I had to stick to my decision. With Shema in my room, what was a dream could turn into our usual reality. I washed my face and walked him to the gates. We looked at each other as if we did not know how to say good-bye.

"Please, take time to think about my text message," Shema said. "Do you promise?"

"Yes. I will think about it."

He put his hands on my cheeks, invited me to look at his eyes, and pulled my lips for a kiss that lasted two seconds. Before I could understand what was happening, I was already sucking a few drops of his saliva.

"Karabo, I love you. Please, say you love me too."

"Good night," I replied.

"Good night."

I rushed to my room, took my red pillow, and squeezed it tightly. I did not know what to make of my emotions.

Ten

On the first of April 2004, early in the morning, we went to Biryogo to the mass grave where the Hutu militants had buried Papa, my younger sisters, and many other Tutsis. We did not have wreaths of flowers, but hoes and shovels. The men delicately dug for the exhumation, while the ladies prepared the plastic sheets on which we would lay the remains of ours. Shema and Sugira, as well as Muhire and his friend Karega, were among the men. Mugabo, my Hutu cousin, whose father had killed many Tutsis in Nyamirambo, also joined them. After about four hours, we reached the remains. They had no flesh, their bones had been torn apart, but their souls and their spirits claimed their names' dignity.

On the morning of the third day of exhumation, I saw the little red dress of my sister Fifi, as well as the Bermuda shorts of my sister Doudou. The memory reproduced the image of Papa and my sisters lying in a river of blood with those same clothes. I showed Papa's shirt to Uncle Kamanzi. He took it in his hands as if he wanted to kiss it.

"Tss, the Hutus will not get away with it," he said before

putting on his shades and moving away from me a little further.

My other uncles—Rutayisire, who lived in Kenya, and Mugenzi, who lived in the UK—and many other members of my paternal family shivered as they stared at the skull that was believed to be of Papa.

I approached Gatarina to ask her if she had seen my maternal uncle Gasana.

"Even today, he has not come," replied Gatarina. "Yesterday, I called him. He told me he has too much work. He has sent Mugabo."

"Hmm? Doesn't he have a few minutes for the exhumation of his nieces?" I asked. "And on the seventh, we will see him at the Genocide Memorial Center, in shades, behind the president, pretending to be saddened by the tragedy of the genocide."

"Of course, as a minister, he will accompany the president of the Republic," declared Gatarina.

"Tell me, should he come as a minister for the funeral of his own nieces? I shall never understand what goes on in my uncle Gasana's heart and mind."

"Karabo, forget your uncle. Time will teach him a lesson."

While I was talking to Gatarina, I saw Shema sitting under a mango tree a hundred meters away from us. He had bent his head between his legs. I walked toward him, sat down by his side, and put my arms on his shoulders. His eyes were as red as blood. The smell of his body told me more.

"Shema, what's going on?" I asked. "Don't tell me you're smoking. Apparently, it's stronger than marijuana."

"I begged you not to ask me any more questions about

weed," he said, clenching his teeth and narrowing his face. "I must take something. Otherwise, I would take my own life or that of all these people who walk freely on the streets without paying for the blood they shed."

"I don't agree with you. You are destroying yourself by smoking weed."

"Please leave me alone," he said.

"Get up," I said. "Let's take a walk."

"A walk?"

"Yes, I'm in my neighborhood. I want to show you some Biryogo weed. You've never tasted *Asusa* beans, have you?"

Shema stood up and ambled with me.

"Who is that Hutu bastard?" he asked, after taking a few steps. "Do you know him?"

"Yes," I replied after turning back to look at the person who was following us.

"Please, tell him to get lost. I don't want to see his gorilla-like face. Why is he calling your name?"

"I don't know," I said, before turning to Mugabo and telling him, "Please, I don't have time to talk to you. I'll talk to you later."

"I'm going home," Mugabo replied. "I wanted to give you your message. A letter for you."

"Wait," I said.

While I tried to figure out what to do, Mugabo threw the letter to me, but Shema seized it before I could. On the back of the envelope, it was written the letter had come from Malawi. My hands shivered. My tongue jerked between my teeth. I felt a stomachache as if I needed to use the toilet.

"Who has sent you this letter?" Shema asked. "Who is that Hutu who has brought it to you?"

"That boy who has brought the letter is… His name is

Mugabo. His sister was my classmate in primary school. She is the one who has written to me. She... She lives in Malawi."

"Karabo, please, you must never have friendships with those Hutus. You have nothing in common with them."

"Hmm? Shema, not all Hutus are bad people."

"If they aren't evil, why are we here then? Who massacred our families? Didn't they kill your father, your mother, and your sisters? How dare you say they aren't evil?"

"That's not what I said. But what's telling you Mugabo is a Hutu? I have told you his sister was my classmate in primary school. I don't know anything else about their family. I beg you. Please, give me the letter. It's addressed to me, not to you."

Instead of handing me the envelope, Shema tore it up to read the content. I attempted to snatch the letter from his hands. As I pulled, he stretched more until the paper was torn into pieces. With all the strength I was using to pull, I fell to the ground and banged my head on a big rock. It felt as if my head had broken into pieces.

"Karabo," Shema shouted. "Sorry, you're bleeding..."

Many people galloped toward us. Uncle Kamanzi picked me up, put me in his car, and drove off to Kigali General Hospital. My head strained my neck, but that was not the reason why my heart was beating so fast. Mama's letter was in Shema's hands. I could not imagine his reaction after learning the sender was not my old classmate, but my own mother, whom he thought was killed by Hutu militants. Maybe Mama had detailed the reasons for what she had done. Maybe she had acknowledged her failure and asked for my forgiveness. Maybe she had learned that we were exhuming the remains of Papa and my sisters and sent me words of encouragement.

In the hospital, my wounds were treated. The nurse gave me sleeping pills. When I woke up, many people were in the room. I hid my face from the quizzical looks of Sugira and his mother. By their right side, stood Muhire and Karega. Maybe everyone was aware of my romantic relationship, which had gone wrong. After a few minutes, my paternal uncles Kamanzi and Rutayisire came in.

"Thank you for passing by," said Uncle Kamanzi. "You can now go out. We want to be alone with Karabo."

I was dismayed by the way Uncle Kamanzi sent them away. He had no right to despise my friends. They said good-bye and left. Uncle Kamanzi hated all those who looked like Hutus. He only showed empathy to those of his small circle of the Tutsi elite.

He pulled his chair closer to my bed and said, "Karabo, I have asked them to go out because we want to talk to you."

"Talk to me? Is there a problem?"

"We are worried about you," said Uncle Rutayisire. "We know these moments aren't easy. But please, take heart. We are your parents and will always be by your side."

"Uncles, I'm fine. Don't worry,"

"You don't have to say that," said Uncle Kamanzi. "Even at our age, the experience of these last days has left us devastated. We can't comprehend how Hutus killed their compatriots with that brutality. Your father had married from Hutus, but they didn't spare his life or the children of their own sister."

"It's over now. No need to talk about that," I said. "What is important, for now, is to honor Papa and my sisters with the decent funeral they deserve."

My heart was too burdensome to bear the Hutu-Tutsi conversation.

"Okay, just know that as your parents, we feel your

pain," said Uncle Kamanzi. "You are saddened by your dad's death. You are disheartened by your mother's betrayal. We will be both your father and your mother. Do never worry about anything."

As my eyes let out the tears, my chest blew a bit of force to respond to Uncle Kamanzi.

"Mama didn't betray Papa," I said. "When she left our home, Mama was going to ask her brother to protect us. She did not come back. Do you know why?"

"She didn't come back because she didn't want to," replied Uncle Kamanzi. "She was with her Hutu family. She was spared from the killings."

"Please, let me bury my father and don't talk about Mama," I said, blues tearing my chest. "You don't know anything about them. You don't care about my sorrow. The Hutu militants killed my father and my sisters. And as if that wasn't enough, they took my mother and made her their captive. I am alone and lonely in this Rwanda. I don't have a family, and you can never replace them."

"Please, Karabo, my daughter," said Uncle Rutayisire. "Try to understand. Don't take it the wrong way. We share your pain."

"Uncle, I respect you both. Please leave me alone. If you felt my pain, you would understand I am absolutely orphaned with neither a father nor a mother. The Hutu militants killed my father, and soon we will be organizing his funeral. They also killed my mother, even though she is still standing and not ready to be buried; to me, she is as dead as the rest of my family. Please, let me be."

After they left, a nurse came in and closed the curtains. I closed my eyes to fall asleep.

The following day they released me from the hospital. Uncle Kamanzi begged me to go to his home.

"No, Uncle, please, take me to the campus."

"Karabo, you must listen to me. Come stay with us during this time of mourning. You shouldn't be alone."

"I am sorry. I don't want to disobey you, but I have to go to my room at the campus. There, I'm not alone. I am with my family, those who share my pain."

"Those who share your pain? Who are you talking about?"

"I'm talking about other orphans, survivors of the genocide against the Tutsi."

I had so many other problems to deal with, including what Shema had done with Mama's letter.

Uncle Kamanzi took me to the campus. Nobody was there except my roommate Karigirwa. My heart wanted to call Shema, but my head advised me not to. Maybe he had crushed himself with drugs after reading the letter. The idea that Shema could explode was giving me paroxysms in the heart. The ringing of the phone interrupted my dismay.

"Karabo, how are you today?" Sugira asked. "Are you still at the hospital?"

"No, I have been released. I am at the campus."

"Where? Who is taking care of you there? Anyway, I'm coming."

"Do not worry. I'm fine."

In less than ten minutes, he was in my room with a bag containing milk, juice, and fruits. He made me a fruit salad and encouraged me to eat.

"Sugira, you didn't have to bother yourself," I said.

"Bother myself? Or bless myself by doing something for you? I cannot give you the joy your heart longs for, but I can at least give you my ears when you want to talk to someone, and my chest when you want to lean on something."

"Thanks, Sugira. You are such a nice friend. I don't

know what I can tell you. You are the only person I speak to without pretending to be the person I am not."

"Thanks for looking at it that way. I pray to God to make me a friend you can always count on. You are an important person in my life. Whenever I am with you, serenity surrounds me."

I had a lot of esteem for Sugira. Sometimes he played the role of a brother I had never had, and at other times he played the role of a best friend. My heart and body did not push me to lie on his chest, but my head wondered why not. Maybe he could have helped me forget about Shema. Maybe I could have in him a lover from whom I wouldn't need to hide the details of my life. If I could find a good wizard, I would ask him to kill in me all the love I had for Shema and transfer it to Sugira.

I joined the others in Biryogo the next day, and we posed the remains of our relatives in coffins. I had forgotten my phone in my room at the campus. My uncles Kamanzi, Rutayisire, and Mugenzi were already there. In the afternoon, the priest led prayers and poured holy water on the coffins. We lit the fire and spent the night in a tent in Biryogo, singing mourning hymns. Sugira, Muhire, and Karega spent the night with us, but Shema had disappeared from the scene. Mugabo, my Hutu cousin, had not come back.

We left Biryogo around 4:30 in the morning to sleep one or two hours before getting ready for the big day. I had missed five calls from Shema. Fear pinched me in the stomach. Maybe Shema had called to bombard me with wrath after reading Mama's letter. I ignored his calls and placed the phone on the small table in my room.

In purple, black, and gray clothes, we headed for the Genocide Memorial Centre. The ladies were in *imisha-*

nana and the men in black suits. With white flowers in our hands, we arrived around 7:30 in the morning. As I had guessed, a few minutes after, Uncle Gasana, wearing his gray suit and black sunglasses, rushed to take one of the VIP seats reserved for the ministers. I went to talk to him, but a policeman stopped me and told me I was not allowed to go there. I made some noise to get my uncle's attention. Uncle Gasana gave a signal to the policeman to let me pass.

"Hello, Uncle," I said. "I wanted to tell you my family is among those whose lives we are honoring today."

"Oh, okay, go back. Please, don't argue with the policemen. They will show you where to stand." Maybe another minister had heard our conversation. To cover himself, Uncle Gasana told him: "She is the daughter of my sister. She is the only survivor of her family. They are among those we are laying to rest today."

"Oh, so sad. Take heart, my dear," said the other minister.

"Thank you."

Uncle Gasana was less concerned with the funeral of his nieces, but he had found it essential to use them as a card to gain acceptance from the other minister. Maybe he also told lies about my mother, his sister.

His Excellency, the president of Rwanda, arrived after a few hours. He lit the fire. In his speech, the president recalled the context of the genocide. He spoke of the hatred against the Tutsi. He talked about Hutu power, the slogan of Hutu extremists. I hid my eyes until he added:

"No Rwandan should ever be ashamed of who he is, his ethnicity, his sex, or his religion. Never again."

After the president's speech, we placed the coffins of our loved ones in their graves, while five men in white T-shirts with the words *Never again* read the names of all the victims we were burying. After the burial, the choir of the Catholic Church sang '*Nzataha Yeruzalemu,*' which translates as 'I will return home to New Jerusalem.'

After the event, Uncle Kamanzi invited members and friends of the family for the customary *gukaraba* at *Bar des Soirées Familiales*. From my maternal family, only my cousin Mugabo was with us. Uncle Gasana had gone with other senior government officials without even greeting my paternal uncles. A tall silhouette plodded a few steps from me. His sunglasses were hiding his eyes.

I approached and said, "Hello."

"Karabo, how are you?" Shema asked. "I have called you many times but in vain. I was worried about you."

"I'm fine. Don't worry."

"Please, forgive me. Everything was my fault."

"No. It was an accident. Don't blame yourself."

Has he read the letter? I wondered. *Maybe he is waiting for the right moment to teach me a hard lesson.*

"I don't recall how it happened. How did I push you?" Shema asked.

"Eh, did you push me?" I asked.

"Didn't I?" Shema asked. "I thought it was the reason why you fell. Karabo, maybe you're right. I should stop smoking weed. I was in my swings. I don't even remember what happened."

"Don't you?"

"No, I don't. Please tell me why and how you fell down."

"You were trying to pull a piece of paper from my hands."

"A piece of paper...?," he asked. "Oh yes, I remember... It was a letter sent to you by a Hutu woman living in Malawi. Why didn't you want me to read it?"

"Have you read it? Give it to me," I said, pulling his shirt.

"Hey, gently. I didn't read it," replied Shema. "I am sorry. I think I lost it. I was more worried about you."

"Don't worry. If it is important, she will write to me again."

My heart resumed its rightful place in the middle of my chest. Shema had not read the letter. Fate did not want me to read messages that Mama was sending to me.

After we washed our hands, we took seats on chairs in the tent. Uncle Kamanzi thanked all those who came to support us. He narrated, with sadness, the story of our family. He talked about how his father was killed in 1963, how his family went into exile, and what his brothers experienced in 1973. Then, he went silent, clenched his teeth, and turned his grief into rage.

"We thought it was over. We were discriminated against, but not exterminated. We were refugees but were not corpses. The apocalypse was waiting for us in 1994. I had warned my brother Kalisa about his marriage, but he had not listened to me. In 1978, he sent me a letter. He was announcing his marriage to Musanabera and told me their love was stronger than the hatred that flowed in the veins of Rwandans. He was wrong. They didn't spare him. They killed him and his innocent children."

The organs of my stomach crumbled. What was Uncle Kamanzi talking about? What if he was about to spill it all? Shema stroked my hands to calm my grief.

After a few seconds of pause, Uncle added, "Anyway, he's gone. He didn't receive the love he had given. Love didn't save him. Love destroyed him." Uncle took a handkerchief from his pocket and wiped his eyes hidden by the black sunglasses. "Please excuse me. I thank you for being here during these important moments of our family."

A sob escaped my lips. Shema invited me to lay my head on his lap. Maybe he had not understood what Uncle had said about Papa and Mama. After a few minutes, Uncle Rutayisire thanked and released our guests.

Uncle Kamanzi called my name, but before getting to his car, Shema ran to me. "Karabo, are you going to campus?" he asked.

"Yes."

"Do you have to go with Colonel Kamanzi?"

"Why do you ask?"

"I wanted to go with you. Why don't you join me in a taxi?"

As usual, my head advised me to say no, but my heart had already said yes. I said good-bye to Uncle Kamanzi and footed it with Shema. After a few minutes, a taxi stopped in front of us, and we entered.

"How are you?" Shema asked, massaging my fingers.

"Don't you know how I'm doing? I cannot paint it. I feel as bitter and sour as a lemon that can't even be used for lemonade. I don't have life in me. I have died inside."

"Yes. I see what you mean. It's as if the world rotates around us, and we fly like birds without a nest. The rope that connected us to the world was broken the day we were lost without parents or brothers and sisters." He stopped talking for a moment before saying, "Karabo, may I ask you a question?"

"A question?"

"Yes. There is something I have failed to understand. Why did Colonel Kamanzi say he had cautioned your father about his marriage to your mother?"

"I don't know. Only Uncle knows why. You know how he is, don't you?"

"Yes, but I didn't get what he was insinuating."

"Shema, I have told you I don't know. Uncle Kamanzi has never met my mother. He knows nothing about the relationship between Mama and Papa. I don't care what he said about their marriage. Can we change the subject please?"

"Don't get upset. It's okay. Don't think about it."

My heart rested well in my chest. Shema had not understood what Uncle Kamanzi had said about my family, but I could tell he was not convinced by my replies. Perhaps he expected me to wonder why Uncle Kamanzi had not approved my parents' marriage. I had understood everything. My mother's only sin was that she was a Hutu.

Shema accompanied me to the campus, and when we arrived at my room, he asked for answers to questions that had been hoarded for days.

"Karabo, maybe it's not a good day to talk about it, but I wanted to remind you of the text I sent to you. I'm still waiting for your response."

"Don't worry, I am still thinking about it."

"After all these years?" he asked, putting his hands on mine. "It's been more than nine years since we met for the first time. I fell in love with you the minute you walked into Colonel Kamanzi's house. Although life hasn't given me enough time and space to love you, my heart has always kept a VIP seat for you."

"Shema, I love you too. All that I am loves you. Never doubt my love for you. You've been everything that my heart, soul, and body desired. You have loved me as if I were the most precious princess of the *Kalinga* kingdom. You taught me how love can turn a person into a bird that flies in the sky without knowing where her winds can take her. But now I want to put my feet back on the ground. Shall you walk with me on this land full of mountains and valleys? Will you be able to climb all the mountains of my life with me? Will you stand beside me even when I will be pushed from left to right by the winds of the sturdy trees of this world? Will you come down with me to the valleys and never leave me alone?"

"Even though you sound so poetic, I would like to tell you, once again, that I decided to change my life and become the best I could be. Please allow me to climb the mountains of life with you. When you get tired, I'll carry you on my shoulders, and we'll walk together."

"Shema, it's serious. Some mountains aren't easy to climb, especially when hearts are weary."

"By the way, tell me. What kind of mountains of life do you plan to climb alone without me? What don't I know about you? We have already gone through a lot together."

I wish I had attempted to respond to his question, but the time did not seem appropriate. It was a matter of a few days before Shema learned the truth about my mixed ethnicity and my mother, whom I had declared dead but who was living in Malawi with her Hutu husband and children. I could not throw that atomic bomb at Shema.

"We haven't climbed all the mountains of my life. We are no longer teenagers. We must be ready to face the challenging life ahead."

"Okay, I believe I have understood. You're insinuating you'll soon graduate from university, and I, your boyfriend, don't have a clear plan for my future, isn't it?"

"No, that's not what I meant. There are many more unanswered questions about the future of our relationship."

"I get it. If you're ashamed to have a relationship with

me, that's indeed a big problem. I won't blame you because you're not the cause of my misfortune. You didn't make me an orphan without a parent or relative, and a poor guy with an empty pocket. Pursue your life. I wouldn't forgive myself for being the cause of your failures in life."

Shema got up to leave my room with a pleated face. I pulled his shirt.

"Shema, you're wrong. That's not what I meant. Please, forgive me. I love you. In you, I see treasures more precious than anything people around the world could offer. Even though riches and diplomas don't form the basis of a good life, I know you have everything you need to get the gold and diamonds of the world. My problem is that I have too much love for you. It makes me sway to the left and right, and lose the sense of the person I am. I want to be convinced of the future of our love both in my heart and in my head, but my heart dominates the brain."

He stopped and looked at me as I talked about my love for him. He invited me for a hug and a kiss. I refused. I could not allow myself to enjoy the pleasures of my body the day I had buried the remains of my family. I asked him to leave but begged him not to think about what I had told him.

"Why shouldn't I think about it?" he asked.

"In your phone message, you wrote that love could destroy or heal. We will let our love do what destiny has planned for us. If it's death, we'll die."

"Karabo, please, allow me to love you. Don't worry. Our love won't destroy us. It will restore us. But if you break the rope of love that unifies us, I will fall and crumble, and you won't be spared."

"And when you shall betray our pact of love? What will I do with my life?" I asked.

He put his hands on my cheeks and said, "That will never happen. Nothing or nobody will ever separate us. I promise you."

He gave me a peck and left. I slammed the door.

Mixed feelings danced in my head. I had offered Papa and my sisters the decent burial they deserved. But I had not taken the time to listen to the gratitude of their souls. Exhausted, I laid my body on the bed, held my red pillow, and whispered, "Papa, forgive me that I did not wait for Mama. She left. She betrayed the pact of love."

I calmed my heart and ordered it to listen to Papa's answer. He said, *My love, it's okay. I love your mother, and I will always love her. There could be reasons why she is where she is. I know her very well. She can never betray the pact of our love.*

Papa's response dumbfounded me. I could not sleep. I got up, looked for the notebook, and started writing about Mama. It was a therapy Doctor Baziga had prescribed for me. A soft voice from afar told me she missed me too. She whispered in my soul's ear that deep down in her bone marrow, she was still Musanabera, Mrs. Kalisa. No, Mama could not be a wife to Kalisa; he was no more. She could not be the mother of Kalisa's children; the Hutu militants had exterminated them. She had become Mrs. Hagira, the wife to her Hutu rapist and the mother of his Hutu children. I wept. I hated my mother. She was away from me. I could not call her. I could not stroke her hair. I could not lay my head on her chest. She was not there for me.

In the morning, the ringing of the phone woke me up. Sugira was on his way, and in a few minutes, he knocked on my room. I opened it and invited him in. I offered him mango juice.

"Yesterday, we didn't have the opportunity to speak," he said. "How are you?"

"I'm fine. Thank you."

"I have so many questions. But if you don't want to answer, it's okay. I'll understand."

"Why wouldn't I answer?" I asked.

"The period is difficult for you. Maybe you don't want to discuss other topics."

"What do you want us to talk about?"

"Many things. For example, how did you fall the other day?"

"How did I fall? I slipped."

"Karabo, who was that guy with you the day you fell?"

"Hmm? Don't you remember him?"

"His face is familiar. Who is he? Is he a member of your family?"

"No. But I can consider him as one. We lived together at Uncle Kamanzi's place. He was one of his escorts."

"Yes, of course. He is the guy who refused to shake my hand the first time I came to visit, isn't he? But you haven't answered my question. Who is he for you?"

"Sugira, I don't understand what you want to know."

"Karabo, I saw everything," he said, rubbing his eyes. "After you fell, the guy became like a bird with broken bones.

"And how does that explain your questions?"

"I'm not yet done. The biggest scene was yesterday. You laid your head on his lap as if the game was going to start. He didn't hold back; his hands brushed your hair. You didn't even worry about the fact so many people, including your uncles and aunts, were there—"

"Sugira, I don't want to talk about that."

"Why not? When I approached you, you left to take a taxi with him. Where did you go with that guy, instead of getting into your uncle's car?"

I remained silent for a while. Sugira made the tss sound.

His face looked dry. I cared less for his feelings, but for our friendship. I didn't want to lose the friend in him.

"Sugira, let me tell you the truth," I said.

"Please, go ahead."

"Yes, you are right. Shema was my boyfriend. But it's over now."

"It's over? So, what I saw yesterday was a replay, right?" he asked.

"He was there like all the other people who had come to comfort us."

"Anyway, whatever relationship you have with him, he has the eyes of a mean person."

"Why do you think he's not a good person?"

"Don't ask me what I think. If I were your friend, you would have told me you had another boyfriend. Karabo, how could you do that to me?"

"What did I do to you?" I asked. "What do you have to do with my relationship with Shema? I'm sorry to say, but you're talking like a jealous person."

"No, I'm not jealous." He looked down, picked at his nails, and said, "I have to go. Have a good day."

"Sugira, please, don't leave. Let me tell you the whole truth...I beg you."

I held his hands and directed him back to his seat. I was not indifferent to Sugira's sadness.

"Yes, Shema is my boyfriend," I said. "But please, lend me your ears. I won't lie to you. I love Shema with all my heart, but our love is impossible. It's over between us."

"Why is it impossible? Why is it over?"

"Sugira, don't give me that look."

I told him about the day I met Shema for the first time, and how we had become lovers in secret. I told him that since the day Hutu militants exterminated his family,

Shema's life had become blurred. I did not tell him about Shema's drug addiction.

He held my hands, looked me straight in the eyes, shook his head, and said, "I'm shocked by this nightmare. But don't worry, I'm listening. Why is your relationship with Shema impossible?"

"Shema has not yet digested his family's death. He hasn't forgiven the Hutus. He doesn't want to mingle with them or someone related to them in one way or another."

"What does that have to do with your relationship?" Sugira asked.

"I have never told him about Mama, lest he does something terrible to me if he found out that Mama was a Hutu who lives somewhere in the Hutu refugee camps."

"Maybe you're wrong about Shema," said Sugira. "He can't put you in the same basket with those who killed your father and your sisters."

"Let's stop talking about Shema," I said. "Let's talk about us. Whatever happens between Shema and me, I will never find a good friend like you in this world."

He turned his face to swallow the tears that were trying to blind his eyes. His chest was swollen as if he was taking in too much air.

"Yes, I am your friend, just a friend," he said with a sarcastic smile. "For you, I'm not a man, or I'm a man without a heart nor a body. Karabo, I'm a man, not just a friend."

"I haven't said you're not a man. I've said you're my best friend."

"Okay, I get it. Now that you've told me everything, may I leave? Please, my best friend," he said with another insincere smile.

"Do whatever you please. Maybe this isn't the right time to talk."

He gave me a handshake and left.

I rushed to hold my red pillow. In addition to losing my parents, I was about to lose the two boys who had kept me moving for years. For the whole night, I was in nightmares that seemed so real. I was alone without parents, without sisters, without relatives, without friends. My father's family was standing on my right side, pointing fingers at me, making me ashamed of having a Hutu mother. My maternal family was standing on the left, reproaching me for not being compassionate for what Hutus had also experienced in Rwanda and Congo. I wanted to run away and forget about it all. I wanted to forget the Hutus. I wanted to forget the Tutsis. I wanted to forget Shema. I wanted to forget Mama. I wanted to fly and go to another planet. I called Devota's ghost, but her ears had been buried with her. I got up, cleaned up all my sadness with a warm shower, and went out for a walk in the campus arboretum. My nightmares and dreams continued to dance in my head. Maybe I was going insane.

I called Doctor Baziga for an appointment, and he said I could drop by right away. I took the bus and went to the Ruhuka Centre to meet Doctor Baziga. I did not know what to discuss with him. Was I going to ask him to bring Mama back to Rwanda? *Why do you want your mother? Have you forgotten her betrayal?* My brain asked. My heart interrupted, *I know you better than the brain. I will grow bigger and heavier in your chest until the day you shall meet your mama. Your eyes will shed tears the day they shall cross your mother's. You will hug her, and you will feel the heartbeat of the chest that breastfed you. From that hug, you will renew the pact of your love.* I agreed with neither the brain nor the heart. I told both to shut up.

The bus stopped, and I entered the gates of *Ruhuka Centre*. Doctor Baziga was in the garden. He offered me a welcoming smile, gave me a handshake, and invited me into the usual small room.

"Tell me, how are you?" he asked.

"Fine."

"Your eyes don't agree with you," he argued. "What happened?"

"I wanted us to continue our conversation."

"Yes, last time we had agreed that we would talk about Shema. Okay?"

"Yes, but I would prefer we talk about me instead."

"About you? What do you mean?"

"Doctor, I'm afraid I'm going crazy. Our conversations have made me mad."

"How?"

"Last time I had told you I didn't want to think about Mama. My brain tells me I should forget her, but my heart wants to lean on her chest, smell her perfume, and listen to her heartbeat music. I am confused. I don't know if I have to obey my brain or my heart."

"What's the reason for the disagreement between your heart and your brain?"

"I have to stop being naive. I must not follow the madness of my heart. I have to reason with the brain. I must not behave like a butterfly in the sky without knowing where I'm heading. For example, my brain had convinced me to break up with Shema, but my heart disobeyed. What's wrong with me?"

"Some people say when you really love someone, you feel it in your heart," said Doctor Baziga before asking, "Do you mind talking to me about Shema? What kind of relationship do you have? How long have you known each other?"

I told him about our love story. I spoke about our love at first sight. I described his tall figure, his cow-like eyes, and long white teeth adorned with a chocolate gum. I recalled our walks under the Kiyovu trees on our way to and from St. Michael Cathedral. I told Doctor Baziga that Shema's charm had been stifled by the burden of rage and hatred against the Hutus, who had deprived him of the warmth of his family.

"Doctor, I cannot. I can't abandon Shema. To leave him would be like sacrificing my own soul. I need Shema as much as he needs me. He told me our love would heal us or kill us, and that our love is the cure for our sorrow. The appearance of Mama in my dreams makes Shema's love lose its rigor. Shema doesn't have a mother. I cannot forgive myself for abandoning him because my own mother has reappeared."

"How can I help you?" asked Doctor Baziga.

"Doctor, if you can, give me the magic to hide from Shema I have Hutu blood in me. Or, if you cannot get that magic, please give me the one that will make Shema love me for all eternity despite the person I am and the names I identify with."

"How about having Shema and your mother, both, in your life?"

"How? It's impossible. I love Mama, but I don't have her. I love Shema, but I don't have him for long. Please, help me erase or hide Mama from my memory and my life. And if she must show up, let Shema realize I am *Uwase*, the daughter of my Tutsi father. I have no connection with the Hutus, who made me an orphan. Can you make Shema love the Tutsi I am and ignore my Hutu blood?"

Doctor Baziga had his own list of questions.

"You've told me you miss your mother so much, and that you call her in your dreams."

"Yes."

"Do you want me to give you another exercise?"

"Exercise? Another...?"

He went out for a few minutes and came back with two baskets, one red and one white.

"Take these two baskets," he said. "The white is your mother, and the red is Shema. In each basket, you will place at least one picture. Put your mother's picture, if you have one, in the white basket and Shema's photo in the red basket. Whenever you need to talk to your mother, open her white basket, and tell her whatever is in your heart. Whenever you want to talk to Shema, you will do the same thing—open his red basket and talk to him. Tell them everything you have in your head and heart, including what you may not want to tell them in real life. After talking to them, stay silent and allow them to respond. Answer their questions and, if they argue, please explain to them. Next time, you will tell me what you have learned from the exercise."

"This is the funniest exercise I have ever had. Will I be able to talk to baskets? Now I understand I am really going crazy."

"Don't worry, it's not complicated. Take it as a game. A girl of your age needs to have a conversation with her mother, and you miss it. On the other hand, you're old enough to deserve a healthy and true romantic relationship. You love Shema, and you have been together for a long time. There should be no secrets between you. You shouldn't hide anything from him."

"Are you talking about Mama and Shema in the baskets or the real ones?" I asked.

"I'm referring to the real ones. But for the moment, I would like you to tell those in the baskets all that you haven't managed to share with the real ones. You will learn to communicate with them and listen to them speak with you. Please agree to try this game."

"Yes."

I asked him more questions about the task before saying good-bye. He gave me another appointment. I took my two baskets and left.

All the way back to the campus, I recalled I had Mama in one hand, and Shema in the other. I laughed at the way I carefully carried the two baskets as if they were full of fragile eggs. Why are real human beings not so calm? Why don't they let me put their love in my heart without pushing me to let it go?

At the campus, I looked for photos and put them in the baskets. I looked at the white basket and said to Mama, "Please, come back from those distant lands. Leave every-thing, come stay with me in this room. I will protect you from the Hutus who murdered your husband and your children, raped you, and made you their captive. I'll protect you from the Tutsis who do not know anything about your nobleness if you still have some."

I opened the red basket, put a picture of Shema in it, and said, "I was talking to Mama. I never lied to you about her. She is indeed dead, but she died a different death. She is dead but not buried. She is far from Rwanda, but I have brought her back in this little white basket. Maybe since she is not buried, she can hear me talk and come back to life. Do you want to help me bring her back to Rwanda? Don't say no because you told me we will climb the mountains of life together. This is the first mountain we will have to climb."

While I was talking to Shema, someone knocked on the door. She entered immediately. It was Karigirwa, my roommate.

"Who are you talking to?" she asked.

"Was I talking?"

"Yes. Karabo, what's going on? And these baskets?"

"Hmm? Maybe that's why I was talking to myself. These baskets are so beautiful. But I don't know where to put them in this room. There are so many papers and books on this desk."

"Yeah, that's true. You have to rearrange your desk. Maybe you need to throw some of the less important things away so you can find a place for your baskets."

"Uh, yes."

"Before I forget. I was looking for the other book I lent to you. I want to read it."

I looked for her book from that mess, and I gave it to her. She left.

I could not help but think there could be a drop of truth in what she had said. Indeed, the two baskets of Mama and Shema were of value to me. But I needed to remove a lot of clutter in my room to give them the space they needed. In cleaning my room, I also thought about how my life, in general, should be cleaned up. My brain whispered to me, Mama and Shema also needed to do some cleaning in their own lives to be able to enter the space reserved for them in my life.

After that day, whenever questions arose in my head about them, I threw them into my little baskets and waited for their answers. Mama always replied with words of hope. She told me I should not be trapped in my own sadness. And Shema, on the other hand, kept telling me he loved me and that he would climb the mountains of life with me. My red pillow became jealous of the baskets.

For several days, Shema did not pay me visits. I didn't receive his phone calls. I was worried. Even though we had

had a troubling discussion, we had concluded that we would allow our souls and our bodies to go with the flow of love. My head whispered to me I should let him go. I needed time to solve the puzzle of our love. I opened the red basket and spoke to Shema's photo. I told him how much I missed him. He murmured to me he missed me too.

One morning, walking to the library, I met Sugira. His big smile lashed my heart.

"Karabo, I was looking for you."

"Hello, Sugira. I was going to the library. Do you want to tell me something?"

He scratched his head, looked down, and said, "Yes, if it's possible."

"Okay. Let's sit under this acacia," I suggested.

He looked left and right. "How are you?"

"I'm fine. And you?"

"Karabo, I'm sorry. Please, forgive me."

"Why?"

"Forgive my behavior. I shouldn't have been mad at you. I am sorry."

"Hey, don't you think it's me who should apologize for having made you angry? Sugira, as I told you last time, you're my best friend. You are like a brother I have never had. You know I don't have a family. You are my family…"

Sorrow repealed my voice, but I held back my tears.

"I'm sorry," said Sugira. "The love I have for you is different from brother-sister love. But for the moment, I'll be satisfied with our friendship, as long as I still have a chance to be with you and talk to you. Whether you decide or not to love me the same way I love you, I will always understand. I respect the fact you have another boyfriend."

"Sugira, listen… I told you Shema and me, it's…"

"Please, stop talking about your relationship with

Shema," he interrupted. "If you are still together, it's good. If you broke up, that was your decision too. As for me, all I want, for the moment, is to offer you my friendship or fraternity, whatever you call it."

He smiled, then invited me for a hug of reconciliation. It was good to finally have a conversation with Sugira. I had missed him. I asked him about his mother Gatarina and Devota's daughter, Mbabazi.

"Why don't you find some time to visit my mom one of these days? She always asks me how you are doing."

"I miss her too. You know she's like a mother to me."

"A mother to you? You mean your mother-in-law? … I'm kidding."

"Please, stop. She is my mother. Let's go see her next Friday."

"Yeah. After school?"

"Good."

Eleven

For my thesis, the campus library had some books on ethnicity and the Rwandan context in particular. It was thought-provoking to learn that ethnicity was built and created by human imagination. I discovered that it could be born of palpable and historical forces or disappear when the situation of those who considered themselves to belong to an ethnic group changed. As a political scientist, it was vital for me to understand how ethnic identities could be accentuated by political leaders and how they would evolve over time, depending on the circumstances. The narrow vision of who the Rwandans really were led to their failure to objectively study Rwanda's history and culture and find solutions to the challenges and conflicts that characterized the twentieth century. Most Rwandans thought that people belonging to the same ethnic group necessarily shared the same fate. Many cared less about what they shared as a community that lived on the same land, connecting to other nations and waters that make our beautiful planet.

The ringing of the phone interrupted my reading.

"Hello, it's Muhire. Long time. How are you?"

"Oh, fine. You?"

"I'm fine. Karabo, I wanted to talk to you. May I come to see you today?"

I had spent several days at the campus without having the chance to go out. I suggested going to his place instead.

The sky was gray. In blue jeans, a black T-shirt, and black shoes,

I took my umbrella and left the campus. It was not long before I took the bus to Muhima. The streets were full of people and cars. While my head was still digesting the literature on ethnicity, I tried to guess the ethnic origin of the woman who was sweeping the road around the main roundabout of the city. Nothing suggested she was Hutu, Tutsi, or Twa. The ethnicity of the bus driver was also not apparent. The policeman in the street was as small as the woman who swept the road, but with eyes and nose similar to those of the tall bus driver. Perhaps the author of the ethnicity had another magical way of categorizing Rwandans.

At Muhire's house, I knocked on the door. He greeted me and offered me fresh pineapple juice. He asked how I was doing, and I told him I was okay.

"How's your friend Sugira?" he added.

"He is fine."

"Recently, I met Shema. God has worked miracles in his life. I couldn't believe my eyes."

"Why? How was he?" I asked.

"He was wearing a well-ironed white shirt, navy-blue polo pants, with polished shoes. He was coming from work."

"Work?" I asked.

"Don't you know that your boyfriend has a job?"

"No, these last days, I was too busy with my research. We haven't spoken for a few days."

"Not even on the phone? Or you… Did you break up with him?" asked Muhire.

"I love Shema with all my heart. I could never find the strength to break up with him, even if I wanted to."

"What happened? Why don't you talk?"

"Muhire, I cannot hide anything. You are like a brother to me. I didn't break up with Shema. We are still together. But I want to let him go. I have a lot to do in my life before I can consider a love relationship."

"Oh, why now? He needs you today more than ever. You must support him in everything he undertakes. Has he stopped smoking drugs?"

"No, he still smokes weed. I am so happy he has finally understood the difference between living and surviving. But in addition to smoking weed, he continues to carry the burden of hatred against Hutus."

"It's a burden that many of us carry. It can only be released from his shoulders if he abandons himself to God, the Creator of humans. But that shouldn't be the reason you would break up with him. You have nothing to do with those he hates."

"Don't you know Mama wasn't killed together with Papa?"

"No… Yes… Devota told me about it. Wasn't she killed later?"

"No. She lives in Malawi. She is the reason for my breakup with Shema."

"Why?"

I told Muhire Mama was a Hutu, and that I hadn't forgiven her for having not returned to Rwanda, at least to offer Papa a decent funeral. She followed her Hutu relatives and married one with whom she lived in Malawi. Muhire asked me if I knew why Mama hadn't come back. I told him that she didn't want to leave her new children.

"Muhire, please, let's stop talking about Mama," I said. "She isn't my main concern. The problem is that even if Shema loves me as much as I love him, our love is impossible. He will disband the day he shall learn that I am the daughter of a Hutu woman."

"Why? Is it a sin to have a Hutu mother?"

"For Shema, yes. Besides, he would hate me for having hidden the truth from him. I told him Mama had been killed the same day as Papa and my younger sisters. I don't want to be the cause of his collapse the day the truth shall fall right in front of his eyes."

"To be honest, I understand the state in which Shema is. I was there before I was enlightened by the Word of God. I abused Mbabazi because she was a child of a Hutu. I shouted insults at her. I spit on her. I had even led her mother to hate her own daughter. I couldn't understand how to live under the same roof with the daughter of the murderer of my sister Uwera and the rapist of my sister Devota. God taught me Mbabazi had nothing to do with what happened to my family. In fact, it was because of her I wanted to talk to you."

I could not share with Muhire that Mama had not chosen to marry the Hutu she was living with. I did not tell him Mama had been raped.

"Did you want to talk to me about Mbabazi?"

"Yes, I want to ask the Kamana family to give me Mbabazi. It's time for her to be raised by her own family."

"Do you want to live with Mbabazi? Will it be easy for you?"

"It cannot wait for the day I will get married. My future

wife will have to understand I have a child of my sister, whom I consider as mine. In this world, I have no one but Mbabazi. What does Devota think of me when I eat and sleep, without knowing where her daughter is?"

"You are right. Maybe we could go there together one day to visit them before you approach them and inform them about your plans. In fact, I plan to go there next Friday."

"Let's do it like this. When you go there next Friday, try to talk to them about my plans and see how they react. Tell them I want to come to express my gratitude next week. If they don't mind, I'll look for some people to accompany me with drinks of recognition, and then I'll take the opportunity to tell them I'm ready to take Mbabazi to live with me."

"I wish Shema had also made the same steps of life as you have. He must forgive the Hutus for what they did to his family."

"Forgiving is not an easy and simple thing," Muhire replied.

"Especially when the person who needs to forgive hasn't yet freed himself from the chains of his sorrow. Shema must free himself from the captivity of those who hurt him."

"How?" I asked. "I don't understand."

"He shouldn't allow the genocide against the Tutsi to be the point of reference for all decisions in his life. He must know there was life before the genocide, and there will be life after the genocide. To live is to reject the plan of the Hutu militants who wanted nothing but to exterminate us."

"Yes, you are right," I said. "I'm glad Shema has started to take a few steps towards a better life."

"That's the most important thing. But it will be difficult for him to keep moving forward if he is still drawn by the hate he feels. If he loves you, he loves you, whether you are Hutu, Tutsi, or Twa or even a foreigner. His problem is that he lets Hutu extremists' hate reign and continue to destroy him day after day. He's allowing the same hatred that separated him from his family to separate him from his girlfriend."

"It's a sagacious way of looking at things, Muhire… So, what can I do?" I asked.

"You aren't different from him. I also want to tell you that you should never allow anything, or anyone, to make you trapped in our tragic history. Shema shouldn't separate you from the mother whose breasts fed you milk and love. And your mother shouldn't separate you from the guy you consider to be your first and true love. It's up to you to say no and yes to both of them."

"It's up to me? How?" I asked.

I could not believe Muhire was going to be another therapist for me.

"Yes. You disappointed Shema. You have built your relationship on a big lie. You have deceived his trust. You shouldn't have told him your mother was dead… But please, don't think I don't understand. You had pushed your mother in the back-sphere of your heart where only bitterness and confusion reign. You didn't want the world to notice her in you because the name she bears had been made dirty by what the Hutu militants did."

Muhire was scratching the same scars Doctor Baziga had already made fresh. I had to leave.

"Muhire, I'm sorry. We will continue this conversation next time."

"Karabo, let me give you an important suggestion…"

"A suggestion? Go ahead."

"Please, learn to pray to God. You must pray for the

two most important people in your life. You must pray for Shema so that he may drop the burden he bears and find the strength to forgive Hutus even though it may be humanly tricky. You must pray for your mother the same way a child would pray for a parent in danger. Send love to both of them. It will come back to you in abundance. Please, know that loving them should never be an excuse to deprive you of loving yourself. You cannot give what you don't have."

"Thank you for your words of wisdom. I have to go. It's already dark."

He held my hands, asked me to close my eyes, and prayed for me before accompanying me to the bus stop.

On the way to campus, I digested Muhire's words. They had all kinds of taste, sweet, bitter, and sour. I could draw the link between his words to the exercise Doctor Baziga had given me. They had both read in my eyes that I missed both Mama and Shema. Several days had passed without speaking to Shema. Why had he not called?

When I arrived in my room, I opened my red basket and said, "Shema, I am sorry. Please, forgive me for having lied to you about Mama."

I turned to the white basket and said, "Mama, please forgive me for having confused you with the name of a Hutu woman, and ignored the fact that I had never smelled in your belly or tasted in your breast the hatred towards any living thing, human or non-human. I didn't care about your sadness the day you heard that your husband and daughters had been killed by those who called themselves your relatives. I didn't give you my ears so that you could talk to me like a mother to her eldest daughter. I didn't want you to disturb me with your grief because my chest was already heavy with my own sorrow. I love you, Mama. I miss you…"

I fell on my bed, squeezed my red pillow, and, after some minutes, I picked up the phone and dialed Shema's number.

"Hey, sweetheart," He said. "How are you? I am happy to receive your call. Kisses."

"Shema, how are you? It's been a long time…"

"Hey, Karabo, what's the matter? Don't tell me you have wept again…"

"No… I mean… yes. But I'm fine. Don't worry. I missed you."

"Is that the reason you're sad?"

"Yes. Don't you miss me too?"

"What do you want me to say?" asked Shema. "Last time, you told me tough words. Maybe you needed time to think. How should I make you understand I love you with all my head and all my heart? Shouldn't that be enough?"

"Why didn't you call me all these days?" I asked.

"If you want me to come to your place, in two seconds, you'll see me in your room. I want to come to wipe your tears."

"No. It's okay, I'm fine. You may come tomorrow if you want."

"Are you sure you want me to come?"

"Yes."

"I will come tomorrow at around three. But please, dream of me tonight…I love you so much. I don't think I'll need to repeat it every day after all the years we've spent together. We will talk tomorrow. Sleep well, and have the best dreams."

"Thank you. Good night."

All night, my head and my heart were playing Ping-Pong in my dreams. I practiced how I would tell Shema the whole truth. I would say, Shema, I'm sorry for telling you lies…

No, it would be a bad start. I would start like this: Shema, wouldn't you hate me if I told you something? It would be very alarming. I'd get right to the point and say, My mother, lives in… No, it wasn't about Mama. It was about Shema and me. I failed to draft the apology speech.

In the morning, at the library, I wrote another chapter of my thesis. My research focused on the origin of Tutsis, Hutus, and Twas. I read a lot of confusing theories about their origin. Most of what was written did not make sense. It was about the usual stories of the nomadic man. It was about the invasions or occupations of kingdoms by other kingdoms. It was about the stories of the haves and the have-nots. I could not find any research that explained what the morphology had to do with ethnicity in Rwanda. I did not learn anything particular about the history of the Tutsi people nor the Hutu people. All I understood was that they shared the same land, the same culture, and the same language. Over time, they became blinded by the conflicts that characterized the times before, during, and after colonization; disputes about power, conflict over resources and geopolitical conflicts of the twentieth century. After a few hours of the research, which did not explain the hatred, the wickedness, and the killings, I closed the books.

At around 2:30 p.m., someone knocked on the door. I rushed to open it. It was not Shema, but my cousin Mugabo. What the hell was he coming to do?

"How are you, Mugabo?"

"I'm fine, thanks. How about you? Aren't you letting me in? Are you going out?" he asked.

"Yes. I'm… Yes, I'm going out. I am sorry."

"Okay, where are you going to?"

"The city center."

"Let's go together then. I'm going to see one of my friends in the Matheus shopping center."

"No, please, you may go alone," I said. "We'll talk tomorrow."

"Okay, I understand. When will you stop avoiding me? When shall you realize you are the only member of my family in this world? I have a lot of things to discuss with you, but you never give me a chance."

Mugabo looked as if he did not like the fact I did not want to welcome him. Lest Shema finds us there, I invited Mugabo for a walk in the campus garden, so he could tell me what he had in mind. I waited for him to speak, but he picked at his nails.

"Why are you so silent?" I asked.

"Karabo, I wanted to ask you something," he said. "Why don't you respond to your mother's letters?"

"Is that why you came to see me?" I asked.

"Yes, please don't be offended. Your mother suffers, and you are the only person who can wipe her tears."

Even though I was touched by his words, I did not want to show him my discomfort.

"Is she more miserable than the girl she left alone and lonely?" I asked. "Don't worry about her. She is fine. She is with her husband and her children."

Hiding his eyes, Mugabo said, "You don't know what you're talking about. Have you read her letters?"

"No. I haven't. Please, if you've come to talk to me about Mama, today isn't the right day. I've told you I wanted to go—"

Before I finished my sentence, my phone rang.

"Karabo, where are you? I am knocking on your door. Are you there?"

"Yes, I'm coming." I hung up the phone, turned to Mugabo, and said, "I must go. Please, take this path."

I hurried to my room. Shema was standing in front of the door with a bouquet of red roses in his hands. He also had a pack of ice cream. He did not give me a second to say a shy hello. He pulled my chin and kissed my lips with passion before giving me the bouquet of flowers. Before I could thank him, he turned his head and asked, "Karabo, who is that guy?"

"Who?"

"I don't know. A guy was watching us. His face looks familiar… He looks like the one who brought you the letter from Malawi. What is he doing here?"

"Who…? No, it can't be him."

"Anyway, that's his business. Tell him and his sister you have nothing to do with their flat noses."

I did not answer. I invited Shema to enter my room. Putting the flowers in the vase, I noticed I had forgotten to hide the baskets. I prayed to the Lord that Shema did not open the baskets. *Irresistible curiosity*! Before sitting down, he opened the red basket and gave me a big laugh.

"What? Don't tell me you have become like an old single girl who cannot live without the picture of her lover?"

"What can I say? I missed you. I had to find a way to have your copy here in my room, near my heart."

"And this other white basket?"

Fear tore my bones. I rushed to grab the basket, but Shema was faster. He opened it and removed the picture.

"It is…"

"Tell me. Who is this stunning and gorgeous lady?" Shema asked.

Maybe it is a kind of irony, I thought. Many people said

Hutu women were less attractive. I was convinced Mama was beautiful only to me, but no one else found her attractive.

"Guess who she is," I said.

"It's easy to guess. If she isn't your mother, she's your aunt," Shema replied. "She doesn't look like your uncle Kamanzi. She must be your mother. She had a placidly graceful face that didn't appeal to bad guys, but men who knew how to appreciate a wild and serene beauty. Is she your mother?"

"Yes," I answered with heaviness in my voice.

Shema examined Mama's photo, shook his head, and invited me to lie on his chest.

"Dry your tears," he said. "Your mother's spirit is always with you. She can never abandon you. Even me, whenever misery fills my heart, I look up at the sky and call my mother."

He kissed Mama's picture and put it back in the basket.

Like Doctor Baziga and Muhire, Shema also sided with Mama. I wanted to scream and tell him he was wrong. I wanted to say to him Mama was not in heaven, that she lived in another country, and that she had left me alone to mourn the death of Papa and my sisters. My brain told me I should be glad Shema had seen in Mama's photo something admirable. I calmed down and let fate take its course. I took my ice cream and gave another to Shema. We fed each other like little darlings.

"Karabo, may I take you somewhere?"

"A date? Where do you want to take me?"

"Come, I will show you."

I wanted to change my clothes, but he said my dress was beautiful, no need to change. We went out, sucking our ice cream. The spy eyes of the campus made me shy. At the gates, he stopped a taxi and asked the driver to take us to Lake Nyandungu.

"Lake?" I asked, thinking he meant a valley.

"Yes, there is a large artificial lake at Nyandungu, with a beautiful sandy beach."

"Hey, I didn't know. Kudos to the person who made it a lake. The city of Kigali wouldn't do better with the Nyand-ungu Valley."

In the car, the driver spied on us through the rearview mirror. I held Shema's hands to prevent them from taking advantage of the shortness of my dress.

"Now I know, the only thing you inherited from your father is your lean nose," Shema said, putting his hands on my lap. "You inherited from your mother all the other characteristics of your beauty. But she, on the picture, seems calmer and wiser."

"What do you mean? Am I not wise?"

"No. If you were, you wouldn't be in a relationship with a street boy."

"Okay. Leave me alone if loving you is a sign of credulity."

"Don't worry. I like your audacity." He kissed me on the cheek to calm me down before adding, "You'll be as wise as your mother when you give birth to our children."

Shema's face was embellished with an obliging smile. He had changed so much that I could not conceive. He was joking as before when we both lived with Uncle Kamanzi. I wanted to ask him questions, but maybe it was better to wait until he took the initiative to talk to me about it. I was wondering what kind of work he was doing. I was wondering if he had stopped smoking weed. We arrived at Nyandungu and got out of the car. Shema held my hand and invited me to follow him. We walked to a small bungalow house where they were selling sportswear.

"Please, take everything you need for swimming," said Shema. "We are going to turn into fish and sail on the lake, just the two of us as I promised you."

"No, please. I can't swim."

"Don't worry. I'm going to train you. Take floats."

"Shema, don't make fun of me. Or you'll forget about this swimming idea."

I took the swimsuit and went to the locker room as Shema headed for the men's. In a few minutes, we were in the lake, swimming like little fish.

"Didn't I tell you that if becoming birds was hard, we could become fish and sail in the ocean? No need to climb the mountains. Leave the climbing to those whose childhood plates were full of sweet potatoes."

"Shema, please, it wasn't a joke. I meant to climb the mountains of life."

"Which mountains? Aren't we already at the peak?"

"As long as we are still in this world, there will be more mountains of life to climb."

He remained silent. His hands held my hips, I threw my chest into the water, and let myself be guided by my lifeguard. As my body fled into the water, my heart flew in the sky every time my eyes met Shema's smile. His chest commanded authority and attracted the attention of my innocence. White ladies covered with sky-blue towels ogled us. The shyness of the girl I was pushed me to sit on one of the bamboo chairs.

Shema joined and asked, "May I tell you a story?"

"A story? Do you mean *umugani*?"

"Yes. Look, it's already sunset… It's time to tell bedtime stories…or bamboo chair stories… Stop laughing. Listen…"

"I am listening. Go ahead."

"There was once a man and a woman. They gave birth to a little girl. They called her Flower. She grew up to be as beautiful as the seedtime blossom. They lived near a forest where life resembled that of a real jungle. Because the girl was so beautiful, all human and non-human beings of the forest wanted to touch her. Some managed to break a piece of her to decorate their lives. Even the other girls did not pity her. They used her beautiful aroma to make perfume. Nobody understood her pain and sorrow. Nobody realized that she was not happy to be pulled left and right. Everyone wanted to have a piece of her. Bees seemed to have a better way to taste her beauty. They kissed her, sucked the seeds of her beauty, and produced a sweet puke that human creatures could not resist sucking. One day, a prince named Pride of Boys, Symbol of Dignity, came into the forest. When he saw Flower's beauty, attracted by her beautiful rainbow colors, he decided: 'I will not break her like the humans and animals of this jungle. I will not take a piece of her. I want her wholly and entirely. I will live with Flower in my secret and apparent life. I want these colors to illuminate every room in my life, and when life shall become bitter, I'll kiss her like bees, but instead of throwing up her sweetness, I'll keep it in me, softening all my organs. Her beautiful aroma will be the fragrance of my thoughts and feelings so that my actions shall never pollute the world.' Shema took Karabo, and they lived happily ever after... That's the end of the story."

He deserved nothing less than a big hug, or maybe a punishment for having made me laugh to death. That day was so special. My big decision was made. Between Mama and Shema, the choice was clear, either both or Shema. I did not have anything to say to him. The only truth he had to know was that I was crazy in love with him. The madness of our love was enough to make us go against all the perspectives of the world, to face the sun without being afraid of the precision of its brightness, and to wait for the rain without being fearful of the cold. We left Lake Nyandungu with our feet on the ground, but hearts flying in the heavens of love.

———

Friday knocked on the door. As I had promised Sugira, after school, I went to visit his mother. It was not a simple visit. I also had to deliver Muhire's message.

Mr. Kamana was sitting in the garden with a newspaper in his hand. He stood up to give me a handshake.

Gatarina came out of the house and said: "Welcome, it's been a long time. Is it because of the studies?"

"Yes, I am combining studies with my end-of-program research."

She invited me to follow her into the house.

"Let's sit here," said Gatarina. "If you hadn't come today, I would have come to fetch you at the campus. How are you?"

"Good."

"I always asked Sugira if you were okay, but you know him—his words can be counted on the fingers. He wouldn't tell me anything. Did you say you are writing your graduation thesis?"

"Yes. I am writing about the impact of the social and political integration of people from different ethnic groups on conflict prevention, in Rwanda. It's hard to find all the answers to my questions. There isn't enough literature on Rwanda. For example, I still don't understand the origin of Rwandans."

"And that," said Gatarina. "I hate the fact that even the so-called scholars answer that question with total ignorance and stupidity."

"How?" I said, curious to know her opinion on that much-debated issue.

"Never consider what people say about racial or ethnic origins. Before talking about Rwandans, no one can ever tell the true origin of human beings. No scientific research has been able to answer this question."

"I'm sorry. I don't understand."

"My dear, the truth is that human beings have always been nomads. Even today, we are nomads. In early times people moved from place to place looking for greener pastures for their livestock or more fertile land for their farming endeavors. Some fled dangerous wild animals or natural disasters such as earthquakes or floods. We can't forget those who were taken as slaves or servants or those who were expelled from their kingdoms for having offended their kings. Kingdoms invaded other kingdoms and took captives. There were many reasons for leaving one place for another. It is essential to understand there is no indication that members of the same clan or family moved from one region to another at the same time. Maybe they didn't even take the same directions."

"That's an interesting way of looking at things," I said.

"What I laugh about is that in Rwanda, some ethnic groups claim to be more Rwandan than others but contradict themselves by saying that Africans who have migrated to Europe, Europeans who have migrated to America, or Africans who have been taken as slaves, or for other reasons, have the right to claim citizenship in their countries of residence. Apart from the language and culture, we should be unified by the fact that we all call Rwanda our heritage."

Perhaps her perspective could guide my research on ethnicity, but as a political scientist, I had to consider many other hypotheses. I had to study how and when Rwandans had created the Tutsi, Hutu, and Twa identities, and what these identities meant in the twenty-first-century Rwanda. Why did Rwandans not learn to live in harmony in their country of citizenship? I wanted to ask her more questions, but Sugira walked into the living room and asked what we were talking about.

"I'm talking to my daughter." She turned to me and added, "Do you understand?"

"Yes. Thank you very much."

"Karabo, let's continue our conversation another day. I have to give Kamana a drink."

Before saying good-bye to them, I conveyed Muhire's message, and they said he was welcome, but did not comment about Mbabazi.

On November 28, 2004, I had to present my thesis to the jury, composed of three professors, and an audience of classmates and some outsiders. I was about to open a box full of pain and let it fly over the skies of Rwanda. The fear that the wind would blow on those wounded hearts crumbled my stomach. How can I stand in front of the Hutus and tell them that singing and praising their Hutu identity is like worshiping a hoe while their children are dying of kwashiorkor? How can I say to the Tutsis that before talking about cows, my Tutsi father had not even a single hen? Time was running out. I decided not to wear a red dress. A black suit would better invite the professors to consider the importance of my research. As a true academician, I took my books and headed for the large conference room.

Three professors had taken seats around a large round table. One of them, Professor Simon, had swallowed the history of Rwanda. Perhaps he would ask me if I had read the books of Belgian and French writers who called themselves '*experts on Rwanda.*' I would say, '*Yes, I read them.*' But would add, '*I did not believe everything they wrote.*'

After his verbose introduction, Professor Simon said: "Miss Karabo, the floor is yours."

I looked left and right, and sent my hands under the desk to pinch my fingers while my heart whispered, '*Be brave, you can do it.*'

"I did this research in Rwanda. My objective was to study the impact of the political and social integration of all ethnic groups on conflict prevention in Rwanda. A thousand Rwandans responded to my survey questionnaire."

"What were your findings?" asked Professor Simon.

"Rwandans have a lot in common that should push them to interact socially and politically, whether they like it or not. For example, in Rwanda, we do not have wells from which only people from a specific ethnic group can fetch water. There is no road or pathway used by one group of Rwandans and not the other."

"How does that contribute to your research?" asked Professor Mutoro.

"Ninety-five percent of respondents to my survey said they understood the meaning of a good neighbor only when they tried to interact with those they did not consider theirs."

"Weren't they good neighbors before? If not, is that what led to the tragedy of 1994?" asked Professor Mutoro.

"Maybe I have not explained my point very well. I didn't say neighbors cannot have conflicts. The spirit of good neighborliness should be accompanied by social and political initiatives by which Rwandans of different ethnic groups are called to meet and work together for the development of their slice of Rwanda."

"Do you confirm there are ethnic groups in Rwanda?" asked Professor Mukamurego.

"The answer to that question is no and yes. The no hypothesis is supported by the fact that Rwandans live together, speak the same language, share the same culture, and have, or instead had the same religion, and all these confirm that they should be regarded as one people, and not distinct communities or ethnic groups. On the other hand, the yes hypothesis is supported by the fact that an ethnic group can also be formed based on experiences shared by a group of people. Thus, in Rwanda, recent history has led some to identify themselves as Hutus, Tutsis, or Twas. Perhaps Rwandans may not refer to these identities as genealogically, geographically, or culturally distinct ethnic groups, but identities stressed by the recent history of Rwanda. The history of *ubuhake*, *ubukonde*, *uburetwa*, and *ibikingi*, comparable to feudalism and manorialism in other cultures, which created superiority and inferiority complexes. The history of exile, marginalization, discrimination, killings, and genocide, which left many hearts wounded, and many brains fretful. The history of revolutionary movements and liberation wars, which listed some Rwandans on the walls of fame, and others on the walls of shame."

"What is the conclusion of your research?" asked Prof. Simon.

"I concluded that the only way to prevent conflict in Rwanda is by reversing the footprints of that past. Every Rwandan should be allowed to exercise his or her citizenship rights socially, politically, and economically despite the group with which he or she identifies. Political leaders need to aim at policies that make all Rwandans feel safe and valued in the country they call home. Nobody should be treated as a second or third-class citizen. Nobody should be discriminated against or marginalized socially, politically, or economically. Nobody should be killed for whatever pretext."

Some applauded my speech, and others whispered. Professor Simon thanked me and announced the jury would meet for the deliberation.

I fled to my room. *The presentation has not achieved its goals*, I thought. The broken hearts had not been restored, and the confused brains had not recovered their senses. I was afraid that by simplifying a rather complex phenomenon as ethnicity in Rwanda, I had condemned the victims to be cowards, and described as mad those who tried to escape the reality of Rwandan ethnic groups.

Someone knocked on the door.

"Who is there?" I asked.

"Karabo, open for me. It's me, Sugira."

"A second..."

"What's wrong? Why that grayness in your eyes?"

"Nothing. I am tired, and I want to go to bed. I'll see you tomorrow if you don't mind."

"Don't worry. I just wanted to give you a letter from your mother."

"A letter? Who gave it to you?"

"Yesterday, I met Mugabo... Please, read it. I beg you."

"Okay. At your command."

"Thank you. Let me go. Please, don't cry anymore."

"Good night."

I closed the door. The letter in my hand, my heart pounded as something ran through my intestines. It had been a long day that I didn't want to add any more to. I opened the white basket and said, "Mama, thank you for writing to me." I threw the letter into the basket and threw myself into bed to sleep, squeezing my red pillow.

Twelve

In the morning, as I pondered where I would go to live after graduation, the orphan's bones cracked. My age and way of living had changed in such a way that they could cause disarray in Uncle Kamanzi's home. To live in the house of my maternal uncle, Gasana, would be like living in the hell that burns wounded hearts. Being an orphan hurts, but the pain becomes much more severe each time an orphan looks to the left and right, only to hug the loneliness, despite being surrounded by many people. I opened the baskets of those I loved. To my love in the red basket, I said, "Hello, darling. Yesterday, I presented my thesis. I finished my undergraduate studies. The time has come to climb the mountains of life together. Are you ready?" I waited for him to answer, and a voice in my heart murmured, *"Yes, my love, we'll climb the mountains of life together, just the two of us, with no one else."* Why would I receive that answer from Shema? Doctor Baziga and Muhire had told me I needed both Shema and Mama in my life. I turned to the white basket, took a picture of Mama, and asked, "Have you heard Shema? What do you think?" With trembling hands,

I took the envelope I had dropped in the basket the night before and began to read Mama's letter:

"Karabo, my daughter, tears are running down my cheeks as I write you this letter. My darling, every time I remember you're alone in Rwanda, my head goes crazy. In my last letter, I told you about my ordeal. It's like I'm paying for the sins of humans who have turned into wild animals to destroy theirs. I am in prison. Those with whom I live in Malawi warned me that if I ever dared leave our village, they would kill me. All my escape plans have failed. Maybe I could have taken the path to the forest, but I didn't want to leave behind my innocent children… My darling, I don't have to bother you with my own problems. Whenever I remember I was twenty-two years old when I married your father, and that you are already twenty-five, I pray to God to bless you with a husband who shall fill you with the same love I have lived with your father. Tears are falling on this paper. I cannot talk about my love relationship with Kalisa, your father. The kind of love that people in this world shall never understand with their little brains. Every day, I pay for the death of Kalisa, who was killed by those whom I called my people. The animal husband with whom I live abuses me every night before he jumps on me like an enraged pig. Every morning, he spits dirty saliva on my face and says I hate him because of who he is. It's the life I've lived for six years. The only blessings I have received from all these years are my three children. They are your brothers and sisters, Karabo, and they laugh, play, and jump like all other kids. Without them, my heart would have burst. I owe my life to the beauty of their smiles, and their dirty, sweet hands that they love to place on my cheeks to resurrect my belief that everything will be fine. I cannot stop writing... My love, shall you write me a letter? I will be happy to read that you are all right. My eyes shall read your writing, but the ears of my soul will listen to you, whispering that God has answered all my prayers. He never abandoned you. He promised to keep you straight in his chest and that his spirit will surround you with love and grace. I was told you are about to graduate from university. I wish you many more blessings. I didn't lose my trust in God. One day he will make me free. He will take me back to Rwanda to hold you in my arms and cuddle you with the longest hug ever. Maybe I won't be able to wipe away all the tears you have shed for the last ten years, but I'll give you a chest to lean on and let all the tears flow on the breasts that fed you love and milk. I love you, sweetheart. Take care of yourself."

By the time I finished reading the letter, I was wet with tears. I wished I had a visa and a plane ticket to Malawi. But where exactly? My mind was short of ideas. My mouth did not have words. The only thing that could save me was going out somewhere important.

A few minutes later, I was on a motorbike.

"Let's go," I said to the biker.

"Where?"

"Nyarutarama."

"Where exactly?"

"Please, start the bike. Are you already in Nyarutarama to ask if you should turn left or right?"

"Miss, what happened to you? Why the tears?" he asked.

"Nothing. Please, bike faster."

My arms clutched his midriff tightly, and every time he felt my strong heartbeat, he forgot the brake pedal and drove faster than the traffic police allowed. In just five minutes, we were in Kagugu.

"Turn around, I told you, Nyarutarama."

"Where? Madam..."

"Miss."

"Sorry, miss, you should have told me we had arrived where you were going."

At the big scary gates of my uncle Gasana's place, a security officer asked me who I was. I introduced myself, and he let me in. The minister and his wife were sitting in the living room.

"Hello," I said.

"How are you? What happened to you?" asked Uncle Gasana.

"Hmm? Nothing. Is Mugabo around?" I asked.

"Yes. He is. Have you come only to see Mugabo? You haven't even greeted me. What is it, my daughter?"

I threw myself in his arms but did not say a word. He called Mugabo.

Before I told Mugabo I wanted to talk to him, my uncle's wife said, "Mugabo, please, offer your cousin some juice or tea. Karabo, what would you like to drink?"

"Thank you. I am not thirsty."

"You cannot refuse," she insisted.

"Okay, maybe tea. I'm going to drink it after talking to Mugabo. There is something I want to discuss with him."

I pulled Mugabo's arms and directed him to the garden for a discussion. He followed me like a sheep to the slaughterhouse.

"I have read Mama's letter," I said, sitting down in that green garden.

"Which of the letters?"

"The one you gave to Sugira. It's the only letter I have read. I'm sorry I never listened to you when you wanted to tell me more about Mama. Please tell me."

"What do you want me to tell you? Hasn't she told you everything in the letter?"

"Yes. She has told me something but not everything. Please, tell me everything you wanted me to know. I'm sorry to repeat it, my maternal family did the unspeakable, and it was hard for me to forgive them. But Mama's letter made me shed tears. You've always told me she has gone through incredible experiences, but reading her own words, I understood the degree of her sorrow. How did she get married to that man? Why didn't she come back to Rwanda much sooner? How did you go to Congo? And your father, Uncle Rwasibo? Is he still alive...? Tell me everything."

"Hey, you are asking a lot of questions. Go slowly. After leaving Kigali in May 1994, we moved to Gitarama, but as the Patriotic rebels advanced, we followed others to Congo after a few days. Dad was the mastermind of that plan..."

"Mugabo, can you tell me from when you were still in Kigali? Why didn't your dad send soldiers or militiamen to help us escape? Hadn't Mama asked him to do it?"

"I don't know. All I know is that... Um ..." He bent his head between his knees as he fought with tears. He had no reason to cry. He swallowed his grief and continued, "Your mother began her ordeal the minute she entered our house. Dad told her she should never go back to the Tutsi that she had married. She was subjected to abuse, insults, and sometimes slapping whenever she worried about her husband and children. Dad had told her she should never mention Tutsis in Rwasibo's house... Karabo, I am sorry. I didn't know Dad was so wicked until he became a monster during the genocide. I will never forgive him. I hate him. He is evil."

"Please, go ahead, tell me everything he did to Mama."

"The worst was how he treated her because she carried a Tutsi in her womb. Nobody was allowed to give food to your mother. Dad wanted the child to die in the womb, but it didn't happen. The baby was born, but..."

Mugabo could not hold back his tears. I could not stop him.

Something squeezed my back as I guessed what he was about to say.

"Uncle Rwasibo killed the baby, right?" I asked.

"Yes. How did you know?" Mugabo replied.

"Mama was pregnant when she left our house, and in her letter, she didn't tell me I had a brother. I assumed the baby was dead."

"Karabo, I can't hide anything from you. I have always wanted to tell you everything, but I didn't know where to start. I don't know how to tell you I hate my family for what they did to those they called Tutsis." He continued to pinch his fingers and dismantle the grass in the garden as if he was afraid to cross his eyes with mine. "Yes, Dad killed your brother. The day the baby died, I heard my mother telling Dad that the blood of that innocent child shall haunt him forever."

"Does that mean your mother didn't want Tutsis to be killed?" I asked.

"No, it doesn't. She was as devilish as Dad. Mom abused your mother with a lot of insults. But she told Daddy he shouldn't be directly involved in the killings. She told him he should leave the job of killing to the market boys, the handlers."

Wrath and nausea strangled my throat as I listened to Mugabo tell me how his mother had no mercy for a mother who was losing her only son to death. She had no empathy for those whose lives were being extinguished. Her only concern was that her husband had become a butcher of human flesh, while she believed that killing Tutsis was only a job for low-class people. It reminded me of some former Hutu militants who pleaded not guilty, simply because they did not physically kill Tutsis, while they were among the many supporters of the killings, whose job was to lead the killers to the hiding places of the Tutsis. To turn the page, I encouraged Mugabo to continue his story.

"So, you left for Congo…"

"Karabo, I won't be able to talk about our long way to Congo. Your mother didn't want to go with us. When she tried to run away, Dad threw a big knife at her and injured one of her legs. All the way to Gitarama, your mother's leg was bleeding, until she was able to apply cobbler's pegs on it and cover the wound with a little cotton… Hey, Karabo, wipe your tears."

I could not bear to listen to how Mama had gone to Congo with both emotional and physical pain. Mugabo told me how my uncle continued to torture Mama in Congo, where he had kept her captive. He told me about the day Uncle Rwasibo had beaten Mama severely because he had learned that she had tried to leave the refugee camp to return to Rwanda in 1996. He told me about the war in Congo and the horrible experience that he, his family, and Mama had lived.

"I had already approached your mother and told her I did not support the hatred my family had against the Tutsis. We had agreed we would take any opportunity to return to Rwanda. When the camps got attacked by the soldiers, many people identified as the new Rwanda army, I mean the former Patriotic forces, the refugees started to flee, but your mother and I decided to take another direction, with the idea we could meet those who were heading back to Rwanda. After running for kilometers, we were exhausted and thought maybe it was better to fall, close our eyes, and die. It was so terrifying."

"Oh, Mugabo, I can only imagine what you went through. Did you lose your way back to Rwanda? What happened then? How did you end up in Malawi?"

"Instead of heading to Rwanda, we found ourselves at a crossroads that linked us to the other refugees' path... But they were all corpses."

"Dead?"

"Yes. Among them were Mom and my sister Ngabire..." He burst into tears again, before saying, "I'll never forget how your mother took off her African loincloth to cover my mother's body, despite the pain she had caused her. That's where we met Hagira, your mother's husband. We thought he was our savior, but his only goal...was to abuse your mother."

Mugabo was silent for a moment, then said, "Karabo, I beg you. Please. Let me stop here. I'll tell you more next time."

"Mugabo, I am really saddened by what you experienced. I blame myself now because I had not wanted to lend you my ears. Forgive me."

Before Mugabo could react, a voice interrupted us.

"Are you joining us for lunch?" Mrs. Gasana asked. "Your eyes are red. Has Mugabo told you how Hutus were killed in masses in Congo?"

"No, Aunt," replied Mugabo. "Why do you always talk about that?"

"I haven't said anything bad. I just wondered if Karabo now understands Hutus were also killed by Tutsis."

"Who told you they were killed by Tutsis?" Mugabo asked. "Why do you pretend to know a lot about what happened in Congo?"

"If they weren't killed by the Tutsis, who killed them?" Mrs. Gasana insisted. "Did they commit suicide?"

"As far as I am concerned, my mother, sister, and those who died with them are victims of the war in Congo. I don't know the identity of those who killed them."

"Come for lunch," said Mrs. Gasana. "You know what I'm talking about. Many books and reports have been published. Read them."

I got up and told Mugabo that we would resume our conversation another day. I couldn't find the appetite to eat the food of my uncle's so-called wife.

"Karabo, are you leaving before having lunch with us?" Mrs. Gasana asked.

"Excuse me," I said, hurrying to the big gate. "We'll share lunch next time."

My heart was so heavy that it was jumping out of my chest to explode on the road.

When I arrived in my room, I took Mama's picture out of the white basket, pulled out a piece of paper and a pen, and began to write:

"Mama, I am sorry. Please forgive me for having taken you for a wicked woman. May the tears that are flowing on this paper prove to you the love I feel for you. My sadness followed you. It never allowed you to breathe. You have always borne my sorrow in your chest and held the right breast to pray for my protection. Mama, let me cry and cry again, scream and scream until my voice reaches where you are and tell you how much I miss you. Papa had told me you're a noble person. But I let myself be blinded by how those with whom you share the name shattered Papa's life and let his blood run. You did not come back to stop his soul from bleeding. This is how I concluded that being Hutu was synonymous with being cruel. Yes, Mama, I am now a big girl, maybe a young lady. Your letter made me cry. I have talked to Mugabo, my cousin. You are the only person who can free me from this heavy burden that I carry on my shoulders. When will you come back to Rwanda? Maybe we could start a project to heal the hearts of Rwandans? Cardiologists and psychologists have failed. We will begin with ourselves. You will heal my heart, and I will heal yours, before going to those Hutus who call themselves your people, and the Tutsis with whom I identify."

I read the letter. No, it was too early to write all those words. It was necessary to wait until the day when my eyes would cross Mama's eyes. I tore the paper and took another:

"Mama, I have read your letter. When will you come back to Rwanda? I pray for the end of all your problems. I miss you. Yes, I will soon be a graduate of the university…"

I couldn't write a letter. I couldn't find words. I called Mugabo and asked him to contact the person who brought the letters so that I could ask that person more questions about the town or village where Mama lived and how I could contact her. I was determined to bring Mama out of that faraway country of Malawi. I dreamed of a day when she would return to Rwanda. Our eyes would communicate even when our mouths would not open to say a single word. Our tears would explain the feelings of our hearts. All evening, I was in my dreams of the day when I would meet Mama after many years of separation.

The following days, I bought newspapers to look for job offers to consider. I wrote many job applications and sent them to those who had vacancies and those who hadn't. I applied for all the vacancies, either a waitress at a restaurant, a manager at a bank or a secretary at a government institution. I was applying for managerial positions as well as subordinate positions. My goal was a job. I walked Kigali from north to south and from east to west, distributing the letters. The answer was the same: "We shall contact you soon." The wait became interminable.

To fight against loneliness, I visited Uncle Kamanzi to be distracted by the smiles of my cousin Neza. And then, I went to Cyahafi for an adult game with my Shema. I had surrendered the fate of our love to the will of the Almighty. It was not for me to hate Shema. It was up to him to choose between being my hero and climbing mountains of life with me and being a coward to leave me when I needed him most.

My days always ended with a conversation with Mama and Shema in the baskets. I would tell them how much I loved them both and that living without one or the other would make my life bitterer than it already was.

On December 20, 2004, I had spent the whole day with Shema in our rough and soft game that had made me lose my sense of time.

When I came back to my senses, it was already too late to return to campus.

"Don't worry, you'll leave tomorrow," said Shema.

"No. Shema. I have to go to sleep in my room."

"And this one? Whose room is this?"

"It's not mine, but yours."

"Tell me, what are you afraid of? What would we do in the night that we haven't done during the day?" Shema asked.

"Stop it. What are you talking about?"

He had his way of making me shut up. The nuzzling resumed, and before I knew it, I was lying on his chest again with my eyes closed. He would wake me up to make love again. I would sleep, then he would wake me up to do our third, fourth, and for the whole night.

In the morning, I woke up to the ringing of my phone, and with a body as light as Dodo green vegetables, I couldn't get up. Shema picked up the phone, but instead of giving it to me, he took the call.

"Hello… Who…? Her mother…? Um? Who are you…?" Shema said on the phone.

I jumped out of bed to snatch the phone from his hands. With an elephant's rage, he pushed me so hard as if the sky of hell had fallen on me. I banged my cranium on the head-board.

"Do you have a letter from Karabo's mother?" Shema asked the person at the other end of the line. "Oh, wonderful. How is she?"

With an intense headache and a beating heart, my mouth refused to open to say a word. I could only hear Shema agreeing with the person on the phone, pretending not to be surprised by Mama's news.

"Did you say you are Sugira?" he asked after a few minutes of conversation. "Thank you for letting me know that Karabo is nothing else but one of yours."

He threw the phone on the floor, pulled me out of bed, opened the door, and pushed me out. I sat down and refused to go out.

"Karabo, please don't push me to do what I don't want to do… Do you want me to send you where your relatives sent my family?"

"Shema, let me tell you the whole truth…"

"Which truth? That your mother was killed during the genocide against the Tutsi? Do you want to tell me that, unlike our families, she has been resurrected or reincarnated in Malawi? What truth do you want to tell me? That you managed to lie to me during all these years? You told me you were a survivor of the genocide, and I believed you when you are nothing but a heartless Hutu… Please get out of here."

He scratched his head and pulled my arm from the armpit to throw me out of his studio. His eyes blazed. His teeth made noises, and his chest was becoming swollen as if he wanted to turn into a lion and roar on me.

"Shema, forgive me. I didn't tell you lies. The Hutu militants killed my father and my sisters. They killed me too, even though God didn't want me to blow my last. Please, calm down and listen to what I have to tell you about Mama."

My tears fueled his fury and turned it into shards of fire. Shema gave me a hot slap on the cheek. When I tried to open my mouth and beg him again to forgive me, I had another slap. He thumped me on the head, pushing me out.

"Get out of my room if you don't want me to kill you this minute!"

He pushed me out of his studio, locked the door, and threw my clothes, the bag, and the phone out of the window. I sat in front of his studio, wearing only the ikanga loincloth around my body. Inside the studio, there was a lot of noise. Shema screamed and broke things. I shouted, but nobody came to the rescue. The phone rang. It was Sugira.

I did not pick it up. He sent a text: "Where are you? You're okay?" *Why does he care after what he has just said to Shema?* I wondered. After a few minutes, there was total silence in Shema's studio. My right leg shook. My hands quivered. An inner voice whispered to me, perhaps Shema had ended his painful life. My heart would die. I knocked on the door.

"Shema, please, open for me," I said. "I want to say one word before leaving."

Shema didn't respond. I knocked and called his name again. But apparently, his ears were no longer functional. I hit a small stone on the door. Shema opened the door. He was still alive. He pulled me inside his studio. The table was full of drugs in white powder and a bottle of whiskey.

"Shema, what are you doing? Please, stop," I said.

He did not answer with words, but with punches. He hit me on the walls of his room. He pulled me one more time, slapped me, and hit me again on the walls. I lost the sense of what was happening. At least I was dying in the arms of my only love.

Thirteen

One morning, I opened my eyes and looked at the ceiling of the room where I was. Everything was strange. Some plastic material covered my nose. There were ropes everywhere, including those that stretched to the bottom of my body, between my legs. The room smelled of death. A woman shouted Hallelujah, and her voice was familiar.

"Doctor, Doctor. She has woken up. God is good."

The doctor came with his tools. He placed them on my chest and said, "Let her rest. She is still weak."

I closed my eyes and went back to sleep. Shema's hands were in my hair, while his rocky voice was singing French slow songs, including the one with the words *Je t'aime à l'infini* by Benny B. He circled my neck with his protective arm, while his rebellious hands tried to get my nipples, and when I tried to push him away, I found myself stuck with the chemistry of electric love. He went down to my navel and gently inserted his organ between my legs. And as he pushed hard inside me, I moaned: "Mmmm, eh, mmmm, Shema, Shema… Hmmm, Shema…"

"I'm not Shema," a voice responded. "Karabo, it's me."

I could not believe my ears.

"Hmm? No. Sugira, what did you do?"

I struggled to get up from the bed, but ropes held me down.

"Karabo, what is it?" said Gatarina. "Sugira, what did you say to Karabo? Why is she scared?"

"Nothing. I guess she was dreaming," Sugira replied to his mother.

Uncle Kamanzi entered the room in his military uniform, accompanied by a tall gentleman in a white coat.

"Please give us some space," he said to Sugira and his mother.

Gatarina covered me with the bedsheets and ordered her son to follow her. Tears danced in Sugira's eyes. Apparently, he did not want to go. Uncle Kamanzi pushed him with a hand on his shoulders.

"When did she come out of a coma?" Uncle Kamanzi asked the doctor.

"About an hour ago."

"Have you finished with the report? I have to take it to the prosecutor's office so that the bastard may learn a lesson he will never forget."

"It's already signed. You can take it," replied the doctor.

"Thank you. Maybe the prosecutor shall want to talk to Karabo for a testimony. When shall she remember exactly what Shema did to her?" Uncle Kamanzi asked the doctor.

"We need more than three days to determine if she is ready to talk about it. She keeps repeating the name of Shema. Apparently, she has not fully regained consciousness."

"I don't know what kind of poison he gave her. I have to go. I'll be back in the evening." Uncle approached me and said, "Darling, don't worry. The police arrested the bastard. He won't hurt you anymore."

I turned my back to hide my eyes. Shema had been arrested. Sharp spears wounded my heart. Shema could not be the cause of all the painful sores on my body, I thought. They did not know what they were talking about. Penetrating very far into my memory, some pieces of the image of what had happened to me appeared, but I could not assemble them to make a whole. A picture of Shema talking on the phone and mentioning the words Sugira and Mom, and the last picture of me sitting in front of his studio crying. Had Shema learned the truth about Mama? Maybe yes. What had he done to put me in a coma in an intensive care room? It was easy to understand. I closed my eyes until the evening of hospital visits.

"How are you, Karabo? Sorry for what happened," said Mugabo.

"Thank you."

Before I could ask him the details of what had really happened, Gatarina and Kamana came in. They praised the Almighty for having saved me before engaging in their own conversations. Nobody wanted to discuss what had happened to me. Maybe Sugira could have enlightened me. Gatarina approached to give me some milk.

"Where is Sugira?" I asked.

"Since morning, he has locked himself in his room. He doesn't want to talk to anyone."

"Please, come with him tomorrow. I beg you."

"I will tell him."

Birungi was sitting on a chair in front of my bed.

"How's Neza?" I asked.

"She's fine." Birungi pointed to Mugabo. "Who is this young man? I don't think I've met him before."

"Don't you know him?" responded Gatarina. "Mugabo is Karabo's maternal cousin." She turned to Mugabo. "And your uncle Gasana? I haven't seen him here. Isn't he aware of what happened to Karabo?"

"I told him," Mugabo replied with a low voice, staring at the floor. "Lately, he has been too busy with his work. I'm sure he'll be here as soon as he can."

"Karabo has been in the hospital for two weeks, and her uncle hasn't found time to pass by?" Gatarina asked, signifying that she couldn't stomach the excuse of Uncle Gasana.

My ears were open to note that I had been in the hospital for two weeks. I realized maybe Shema had also spent two weeks in prison.

I wanted to break the chains of the hospital bed and go to plead for his release. Nobody had the right to put Shema in prison. There were only two options, either to release him or put me in jail with him. After the visiting hours, the nurse asked everyone to go out and encouraged me to close my eyes and sleep.

The next morning, Sugira was the first to enter the room.

"Hello," he said.

"Hello," I replied.

"Milk, from Mom."

"Thank you."

He sat on the chair, his mouth muted as if he didn't want to talk to me. His wrinkled eyes avoided mine.

"Sugira, what happened to me? I don't remember anything."

"Don't you remember? Hmm, leave it, nothing is interesting to remember."

"Why? Don't I have the right to know why I'm lying on this hospital bed, with wounds on my whole body?"

"Please, don't talk to me as if I'm the cause of your

injuries… Maybe you have to remember where you had spent the night, and who you were with."

"That, I remember."

"Karabo, I had never considered you like a girl who would spend a night in a bed with some kind of a boy, as if you were…I was going to say a married woman, no, a prostitute."

"No, Sugira, please. It wasn't what you think."

"Okay, I'm still wrong. You hadn't spent the night in his room, right?"

"Sugira, I only want to know one thing. Is it Shema who hit me? Why? How did I get to the hospital? Please, tell me."

"The most important thing is that you are alive. Take the time to heal. I will tell you everything when you leave the hospital. I am the one who brought you to the hospital. I called you on the phone in vain, until some ladies of that shitty neighborhood you call Cyahafi took the phone to tell me you were unconscious. Only God knows what could have happened if I hadn't appeared in time…"

He hid his eyes as he clenched his teeth. I remembered an important detail.

"Shema had spoken to someone on the phone. Was it you?" I asked.

"I've told you it would be better if you could wait until you completely heal. I will tell you everything."

"No, tell me, did you talk to Shema on the phone?"

"All I know is that I never called Shema's phone. I didn't know he was your secretary. Besides, it's not what we talked about that drove him to do what he did to you. You can blame it on drug addiction. How on earth, among all men, did you choose a drug addict who lives in a studio surrounded by garbage cans, shit holes, and women in dirty clothes?"

"Sugira, you've said we must end this conversation."

"Yes, but maybe I should tell you that I was at the prosecutor's office to testify yesterday. Whether you're madly in love with him or not, he can't do that to you and go unpunished. Notwithstanding your indifference to my feelings, I will protect you from that Shema to whom you've given your dignity and body."

"Please, don't get involved in that dossier. I am the only one who can understand why Shema did what he did. Tell those doctors to discharge me. I've got to get out of this hospital."

Before Sugira could respond, Uncle Kamanzi entered the room and said, "Hello, Karabo." He turned to Sugira and added, "Why can't you leave Karabo alone? She needs to rest. Please, go out."

Sugira seemed to be strangled by frenzy, but he failed to respond. He got up and went away.

"What did he do wrong?" I asked. "Isn't he actually the one to whom I owe my life? He brought me here. Not true?"

"Yes. He did, and we thank him. But now he should leave us some space."

"He had brought me milk sent by his mother. I don't like the way you talk to members of that family. It's high time you understood I am now mature enough to choose my friends."

"We saw the kind of adult you are," said Uncle Kamanzi. "Was Shema one of those friends you picked? Look at the condition in which you are. These Hutus you mingle with shall do worse than him. When they shall show you their true face, you won't lose consciousness; you will die."

I looked at him and felt pity for him. This time, I didn't remain silent.

"Please, don't think I am disrespecting you," I said. "You aren't so different from Shema. Maybe he learned to hate Hutus from you."

"What are you talking about?"

"When Shema was a *Kadogo* soldier, you took him to live with you as one of your favorite escorts. The only thing he learned from you is the hatred against Hutus. But I sometimes wonder what kind of love he has received from you, a noble Tutsi for whom he had a lot of consideration. It is tormenting that you pursue him for having assaulted me, while you kill me every day with your words full of animosity towards Hutus you call my relatives."

"Karabo, please. What are you talking about? You are comparing the incomparable. I have never hit you. Shema is a drug addict. He is a danger to our society. Anyway, it's over now. He is in prison."

"Yes. He is a drug addict and in prison. Do you know why he is being punished? Because he is an orphan without a parent or relative. Did he smoke drugs when he lived with us? The day you decided to throw him out in this world jungle, alone without a protector, what did you expect? That his mother would send magic birds to teach him how to live? Anyway, I don't know what to say to you. Please, leave Shema and me alone. I am the only one who understands what he is going through. He doesn't deserve to be in prison."

"Karabo, how dare you talk to me like that? Why should I be blamed for the misfortune of that bastard you call Shema?"

He stared at me as if he wanted to slap me.

"Uncle, I'm sorry. I didn't mean to disrespect you. Maybe I'm confused. I want to sleep now if you don't mind."

"I'm leaving. But please, you have to come back to your senses. Shema isn't what you deserve. What did he give to you to make you so crazy about him?"

"He gave me what I needed the most. Love is what he gave me."

He pulled the chair near my bed, held my hands, and said: "Tell me, what happened that made the love of your life assault you in a pugnacious way? Stop crying. It can give you headaches. I am your uncle. Please, tell me what happened."

"Shema hit me because my mother is a Hutu. I had told him Mama was also killed by Hutu militants in 1994. I lied to him. He has every right to be angry. Do you understand?"

A hand on his forehead, Uncle, moved his eyes left and right before saying, "You should rest. We will talk about it again next time. I need to go to work. Birungi will bring you lunch."

He kissed my forehead and left. His face looked dark. Perhaps I had just reminded him that everything had started the day my father married a Hutu.

A week later, I was discharged from the hospital. Uncle Kamanzi put my stuff in his four-by-four car and invited me to sit in the backseat.

"I'm going to the campus to take my belongings, then hand the key to my room to the dean," I said before jumping in his car. "And if you don't mind, you'll drop me off at the Nyamirambo Catholic Sisters Hostel."

"Hmm? Do you want me to drop you at the convent? Are you going to become a nun?" he asked with a big apocryphal smile.

"No. I will rent a room in their inn. Please, don't get me wrong. I think the time has come for me to leave the parents' nest. I am mature enough to take care of myself."

"I'm sorry to say, but your decision shows rather a lack

of maturity. You don't have work. How will you pay the rent? Who will give you food? Will you become a beggar?"

"Don't worry. I will live like all other orphans."

"Absurd. Let's go get your suitcases from the campus. I'll show you where to take them."

Gatarina, who was not far from us, gave me a warning signal that I should not argue with my uncle. I got into the car, and Uncle started the engine.

"Why is that woman following us?" Uncle asked after driving about three hundred meters.

"She is accompanying us to the campus," I replied.

"Karabo, what kind of relationship is between you and that woman?"

"God knows that I have neither a mother nor an aunt. So, he sent me that lady to be my guardian angel."

"Aha, those are the people who inject their bad ideas into your soul."

I kept silent. I didn't need to tell him Gatarina wasn't what he thought she was, but a Tutsi who, after losing all of her family members during the genocide, had decided to be the mother or the sister of other survivors.

At the campus, I entered my room alone and asked Uncle Kamanzi and Gatarina to wait for me outside. My room deserved a proper goodbye. All my secrets were buried in that two-square room. I removed the bedsheets and put them in my suitcase. I did the same for my books and my clothes. I opened the white basket, took a picture of Mama, and said, "It's done. It's over. You are the only person I have in the world." I opened the red basket, took Shema's picture, and said, "Forgive me for having built our relationship on a lie. I will never forgive myself for having broken your heart. The mountains of my life are covered with very sharp spines. I shouldn't have asked you to climb them with me." I pulled out the bags, my red pillow, and my two baskets. Uncle Kamanzi helped me put them in the trunk of the car. I took the room key to the dean's office, and on my return, I got into the car.

At Rugunga, instead of taking the road to Nyamirambo, Uncle Kamanzi drove toward his house in Kiyovu.

Gatarina called me on the phone and said, "Karabo, I beg you, please. Don't argue with him. Go to your uncle's house. He is like your father. You will find the best time to talk to him quietly."

"But, I don't think he—"

"Calm down for the moment," she interrupted. "Prove him obedience. I am going home. We will talk later."

I never knew how to question Gatarina's judgment, but this time I was confused.

"Why are you taking me to Kiyovu, and not to Nyami-rambo?" I asked Uncle Kamanzi.

"As long as I'm your parent, I'll take you where you belong," he replied firmly. "Don't worry, my house is not a prison. When you shall want to leave, the door will be open."

I followed Gatarina's advice and kept silent.

At my uncle's house, I put my stuff in the room. All its corners stared at me with irritation. To prevent tears, I left the room and joined Uncle Kamanzi, who was sitting in the living room with a glass of water in his hands.

"I'd like to talk to you before you go back to work," I said.

"Karabo, please, go get some rest. You haven't yet fully recovered. We will talk tomorrow."

"Give me only a few seconds of your time. I would like you to do me a favor if you want me to stay in this house…"

"A favor? Okay, tell me."

He sat down again to lend me his ears.

"I have three requests."

"Go ahead, please. What are your requests?"

"Please, help me get Shema out of jail. He is innocent."

"I can't. He must pay for having abused you. What's your second request?"

"Is there any point in making it if you are not ready to listen to me? Anyway, I also wanted to inform you that I now know everything about Mama, and I would like you to help me bring her back to Rwanda."

"Karabo, what are you talking about?" Uncle Kamanzi asked.

"Third, if you want me to stay in this house, you will have to understand that apart from my paternal family that we share, I also have a maternal family, and friends, whom you don't necessarily consider yours. They can only visit me at the house where I stay. Will you welcome them to your house as your daughter's visitors?"

"Okay, I understand now. You think you're old enough to impose your game rules. Kalisa, my brother, won't blame me. I'm sorry to tell you I won't grant any of your three requests. Please, be patient only for today. Tomorrow I will take you to the hostel of the Catholic Sisters. I can never allow you to make my home a meeting place for your Hutu relatives, including the woman you call your mother."

He got up and walked to the door.

"Uncle, please," I said. "Tell me in which prison Shema is."

I did not expect much from Uncle Kamanzi. I had to take charge of my life.

Birungi approached me and said: "Please go to your room and rest. You will speak to your uncle another day when he will be calmer, and after he will have digested all that you have told him."

"I don't care. It's my life, and it's only me who knows what's best for me. Please tell me. In which prison is Shema?"

"I guess he's still at the Remera police station."

"Four weeks in police custody?" I asked.

"No. I don't know… I guess… I mean, maybe they took him to Kimironko Prison."

"Okay, thank you, I have to go," I said, heading to the door.

Birungi followed me, shouting, "Karabo, you cannot go anywhere in that state. What if you asked your uncle to take you there tomorrow?"

"Don't worry. I will take a taxi."

Braver than my problems, my head firmly on my neck, and my heart larger than my sorrow, I headed to Kimironko. It was the first time that my head and my heart spoke the same language. Without a doubt, I loved Shema, but it was up to him to love me or to hate me after learning that I was of mixed ethnicity. I loved him, but I loved myself too. I loved his caresses, but I also dreamed of laying my head on the chest that had fed me with both milk and love. Whatever decision Shema would make, I would offer him support, not only as my first love but also as the brother who needed me in his moments of distress.

The taxi driver stopped. I had arrived at Kimironko Prison. I paid and got out of the car.

"Who are you looking for?" asked a policeman at the door, scrutinizing my identity card.

"The person in charge of this prison," I replied.

"Why?"

"He must urgently release one of the detainees. He is innocent."

"Now that's funny; who are you to give such orders?" he asked with a scornful look.

"Show me the prison officials. I have to talk to them."

"Go to that office, and they will explain how it works."

They explained that Shema's case was already before the court and that only the prosecutor's office could advise me. I asked them for permission to speak to Shema.

"What relationship do you have with him?" the officer asked.

"He is here because of the misunderstanding I caused."

"Are you the one he assaulted?"

"Yes, he is accused of having beaten me, but it isn't true."

"So, you are the daughter of—"

"Colonel Kamanzi," I interrupted with great pride.

"This way, please."

He showed me a bench to sit on; then he went to call Shema.

"You have a visitor," the policeman told Shema, pointing fingers at me. When Shema caught sight of me, he tried to return to the cell. I shouted his name. He approached.

"What are you doing here?" he asked. "I have nothing to do with you or any member of your family. Please, leave me alone. Forget me the same way I cursed the day I learned to pronounce your name."

"I'm not here for my boyfriend, Shema. I have come to help a prisoner in need. I have come to express my sympathy to the innocent punished for my own disloyalties. Let me promise you something: I'll get you out of this prison, whether you like it or not."

"Don't try anything," Shema replied, grinding his teeth.

"I don't need your help. In fact, it is here that I want to stay until the day the earth shall vomit me into another world. Go live your life with your relatives. Don't worry about me."

"You must know three things: One, I am not a Hutu, and my mama doesn't share the shame of those she shares the name with. Two, I love you, and I will love you forever. Three, be ready to pack your things. I will soon get you out of this prison. Don't worry, when you get out, you will be free to live your life as you understand it. I won't bother you anymore."

I did not give him time to respond. I got up and rushed to the door.

He returned to his cell, scratching his head.

I went to the prosecutor's office and told the people sitting at the reception that Shema was innocent and that they should not keep him in prison.

"Do you want us to release a criminal?" asked the slender gentleman with interrogative glasses.

"A suspect, you mean," I replied. "He is presumed innocent until proven guilty. What tells you he abused me?"

"Your wounds say everything."

"Did you test them to confirm they were caused by Shema?" I asked.

"No, we didn't. Tell us what happened."

"I had spent the night with Shema. In the morning, we woke up drinking whiskey. Whatever happened was because we were drunk."

"Miss, don't try to tell us lies. We have evidence and statements from other people. Go. You will be called to testify in court."

They did not want to listen to me. I went out without being able to release Shema. Only two people could help me get Shema out of prison: Uncle Kamanzi and Sugira. They had pushed his file to the prosecutor's office, and perhaps they could contradict their statements, and say that they did not have all the details about what had happened.

I went back to Kiyovu to Uncle Kamanzi's house. I would have a quiet conversation with him, apply effective negotiation techniques, and humbly ask for his help.

At the sound of his car horn, I tried to arrange my skirt, pinching my fingers and wondering where I would start our conversation.

Uncle Kamanzi entered the house, saying, "Karabo, how are you? We have to talk."

"I'm listening to you," I replied.

He kissed Birungi and gave her his laptop bag before taking a seat on one of the chairs around the coffee table, and saying, "Karabo, I wanted to tell you again that I am your parent. The only thing I could do for my late brother Kalisa, whose life had been ended by the Hutus, was to raise his daughter. I fulfilled my obligations as a parent. Didn't I?"

"Uncle, I didn't mean to be ungrateful. I can never find words to thank you. But—"

"But you are now an adult. That's what you want me to understand. Isn't it? I have understood it. My darling, the responsibilities of a parent remain forever. I am not only your uncle; I occupy the place of your father."

"You are right. I didn't mean you aren't my parent. Maybe I just need more freedom."

"Karabo, don't worry. I have a suggestion. What if they arrange the annex house for you? There, you will gain the privacy and independence you want. Of course, that doesn't include bringing in night companions," he said, slapping me on the shoulder.

Touched by the way Uncle Kamanzi was speaking to me,

I wept and said, "Uncle, I am sorry. What would I have become if you had not brought me to live with you as your own daughter? I never missed anything. You covered me with your love. I'm sorry I was insolent this morning. I am grateful that you have heard the meaning of my feelings, even when the words could not explain my fears."

He interrupted me, pulled me to his chest, and said: "It's okay, my daughter. Thank you for making me realize I may have focused on my own bitterness. I forgot that we are indeed two individuals. I am your parent. Never hesitate to discuss your concerns with me. As an adult, you will be free to take or reject my advice, which I will continue to give anyway."

I told my uncle the ordeal that Mama went through.

"They also suffered," he said, referring to Hutus, but avoiding talking badly about Mama.

He took the opportunity to ask me questions about my relationship with Shema and, with coyness, I told him that my love for Shema was stronger than what my head and heart could comprehend.

"Uncle, I beg you, help me get Shema out of prison," I said. "It's over between him and me, but my heart will never find peace knowing that Shema is in prison because of my betrayal."

He was silent for a few seconds before saying, "Okay, tomorrow I will call the prosecutor's office. But I'm afraid that, now that his case is before the courts, we can only ask for his release on bail. Then we will seek a lawyer to defend him."

"Thank you very much, Uncle. I don't know what to say… Thank you very much."

"Now, let's go for dinner, Birungi is calling us," Uncle said.

We shared dinner with smiles that we had not exchanged for so long. I once again felt like a princess in my Uncle's kingdom. I was looking at little Neza smiling at me, and I wanted to remind her that I, too, was with my own parents.

Uncle Kamanzi kept his promise, and only two days later, Shema was released. Even if it was over between us, I had to talk to him. I was afraid to go alone. I called Muhire on the phone.

"Hello, Karabo," he said. "It's been a long time."

"Don't you know what happened to me?"

"No. What happened to you?"

"Muhire, I spent four weeks stuck in a hospital bed."

"Hospital? Why didn't you tell me? Tell me, what happened to you?"

"Muhire, calm down. I'm fine now. But I need your help… I mean, I wanted you to go with me somewhere."

"Where?"

"Just tell me where you are. I will tell you more."

He told me he was at his carpentry workshop in Gakinjiro. I took a taxi.

Alarmed by the scars on my face and body, he asked me: "Karabo, it looks like you've been assaulted by bandits. Who did this?"

"That's the reason I'm here," I replied. "My assailant is none other than Shema. He hit me after learning everything about Mama. That's what happened to me."

I told him everything that had happened and how I had found myself in a hospital and Shema in prison.

"Oh my God, this is the work of the devil."

"Muhire, I need your help. You are the only one who can understand me. Please say yes."

"Yes, to what?"

"Aren't you a born-again Christian? God, didn't he ask you to help all those in need? Shema needs you. You must be his friend or his brother. Please, stay by his side, and never leave him as a lost soul wandering alone in this wicked world. Shall you accept my request?"

"Karabo, you're somehow right. Shema needs God; otherwise, the devil will ruin his life. I did everything I could for him to change, but I don't know what to do about his drug addiction."

"You helped him, and there were changes. But because of my betrayal, he's going back to square one. I will never forgive myself for having lied to Shema about my family. But why me? Why should I carry the heavy burden of ethnicity in this Rwanda? I share the pain of the Tutsis with whom I identify, and whose lives have been hunted like serpents. I carry the burden of the Hutus whose blood runs in my veins, even though I should share neither their name nor their shame. Muhire, I'm tired. I can't take it anymore."

Muhire pulled me to his chest. "Karabo, stop crying. The problem is not you. This world is amblyopic and cramped. You won't be able to change it with those tears. You shouldn't carry any other burden, but love."

"Muhire, let's go. We have to go to Shema's house."

We descended the road to Cyahafi. I hid behind Muhire's back as he knocked on the door of Shema's studio. He wouldn't open if he saw my face. Nobody answered. Muhire knocked on the door again, but there was no sign anyone could be in that room. We concluded Shema wasn't there.

"Excuse me, have you seen the occupants of that studio?" I asked the neighbor who was doing laundry by the door of her flat.

"One of them has gone to work, but the other is in. He

was away for many days. He has come back this morning, entered the room, and locked the door. He looked troubled."

Muhire held my hand, and we went back to Shema's door.

"Shema, it's me, Muhire. I know you're there. Please, open for me."

"Not today, please. I don't want visitors."

"It's been a long time. I just wanted to know how you are doing. Open for me. It will only be for a few seconds."

Shema opened the door. Muhire and I hurried inside.

"Karabo, what do you want from me?" Shema asked. "Can't you let me live in peace?"

I was mute. Muhire had warned me.

"She has told me everything," said Muhire. "Karabo has done you wrong. She shouldn't have built your relationship on a big lie. I'm not here to ask you to forgive her. That, she will do for herself. I'm just here because I can imagine what you went through. You understand what I'm talking about. Don't you?"

"Please don't talk to me about my love relationship with Karabo. It was just a nightmare, which finally ended. I am now awake." Shema turned to me. "Karabo, you have no shame. How do you dare come to my place? You had made me believe your big lie for ten years. Every time I cried because I was an orphan, you cried with me. I told you I loved you; you told me you loved me too… Karabo, what did you want from me? Your Hutu people killed my parents and all my brothers and sisters. You found me in my own life where my mother could never hear my cry. You made me forget the person I was, an orphan alone in this world of the wicked. My love for you has only caused me misfortunes. I left the army because of this love. I left school because of this love. I was sent by your uncle to the streets just because I was in love with you. You made fun of me, making me believe you shared my pain, when you knew that one day, your Hutu mother would reappear I don't know where from. Karabo, please get out of my room. Muhire, help me beg Karabo to get out of here."

"Shema, please forgive me," I said. "Forgive me for all the pain I have caused in your life… I don't know what to say…I'm simply asking for your forgiveness."

"Forgiveness for what? What will I do if I don't forgive you? Stop crying, or the orphan I am will be sent back to prison for making you cry. Go live your life… Leave Shema, who has neither the past nor the future. Go wait until your mother, who has risen from the dead, shall come to take care of you, while mine has refused to come back to life. Get out of here, please."

"Shema, I'm not asking to come back into your life. I'm ashamed. I beg you to forget me and pursue your life."

"Karabo, please, stop. What life are you talking about? I've done everything I had to accomplish in life. I'm only waiting for death. Tell me what remains to be done."

Muhire approached Shema, put his hands on his shoulders, and said, "Don't say that. You have a whole future ahead of you. Life goes on."

"Muhire, you know I've already tasted all the bitterness of life on earth. What else haven't I lived yet? Will I be orphaned for the second time? Will I have to go back to the street to smoke weed? Is it the prison that I haven't experienced yet? Oh no, maybe you meant finding love and its disappointments."

"Your future is bigger and longer than your past," said Muhire. "God has good plans for you."

Shema stood up, opened the door, and showed us the exit, "Thank you for your visit. Now, you can get out; if not, it's me who will get out."

We did not insist. We said good-bye to him and got out of his room. Outside, Muhire asked me to wait for a few minutes. I waited for him, stabbing hard my trembling body with my fingernails. The earth was falling on my neck. He returned after about ten minutes.

"Karabo, may I tell you something?" he asked.

"Yes, go ahead, please."

"Shema has been deeply hurt by what you did, but he still loves you. Give him some time to digest everything. He is still in shock."

"I will never forgive myself for having kept him in the dark. I could have ended our relationship a long time ago. Perhaps he would have found another girlfriend who isn't condemned to carry the weight of ethnicity. Now I don't know anymore. Muhire, tell me, is this love? Is this how it ends? I will never find the strength to forget about Shema. I love him so much. The whole person that I am is only in love with Shema."

"In all that he has just told me, I appreciate one thing. He's sorry to have hit you. He has told me he didn't know what he was doing, and that everything was because of the drugs. He has added he decided to quit."

"Shall he really be able to stop smoking? Please help him."

"Yes. I will link him with the doctor who helped me as well as the drug addicts with whom I was in prison. Shema can't fight addiction by himself. He needs both clinical and psychological support."

"Thanks, Muhire. I knew I could count on you."

We climbed the road to Gakinjiro, and when we got

to his workshop, I gave him a good-bye handshake before hurrying to Kiyovu.

Lying on the bed of my room of the annex house, I replayed the flashbacks of the life I had shared with Shema. I missed everything already, his hugs, our love games, and how I used to lay my head on his chest while listening to the music of French slow songs. My red pillow was all I was left with. I squeezed it hard and wet it with tears.

From that day, my life became boring without my boyfriend, Shema, and my friend Sugira. Apart from Mama's photo, which I had a lot to say to, I had nothing but Neza's smiles, the tea served by her mother, Birungi, and the life lessons Uncle Kamanzi gave me every evening.

Fourteen

On January 14, 2005, the day before graduation at the university, which I did not care so much about, Uncle Kamanzi brought me a toga and a hat to wear on that day he considered special.

"Take it, please," he said. "That's what you'll put on tomorrow."

"Hey, you brought it," I said. "I didn't want to go to the graduation ceremony. What matters to me is the certificate."

"Why? Tomorrow is a big day. Look, we have our invitation cards. Birungi and I will accompany you. It calls for a celebration, and everyone in our family is invited to the party tomorrow. You must also invite all your friends."

"My friends?"

"Yes, don't worry," Uncle Kamanzi said with a big smile on his face. "Everyone is welcome. It's your big day."

After lunch, I entered my room to write the potential guests' names, sad that Shema couldn't be there. I picked up the phone, and with trembling hands, I dialed Sugira's number.

"Hey, how are you?" he said.

"Good, and you?" I replied.

"I am doing very well. Please tell me, are you feeling better now? The last time we saw each other, you were in the hospital. Have you healed well?"

"Yes, thank you. Sugira, I…I wanted…I would like to talk to you."

"Talk to me? Go ahead, please."

I could not tell him about the party as if nothing had happened. How could I ignore that he was angry at me for having chosen Shema over him?

"What if we meet somewhere to talk?" I asked.

"No problem. I also wanted to talk to you."

"Where could we go then?"

"You just tell me what time you'll be ready, and I'll come to get you," he said. "I am driving Dad's car today. Don't worry. I'll come to pick you up."

I did not understand the meaning of his mood, with a smile that could cross the telephone wire to my ears.

In the evening, I wore black denim leggings and a gray T-shirt, and when the horn of Sugira's car made noise, I told Birungi I was going out, and that I would not be late. Her lips tried to open, but I guessed her mind reminded her I had been given an annexed house.

"Hello," I said, getting in the car.

"Hi," Sugira replied coldly.

He did not kiss me on the cheek as he used to. He instead started the car. He was different from the Sugira I had spoken to a few hours ago on the phone. His smile and his words had become so rare. I did not ask where we were going. To my surprise, he headed for Corners of Lovers, the same place he had brought me for our first date.

He parked the car, got out, and waited for me. He did

not open the door as he had the day we had come to the same place for the first time. After I got out of the car, he locked it, and, by a show of hands, invited me to be the first to enter.

"We'll take a seat next to the water fountain," said Sugira, before the waitress could direct us to a few seats.

Our eyes met, but neither of us moved our lips to make a smile.

After we had taken our seats, the waitress brought the menu. I chose a lemonade cocktail. Sugira asked for a glass of red wine.

"You said you wanted to talk to me," he said.

"Yes."

"Here I am, go ahead, please."

"Later, but I wanted to tell you…I missed you."

"Did you miss me?" he asked. "How?"

"Sugira, please forgive me."

"For what?"

"For everything," I said. "Please, forgive me for everything."

"What do you mean by 'everything'?"

"Sugira, you know what I'm talking about. You were mad at me because… Because I had spent a night with Shema."

"Hmm… didn't you tell me I should never be jealous of Shema because I'm only a friend to you? Why should I get angry when you decide to spend a night with your lover? Besides, however sad it makes me, I can handle my pain. You have nothing to do with that."

"Sugira, I never said that. But please, forgive me."

He took a sip from his glass of wine before asking me if I wanted to eat something. I ordered fish brochettes. He called the waitress and asked her to bring two brochettes for each of us.

"Karabo, don't worry. I took the time to think about it. You chose Shema. The only thing that saddens me is that I'm afraid he doesn't love you the way you love him."

"Maybe you're right. But—"

"Karabo," Sugira interrupted me. "The first time we came to this place, I had planned to declare my love for you. I loved you since we were little. I love you with all my heart, soul, mind, and body. That's what I had intended to tell you. But as soon as we got here, I realized your heart wasn't ready for me. I buried my words deep in my heart and waited for the right moment to take them out. Now, I guess it's too late."

"Sugira…not now, please… I—"

I did not want him to start again. My head and my heart were not yet ready to hear the word love. He scratched his head. His eyes moved left and right as if they were going to let rivers of tears fall.

"I will never forget the day I found you unconscious in front of Shema's room. You were pitilessly beaten, blood running on your torn clothes. That's when I realized how weak I was. I avoid thinking of myself as a coward, but that's what I am."

"Sugira, you aren't a coward. You are the kindest person I have ever met."

I wanted to be clear and tell him that Shema had given me the poison from the tree of love fruits, but I could not face his miserable eyes. I wanted to say to him that Shema was not always cold and angry but a romantic guy with a seductive smile. How could I tell him that everything had started in my uncle Kamanzi's house, Shema singing love songs for me, caressing my hair, and cuddling my skin from chest to navel and the organ below? Maybe I could tell him how helpless my body was every time Shema's eyes went through my heart. I decided to keep my mouth mute.

"Karabo, I love you… I love you so much," said Sugira with a frail voice. "What can I do so you can open for me the doors of your heart? I want to reveal to you the lover in me, not just a friend."

"Hmm? What kind of lover are you?" I asked.

"You still don't get it. Are you asking me how I can shower you with love? Karabo, I am a boy. If you doubt, ask me to take off my pants and show you."

Irritated by the fact that he could think of me as someone who values only sex, I raised my voice, "What do you take me for? A bitch?" I asked. "If you think I sleep with all the men who cross my ways, you don't know me. In fact, you shouldn't pretend to love me if you take me for a slut."

"Karabo, I am sorry. That's not what I meant. I love you so much that even if you had done something wrong, my eyes wouldn't notice."

"What do you mean then?"

"I'm not your brother, nor your cousin. When I invite you to share lunch with me, it's because my heart and body aspire to be by your side. When I come to your house to visit you, I want to admire your smile. When I look at your beauty, I hold my boy's organs so they won't disrespect the girl you are. My love for you is the one that doesn't dare to call you names. May I ask you something?"

"Yes."

"I heard Shema was released from prison. Are you still together?"

"No, it's over."

"Never go back to him. You won't have anything good from that relationship. Karabo, please, give me the chance to love you. I am kneeling down to beg your love."

"Sugira… don't do this to me, please."

"Karabo, you don't have to say anything except yes."

I looked at the sky to hide my eyes, and said, "Sugira, my biggest concern now is to bring Mama back to Rwanda." I did not know what else to say.

"Yes, I know. But that doesn't change the fact my heart is thirsty for your love."

He brought his chair closer, put his hands on my cheeks, made his eyes meet mine, and tried to kiss my lips. I pushed him.

"Karabo, do you feel at least a bit of love for me?" he asked. "We can build on that drop of love. I promise you it will flourish."

"My head is full of other worries," I replied. "I'm not ready for another relationship yet."

"Okay, I have given you the message of my heart. May I make another request? Would you give me the time and the space to prove to you how much I love you?"

"Sugira, I have told you I'm not ready for a relationship. Try to understand, please."

"I'm not asking you to commit to a relationship now. There is no remote-control button I could press to command your heart to love me. I am only asking for time and space to love you. I will wait for you as long as it takes. Do you want to give me a chance to splash you with my love?"

I did not feel any electrical chemistry that linked my heart to Sugira's, but my brain liked the kind person he was. Nor could I ignore the fact that, contrary to Shema, Sugira shared the weight of mixed ethnicity. He understood the pain I had been caused by the Hutu militants who killed my father and my sisters because the same Hutus had also exterminated his maternal family. He did not doubt my Hutu mother's nobility because he testified to the nobility of his Hutu father. The authors of the compatibility rules would not have taken a second to approve my relationship with Sugira. But why didn't my heart open to Sugira?

As if I were a shy teenager, I looked at Sugira and said: "Yes."

"Are you giving me the chance to water you with my love?"

"Yes, I am giving you the space to prove to me your love, but we cannot talk about a relationship at the moment."

"Karabo, thank you very much. I don't know what to say."

He approached me for a passionate hug. His heart played afrobeat. In a few seconds, his lips were on mine, but I rejected the kiss as soon as his saliva reached my tongue. The idea that I could kiss another boy made me sick. Only Shema had the right to kiss me and touch my body. I lowered my eyes and picked at my nails. Fortunately, the waiter interrupted. He brought us the brochettes we had ordered. While eating, Sugira looked at me and smiled. I paid him a fake smile. Sitting next to Sugira was not my concern, but the idea he would be my boyfriend was troubling. Maybe I had not given Shema enough time to digest everything that had happened to us. Maybe there was hope that Shema would come back to me as my first and only love.

After eating, I looked at my watch, and said, "Oh, it's late. I have to go back before Uncle Kamanzi wonders where I am."

"Yes. It's 8:30. Let's go."

Sugira paid the bill, and we left the restaurant.

He opened the car door for me, took the driver's seat, then turned on the radio to play Rwandan music. The happiness in his eyes worried me. Maybe I have given him false hopes.

"Karabo, listen to this song," Sugira said. "I dedicate it to you."

He helped Utamuliza to sing, '*Kunda ugukunda! Oooooh! Ooooooh...*' which means, 'Give your love to the one who truly loves you.'

I did not agree with Sugira that Shema did not love me. But I knew our love was impossible. Maybe the Rwandan singer Utamuliza was right. Perhaps I should have learned to love Sugira. He had shown me his love since we were young in high school. He was a boy with whom many girls would have loved to be. He was from a decent and comfortable family. He was about to complete his university studies and, more importantly, our ethnic destiny had more similarities than differences. There was no doubt that our future together would be bright. I wanted to forget the mantra *follow your heart*. I had to obey my brain. I was scared. In love, my body could only follow the heart's instructions and not necessarily those of my brain.

He dropped me at home. I kissed him on the cheek before entering my uncle's compound. He took a few minutes before restarting the car and leaving.

"Good evening, I'm sorry to come back so late," I told Uncle Kamanzi and Auntie Birungi.

"Where were you?" Uncle Kamanzi asked.

"I was... I was inviting my friends to the party," I responded.

"Okay, please go to the dinner table. We haven't waited for you."

"I'm not hungry. Thank you."

Uncle Kamanzi moved his lips to speak but held his anger after receiving a warning peep from Birungi. I wished them good night before going to my room in the annex house.

In my room, I looked at myself in the mirror and hated the shame I was reading on my face. I opened my red basket and took Shema's picture to ask him questions: "Shema, tell me. Why are you separating from me because of the history we haven't written? Do you want to change my name to *uwanyina* (Mom's daughter) when my father called me *uwase* (Dad's daughter)? Are you throwing me in the hands of another guy? Tell me. Please tell me…" I changed my clothes, squeezed my red pillow, and closed my eyes to pretend to sleep. Dreams did not solve my puzzle. Instead of pulling Sugira alone in my thoughts, he appeared there with Shema. I could visualize myself in bed with Shema while Sugira stood by the door, calling my name out loud, begging me to get out of that room. And without my noticing, my dreams reversed the image. I could visualize Sugira holding my hands and telling me how much he loved me, while Shema stood on the other side of the road calling me to cross and fly with him. The two guys continued to disturb my sleep and dreams until the next morning.

"Karabo, wake up and get ready. You'll be late," said Birungi in the morning.

"Eh? What time is it?"

"Six thirty. Graduands and their parents should arrive at 7:30."

"Let me get up then."

I took a shower and prepared to leave. In the living room of the main house, Uncle Kamanzi was ready in his navy-blue suit. He looked so handsome without his soldier's costume. Birungi was in the traditional Rwandan *imisha-*

nana. Looking at how they painted the image of Papa and Mama, tears attacked my eye makeup. The joy I felt because my uncle had taken seriously my graduation crossed with the sadness that my parents were not there to witness the day of my graduation from university.

"Here is the most beautiful and intelligent girl in the world," said Uncle. "You are splendid, darling."

"Thank you," I replied.

"We are late," said Birungi.

We got into Uncle's car.

At school, it was a big ceremony but so tiresome. The sun was unbearable, and the academicians shared the floor to make their long speeches instead of calling our names. I was called among the category of second-class honors. Sugira was sitting not far from me with those who had not graduated. He was pursuing a program of engineering studies, which lasted for five years. At the end of the ceremony, Birungi approached me to give me a beautiful bouquet of flowers, followed by a kiss on the cheek. Uncle Kamanzi gave me a big hug.

"Congratulations, stop crying," he said, wiping my tears. "Today is a day of joy."

We got into his car to go back to Kiyovu. There was a large, well-decorated tent. All the members of our family were there. It was like a dream, looking at members of my paternal family sitting in the same tent with my maternal uncle Gasana. Sugira's parents were also there.

"Congratulations, my daughter," said Uncle Gasana. "I'm so proud of you."

"I should be the one to thank you," I said. "Who told you about the graduation?"

"Colonel Kamanzi called me yesterday," Uncle Gasana replied. "He invited me to the party."

"Is he the one who invited you?" I could not believe my ears.

"Yes."

I greeted other visitors before escaping. It was too heavy for my heart. I hurried to my room, took my red pillow, and let the tears flow. I cried and cried until I forgot everything that was going on outside. I did not understand why I was crying, but I assumed it was just the crossing of my grief and joy. I opened my white basket to talk to Mama. "Mama, where are you? Please come back. I want you by my side. Come and witness what's going on outside. Uncle Kamanzi is with your brother Gasana. Mama, it's possible. We can become a family again." I sat on the bed until someone knocked on the door.

"Who is it?" I asked.

"It's me. Please, open."

I opened.

Sugira entered and immediately grabbed the picture from my hands before saying, "Karabo, what are you doing in your room looking at your mother's picture? What's the matter? Please, stop crying."

"Sugira, everything is fine. Please, go outside. I am coming in a few seconds."

"No, I'm not going anywhere without you. Wipe your tears and come with me. Your mother will come back soon. I promise you."

"Do you promise? How?" I asked.

"Karabo, if you have a bit of confidence in me, please leave it to me. I will do my best to reunite you with your mother."

"Eh? Are you sure?"

"Yes. But for now, please, come out of this room. Your uncles and aunts are wondering where you are."

He held my hands and took me back to the tent. It was indeed a big party. The guests were eating and drinking before they started singing and dancing. After a while, Uncle Kamanzi interrupted the songs to make his speech.

"Today is a day of joy for our family. It's a big day for Karabo. I am a happy and proud parent. You all know the tragedy our country has gone through. Karabo's father was my little brother. I lived in Uganda as a refugee. My best memories of Rwanda were the childhood moments I had shared with Kalisa. We were like twins, and we loved each other so much. I dreamed of the day when I would see my younger brother. But the day I returned to Rwanda, the only picture of Kalisa I was able to recuperate was his daughter Karabo. Kalisa loved his family so much. He had great plans for them. I thank the Almighty for having given me this opportunity to attend a university degree graduation by the only child Kalisa has left in this world. I thank my wife for all the support she has given to Karabo. Thank you all, including those I do not know, who stood by Karabo in one way or another. She is surrounded by a big family. Thank you. Please, refill your glasses."

Uncle's words kindled my heart. He chose not to ruin my day by talking about my mother, associating her with what Hutu extremists did to our family.

After a few minutes, I was invited to say a few words.

"Thank you all for honoring our invitation. I would like to express my gratitude to Uncle Kamanzi, I mean Papa Kamanzi. I thank him for having protected me from the bitterness of an orphan's life. I have never lacked anything, water to drink, or a bed to stretch my body on and sleep. This university degree is the result of his actions, and I will always be grateful to him. I would like to thank so many others. I could start by Devota, who is no longer of this world. I do not have enough time to tell the story of Devota and me. Her brother Muhire is here, and he knows how much I am indebted to Devota. Today, I'm happy that Uncle Gasana is celebrating with us…I'm sorry that despite the fact I have a lot to say, I'm afraid I may not put my words in the right order. I thank Mr. Kamana's family for having been by my side even though they had never met my parents. I say thank you to all of you."

I avoided crying in front of all those people and quickly returned to my seat. After a while, Uncle Kamanzi gave his speech signaling the end of the party.

As the visitors got up to leave, Sugira called me and asked me to follow him to the backyard.

"My sweetheart, I just wanted to say good-bye. I have to go with Dad and Mom."

"Okay, 'bye."

"Please, don't cry anymore. Do you promise me?"

"Yes."

"Keep in mind what I've told you. I'll make sure your mother comes back to Rwanda. This is my promise to you."

"Thank you."

"I have to go now."

He kissed me and left. After having accompanied the visitors to the gates, we entered the living room. I had to thank Uncle Kamanzi and Aunt Birungi in a more particular way.

For once in life, blessings were crossing my way. One week after graduation, I received a phone call.

"Hello, may I talk to Karabo?"

"Yes, I am Karabo."

"This is HROR, the chapter of the Human Rights Organization in Rwanda. It's about your application for the position of mobilizer for women's rights. You are invited for an interview on Friday, January 21st, 2005, at 10:00 at our Kimihurura office."

"Thank you. I will be there on time."

"Thank you."

I did not know how to prepare for a job interview. I called Sugira. He promised to help me. We spent the whole afternoon together. He asked me questions, pretending to be the interviewer, and I played the role of the interviewee.

"Who wouldn't give you a job, Karabo? You're so smart," he said.

"How?"

"You talk about women's rights with a lot of passion. You are so convincing."

"Maybe it's because of what Mama went through. I have read a lot of books and reports about what women experienced during the war in Congo. If I had the means, I would defend women's rights."

"That reminds me," said Sugira. "Yesterday, I went to the Ministry of Refugees and Returnees. But unfortunately, the head of the Rwandan refugee unit was not there. The assistant scheduled my appointment with him on Tuesday next week."

"Sugira, thank you very much."

"Please, don't thank me. I am doing it for my mother-in-law," he said with a smile.

"Sugira!"

He put his arms on my shoulders and said, "I mean my future mother-in-law."

In the early evening, he kissed me and left.

The following Friday, I put on my long-sleeved white

shirt, a black skirt, and black high heels. I headed for Kimihurura to HROR. The interview questions were not difficult at all. I answered with confidence. After the interview, they asked me when I would be ready to start. I told them I was immediately available. They said they would call me as soon as a decision was made. Before I arrived home, they had already called me to tell me I had been selected for the job and to ask if I could start work the following Monday. Uncle Kamanzi could not believe how only a week after graduation, I was hired. I told him I owed him all those blessings.

On Monday, I wore a navy-blue skirt, a sky-blue shirt, and high heels in blue and black colors, and Uncle Kamanzi dropped me off at the workplace. The first day at the office was for orientation, which included reading numerous reports on women who have been victims of sexual violence. In each story, I visualized what Devota had endured when she was raped by the Hutu militant Abdullah during the three months of darkness. I recalled Mama was still going through the same horrible experience, and tears stung my eyes.

At 5 p.m., I left the office and took the bus to Kiyovu.

After taking a shower, I joined Uncle Kamanzi and his wife Birungi in the living room for tea-time, and later dinner.

On the second day of work, I decided to take a pen and write each story's particularities. To read about women who were unable to free themselves from the hands of their captors made me think about Mama. Maybe she had also surrendered to her hijacker, Hagira.

Exhausted, I left the office around 5:30. My first priority after arriving home was to rest for a while. But the ringing of the phone did not allow me to.

"Hello, Sugira," I said.

"Hello, darling. How is it at work?"

"Great. I am getting used to it little by little."

"I have good news for you," he said.

"Good news? Please tell me."

"Have you forgotten my appointment at the ministry was scheduled for today? I have told the in-charge about your mother's story and everything she's going through to this day. He has expressed sympathy and promised the ministry will do everything possible to bring back your mother and her family to Rwanda."

"Her family? Didn't you tell him Mama lives with a genocide perpetrator?"

"Yes, I have told him. Maybe he meant your mother's children. The husband can also come to face justice."

"Sugira, it scares me a little. If that man learns Mama is planning to return to Rwanda, he will kill her."

"What did I tell you? I begged you to trust me. The official has told me the ministry works with other international organizations specializing in the treatment of similar cases."

"Okay, I count on you. But they should leave the husband in Malawi, or bring him later."

Sugira promised me to follow the case up with the ministry every week.

"What plans do you have for next weekend?" Sugira asked.

"Nothing yet."

"May I suggest something?"

"What?"

"I wish we could go somewhere next Saturday."

"Corners of Lovers?"

"No, somewhere else. Please, say yes," Sugira begged.

"I will not say yes before you tell me the name of the place."

"It will be a surprise. All I can tell you is it's a great place you will love."

"Okay, I accept."

He said good-bye and hung up. I took a shower and joined Uncle Kamanzi and Aunt Birungi for dinner before going to bed.

The week's routine was the same: waking up to go to work, a whole day at the office, and going home at night to take a shower, have dinner, and sleep.

On Friday, I received a phone message from Sugira, "My sweetheart, are you ready for tomorrow?"

"Hey, yeah. Where will we go?"

"Karabo, don't tell me you have forgotten."

"No. Sorry, this week was busy. The syndrome of a new employee. I had to prove the excess of zeal at work. Where will we go?"

"Don't worry. You'll see it tomorrow."

On Saturday, around 9 a.m., Sugira was already at the gates of Uncle Kamanzi's place, driving his father's Mercedes-Benz.

"Sugira, where are we going? Tell me please," I asked him after giving him a hello kiss.

"Be patient, you'll see," he replied. "I like this dress, but today, I would advise you to wear jeans and safari shoes instead."

"Why? Are we going to volcanoes?"

"You got it well. We are going to climb a mountain."

"No, please. Don't talk about mountaineering. I will not be able to climb a mountain."

"Don't worry. When you're tired, I'll carry you on my shoulders."

"Okay, I hope your mother gave you enough dry corn when you were a child."

He drove toward Muhima. On reaching *Giti cy'Inyoni*, we took the road to Shyorongi, but immediately turned left on to a small muddy street. We drove for several minutes until we reached somewhere where we were facing Mount Musasa. He parked the vehicle, opened the door, and invited me out of the car. We were in the middle of nowhere, in the countryside surrounded by magnificent mountains. He led me to a small path. My heart was beating so fast. I wanted to tell him I could not climb that mountain, but I did not want to disappoint him. After five minutes of climbing, I could not move. He placed his hands on my waist, trying to help me move forward. I jumped and pushed back his hands.

"Karabo, why don't you want me to touch you?"

"It's not that I don't want you to touch me."

"But when shall you get it?"

"Get what?"

"I want to touch you."

"Let me sit down. I'm tired," I said.

"We still have a long way to go. We have to reach the top of this mountain."

"Is it a punishment?" I asked.

"No, a metaphor."

"A metaphor? How?"

"I'll tell you when we reach the top. The place is called *Bwiza*."

Eyes to the valley, I felt as if I was taller than all life challenges. Shema had refused to climb the mountains of my life. Sugira had invented a climbing game he called a metaphor. *Did he eavesdrop my conversation with Shema?* I wondered.

"Can we continue?" Sugira asked. Before I could answer, he stroked my legs and said, "Don't worry. You are with a doctor of all aches and pains. I treat hearts and legs."

He gave me a massage from toes to the knees. How I wanted those hands to be of Shema, who mastered the joints of all my body. Sugira pulled a bottle of water from his safari bag and handed it to me.

"Let's get going," I said, getting up.

"We aren't in a hurry. Can I tell you something?" he asked.

"Yes."

He put his hands on my cheeks, his face aimed at the middle of my eyes, and as I tried to hide my shy face, he said: "I love you." He looked down at the grass, then up at the sky and shook his head. "Have you ever tasted the pain of loving someone in secret?"

"Thank you." Those were the only words I could say to him.

"Please, don't thank me. I made the decision to love you in secret or in public. My heart will rejoice more the day you shall say you love me too. But even if you decide it stays this way, I will continue to love you as on the first day you gave me your smile."

"Sugira, I...I love you too."

"I know, but I also want the love of your eyes and your heart."

He got up and invited me to move on. Climbing the mountain seemed less disturbing than the conversation about love. After a while, we reached the top of the mountain, a flat place known as *Bwiza*, a beauty like Eden with many acacias that cast different shadows on the grass. He opened his safari bag and pulled out something that looked like a big balloon and started to push some air into it. The thing turned into a practical mattress. He stretched his body on that mattress and said: "Here we are on *Bwiza* Square. I invite you to lie down beside me."

"By your side?"

"Yeah, don't worry. Your jeans are tight enough to protect you from my stubbornness."

"Let me take a look at this beautiful garden."

I strolled, pretending to admire the beauty of the land of a thousand hills leading to valleys decorated with rivers of water flowing to all the peoples of the nation. A voice interrupted.

"Karabo, help me, please!"

I ran to him.

"What is it? What's wrong?" I asked.

"Look here…"

"Where?"

"On my back. Something bit me."

I bowed to check if it was an insect.

Sugira seized me and pushed me to lie beside him on the mattress. "It's gone. Please, don't leave me again. It could come back."

"Please, stop," I said.

"Let me help you take off your shoes," he said. "Don't worry. I will keep my hands off your jeans."

I placed my body next to his, and we both admired the shades and shapes of the clouds in the blue sky.

"Have you seen the beauty of the skies?" he asked.

"Yes, it's incredible."

"And what if we could fly there like birds?"

"Fly like birds? You and me?"

"Yes, let's try next time. We should fly like two little birds in the sky where there is no one else. Maybe there you could listen to the songs of my heart."

After some jokes full of metaphors, we shared the food he had packed and spent a few more minutes digesting before resuming our sightseeing trip. He behaved like a gentleman, as he had promised. With his help, it did not take long to go down the mountain and reach the car. While driving back to the city center, we talked about life, laughed at life, and the mess that decorated the Giti cy'Inyoni road, including how a headscarf flew from a woman's head on a motorcycle at Nyabugogo crossroads.

At Uncle Kamanzi's, Sugira gave me a good-bye kiss.

"Good night."

"Thanks a lot for today," I said.

"There is nothing to thank me for."

"Good night."

I got out of the car and hurried to my little room. For the whole night, I could not answer questions from my brain. Maybe the red basket of Shema in my room was the container of all the poison of love. I took it off the desk and put it in the closet. I did not have the strength to throw it out. I closed my eyes to pretend to sleep despite my dreams and nightmares.

On Monday, the director of HROR told me the NGO had a chapter in Malawi. I told her about Mama's fate. She promised to ask the NGO office in Malawi to look for Mama. I did not say anything to Sugira about the promise of the NGO.

A few days after, the director of HROR entered my office. "Karabo, look at this picture. Is she your mother?"

"Let me see."

Her face was like that of an old woman from the village.

Her shiny skin had turned gray. She was so thin, with a head covered with a scarf as multicolored as her African loincloth. She was no longer the classy woman with a chignon and a slinky blouse in a black straight skirt, marching in high heels and waving good-bye to us, before walking through the doors to work every morning. The woman in the picture had nothing in common with Mama except her eyes and her lips, despite their cigarette look.

"Stop crying," said the director.

"Mama has changed so much. She had to suffer a lot."

"It's been a long time, and she went through a lot in her life. The good news is that our social workers spoke to her in secret. She confirmed she wanted to return to Rwanda, but she doesn't want to leave her children. We are discussing how we can bring her back with her children."

"Please, be careful. Her husband is ruthless. He can kill her."

"We also talked to her husband."

"Did you?" I asked.

"Yes, we talked to him separately, but we didn't tell him we had talked to his wife. We encouraged him to return to Rwanda with his family."

"Did he accept?"

"No, he thinks he will be killed as soon as he arrives in Rwanda. We will continue to talk to him. If he committed the genocide, he should come back and face justice."

That day tasted like bitter honey. My heart wanted to see Mama again, but my brain was confused with all the questions I had about her. I could not imagine what I would say to those who knew me as a genocide survivor whose entire family had been exterminated. *How can I tell them I am welcoming my Hutu family returning from a refugee camp in Malawi?* I wondered.

Back home, while I was getting ready to take a shower, the phone rang.

"Hello," I said.

"How are you, Karabo? It's me, Muhire. Hey, listen, are you watching TV?"

"No."

"Please, go quickly to Celebrity TV. I'll call you later."

He hung up before I asked him why.

Uncle Kamanzi and Birungi were not at home. I turned on the TV in the living room. Shema had been invited to the Fashion Stars Show. He was in blue jeans fashioned with a blue T-shirt and a gray blazer. I could not believe my eyes. I sat like a dog watching a movie.

"So, how do you intend to make use of the prize?" asked the host of the show.

"I intend to invest more in my fashion business," Shema replied.

He had become a fashion designer with his own company. Shema had won a 100,000-dollar prize at a fashion design competition in Atlanta, Georgia, in the USA. I could not conceive how Shema had changed so much in a short time. I continued to listen to him talk about his fashion creations.

"Many young Rwandans want to be able to do something on their own, but they think it's always difficult to get funds. Do you agree with them?" asked the host of the show.

"Yes, I was like them. The only advantage I've had is that I graduated from a fashion and sewing school. I learned a lot about why people choose one style or the other. I liked to observe the people I loved, I mean the person I loved. Whenever I was alone, I drew dress patterns that could match the shape of her body."

"Wow, is she your girlfriend?"

"No, we broke up. I loved her, and I will always love her. But it's over between us. However, every time I want to inspire myself, I pull her picture from my consciousness and draw it on a piece of paper. Each of my creations tells a little story of our lives or her own life."

"So romantic. If you don't mind, could you tell us why you broke up?"

"No, it's not necessary. She has her own life, and I have mine. I can only say I owe her a lot. She was at my side when I didn't have anyone else. I wouldn't be here if she hadn't encouraged me to live when there was nothing more in my life than waiting for death. I want to respect her private life. She is in another relationship. I wish her the best."

"Thank you. We look forward to other Shema designs."

I turned off the TV and ran to my room and squeezed my red pillow.

A phone call interrupted my weeping.

"Have you seen him on TV?" asked Muhire.

"Yes, I have seen him."

"That's Shema you asked me to take care of as if he were my little brother. He stopped smoking weed. He has a business he calls Shema Designs. At first, I didn't think it was a good business until he won that jackpot. I am proud of him."

"I'm happy for him," I replied, my voice almost refusing to come out of my mouth.

"Karabo, Shema still loves you."

"Perhaps, but our misalliance is stronger than our love."

"I cannot hide anything from you," said Muhire. "Shema told me he loves you so much. But he added he can never forgive you for having lied to him about your ethnicity and your mother. Shema still suffers from heart wounds. He still curses Hutus for having killed his family."

I said good-bye to Muhire and hung up the phone. I did not want to open that Hutu-Tutsi box.

I woke up in the morning with an important decision. At 10:00, I picked up my phone and called Sugira. I invited him for an evening at Corners of Lovers. After hours, we headed over there. We ordered drinks, and before the waiter brought them, I looked at Sugira in the face and said:

"I accept."

"Hmm? What do you accept?" he asked.

"To be your girlfriend."

I waited for him to jump for joy to kiss me, but he did not.

"Karabo, you look sad," he said. "What happened?"

"Nothing. I have considered your proposal and concluded we must give ourselves a chance."

"Your eyes don't agree with you. They communicate a message of heartache. They don't tell me they love me."

"Okay, you will choose to believe me or believe my eyes."

"Thank you, Karabo," Sugira said finally. "You know I love you so much, and I always dream of hugging you until the end of the world."

He got up, moved behind my back, and wrapped his arms around my neck before sliding his hands to my chest and his lips on mine. I told my heart to shut up and follow the instructions of the head. The only way to punish Shema was to kiss another guy passionately, whether my heart wanted it or not. I closed my eyes and let myself go.

After the kiss, Sugira put his hands on my cheeks, looked at me, and said, "I love you."

"I love you too," I replied.

As we shared drinks and food, he told me how he had loved me since we were in high school and continued to promise me that nothing or nobody would ever separate us. Many people say that women follow the voice of their hearts to make decisions, but I had to follow the advice of my brain for the most critical decision of my life. Life could never offer me a guy who would love me more than Sugira. My mind had convinced me that although Shema loved me, his love was not complete as long as he continued to put me in the same basket with the Hutu militants who had made him an orphan.

After dinner, Sugira dropped me off at Uncle Kamanzi's, and when we got there, he kissed me before I got out of the car. My heart was still heavy. Shema's smile was permanently painted on my memory, but I had to force myself to erase it and replace it with Sugira's.

Fifteen

The mission to repatriate Mama to Rwanda was complicated despite the efforts of the ministry and the NGO. Her husband had made her his prisoner. One day in November 2005, the HROR director called me into her office. She informed me she had learned the ministry was working on the same file and that they had agreed to join their efforts.

"Your mother's husband agreed to return to Rwanda with his family."

"Will they come together?"

"Yes, it's the best solution. Your mother couldn't bring the children with her without the permission of that man."

"When will they come?"

"No later than next month."

I had already told Sugira that HROR was helping to bring Mama back to Rwanda. After work, I went to tell him the good news. We concluded it was the right time to talk to other family members. I promised to announce the news to Uncle Kamanzi before going to Uncle Gasana's place the following weekend. However, I had to warn Sugira about something.

"We will only tell them Mama is coming back. We shouldn't mention those who are helping us."

"Why?"

"We should be careful. I'm not sure Uncle Kamanzi wants Mama to come back to Rwanda. Moreover, if Uncle Gasana had wanted to help his sister, he would have done so long ago."

At home, I took a shower and joined Uncle Kamanzi in the living room for a conversation.

"Good evening," I said.

"Good evening. Long time. Do we still live in the same house?"

"Yes, too much work. I wanted to tell you something."

"Tell me."

"Mama is coming back to Rwanda soon."

"How? And her husband?" Uncle Kamanzi asked.

"I don't know about her husband. All I know is that Mama is coming back next month. She will need housing. Maybe I will have to rent a house for her."

"From your little salary?"

"I will look for cheaper options."

"Okay."

Uncle Kamanzi did not want to say much about it. I rushed to my room.

The next Saturday, Sugira accompanied me to Uncle Gasana's house. He asked me if I was getting used to my job with HROR. I told him I was becoming an expert in the field of women's rights.

"Mama is coming back to Rwanda next month," I said.

"Oh, that's good news," Mugabo replied before Uncle Gasana said anything.

"Wait, Mugabo," said Uncle Gasana. "Please tell me.

Did you say Musanabera is coming back to Rwanda?" How about her husband? And the children?"

"I don't know about them. All I know is that Mama is coming back."

"That would be the biggest mistake of her life. Anyway, I don't think Hagira, the man I know, would let her come to Rwanda."

"The man you know, did you say?" I asked.

"Yes. I met him the last time I was in Malawi. I paid them a visit."

"The last time you were in Malawi? You never told me you were visiting Mama."

"Don't get me wrong, Karabo. I only saw them twice. As a representative of the government, I absolutely couldn't come back and say I had visited Hutu refugees. I am the one who brought you some of her letters."

"Mama isn't just any refugee; she is your sister. Why don't you want her to come back to Rwanda?"

"Don't ask me questions. You didn't ask for my opinion before you planned to bring her back. She is a married woman with children. They need her."

"And me?" I asked before turning to Sugira. "Let's go. We have nothing left to do here."

"Karabo, hold on," Sugira said, holding my hands.

"If you don't want to go, you stay. Good-bye."

I got out of that house. Sugira and Mugabo followed me. Anger strangled my throat. My brain could not grasp why Uncle Gasana did not want his sister to come back to Rwanda when he enjoyed the glory of being a minister in a government he despised.

"What's wrong with you people?" I asked Mugabo. "When shall you change? Why didn't you tell me Mama's letters were brought by Uncle Gasana?"

"Please, forgive me," replied Mugabo. "Uncle Gasana had warned me I shouldn't tell you. He wanted to throw away the letters. I begged him to give them to me and told him I wouldn't reveal the person who brought them."

"Why didn't he want me to know he was the one who brought the letters?"

"He has secrets. He told me he was a good friend to your mother's husband." Mugabo was quiet for a second before adding, "Anyway, let's ignore Uncle Gasana. I'm glad your mother is coming back. I am with you on that plan. Please don't involve Uncle Gasana again. You have no idea what he could do. I don't trust him."

"Thank you, Mugabo."

I concluded maybe not so many people were eager to see Mama back in Rwanda. The idea they would do anything to prevent the plan to bring her back scared me to death.

⟶

On December 17, 2005, I was in my room wondering if Mama would be back before Christmas. Waiting for her had mobilized all the veins in my body. The ringing of the phone woke me up.

"Hello," I said.

"Karabo, I have good news for you," said the HROR director. "Your mother is coming tomorrow."

"Tomorrow? Why didn't you tell me before?" I asked.

"Don't worry. We have made all the preparations to welcome her."

"Eh? Where will she live?"

"She's coming with her family. The ministry reserved apartments for the returnees before they could find permanent housing."

"Oh, thank you very much."

I did not have any other questions. Apparently, they had everything in order. I ran to the other house.

"Mama is coming back tomorrow," I said.

"Tomorrow?" Uncle Kamanzi asked.

"Yes. Please, let's all welcome her at Kigali International Airport."

"Where will she stay? Did you rent a house for her?" Uncle Kamanzi asked.

"No. I don't know," I replied.

Uncle Kamanzi and his wife, Birungi, stared at me as if they were watching a dramatic movie. I ran to my room, picked up a picture of Mama, and thanked her for having agreed to come back to me. I called Sugira and asked him to tell the news to his family. I called a few other people, only those who knew about my mixed ethnicity and that Mama was still alive. Doctor Baziga and Muhire were among them. I was sure they would be happy to know their advice had resulted in something. I secretly informed Mugabo but asked him not to tell anyone else.

The next day, Sugira accompanied me to buy a bouquet of flowers for Mama and some chocolates for her children. Around 2 p.m., Birungi called me on the phone to tell me she and Uncle Kamanzi could not come. She did not have to tell me why.

Sugira and I arrived at the airport early.

"That's the gentleman who works at the Ministry of Refugees and Returnees," said Sugira. "Maybe he's also waiting for your mother."

"Yes. Let's approach him."

I introduced myself to the man. He said I looked like my mother.

After a while, other people joined us. These included

Sugira's parents, Muhire, and his friend Karega. I was surprised to see Uncle Gasana with Mugabo.

"Didn't I beg you not to tell Uncle Gasana?" I whispered in Mugabo's ear, pretending to hug him.

"I didn't tell him," Mugabo replied. "He was informed by your mother's husband. He is coming with her."

Before I could respond, the man from the ministry called Sugira and me.

"The plane has just landed," he said. "Those policemen are waiting to arrest her husband."

"Hmm? Will they take him to jail immediately?" I asked.

"Lower your voice, please. It will be done in the greatest secrecy."

"Is Mama aware of the plan?"

"No. Not really. She was simply told her husband could face justice for his crimes."

After a few minutes, about twenty Rwandans came out of the airport hall. On their white T-shirts, it was written *Karame, Rwanda*, which can be translated as *Here I am, Rwanda*. The Minister of Refugees and Returnees, along with other government officials, approached the returnees. Uncle Gasana had joined his government colleagues. A woman stared at me. She held the hands of three children. She looked like the woman in the picture the HROR director had shown me a few months ago. I ran to her and gave her a big hug. She squeezed me hard and invited me to put my head on her chest. Neither she nor I uttered a word. The ministry official approached and asked Mama to enter the bus. She was going where the ministry had prepared accommodation for them in the Gahanga neighborhood in Kicukiro. The official told us we could follow the bus. I gave Mama the bouquet of flowers, and chocolates I had bought for the children. Uncle Gasana was nowhere to be found. Mugabo told me he had left after learning that Hagira had been arrested. Sugira, his mother, and I followed the bus to Gahanga.

The Ministry of Refugees and Returnees had rented for them beautiful and modestly furnished apartments. Mama was both calm and anxious. I could count her words. She seemed to be afraid of being surrounded by many people. I was not emotionally ready to spend the night with her. My heart was confused at the same time by the love I felt for the woman who was my mother and the fear for the woman she had become.

Sugira and his mother dropped me off at Uncle Kamanzi's place. I went immediately to my room and hid in bed, squeezing my red pillow tightly. I had to breathe hard and water it with all my tears.

When I woke up, I went to Mama's house, but all the questions I had for her refused to slip off my tongue. Mama could not initiate the conversation I had dreamed of. I had to be brave and spill it.

"I missed you," I said.

"I missed you too," she replied. "Have you received my letters?"

"Yes."

"I didn't receive your responses. I thought your uncle had not delivered the letters to you."

"I received them. I didn't know what to write and where to start. We should talk…about many things. Mama, I have been an orphan for almost twelve years, with neither Papa nor Mama…"

Tears began to appear in her eyes. She looked down before turning to me, and saying, "My daughter, I'm so sorry."

"Sorry for what?" I asked.

"I hate the day I left you, you and your dad, at the hour you needed me the most… What was I thinking? I'm sorry. Please forgive me."

"Mama, I know why you had to leave us. But I will never understand why you took so long to return."

"Please forgive me…"

She burst into tears again and stopped speaking. We both wept.

"Mama, stop crying," I said.

"No, Karabo, it's you who should rather dry your tears. Mine will never stop flowing from my eyes. I will pay for the deaths of Kalisa and my children for the rest of my life."

"No, Mama, you shouldn't blame yourself. You didn't cause their deaths. You were also a victim…"

Instead of asking her all the questions I had, I wiped her tears. She was harder on herself. I had nothing else to add.

"Karabo, will you take me to the graves of your father and your sisters?" she asked.

"Yes, we could go there the day after tomorrow."

I had an honest and moving conversation with Mama. I told her how the Hutu militants murdered Papa and my sisters, Fifi and Dudu, and how I survived the genocide. She also told me about everything she had experienced during the genocide against the Tutsi and how her own family had tortured and abused her just because she had married a Tutsi.

She would stop and say, "Sometimes, I think I had to share the pain with Kalisa. I would have felt worse if the Hutu militants hadn't tortured me. I would feel more remorse than I feel today. How I would have liked to share the same death with the only man I loved… Maybe God spared us for a reason. We will have to live for Kalisa, Fifi,

Dudu, and my baby, who was killed the first day he saw the sun."

She told me she was glad Uncle Kamanzi had taken care of me when my own mother was as good as dead.

"Yes, I am also grateful to Uncle Kamanzi," I said. "But it's time for me to fly my own wings. I'm looking for a house where you and I could move in."

"No, I don't agree with you," replied Mama.

"Why?" I asked.

"I will have to find people who could accompany me to officially express my gratitude to Kamanzi for having taken care of you as a father would."

"Mama, what if Uncle Kamanzi doesn't want to welcome you to his place?"

"He will welcome me. Don't worry."

"Mama, Uncle Kamanzi hates Hutus. Maybe you don't know…"

"Hutu militants killed his father and condemned Kamanzi to be a refugee for many years. And as if that wasn't enough, they killed the brother he loved so much, your father, Kalisa. I don't mean he should hate them, but I want to say we should at least recognize his grief. It takes time to forgive."

"And you? Didn't the Hutu militants kill your husband and your children?"

"That's precisely why I share Kamanzi's pain. Anyway, the only thing you must keep in mind is that Kamanzi is your paternal uncle. You owe him the same respect you would give to your father. I owe him respect as my brother-in-law; actually, in Kinyarwanda, he is considered my other husband."

"Hmm? Okay, I'll take you to his place."

Fixing Mama with my eyes, I could not believe my ears. It's incredible how people do not change. Although she looked calmer and bitten, Mama was still the same brave and determined woman. On her face was written a lot of blues, and her skin looked dry. Her voice conveyed both sadness and braveness. She was not happy with life. How I would have liked her to burst, make noise, and tell me how sad and angry she was.

Two days later, as I promised Mama, we went to the Genocide Memorial Center. Sugira took us in his father's car.

In front of the grave of Papa and my sisters, Mama covered her head and face. Sugira was holding her. She laid a wreath of flowers on the grave, knelt, and said, "Kalisa, I beg you. Please forgive me. I have begged for your forgiveness for many years. Please listen to me and free me. Now I know God has welcomed you into his eternity and given you the heavenly power to watch over our daughter Karabo. I thank you."

She wept. We could not help her.

Mama entered the commemorative house. We noiselessly visited all the memorial rooms. She would point out some pictures and say, "Look at this."

From the memorial, Sugira dropped us off at Uncle Kamanzi's house in Kiyovu. I wondered if Uncle would play the hypocrite or if he would spill all his bitterness at Mama. We knocked on the door, and Birungi opened it.

"Welcome. Is she your mother?" she asked.

"Yes," I replied. "Mama, this is Birungi, Uncle Kamanzi's wife."

"Nice to meet you," Mama told Birungi.

Birungi invited us to take a seat before going to inform

Uncle Kamanzi. She came back after a few minutes, sat down, and continued watching TV. She did not serve us drinks the same way she always did for her other visitors.

After ten minutes of silence, Uncle Kamanzi finally came into the room.

"Hello," he said.

"Hello," replied Mama. "Pleased to meet you. Kalisa spoke a lot about you."

"Kalisa also told me a lot about you," responded Uncle Kamanzi. "He sent me a picture of your wedding, but you seem to have changed a lot. How was your journey?"

"It was good, but a little tiring. We had to tour all of Africa before arriving in Kigali."

Birungi got up and asked us what we wanted to drink. We both chose tea. I waited for Uncle Kamanzi and Mama to continue their conversation, but silence reigned in the room.

"We are coming from the memorial to put flowers on Papa's grave," I said to Uncle Kamanzi.

"Have you gone there with your mother?"

"Yes."

Uncle Kamanzi made a tss sound, looked at Mama from toes to head, took the remote control, and changed the TV channel.

Mama picked at her nails before saying, "Rwanda has had the worst of tragedies."

"Do you realize it?" Uncle asked, before turning to me. "Karabo, here is your mother. She has a lot of explanations to give you. Why did she leave her husband and children to be killed by her own relatives?"

"Uncle, please," I replied. "We have already talked about that. I explained to you what happened."

"Karabo, stop," said Mama. "You should never talk to your uncle like that. He is right."

"Is he right?" I asked. "How?"

"Your mother should tell you why the Hutus killed your father when he had married their sister," said Uncle Kamanzi with a sarcastic smile as he crossed his legs together.

"Karabo, would you please give us a moment?" said Mama. "I need to have a private conversation with your uncle. I'll talk to you later."

"No, I won't go anywhere," I replied. "Whatever you have to say, say it in my presence."

"Karabo is an adult," said Uncle Kamanzi. "You have nothing to tell me. Talk to your daughter instead. She has the right to know why your Hutu relatives killed her father."

Mama wiped her eyes and started talking, "Yes, you are right. If I hadn't left Kalisa," said Mama, fighting with tears that were preventing her from speaking, as if she wanted to crumble into pieces, "if I had stayed with him... maybe I couldn't have stopped the killers, but we could have died together, or he could have died lying on my chest. I should have stayed with him until death as we had promised each other."

"Woman, please, swallow your tears," shouted Uncle Kamanzi. "Kalisa loved you with all his heart, but you... you turned your back on him just because... he was Tutsi. I'm sure the killers were sent by you and your brothers."

"Karabo can tell you. Those who killed them were our neighbors in Biryogo, not my family. But anyway, I have nothing more to say. It is only from Kalisa and our children I will always ask for forgiveness. I should have refused to get out of that house. I should have stayed there with them." Mama's voice was as if sadness and anger were fighting in her throat.

"Please, stop talking nonsense," Uncle said. "You are speaking now as the other lead killer who asked for the people he killed to be brought in as witnesses in court. It's cruel on your part… No, this is too much. Woman, get out of my house. Please."

Uncle Kamanzi got up and left us in the living room of his house.

Birungi brought us two cups of tea. I wanted to ask Mama not to drink that tea, but she thanked Birungi and started drinking as if she was not mad at Uncle Kamanzi.

"My conversation with Kamanzi was brief," said Mama to Birungi. "Please, convey my gratitude to him. I am very grateful to you for having been there for Karabo as her parents."

"I'll tell him," said Birungi.

"Thank you. I'll plan a day when I'll come and officially express my gratitude," Mama added.

"No, that won't be necessary," responded Birungi. "We did nothing special."

After drinking her tea, Mama did not get up to leave. I reminded her she had to take the last bus to Gahanga, a lie. She asked to say good-bye to Uncle Kamanzi, but Birungi told her he had already left the house. He was in his room but did not want to talk to Mama anymore.

"Mama, do you understand now?" I asked after crossing the exit of Uncle Kamanzi's compound. "I have to leave his house. If you don't want me to live with you, I'll have to find another place."

"No, I say no to you. Your uncle isn't a bad person. I'm sure everything he has told me today, he would have said the same in 1978 when his brother Kalisa was courting me."

"Why?" I asked.

"Your paternal family condemns the Hutus for all that they have endured since the murder of their father in 1963.

The scars of the heart of Kamanzi have been made fresh by finding that, thirty-one years after his father's death, Hutus killed his brother Kalisa and many other members of their family."

"He must know the brother he loved was your husband."

"He'll get there. But for the moment, these are my battles, not yours. Kamanzi is your uncle. I will never allow you to disrespect him."

I wanted to respond to her, but I couldn't find the right words to say. I could not conceive why she was not mad at Uncle Kamanzi. I moved the focus of our conversation to her own family.

"Will you tell me the same thing about your brother Gasana? Please don't ask me to love and respect him as my uncle."

"Yes. I will never allow you to disrespect him."

"Mama, Uncle Gasana's heart is dark and full of hatred. Don't tell me you understand him too."

"My dear, I will never justify hatred, but I know the hearts of some people are hurt, and some brains are confused... All I can tell you is that your uncle Gasana also deserves your love and your respect. But you must know he isn't so different from his brother Rwasibo, who killed my baby."

"How? Is he also a murderer? Did he commit genocide?"

"No, I've not seen him kill anyone," replied Mama. "He wasn't in Rwanda in 1994. But he also thinks Hutus had reasons to hate Tutsis."

"So, your whole family is of Hutu extremists, yes?"

"No. Some members of my family blame the Tutsis for everything Hutus endured before and during the colonization. But many understand there was no justification for marginalizing and killing Tutsis in all the years that followed the Hutu revolution. Nothing and no one should ever justify the genocide against the Tutsi."

I had many more questions to ask Mama about Rwanda, Congo, and the world in general, but I had a lot to digest for that day. I accompanied her to her apartment in Gahanga and came back with the same bus.

I joined Uncle Kamanzi in the living room. He asked me what I thought about his conversation with Mama.

"I told you what happened on April 7, 1994. Mama has nothing to do with the people who killed Papa and my sisters. And if you want to know why she didn't come back to Rwanda before, you should take the time to listen to her. She will tell you about her nerve-wracking experience with the Hutus whom you call her relatives. I beg you not to blame her for Papa's death. It breaks her heart."

"Okay. I'm sorry for having been carried away by my bitterness. The good thing is that your mother is back. You had missed her, I guess."

"Yes. I…I have asked her to move in with me to another house. But she has refused. She said she will have to come and express her gratitude for all that you've done for me."

"If I could, I wouldn't allow you to leave this house. It's your house. Your mother is very traditional. Did you say she wanted to come and express her gratitude?"

The smile on his face and his attitude made me more confused. We shared dinner before going to sleep.

On December 25, 2005, Sugira accompanied me to Mama's to celebrate Christmas with her. She had prepared my favorite meat with cassava leaves and pilau rice. At about 6 p.m., we said good-bye to Mama. After starting the car, Sugira told me he had good news.

"Good news?" I asked. "Please, tell me."

"No, I won't tell you. I'll show it to you."

"Okay. Show me now."

"Be patient."

We passed through the city center. He held my hand as we climbed the stairs of the gray building next to the post office. He took a key out of his pocket and said: "Here we are. I present to you my new office."

"Eh? Your new office? What will you do in this office?" I asked.

He told me his father had given him money to start a construction business. I congratulated him with a peck.

"I haven't finished showing you yet," he added.

"More surprises?" I asked.

"Yes, let's go back in the car. We are going to celebrate our we-two Christmas."

He started the car and headed to *GrayStyle*, a five-star hotel. When we took the elevator, fear tore my bones. *Is Sugira taking me to a hotel room?* I wondered. We went up to the rooftop, covered with darkness. I lost sight of Sugira in that blackness. I made noise calling for help.

Musical voices sang in Kinyarwanda a song that translated, "*The rain comes but stops to let the soil dry out again, the sun shines but disappears again to give way to night-time, but my love for you is like the rain that never stops and the sun that lasts forever.*"

The lamps turned on, and Sugira was kneeling before me with a silver ring.

"My Karabo, I want to live in your heart and you in my heart for eternity. Would you marry me, please?"

I wanted to run away, but I did not know which way to

go. Yes, I had agreed to try to be Sugira's girlfriend, but it was too early to talk about marriage.

"Sugi… Sugira…"

"Karabo, please."

"Yes…I say, yes."

He put the ring on my finger, and the waiter of the hotel opened the champagne. Sugira put his glass on my lips for a sip, and I did the same for him. Our lips met, and as we kissed, the singers became Frederic François. "*Mon cœur te dit je t'aime, il ne sait dire que ça…*" I could not help myself. French songs were not a signature of Sugira, but Shema's. I could not imagine myself dancing them with another guy. Sugira noticed my discomfort, took my hand, and sent me back to my seat. He told me more about his plans. He wanted the wedding to take place before the end of 2006.

"Before the end of next year?" I asked. "I don't think we'll be ready by then."

"Why not?"

"For example, I have to find Mama a place to live in. She won't stay in the temporary housing provided by the government."

"Of course," he replied. "That seems very easy."

"Besides, we should take the time to strengthen our foundation before talking about a wedding."

"That's so easy. Do you want me to show you how much I have on my account?" Sugira asked.

"Sugira, it's not just a question of money," I replied.

"But you are telling me about finding a place for your mom and to be more financially ready before our wedding. Right?"

"No. I said we need to take enough time to get to know each other well before setting a date for our wedding. Okay?"

"To know each other?"

"I mean, our courtship should take more time. Marriage is not a joke."

"Okay. Take all the time you need to study me. I don't even need a second more to convince myself you are the one God has created to be the mother of my children."

I waited a long time to leave that rooftop. We ate, we drank, but my heart was not there with me. When I got home, I ran to my room. I had a lot of questions for my red pillow. I could not become Sugira's wife. I needed his love, but not his hands on my body. My whole person was afraid to share my womanliness with him. I could not tell anyone about my engagement with Sugira. He informed his parents, and they called me to congratulate me. In my mind, I was still trying to make him my guy. Mama did not need to know something was going on between Sugira and me, while in my heart, there was still fire for Shema.

On January 5, 2006, I returned to work. At the office, the director informed me she would like me to share my story on television and how I had found my mother after so many years. I refused. She reminded me my testimony could help other women in the same situation as Mama. I told her I should ask for Mama's consent before making her story public. Mama did not make things easy for me. She accepted.

On January 12, 2006, I was in the HPC Television studio telling my story. The journalist wanted to know every detail. He asked me how my family was killed during the genocide against the Tutsi and how Mama had left us. I told him about my family's fate during the genocide, the bitterness that followed, and the grudge I held against Hutus, including the woman I called Mama.

"Did you resent your mother until the day you met her?" he asked.

"No. Things had changed. Although I had many unanswered questions, I had empathy for what she had experienced in the refugee camps."

"What experiences did she go through?"

I told him about Mama's ordeal. I added that after meeting Mama, I could understand how difficult it was for her to leave the Hutu extremists who had held her captive.

Journalists do their research before any interview.

"You had a fiancé who broke up with you brutally after learning that your mother was a Hutu," he said. "Would you like to tell us about that?"

"No. I cannot talk about that," I replied. "I had no fiancé."

"I mean your boyfriend. Weren't you beaten up by your boyfriend after he learned about your mother?"

I took a second before answering. Everything was broadcast live on television, and I did not want to tell a lie.

"Yes, I had a boyfriend... No... I mean, there was a guy I was dating. I'm not sure he loved me the same way I loved him. Otherwise, he wouldn't have done what he did."

"Do you still love him? Have you been able to reconcile?"

"I... Hmm... No. We didn't reconcile. It's over. I'm already dating someone else."

"What if he returns to beg for your forgiveness?"

With a lump in my throat, I said, "Has the theme of the interview changed? I have come here to tell my mother's story, not my love story. Tell me if you are done with the interview."

"It's a TV program about gender and violence against women. That's why I'm interested in how you were assaulted by your lover."

"My experience is different from my mother's. Please focus on Mama's experience. I don't want to talk about mine."

"Okay."

I told the reporter that Mama's experience had made me understand how much the tragedy of our country had affected many women in a world dominated by men.

After a few minutes, he concluded the interview. I left the studio. Crazy I was to talk about Shema on TV, I thought. I did not want to portray him as an aggressor; no, he was not. The second I entered the car of the NGO, my phone rang. I did not recognize the number.

"Hello," I said.

"Karabo, who gave you permission to talk about me on TV?" he asked.

"Hey? Did I mention your name?"

"Does that mean you didn't talk about me?"

"Shema, what do you want from me? Didn't you talk about me the last time you were on TV?"

"Yes, I talked about a girl I loved. But you…you have talked about your assaulter, before adding you're already dating another guy. May I know who that is?"

"It's not your business. If you really loved me, we would still be together. Who ended our relationship? Not you? Did you hide me in a little box where the other guys would not find me?"

He was silent on the phone for a few seconds. I could hear his breathing.

"Karabo, I still need you," he said. "Please, give me a second to tell you one word."

"Hum?"

"I want you. I'm sure, although you pretend, you still love me too."

"No, it's over between us."

"How about your promise? You promised to love me forever, whether I like it or not. But that's not the reason I want you. I have a problem, and you are the only person who can help me. Please, don't say no. Come to my place just for a few minutes tonight. I stay at Kacyiru. Don't worry."

"Okay, after working hours," I said.

He only had to press the button on his remote control to make me lose my sense of everything. With the engagement ring on my finger, my brain convinced me Shema would not try to touch me. Maybe he has a problem. Perhaps he needs my help, I thought.

The hours moved so fast. Five minutes to 5 p.m., the phone rang.

"Hello," I answered the call.

"Sweetheart, are you still at work?" Sugira asked.

"Yes."

"May I come for you?"

"No."

"Why, dear?"

"I still have work to finish…and Mama has sent me somewhere after work."

"I understand. Maybe I could drop you where you want to go."

"No, don't bother. I am taking a taxi."

"Okay."

It came from a sad soul. Sugira might have understood I was hiding something from him.

At Kacyiru, in front of the ministries' buildings, I called Shema. He directed me to his house near the gas station on the road to Kinamba. I was greeted by surprises in his spacious, beautiful, and well-decorated dwelling. I could quickly tell it belonged to a designer. It had brown curtains with creamy and golden shades, wooden furniture, ivory, and coffee-colored rugs, not to mention the different vases and other decorative elements. Shema had metamorphosed into someone else. He gave me a handshake and a kiss on the cheek. I felt the electricity in my body, but I swore to keep my distance. He invited me to take a seat.

"Welcome, I'm glad you have accepted my invitation. What do you want to drink?"

"Water," I replied.

"Water?" he asked. "What kind of water?"

"Just water."

He brought it. Shema mastered the art of disturbing my life. He was wearing khaki polo shorts and a white undershirt. I could not put my legs in order every time my eyes faced his chest. To aggravate the situation, he would giggle whenever he noticed my discomfort. I had to hide my eyes so as not to see his white teeth adorned with a chocolate gum.

"Why are you behaving like a visitor in this house?" he asked.

"Because I am one."

"Karabo, please."

"Shema, who do you think you are? Do you think you can call me at your place, smile at me as if nothing happened between us, and make me forget everything? May I know why you called me?"

"I missed you," he replied.

"Is that the reason you called me here?"

"That's one of the reasons."

"Okay, tell me other reasons. You've told me you have a problem. What is it?"

Shema changed seats, joined me on the couch, and said, "Karabo, I have invited you to my house because I think here we can talk freely. I want… I would like to beg for your forgiveness. Please forgive me for what I did to you. I regret it very much."

"Forgiveness?"

"Yes, I'm serious. Please, forgive me for my madness. The stories you told on the show made me lose the pride of the man I am."

"Are you asking for forgiveness because of those stories?" I asked.

"No. I mean…your mother's story has given me a heartache. One day you tried to tell me about your mother, but my madness couldn't allow me to listen to you."

"And today? Is your madness over?"

"Karabo, please listen to me. I stopped smoking weed. I don't drink anymore. My life has changed. I am trying to become the Shema you encouraged me to be. I owe everything to you."

Shema was getting closer to me. My body was forgiving him before my mind and soul could digest what he was saying.

"Shema, it's okay, I forgave you," I said after sipping water to wet my lips. "But, it's over between you and me."

"I thank you," he said. "Is it true you're dating another guy? You are wearing a ring…"

"Hey? The ring? Yes."

"I understand. But Karabo, keep in mind I love you, and I will love you forever… Please say you still love me as promised."

His eyes stared at mine as if he waited for my answer. Our lips were glued to each other. The electric wires of the love infiltrated my whole body. I sucked the saliva of the only guy who mastered how to waggle me. He ran his hands through my hair. I lost the sense of what was happening. I softened my body and let him do what he wanted with it. We made love as if it was our first time. I called all his names and gave him the cows I did not have. I made noise as if I was a mother of four. After reaching our climax, he pulled the scarf that wrapped the couch and covered my legs. He played French music and let me rest my head on his lap. We remained silent until 10:00. I begged him to let me go.

"Karabo, what should I do for you to forgive me?"

"Nothing," I replied. "Shema, I hate you."

"Are you sure?"

"Yes. Why did you make me do that?"

"Hmm? Didn't you like it? Karabo, I love you. Say you don't love me. It will be a lie."

I hid my face with my hand. It was only a few days after I had accepted Sugira's marriage proposal. I hated the bad cheating girl I was.

"Karabo, you have a fiancé, not a husband. You can always change your mind."

"No, I cannot. He loves me so much."

"And you? Do you love him, too?" he asked.

"Yes, I love him."

"Your eyes don't agree with your lips. Karabo, if you're getting married to someone you don't love, it'll be the worst mistake of your life."

"And how about loving a guy who doesn't love me? Would that be more correct?"

"Karabo, I love you. But now, we aren't talking about

me, but you. I understand you're not ready to give me a second chance, but please don't throw yourself at a guy you don't love."

"Let me do what I judge to be right. Please, forget what happened between us this evening. It was a mistake. It will never happen again. I'm engaged, and very soon, I'll marry the man who loves me."

"By the way, who is that guy you want to marry?"

"You know him. I have nothing to tell you about him."

"Don't tell me it's the other guy you went to school with…"

"Please…I don't want to talk about it."

"Karabo, are you going to marry a Hutu?" Shema asked. "Why?"

Shema's hatred for Hutus was as cold as it had ever been. I regretted having thrown myself in his arms.

"What are you talking about?" I asked. "Do you still keep your hatred against Hutus?"

"That's not what I said. Karabo, the Hutus did the unspeakable to your family; please, don't marry a Hutu."

"Okay. Do you suggest I marry you, a Tutsi who hates me because my mother is a Hutu?"

"It's different. Your mother was also tortured and abused by Hutus, despite the fact they were her relatives. I have asked for your forgiveness. From the bottom of my heart, I'm sorry. Karabo, I love you. I don't care whether your mother is a Tutsi or a Hutu. For me, you are a Tutsi and a survivor of the genocide."

"To love me is one thing, but to accept the person I am is another thing. You must understand my life is related in one way or another to both Tutsis and Hutus. If you choose to share life with me, you will have to prepare yourself to welcome my Hutu relatives and friends to your home.

Before you understand that…I cannot be in a relationship with you."

"But I beg you, don't marry a Hutu you don't love, just because you think he will accept you."

"I have told you I love him. Please, accompany me. I'm going home."

Shema remained silent and went to his room to change. We got out of that house. He opened his jeep door and invited me to get in so he could drop me at my place. We did not speak to each other until we reached Kiyovu at Uncle Kamanzi's house. Shema grabbed my lips for a good-bye kiss. I wanted to refuse, but he held me tight for about five minutes.

"I love you," he said.

I did not answer. I jumped out of the car and ran to my room. I took a hot shower to get rid of Shema's perfume. I cried, insulting myself for having made love to Shema while I was engaged to Sugira. All night I scolded myself, trying to drive Shema out of my dreams.

Sixteen

I woke up to go to work the next morning. My phone in the bag, I had missed eight calls from Sugira. I did not know what to say to him. Around 10:00, he called me again. I told him I had forgotten my phone in the office the night before.

"What plans do you have for tonight? May I pick you up?" he asked.

"Yes," I replied.

My eyes did not want to face his, but I had no choice if I wanted to stay true to my decision to forget Shema and follow my brain's judgment. Sugira was my fiancé, and that was final.

The day was not long. His car parked at the door of my office, he got out to kiss me hello, opened the door of the car and invited me to get in.

"Mom has invited us for dinner," he said. "I hope you have no other plans."

My heart jumped at the idea that his mother's wisdom would read something from my face.

"What if we go there rather next Saturday?" I said.

"No, Karabo, please, don't refuse. Yesterday, I called

you without success before accepting her invitation. I didn't want to tell her I couldn't reach you by phone. I'm sorry I told her you would be available."

"Okay, let's go."

We went to his home. His mother had prepared cassava leaves cooked with meat. There were spicy rice and sweet potatoes, and as if that was not enough, she had added beans mixed with eggplant. Sugira's mother was a perfect woman. I sometimes wondered if Sugira would not expect the same perfection after our wedding. Before we were invited to the dining table, Sugira's paternal aunt, her husband, and her children entered the house. Mr. Kamana welcomed them.

"This is Karabo, our daughter-in-law, Sugira's fiancée," he said.

"It's a great blessing for our family," said Gatarina, Sugira's mother.

"Karabo isn't just a daughter-in-law. She's like a daughter to me."

The aunt hugged me and said, "You may have forgotten to mention something. Her beauty is beyond any pulchritude that can be found on this planet."

At that table, I made many blunders. First, I knocked over Sugira's aunt's glass of water and soaked the whole table. As if that was not enough, when I wanted to add salt to my food, I poured a little too much on the plate. Sugira's mother had to get me another plate. Their eyes made me scratchy. I did not have answers to their many questions.

Everyone chatted about my marriage to Sugira, and what the right choice he had made. Was I really a good choice for Sugira? My heart did not settle with them.

A few minutes after dinner, I said goodnight to the family, and Sugira dropped me off at Uncle Kamanzi's in

Kiyovu. I kissed him good-bye quickly and entered the compound.

In my room, I dialed Mama's number.

"Karabo, is everything okay? Why are you calling at this time of night?"

"I'll come to your house tomorrow," I said. "I would like to talk to you."

"Okay. I'll be at home. I hope everything is okay."

"Yes, I'm fine."

After work the next day, I went to Mama's house. I could not keep Sugira's marriage proposal a secret. It was imperative my marriage to Sugira be concluded as soon as possible so that Shema could forget me forever. At home, my brothers and sisters came to greet me with big smiles on their faces.

"Welcome, Karabo," said Mama. "Glory to Jesus."

"Glory to him for eternity," I replied.

She gave me a cup of milk.

"What's bothering you? Tell me."

"Mama, I'm fine," I replied. "But I have something important to tell you."

I explained to her the meaning of the ring on my finger. She was gladdened.

"The boy who came to celebrate Christmas with us? He is a gentleman. The Virgin Mary has answered my prayers."

"Hey? Did you pray for that?" I asked.

"I prayed to God to give me the chance to be by your side on your wedding day. He answered my prayer. But there is a concern—"

"A concern?"

"Your uncle. We must tell him. He will have to play the role of your father."

"I don't think it's urgent to tell him. We will talk to him later."

"No, he must know. We can't do anything without his benediction. But first, I have to officially express my gratitude to him before talking about the wedding."

"Have you forgotten the way he talked to you last time? Do you think he will receive you with your ceremonies of gratitude? Mama, I don't understand why you don't grasp that things have changed in Rwanda."

"I'll talk to him. Leave that duty to me."

"No, Mama, I'll have to talk to Uncle Kamanzi myself."

I thought Mama had no idea that, after the genocide, things had altered. Social bonds had been torn apart. She was convinced Uncle Kamanzi had a say in my marriage as my father's representative. Yes, Uncle Kamanzi had given me permission to choose my friends, be they Hutu or Tutsi, but I could not envisage him inviting his friends to a wedding in which his in-laws would be a Hutu family, not to mention the Hutu woman who would sit with him as his other wife, as it was culturally interpreted. I gave Mama the money I had brought her, but I did not tell her I was searching for a house where we would move in.

I went back to Uncle Kamanzi's house.

"Hello, Karabo, how are you?"

He made it easy for me by greeting me with a big smile on his face.

"I'm fine, thank you," I replied. "Do you have a minute? I would like to talk to you."

Surprisingly, Uncle Kamanzi was waiting for me too. *What does he want to tell me?* I wondered. We entered the living room, and then he started talking.

"I wanted to talk to you, but our paths don't cross. I

never know what time you leave the house in the morning, or what time you come back in the evening."

"Sorry, I have been coming home late. For example, today, I had gone to Mama's house."

"I wanted to talk to you," he said. "A few days ago, someone called me to tell me you were on TV. Why did you have to say all that on TV?"

"Did I say something wrong?" I asked.

"Was it necessary for everyone to know your mother is a Hutu who was in refugee camps?"

"Yes, it was important to me. I'm sorry to say, you must be one of those who should recognize Mama was also tortured and abused by Hutu militants. They killed her husband and children before taking her captive to those refugee camps. When you internalize that, you will not hurt her heart by blaming her for the death of your brother."

"Karabo!"

"Uncle, that program was about violence against women. I would like to tell you that you add *pili-pili* to Mama's pain."

"How? What did I do to her?" he asked.

"For example, I am coming from her place. Poor Mama, she keeps faith in Rwandan values and considers you a representative of her husband, to whom she owes the same veneration she would stretch to Papa. I had gone to tell her… No. Let's leave it."

"What did you go to tell her?"

It was not the time to talk about my engagement. Uncle Kamanzi would reason it was Mama who had encouraged me to marry a Hutu.

I turned the conversation away and told him I had gone to tell Mama I wanted to move in with her, but that she had insisted she first had to express her gratitude to Uncle Kamanzi before I could leave his house.

"Stop crying," said Uncle. "Okay, she's welcome when she will be ready."

The next morning, I informed Mama that Uncle Kamanzi had agreed she could come for the gratitude ceremony. She told me she would be contacting old friends of Papa's to accompany her. I asked if she planned to ask her brother Gasana to accompany her.

"I already told him about my intentions. He doesn't want to get involved. He told me he has nothing to do with the Tutsis I married."

After two weeks, some of Papa's old friends accompanied Mama to Uncle Kamanzi's house. They brought cans of traditional beer and lots of new beer bins. Mr. Fidel, one of those men in costume, spoke and gave a speech of gratitude on behalf of Mama. Uncle Kamanzi replied he did not expect to be thanked for having raised his own child. Mr. Fidel argued by saying that in Rwandan culture, men gave cows to their wives who, in return, expressed their gratitude at a ceremony known as *gukura ubwatsi*. They exchanged laughter.

Few days after the event, I begged Mama to agree to move in with me to another house, but she refused.

"I have another plan," she said.

"What plan?" I asked.

"The Ministry of Refugees and Returnees asked us to specify the type of support we needed. I chose to be supported for the reconstruction of my house. They told me that since my husband was killed in the Tutsi genocide, the Fund for Assistance to Survivors could join forces with the ministry to help me rebuild the house. I will live in your father's house."

I had never dreamed of living again in Biryogo, in my parents' house.

"Mama, are you sure we could go back to live in our house?"

"Yes. By the way, you must also tell your fiancé to give us enough time to complete it. You will come out of your father's house on the day of your wedding."

"How? How long do you think it will take?"

"I don't know. As long as they will have to wait. If all goes well, construction could begin next month. It will be completed in the 2007 dry season."

Sugira, although he did not like the idea that we should push our wedding plans to the year 2007, said we could not refuse Mama's request. My concern was how I would continue to juggle relationships with my fiancé Sugira on the one hand and my ex-boyfriend Shema on the other. I had to cut off all contact with Shema.

The following months were not easy for me. Finally, I decided to live with Mama in Gahanga. The construction of her house had begun as planned. Mama and Uncle Kamanzi continued to play the hypocrites, but at least they chose their words carefully. I had a big puzzle to solve, Shema's calls. He was doing everything he could to take me to his house. He sometimes came to my office. He invited me for a cup of coffee to discuss his concerns. Whenever he needed to talk to someone, my heart persuaded me I was that person. We swore to respect the limits of our friendship, a kind of "just friends." It did not work, and after a few days, I repented for the same sin, kisses that ended in naughty naps. I reminded him I was engaged. He begged me to cancel my engagement with a Hutu. I refused.

How time flies. By July 2007, Mama had completed

most of the construction, with a roof, doors, and windows. Mama needed only to paint the house and build the annexes.

"Now, you can set the date of your wedding," she said.

"We have already set it," I replied. "Our wedding will take place in December 2007, on Christmas day. It will be two years from the date Sugira asked me to marry him."

"Have you talked to your uncle?"

"No. I will tell him. I will soon go to see him."

Two days after, I went to Uncle Kamanzi's house. I did not know how to introduce the subject.

"I... I wanted to tell you something," I said.

"Please, go ahead," he replied.

"I am soon getting married."

"Wow, congratulations. It's good news. Why do you look sheepish? Who is the lucky man?"

"You know him. He is the son of Mr. Kamana and his wife, Gatarina."

He scratched his forehead, and we endured silence for a few minutes.

"Okay, I get it. Your mother advised you to marry a Hutu."

"Mama has nothing to do with my choice. She didn't even know that family before. I met Sugira at school. Our parents didn't know each other."

"Do you think that changes the fact that he is a Hutu?" Uncle Kamanzi asked.

"No, but perhaps I must remind you I also have Hutu blood in my veins."

"Yes, I know. I've said I've got it. I wish you a good and happy marriage."

I paused for a few minutes before saying: "Mama has told me you will play Papa's role on my wedding day."

"How? Tell your mother to find her Hutu relatives to do

it. There are families with whom I don't exchange cows and brides. Do you understand that?"

He got up and left me alone in the living room. I picked at my nails and warned my eyes not to let tears out. I left his house and went back to Mama's house in Gahanga.

"Don't worry, I'll talk to him," said Mama. "You won't get married without your uncle's approval."

"Why? What does Uncle Kamanzi have to do with my wedding? Why do you continue to attach yourself to Papa's relatives who don't consider you their sister-in-law?"

"Kamanzi is not only your paternal uncle. He took care of you during my absence. He is also entitled to share your joy on the day of your wedding. I can't take that right from him. Do you get it?"

"No, I don't."

I had separated from Shema because he was a Tutsi who loved me and considered me a Tutsi, but who did not appreciate the Hutu blood in me. I was going to be separated from Sugira, a Hutu, who loved me for who I was, because, even though I had Hutu blood in me, I had to keep in mind that my Tutsi family could not exchange brides with Hutus. Apparently, I was still condemned to bear the cross of ethnicity.

The next morning, I called Gatarina, Sugira's mother. I had to talk to her privately about my conversation with Uncle Kamanzi and what Mama had said about it.

"I agree with your mother," said Gatarina.

"You too? Why?" I asked.

"Your uncle Kamanzi loves you so much, and you owe him love and respect. There are many things he doesn't know about our family. I'll talk to him if you don't mind."

I decided to leave the business of convincing Uncle

Kamanzi to the two women, my Hutu mother, and Sugira's Tutsi mother. Neither of them seemed to recognize our country had been invaded by the demons of hatred.

Months passed so quickly. In September 2007, we moved into our house. Living in Biryogo brought back childhood memories. I reproduced our family life before the genocide against the Tutsi. Although Mama had added some modern features to the architecture like an indoor kitchen and bathrooms, she had not changed much the design of the house that the Hutu militants had demolished in 1994. My room was the same. It was opposite the room of Fifi and Dudu, with two small beds as before. My new sisters, Sana and Gwiza, shared a bed, and Mucyo, their brother, another. My room was decorated with my childhood photos, and the other room had pictures of Fifi and Dudu, as well as those of Mama's children. In the middle of those photos, there was a painting of a baby, the little brother killed by my maternal uncle Rwasibo during the genocide. In the living room, there was a picture of Papa and Mama on their wedding day. A copy of the same photo was in her room with some other pictures of Papa.

"Where did you get these pictures?" I asked Mama.

"From Fidel, your papa's old friend. I had instructed him to collect them from all who could have our photos. It's captivating how some people kept our pictures."

I was so glad to live in my childhood home. Our Hutu and Tutsi neighbors came to greet us. Some of them came to ask for forgiveness for what they had done to our family, and others came to gossip about politics.

Mama had a way to prove to them she was still the same Musanabera, able to relate to everyone, big or small, black or white.

In December 2007, my wedding did not take place. Convincing Uncle Kamanzi had been a battle, and Mama had refused to approve the date of the wedding without the blessings of my uncle.

In March 2008, Uncle Kamanzi invited me to his house.

"Karabo, why didn't you tell me Gatarina, Sugira's mother, is from Nyanza?"

"Would that have changed the fact Sugira is Hutu?"

"No, but now I know his parents are good people."

"But his father is a Hutu," I said.

"Yes," said Uncle. "But I was told his wife put him in order. His heart isn't as animalistic as the hearts of other Hutus."

"Uncle, I'm sorry, you don't yet get it. To say his wife put him in order implies all Hutus are naturally wicked people. Is that what you think?"

"No, that's not what I mean. But many of them are evil and ill-mannered, you should recognize it. Anyway, that's not why I called you. I wanted to let you know I have approved your marriage with Gatarina's son. But the wedding shouldn't take place before July. You know why, don't you?"

"I know. We can't organize a wedding during the hundred days of the commemoration."

He was wrong to think some people were evil because of the ethnic group they were associated with. But I judged right to leave the duty to change his bitter heart to Mama and Sugira's mother. I called Mama on the phone to tell her the good news; then, I went to inform Sugira.

"That's good news," Sugira said. "But to be honest, I

don't like the fact that we continue to push our marriage to a later date. Karabo, tell me, when shall we be husband and wife? The first time, your mother wanted to complete the construction of her house, then your uncle didn't want you to marry a Hutu, and now that I am forgiven of the ancestral sin, we should wait until July after the commemoration. I can only hope for July 2008."

"Sugira, don't worry. This is the last time I listen to them. If they come up with other reasons to delay our marriage, we will have to go to the Sector Office for our civil marriage. I hope you won't have any problem with that."

"No. If you could accept, for me, we could even get married tomorrow."

April 2008 knocked on our door, and on April 7, Mama gathered everyone to accompany her to the Genocide Memorial Center to lay wreaths on Papa's grave. The next day, Mama, Uncle Kamanzi, and other members of the *Abatsobe* clan went to Nyanza to pay tribute to the members of my paternal family killed during the genocide against the Tutsi. I did not go with them.

At eleven o'clock, Shema called me. His voice was full of sorrow. He had a headache. Maybe it had something to do with the commemoration period. I dashed to spend the day with him. I had to be by his side to prevent him from talking only to his family's ghosts. I helped him cook and lent him my ears as he spoke about his family and the memories the commemoration period resurrected in his head. Whenever he talked about his mother, I could not hold back my tears. We both wept. I was convinced that if Shema's mother was still alive, our love destiny would have caught the right fate.

That day, although we kissed each other, we refrained from doing the s-action.

"Shema, every time I come here, I swear nothing should happen between us. But I end up flirting on your chest. I will not come back."

"Don't say that," he replied, putting his hands on my lips.

"I sometimes feel like a dirty sinner who shouldn't even pray to God."

"Dirty? Do you get that dirt from me?"

"Shema, please, what we do is called a sin. I'm engaged to another guy. Do you understand?"

"No, we make love, not sins," he replied with a smile, hauling me toward him for another cuddle. He stared at me and said, "You told me you never did it with him. Don't tell me that—"

"No, we never did it. But you must know that Sugira is my fiancé and that we will live together as husband and wife in three months."

"Okay, let me know when you shall have surrendered your body to him. All I know is that before you spread your legs to another guy, you're still mine and for me only."

"But Shema… Please, stop that."

He kissed me again.

"When's your wedding?"

"In July."

"With whom? I haven't yet bought my wedding suit. Who else shall dare to put an alliance on your finger? Tell him to settle for the engagement umt ring. Wedding? It's no. I won't let him take you." He knelt and added, "Please forgive me. Cancel that engagement. I beg you."

"Shema, I told you it's not possible. Please, let's end this conversation."

He was stubborn, but he had to comprehend I was already far away with Sugira.

The sound of the phone interrupted us.

"Hello," I said to the person at the other end.

"Hello, honey," said Sugira. "How are you? I wanted to comfort you. Please, remember I am with you in prayer."

"Hey, Sugira, I'm sorry. I have forgotten to tell you I haven't gone to Nyanza. I am not feeling well."

"What is it, dear?" he asked. "Don't worry. I'm coming to your house in a minute."

"No, not now... I... I don't want to talk to anyone."

"Why? Even me? I am coming."

"Please, don't. I'm not—"

Shema snatched the phone, ended the call, and turned off the device. I begged him to take me home so that Sugira would not find out I was not there. He challenged and told me he would take me home around 6 p.m. I refused, but Shema had his ways to calm me down. He went to the kitchen, brought me an apple, and begged me to take a bite. He told me stories about his fashion creations, grabbed a book, and showed me all the dresses he had designed for me. In the evening, as he had promised, he took me home.

At Biryogo, not far from our house, he parked the car and kissed me good-bye. Someone knocked on the window of the vehicle. Fear crushed my legs, squeezed my stomach, and compelled my brain. Shema got out of the car. I was scared to death to watch their fight.

"Shema, Shema," I shouted.

He pretended not to hear. He approached Sugira and, to my surprise, offered him a handshake. Sugira refused to greet him. He told Sugira words I could not catch. I lowered the window of the car to listen to their conversation.

"Listen to me and listen well," said Shema. "In this

world, I have only loved two women; the first was my mother, and the second is Karabo. Mama is no longer of this world. I only have Karabo. You sell that you're a… I don't know. Listen carefully; the day you shall dare raise your dirty hands to Karabo, you will have to find another planet to live in… I will not spare you."

"Don't worry. I'm not a loser like you who hits women. I am not a drug addict." Sugira turned to me and said, "Karabo, I was worried, but I see you are doing very well. Good night."

He got into his car and started it. I got out of Shema's car, and as I tried to run after Sugira, Shema held my arm. I shoved his hands and shouted at Sugira.

"Sugira, please, listen to me. It's not what you think."

He stopped the car for a second and turned to say: "Maybe it's not what I think, but I don't doubt what I have seen." He pressed the car's throttle again and fled into the dust.

I returned to Shema, and said, "Please, start your car, too. I need to be alone."

"I'm not going anywhere," he replied.

"Shema, if you love me as you say, please leave."

"I love you, but I'm not leaving until you enter your house."

After I entered the house, I begged him to leave. I ran to my room and squeezed my red pillow. Was I becoming like those girls who played boyfriends like joker cards? I mused. I had an engagement ring on my finger, but my heart was ready for Shema's golden ring. Canceling my engagement with Sugira was not an option. It would hurt more than him, but also other people who mattered to me.

A knock on the door interrupted my riddles. I rushed to open and dump it to Shema that he should forget me. It was over between us, and we could not turn back the clock. We had lost forever our chance to be together.

"May I come in?"

It was instead Sugira.

"Yes," I replied.

"Karabo, forgive my behavior. I shouldn't have left without listening to what you had to say to me."

"Hmm… I should be the one to ask you to forgive me."

"Now, tell me, isn't that guy your ex-boyfriend? Don't tell me you see him behind my back. Tell me I was dreaming."

"Yes, it's him, but as I told you, it's not what you think."

"Do you know what I think? Tell me what it is if it's not what I think."

"Sugira, my relationship with Shema is over. You are my fiancé, and soon, my husband."

"How about the one you were kissing a few minutes ago? What kind of relationship do you have with him?"

"None. He kissed me. I did not kiss him."

"What? I don't get it. Please, explain."

"I had a headache, and when I was going to buy pain-killers, I met Shema leaving the pharmacy. He offered to drop me at home. On arrival, he kissed me good-bye. That's what happened."

"That kiss must be the analgesic," Sugira replied with a sarcastic smile on his face. "Anyway, if you think you're lying to me, you're cheating on yourself. Come on, I would like you to go with me somewhere."

"At this hour? I am tired. Can we go tomorrow?"

"No, don't say no if you want us to reconcile. Karabo, maybe I might understand you haven't yet given me your heart, but if you love another behind my back, my heart will break. Let's go."

I accepted his invitation but warned we should not

delay. He took me to his office in town to show me the plan of a house he was designing for us.

"Karabo, we have a plot in Kibagabaga. I intend to build this house. Do you like the plan?"

"It's beautiful," I replied, wondering if that was why he had brought me to his office. He sat on the couch and invited me to join him as he explained the details of the plan to me. After I approached him, he dragged me to sit on his lap. He began to stroke my fingers and hands.

"Karabo, what kind of witchcraft did you apply? Why do I love you so much?"

"Hmm? How?"

"Look at me. Do I look like someone who has just seen his fiancée kissing another guy? I mean, the ex with whom you shared the fruit you never want me to taste. What do you really take me for?"

"Sugira, stop, please. What's going on with you?"

"Why are you breaking my heart? Please, don't tell me you do it with another guy when you don't even allow me to put my hands on your lap."

"I've told you I didn't do anything with Shema. Please, let me get out."

Sugira's eyes went red. The organ in his pants got puffier. His arms firmed. I was scared.

"Kiss me, Karabo, I want you."

He approached my lips for a kiss, and one hand lifted my skirt, while the other looked for my nipple. I pushed his arms hard, but they were too firm. My heart jumped at the sight of his hard-metal organ getting out of his pants. I shouted. He took his hands off my knees and put his cucumber back in his pants.

"Karabo, why do you make me suffer so much?" he asked with a lion's voice.

"Sugira, please, let me go home."

I re-buttoned up my shirt, adjusted my skirt, and ran to the door of his office. I opened the door and ran to the elevator of the building.

Outside, a voice called my name.

"Get in the car," said Sugira. "Don't worry. I'll take you home."

I got in the car. We did not speak to each other until we reached Biryogo.

"Please forgive me," I said.

"Why?" Sugira asked.

"For everything that has happened in your office."

"Should I also forgive you for refusing to do with me what you do with the so-called ex-boyfriend?" he asked. "Go home. We will speak another day. I'm sorry for having tried to force you."

I quickly got out of his car.

At home, Mama was sitting in the living room. I greeted her as I rushed to my room.

"Karabo, what's the matter?" she asked.

"Everything is fine," I replied.

"Come back here."

"Mama, I'm tired. We will talk tomorrow."

I entered the room, took my red pillow, and asked for answers about what was happening to me. That night, I decided. I had to forget Shema. I had to ask Sugira for forgiveness and pray to God for the hormones that would make me accept my fiancé's touch. I convinced myself perhaps after our marriage, I would do it as commanded by the contract signed before God and the State.

After a few days, I managed to talk to Sugira. We became busy with the preparations for our wedding. I disregarded all of Shema's calls. April, May, and June were the best months of my relationship with Sugira. We behaved like a real engaged couple who spent days visiting the various members of our families and distributing invitations to our wedding, scheduled for July 15, 2008.

My happiness could never last. Two weeks before the day of my wedding, Mama entered my room, hands on her head.

"We must stop the preparations for the wedding," she said.

"Why? What happened?"

"Your father-in-law has been arrested."

"Hmm? Why? What did he do?"

"He is accused of crimes of genocide. He has been sentenced by Gacaca courts."

"Oh my God, it's not possible."

It was devastating news for me.

"I don't know. Gatarina says her husband is innocent. They will appeal."

"I have to give Sugira a call."

When I picked up my phone, I noticed I had missed five calls from Sugira. I hastened to his house.

He was sitting in the garden.

"Karabo, Dad didn't kill anybody. He is innocent."

"What is he accused of?" I asked.

"He is accused of the death of my mother's cousin, who lived with us in 1994. When the killings began, she left with her Hutu boyfriend, who had promised to protect her. The Gacaca judges concluded it was Daddy who delivered her to a Hutu killer. Karabo, it's not true. Dad begged her not to leave, but she had a lot of confidence in the guy."

"Sorry, Sugira, your father will be released soon."

"I am not sure. During the Gacaca hearings, they asked Papa to say the name of the person who killed the cousin to mother, if it was not him. All we could remember was that the guy's name was Emmanuel. Nobody knew his last name."

"The most important and urgent thing is to get your father a good lawyer."

"He has already been sentenced by the Gacaca courts to nineteen years of imprisonment. Mom found a lawyer, and we have appealed."

I stayed with Sugira. We could not fathom what was happening to us. We suspended our wedding plans again. I had hope that if Sugira's father was indeed innocent, his mother would not give up fighting for his release.

Mama wanted to break the bad news to Uncle Kamanzi. I refused. I went to talk to him myself.

"Here is the future bride," Uncle said, as he welcomed me in. "How far are you with the wedding preparations?"

"Hello, Uncle, I wanted to talk to you."

"You look troubled. What's the matter?"

"Mr. Kamana has been arrested."

"Why?"

"He is accused of having committed the genocide against the Tutsi. He has been sentenced by the Gacaca courts in Kicukiro."

"I said it," said Uncle, scratching his head. "Karabo, how did you get me involved in all this? Tell me, how will I tell my invitees that there will be no wedding? What will I say to them? That the father of my future son-in-law is a genocide perpetrator?"

"The most important thing to do now is getting Sugira's father out of jail," I said.

"Why release a genocide perpetrator? For you to marry his son?"

"Uncle, Mr. Kamana did not kill anybody."

"Karabo, my daughter, please, how do you know? It is not for nothing that his neighbors condemned him in Gacaca. Many of those Hutus you associate yourself with committed the genocide."

I got up and said good-bye to Uncle.

Yes, I did not know it. But the least burden I could bear in my heart was to convince myself Sugira's father had not committed the genocide against the Tutsi. I could not imagine that I was not only going to marry a Hutu, but also a son of a genocide perpetrator. *Was I wrong about Sugira's parents?* I wondered. I considered them the ideal family. I had to get to the bottom of that case. I had to know if Mr. Kamana was indeed innocent as his son claimed, or if he was a murderer like the Hutu militants who killed my father and my sisters.

My maternal uncle Gasana was a friend of Mr. Kamana's. I was sure that since he was a minister, he would help us follow the case. I took the taxi to Nyarutarama.

It was not news to Uncle Gasana. He already knew that Mr. Kamana was in prison.

"Who told you I worked in the justice system?" Uncle Gasana asked. "I am a minister of water and forests, not a minister of courts and prisons."

"Uncle, but Mr. Kamana is your friend—"

"Your mother has also called me, and Kamana's wife keeps putting pressure on me. Tell everyone I have nothing to do with that case. He isn't the first or the last Hutu to be imprisoned."

"Please, all we want is to follow his case at the level of

the court of appeal. Whatever the verdict, we will accept, but after the appeal."

"Karabo, listen and listen well," said Uncle Gasana in a loud and irritated voice. "Go tell your mother I have warned you both. You shouldn't get involved in that case of Kamana. Be careful, you don't know him enough to defend him."

What he said troubled me. I asked him to tell me everything he knew about the case, but he refused. I left his house with a heavy heart in my chest.

Seventeen

In 2009, Sugira's father was still in prison. One day, I was with Mama in the living room of our house, listening to the radio. We had an announcement that the president had sacked my uncle Gasana from the Minister of Water and Forests position.

"Finally, the president has sacked him," I said.

"Karabo, why are you saying that?" Mama asked.

"Mama, your brother is not a trustworthy person."

"Maybe, but I thought he was an expert in what he was doing as a minister."

On Friday, after a week's work, I passed by Uncle Kamanzi's house in Kiyovu.

"Karabo, do you have news of your uncle Gasana?" Uncle Kamanzi asked.

"Yes," I replied.

"Oh, did you know he's now a fugitive? He left the country."

"How? That, I didn't know. I only knew he has been fired."

"Yeah, he joined the opposition groups. He is now against the government he served for many years."

"And that," I said. "Maybe he is going to reveal his true colors."

"His true colors? Karabo, what do you know about Gasana?" asked Uncle Kamanzi.

"Nothing in particular. Uncle Gasana has two tongues. He never joined us whenever we paid tribute to the victims of the genocide against the Tutsi. Instead, he chose to appear on television, making hypocritical speeches about the genocide, as if he cared."

"What else do you know about him? Has he also committed genocide?" Uncle asked as if he conducted investigations.

"No, I don't think so. He was in Russia in 1994."

$\longrightarrow$

A few days later, I was watching television, only to be informed of shocking news: Grenade attacks in Kigali, the Remera neighborhood. No deaths but a few injuries. Rumors incriminated opposition groups of some Rwandans who had fled the country since 1994. I did not believe my ears. Could my two maternal uncles be part of those groups who wanted to re-destabilize our country? Are we going to experience another 1994? I wondered. Mama was sitting in a small armchair around the corner, an African cloth covering her arms. I told her I needed to go to Uncle Kamanzi's place. He was the only person who could explain to me what was going on in my country. I feared another war.

Upon arrival, I asked Uncle Kamanzi to explain what I had just heard from the television. He told me the police were still investigating the grenade attack. I asked him if the opposition groups, of which my maternal uncles Rwasibo and Gasana were part, were responsible for those attacks.

"Yes, maybe, but we don't know."

"Uncle, who else would destabilize our country, if not the Hutu militants outside the country?"

"Karabo, there are things you can't comprehend. We must wait for the outcome of the investigations." He scratched his forehead before adding, "And besides, this time around, it's not only your maternal uncles who could be involved but... But also, your paternal uncle."

"My paternal uncle? What do you mean? Are you also—?" My heart jumped out of my chest.

"No, not me. I am talking about Rutayisire, my brother."

"Who? What does he have to do with the Hutu militants?"

"They are no longer called Hutu militants. They are Rwandans of different ethnic groups. They claim to fight for the liberation of the country."

"So, you mean Uncle Rutayisire joined some groups of Hutus?"

"Yes, and he isn't the only one. There are a few other Tutsis who claim to oppose the current regime. Rutayisire left Kenya. He now lives in the US. Maybe one day, you will hear him talking on one of the international radios, or you will find what he writes on the Internet."

I could not believe that fifteen years after the genocide against the Tutsi, the saviors could join the perpetrators to form some political groups. My heart and brain were troubled. Why did my family members always have to get involved in that political mess? As if it was not enough to have a Hutu maternal family with members who participated in the genocide against the Tutsi, I was also going to be a relative to a Tutsi uncle who opposed the predominantly Tutsi regime in power.

"Uncle, may I say something?" I asked.

"Yes."

"Papa, before his death, told me that nobility and greatness have nothing to do with a person's ethnicity. Don't you think he was right?"

"Why are you asking me?"

"Uncle, if it's true Uncle Rutayisire is among those responsible for the grenade attacks, isn't he a Tutsi? Shall we say all Tutsis are bad?"

"Of course not. I've told you no one knows who is responsible for those grenade attacks." He scratched his head, crossed his legs, went silent for a few seconds, and added, "Please don't tell anyone that Rutayisire is your uncle. Never speak about him. Do you understand?"

"Yes."

I was not sure Uncle Kamanzi had got what I insinuated. I did not know anything about political games or struggles and could not confirm the identities of those who had thrown grenades. All I wanted to say is that people from different ethnic groups could join forces to do the right thing, in the same way, they could do the wrong thing. It was all a question of choice and not of ethnicity.

Grenade attacks persisted. On September 9, 2009, the radio announced a new attack in the commercial center of Kigali City. The reporter said a person with the name of Shema was dead. My back broke into pieces. With trembling hands, I took the phone to call Shema. His phone was off. I called again after a few seconds. It was still off. I called Muhire. He had not seen Shema for a long time. And as my throat blocked me from screaming, the radio repeated the news, and the reporter said, "Shema, the famous fashion designer, has been seriously injured by the grenade attack. He is not dead, as previously announced. He has been taken to the intensive care unit of Kigali General Hospital."

I rushed to the hospital. Shema had already been taken to the surgery room.

"Are you his sister?" asked the nurse.

"Yes, I'm his friend... No, his cousin... Please, how is he?"

"How about other members of the family?"

"He doesn't have any. All of them were killed. Please, let me see him."

"Oh, is he a survivor of the genocide? Don't tell me he survived the genocide only to be killed by these grenade attacks fifteen years later? So sad."

"Is he going to die?" I asked, goosebumps all over my body, legs trembling, my stomach making gurgling noises.

"I don't know. We must pray to God. He is in a very critical state."

My brain was too small to conceive Shema could die. I had not squawked about everything that had happened to me during the genocide against the Tutsi, but I could never forgive the killers of Shema, my uncles, or anybody else. I wanted to run to the top of a mountain, shout to all Rwandans, wake them up, and tell them they had lost the taste of life. With a heart filled with grief and a head hardened by anger, I waited by the corridor to the surgery room.

After three hours, the nurse came back and said, "Glory to God. The operation has been successful."

"How is he?" I asked. "May I go see him?"

"No. You can't enter. You can only see him through the glass. This way."

I picked up my phone and called Mama.

"Karabo, how are you?" she asked. "Where are you? Sugira and I are worried."

"Mama, listen. Don't tell anybody else. Take a taxi to Kigali General Hospital."

"How? Karabo, tell me, what has happened to you?"

"Nothing. Please come to the hospital."

My eyes could not leave Shema. His head was covered with white bandages. I could not get through that glass to kiss him or lay my hands on his cheeks. The tears refused to sink. If I had pushed them hard, blood would come out of the veins of my eyes.

After a few minutes, Mama was there. At the sight of my face, she understood the magnitude of what I was going through. My hair had stood up like that of the rock stars of the eighties. My face was like that of my grandmother before her death.

"Karabo, what is it?" she asked.

"Mama, look," I said, pointing to Shema.

"Who is he?"

"Hutu militants killed his mother. You are the only mother he has."

"Me?"

"Yes. From today, you are his mother. Don't ask me questions. They told me he could die… Noooo, please, I beg you. Let him smell the perfume of a mother. I'm sure it will save his life."

"Karabo, who is he?"

"He is the brother I never had. He stayed by my side when I was alone and lonely. Please, take care of him as you would for your own son. I will stay here with you, except when I will have to go to work."

"What should I say if nurses ask me questions?"

"Tell them you're his aunt."

Mama did not seem convinced, but my worried eyes and gray skin told her a lot about who Shema was for me. My cheeks had developed pimples I had never had before. I spent the whole day with Mama, our eyes on Shema. In the evening, I asked her to go home to come back in the morning when I should leave the hospital to go to work.

At the office in the morning, my phone rang.

"Hello, Karabo, where were you?" Sugira asked.

"I'm sorry I've missed your calls."

"What happened?"

"Eeeh… Nothing."

"Don't lie to me. You're making me jealous."

"Jealous? Please, stop."

"I'm kidding."

He asked if we could meet in the evening, and I said no.

"Karabo, I hope it's not because you have doubts about my father's innocence. I've told you he isn't a genocide perpetrator."

"Let's wait for the court's decision on the appeal," I replied.

"Please, don't make the mistake of thinking my father is responsible for the death of my aunt, because he is not."

"Okay, Sugira, I have to work. I'll talk to you later."

Although I was not happy his father was in jail, I thought maybe I could use it as a pretext to minimize my meetings with Sugira and concentrate on Shema.

Shema spent several days in a coma. Mama spent days in the hospital, and I did the nights. Doctors and nurses told us we did not need to be there, but we could not leave Shema alone. I had told Mama the truth but not the whole truth. She knew Shema was my ex-boyfriend who had broken up with me after he had learned Mama was a Hutu who lived in refugee camps, but I did not tell her about his drug addiction, nor that he had gravely assaulted me. I only insisted that Shema was depressed because of what he experienced during the nineties when his entire family was exterminated.

"Don't worry," said Mama. "I understand he needs me. I will give him a taste of a mother's love."

"Will you be by his side, Mama?" I could not believe my ears. Mama was so nice.

"Yes, we must restore the hope of people like Shema. When God shall open his eyes, I will be close to his sickbed in the same way his mother would do if Hutu militants had not killed her. I will give him milk, hold him in my arms, and allow him to rest his head on my chest."

"How nice," I said. "Pray that God gives him the strength to get out of that coma."

"The Virgin Mary won't disappoint me. She always listens to me when I call." Mama held her chaplet in her hands, reciting the Rosary in her heart.

"Thanks for praying for him," I said.

I did not know how to thank that angel I called Mama. Although I did not believe in the Virgin Mary, I was sure there was no prayer more powerful than the love and support of a mother.

Shema spent three weeks in a coma. The day he woke up, I received a phone call from Mama.

"Karabo, why do you keep your phone away from you? I have tried to reach you many times without success."

"Sorry, I was in a meeting."

"Shema has opened his eyes," said Mama.

"How? Oh my God, thank you, Lord. How is he? What did he say?" I couldn't find the questions to ask. There were flames of joy in my heart.

"I was by his side. He couldn't recognize where he was. When he asked who I was, I said I'm his aunt."

"So...?"

"He hasn't said anything else. He looked worn out and went back to sleep."

"Oh, Mama, tell me everything. What questions did he ask? Is he still sleeping?"

"Calm down. I'm going back inside, but I have to ask you for a favor. Don't come tonight. He is not yet ready to know the truth."

"Okay, I am going to die of nostalgia. But you're right, it's not yet time for him to know who you are."

My heart was full of love and respect for Mama. I had never met such a merciful woman in my life. She lived the same values she had taught us when we were children during evening prayer times before bedtime.

The next day I went to the hospital, but Mama did not allow me to talk to Shema. She joined me in another room to tell me what had happened when Shema had woken up again. Mama had maintained her lie that she was an aunt whom Shema had never met before. He was cheered to learn that there was a relative of his mother, who was still alive. But Mama's face seemed familiar to him. Shema had told Mama she looked like the girl he loved. Mama was afraid Shema would notice she was not who she claimed to be until Shema added that Karabo's mother on the photo had a brighter, younger complexion. Maybe he had his doubts but chose to persuade himself that his aunt looked like Mama.

Shema spent another week in the hospital. The day he was released, I went to his house to wait for him and Mama. As soon as Shema caught sight of me, the bomb exploded.

I confirmed his doubts were correct and that the woman he called his aunt was actually my mother. He looked left and right to hide his eyes. I was afraid he would strangle me alive.

"Both of you, get out of my house before I call the police," he said.

"Shema, please, forgive me, listen."

"Karabo, do you think my forgiveness comes from a never-dry river? How dare you lie to me again? Your mother told me she was my aunt. Me? Shema? In this world? How dare she tell me that big lie? Both of you are heartless women."

Before I could respond to Shema, Mama put her backpack on and said, "Karabo, I'm leaving." She turned to Shema. "Thank you for having given me the blessing of sharing your pain. I am neither your mother nor your aunt, but a mother. Karabo had told me all she understood of your sorrow, but it wasn't for her I agreed to be with you. Your two mothers had charged me to take care of you, the mother who breastfed you, and the Virgin Mary, the mother who cares for you from heaven. They were there with me at the hospital. You couldn't see them, but they were by my side." She approached Shema, drew a cross sign with her hands on his forehead, and said, "God bless you. I wish you a quick recovery."

She left before Shema could digest everything and respond. He looked touched, but he chose to maintain his anger.

"Karabo, get out of my house. I want to be alone."

"I'm not going anywhere," I replied. "I apologize for having begged Mama to tell you a lie. We did it for your sake."

"For my sake?"

"Yes. If she had revealed to you she was my mother, you wouldn't have allowed her to stay in the hospital."

Shema jumped on the bed, turned his head, and pretended to close his eyes. I went to the kitchen to prepare a bowl of hot soup. I turned on my computer and put on his favorite French songs.

"Oh, Karabo, are you still here?" Shema asked when he woke up at six p.m. "I can never comprehend you. How did you decide to ask your mother to take care of me at the hospital?"

"I'm sorry," I replied.

"I can't forgive you," he said, "but your mother, at least, made me feel as if my mother had risen from the dead. I didn't suspect she was your mother. Please, don't tell me any more lies. Do you promise?"

"Yes, I promise you."

Mama and I had achieved our goal.

"Another thing… Never say your mother is a Hutu. I have never seen a Hutu so beautiful and so kind."

"Hmm? What do Hutu women look like?" I asked.

He gave me a smile and left my question unanswered. I warmed the soup and spoon-fed him like my baby before kissing him good-bye.

My meetings with Sugira had become less frequent. I could not comfort him. Every time we met, he told me his father was innocent. I said nothing about it, lest he could read doubts from my face. Despite the efforts made by Sugira and his mother to get Mr. Kamana out of prison, he was still behind bars. Appeal cases in Rwanda were generally settled in a few days, but because of the synchronization of the traditional justice system with the Gacaca courts, they took longer than before.

Every night after work, I went to Shema's house. Except for some wounds that resisted, he was recovering quickly.

On Friday, after sharing our tea, Shema asked, "How's our mother?"

"Our mother?" I asked. "Oh, she's fine."

"Why doesn't she come to visit her son? You must tell her that her daughter doesn't take good care of me."

"Is that what you say? Okay."

"Stop ballooning your lips. I also need a mother's care."

"Shema, in our culture, it is the children who visit the parents. She will be gratified to welcome you, give you milk, and tell you stories."

"Yes, I will soon go to see my new mother."

"You will be welcome."

He stopped drawing his fashion creations and asked me, "Hey, tell me. What happened to your wedding?"

"Hmm? Something happened." A lump in my throat, "Sugira's father is in prison."

"In prison?"

"Yes. He... He is accused of having committed the genocide."

"Wipe your tears," he said. He invited me to lay my head on his chest and stroked my hair. "I'm sorry to say, but I knew Sugira was hiding something."

My head on Shema's chest, I allowed him to wipe away my tears. His caresses in my hair, on my neck, and up to the chest. As an avid man seeking what to bite, he pulled me by the cheeks, looked for my lips, and sucked them with passion. His hands went to my nipples, to my navel, and before I received him between the legs, he tricked me and went back to cuddling nipples again. After a few minutes, his head was between my legs for a sweet-salty sucking. As an adult African woman, I pushed him to do it the traditional way. As an African man with everything under his control, he drove his organ deep inside and hit it hard to all my corners. Shema mastered the rules of the game. We made love all night long.

The next morning, he prepared fruit and yogurt for breakfast. I hid my eyes, recalling that I was still engaged to Sugira.

"What's bothering you? Forget that loser you call Sugira," asked Shema as if he had read my thoughts. "I can't dictate what you do. But, please, take the time to think about it. I have met your mother, and now I know she is not a Hutu, as you had told me. She will be happy to marry her daughter to her adopted son. Give me a second chance, please."

"Shema, I'm glad you realized Mama is a noble person. But that doesn't make her a Tutsi. Nobility is also found among Hutus."

"The Hutu guy you call your fiancé, is he also a noble person? Why didn't he tell you his father committed the genocide?"

"I'm engaged to Sugira, not to his father," I replied.

"Like father, like son."

Yes, maybe I was beginning to doubt the innocence of Kamana, but not the nobleness his son had proved to me since we were in high school. Shema had no authority over the fate of my engagement with Sugira.

"Shema, you're wrong. First, Sugira's father might be innocent. Second, Sugira is not a bad person as you think. You must recognize that not all Hutus are wicked people."

"I love you so much. But I also pity you. You don't want

to realize you are going to commit the worst mistake of your life. You're not in love with Sugira..."

"How do you know I'm not in love with him?" I asked.

"If you were, you wouldn't be lying in my bed. Anyway, it's not my only concern. You're going to marry a Hutu after all they did to our families. Have you thought about what they are doing now? Who is throwing those grenade attacks that were about to take my life?"

"Let's not talk about the grenade attacks because we don't know who might be responsible. But for your information, I heard that it might have been a group of Hutus and Tutsis."

"That's not true. Anyway, if one or two Tutsis joined those Hutus, they are as wrong as you are."

I got up from bed and put on clothes. I gave up that delicious breakfast and ran for a cab. Shema shouted my name, but I refused to go back. I had to go to my room and think. He was not right about Hutus and Tutsis, but about the fact that I was not in love with Sugira. Shema's heart was still full of hatred against Hutus. It was as if it was painted on the walls of his brain that Hutus were evil. I had thought Mama could change his mind, but instead of changing his attitude towards Hutus, Shema had decided to change the ethnic identity of my mother from Hutu to Tutsi. For Shema, I was no longer of mixed ethnicity, but 100 percent Tutsi. That's not what I wanted. He had to accept me for what I was, not what he wanted me to be.

At home, Mama was sitting by the door.

"Did Sugira get to talk to you on the phone?" she asked before greeting me good morning.

"No, oh my God, where is my phone?"

It was at the bottom of my bag.

"Please, call him. Kamana has been released from prison."

"Has he been released?" I asked, before producing the tss sound.

"Yes, he is innocent. Aren't you glad he's free? What is the meaning of that tss?"

The release of Sugira's father troubled me more. There would be no more excuses to delay our marriage. A knock on the door interrupted my riddles. Sugira carried me in his arms full of strength and swayed me from side to side, singing, "God is always good."

"Mom, our wedding will be tomorrow," said Sugira.

"Tomorrow?" I asked before Mama could react.

"Yes, darling, do you have a problem with that?" Sugira asked. "Dad is innocent. Don't worry. You're not going to marry a son of a genocide perpetrator." He smiled the big one.

"You're kidding, it won't be possible tomorrow."

"Why not? Will tomorrow be a holiday for the priests?"

He stopped the jokes and told us that his parents had suggested organizing the traditional wedding on November 17, 2009. Mama replied that we would consult with Uncle Kamanzi before confirming the date to the Kamana family. In the evening, Mama sent me to break the news to Uncle Kamanzi. It was done. Even Uncle Kamanzi blessed my marriage with Sugira without hindsight.

The following days, Sugira and I were busy shopping for the wedding. He could not leave my side for a second. Every time his hands touched me, I asked him to wait for our wedding day.

One morning, I got up from the bed, grabbed the rosary

Mama had put in my room to protect me, and pleaded with the Virgin Mary: "Has Angel Gabriel changed his ways? Why did he just convince Sugira I was his fiancée? Why didn't he talk to me? He had allowed my heart to fall for Shema. How can I marry Sugira when my heart is with Shema? Please, answer me, Virgin Mary. I am confused." She didn't answer. At least she had kept her virginity. I had given mine to Shema before we were blessed by the heavens. I stopped that absurdity, tried on my wedding dress, and examined myself in the mirror. Maybe I should have chosen a gray dress, not white. There was nothing white about my marriage to Sugira. I removed the dress and went to get my maids of honor for the rehearsal of our steps. All gawked at me as if I were the luckiest. I was going to marry an intellectual guy from a rich family.

Eighteen

Two days before my wedding day, I received a call from Shema. I hesitated to pick it up, but I could not ignore him.

"I wanted to wish you a nice wedding," he said.

"Eh? Who told you?"

"News flies, my darling. But that's not the only reason I wanted to talk to you. I would like to say good-bye. Tomorrow I will go to France."

"What? Why?"

"I have been invited by a Paris-based fashion house called LaBelle. I will spend eight months there."

"Why didn't you tell me? Shema, where are you? May I come to see you?"

"No. Please, don't come. I wish you a good and happy marriage to Sugira. Good-bye."

It was over. Shema had said good-bye. I cried for our love. I had to bury it. My heart collapsed. My head scrambled. I needed painkillers. I decided to go to the local pharmacy to look for analgesics. I took a packet of paracetamol from the shelves not far from the counter and headed to the cashier. Behind the counter, there were some other shelves. A small package on which it was written 'Pregnancy test' caught my attention. A wind of thoughts crossed my brain. *When last did I have sex with Shema?* I mused. What if I was in my ovulation? No. I knew how to calculate my days, and every time I made a mistake, I always took my pills the next day. A voice in my heart whispered: *As a precaution, it would be better to buy the test. Who knows?*

In my room, I stared at the test. Maybe it could be a blessing to have Shema's baby, but it would hurt Sugira's heart. Many people would be disappointed, my family and Sugira's family. As usual, my brain began to make me more confused. You wouldn't be the first or the last to marry a man while carrying a baby of another.

In the morning, I was not only troubled by the headache, but also by stomach pains. My whole body ached. Some friends advised me to drink a lot of milk. It did not help at all. I went to see a doctor. The friends wanted to accompany me, but I refused.

At the small clinic on the Paul VI road, I told the doctor I suspected malaria. He sent me to the laboratory for a blood sample. When the lab assistant was getting ready to take a thick drop, an idea came to mind.

"Would you check for me…if I'm pregnant?"

"Not with a thick drop," he replied. "I will need a urine sample."

When I wanted to shyly say, "Leave it," he handed me the little goblet.

"The restrooms are on your left."

After putting the liquid in the small container, I went back to the laboratory and handed the goblet to the man. He asked me to wait for the results for a few minutes. I had been suffering from headaches and stomachache, but after giving that urine sample to the laboratory assistant, I shivered. Maybe malaria was taking over in my veins and bones. It did not take long before the lab assistant called my name.

"I only have good news," he said. "You don't have malaria. Secondly, congratulations, you are pregnant."

"Pregnant?"

"Is it your first pregnancy?"

"Yes. Thank you."

The stony clouds of the sky fell on me. I ran to the gates of the clinic to stop the first bike.

"Ride as fast as you can. If you can't overtake cars, let them hit us. We are going to Kacyiru."

In just ten minutes, I was at Shema's house. The door was locked. I knocked, but no one responded. I dialed his number. The phone was off.

"Kanombe airport," I said to the biker, "Please, very quickly."

At the airport, I looked left and right, but I could not see Shema. I pushed to enter the building.

"Show us your ticket and passport," said the policeman.

"I'm not traveling. I have to talk to someone. He is traveling with Air Belgolaise."

"Air Belgolaise? The person you are looking for may not be here yet. That flight is at eight o'clock."

I redialed Shema's number, but he was still unreachable. I went back to Kacyiru, and he was not there. So many calls from Sugira and Mama—I did not want to talk to them. I went back to the airport, sat down near the doors, my eyes peering at every person who passed by. At 6 p.m., a group of people appeared. A hand touched my shoulder.

"Karabo, hello, how are you?"

"I'm fine, and you? It's been a long time."

"Congratulations. Isn't tomorrow your wedding? What are you doing here? Don't you have the party to bid farewell to single life?"

"Yes, I'm going home in a moment."

"Lucky you. You aren't like us who haven't yet found our Prince Charming. My dear, I have to go. I wish you a nice wedding."

"Thank you."

After talking to my former roommate Karigirwa, I saw Shema among the people in the departure hall of the airport. I ran to catch him. The policeman stopped me.

"I don't have a plane ticket," I said. "Please, would you call that guy in a black leather jacket? The one who is checking in his luggage."

Instead of going to talk to Shema, the policeman took his time to check the papers of all the travelers before I approached him again.

"Are you going to talk to him?"

"I've sent my colleague to talk to him. He is coming."

Shema did not appear. The headache became more serious. After more than an hour, the policeman gestured to me.

"We're really sorry," he said. "My colleague lost sight of him. He couldn't talk to him. What flight is he taking?"

"He's going with Air Belgolaise," I replied.

"Oh, they have already boarded. Sorry, madam, you cannot talk to him."

I asked them to stop the plane, but they refused. It was very late. My brain could not tell me what I should do. My wedding was in less than fifteen hours. I wanted to sleep at the airport, but that would not bring back Shema. There was no bike. I entered one of the taxis at the airport.

"Biryogo, please," I told the driver.

"Biryogo? You will pay me ten thousand Rwandan francs."

"Start the car. I will pay you as much as you want."

Mama was sitting in the living room, her arms covered with her African loincloth. She had a cup of tea in her hands.

"Karabo, where have you been since morning?" she asked. "Sugira left a few minutes ago. Your friends waited for hours before they gave up. What's going on with your wedding?"

"I am sorry. I had gone to the clinic."

"From morning to this hour of the night? And those red eyes? Karabo, what is it? What's happening?"

"I have to go to bed. We will talk in the morning."

Mama insisted that we talk, but I hurried to my room. She followed me and continued to beg me to tell her why I was getting gray. The words could not come out of my mouth. I forced myself to hold back my tears.

"Karabo, tell me, do you really want this wedding to take place?"

"Yes, Mama. There is no problem."

"I'm not sure anymore," she said. "Anyway, you have to sleep. Kamana's family will be here before 9:00 tomorrow. They assured they won't be late, because you will have to be at the sector office for the civil wedding before 1 p.m."

"Good night, Mama."

"Good sleep."

After she left my room, I sat down on the bed to solve the equation. It was time to think and make an important decision in my life. Perhaps the traditional marriage was not legally recognized, but the civil marriage planned for the same day could only be changed by a legal divorce. Shema was gone, and the probability of returning to Africa for those leaving for Europe could be counted on fingers. The time had come for me to learn that I did not need anyone to put a smile on my life. I took two pieces of paper and a pen, wrote two letters, and closed my eyes, pretending to sleep.

Around 5:30 in the morning, I was ready. I put on my dark blue jeans and a black T-shirt, covered myself with a leather jacket, wore black sneakers, and took my suitcases out of the room. I tiptoed, afraid to wake Mama up. After putting her letter on the dining table, I opened the door and left the house.

"In the city center, near the post office building," I said to the taxi driver.

I stopped at Sugira's office and slipped his letter under the door. I sent him a text: "Go to your office before coming to my house for the traditional wedding. I have slipped a note under the door of your office. I hope you will find in your heart the strength to forgive me. I keep a lot of love and respect for you."

I turned off the phone and told the taxi driver to take me to the bus station. In Nyabugogo, I entered a bus to Butare.

In the city of Astrida, I paid for a room in the hostel called Tekana Holiday Quarters. The clock on the wall read 9:30 a.m. My heart waltzed in my chest. How had Mama reacted after reading the letter? Maybe she had cried. Maybe she did not shed tears. I could not forgive myself for having subjected her to the insults of Uncle Kamanzi. I turned on my computer and wrote a long email to Shema. I thanked him for having spiced up my life with love and romance and blessed me with little Shema, the baby growing in my belly. I clicked on *send* before turning off the computer.

I did not call Mama, Sugira, or anyone from Kigali who wondered where I was. I had to give them enough time to forget me. I had to dry the tears that had been flowing on my cheeks for more than fifteen years. I had to solve the puzzle of my life. I had to reconnect all the points. A small notebook would not be enough. I turned on the computer and began writing the novel of my life. I narrated the story of my family and how my childhood was covered with love and all good things. I recalled the conversation I had with Papa before Hutu militants killed him. I could visualize the blood of my father and my sisters on April 7, 1994. I narrated every detail of my life during all the years I could not lay my head on Mama's chest, full of milk and love. I wrote about the ordeal Mama had gone through. I wrote about Devota. I wrote about Shema. I wrote about Sugira and his family. I deduced the confusion caused by the behavior of my Tutsi paternal uncle Kamanzi and my Hutu maternal uncle Gasana, both with hearts darkened by hatred against those who did not wear their ethnic hats. I described my worries, my doubts, my passions, and my heartbreaks. Why did I always have to stand at the crossroads of Rwanda's tragedy? Why did I have to carry the ethnic burden? Why? I wrote in paragraphs, pages, and chapters.

After five days, I said good-bye to the city of Astrida and returned to Kigali. The trip lasted two hours. My stomach crumbled the second my eyes faced Nyabugogo. The hills and buildings of Kigali looked at me as if they wanted to strangle me alive. I was afraid to look at Mama's face. Uncle Kamanzi would asphyxiate me for having asked him to honor the marriage, which I had to dodge at the last minute. Everything had happened because of them. I was lost and abandoned by a mother who had allowed her Hutu relatives to make her captive and then by my uncle Kamanzi whose resentment towards Hutus made him too blind to notice my sorrow. *If they dare to talk to me, I'll spill it all in front of their noses*, I thought.

At the doors of our house at Biryogo, I stopped. I could not knock, but I had to enter before Biryogo's neighbors could gossip about my return. My sister Sana came out to open the door. She ran back inside the house to tell Mama I was there. Mama did not come out. She waited for me inside.

"Mama…" The words could not come out of my heart filled with grief.

Mama invited me to lay my head on her chest. We both wept.

"My daughter, tell me everything. I am your mother. What happened to you?"

"Mama, why did you leave me alone in this world? Why did you let me be bitten by the sharp teeth of this world?"

"My daughter, wipe your tears," she said, hugging me tightly to her chest.

"Mama, I love you. It all happened because I love you. My head tried to convince my heart to hate you, but I couldn't erase all my childhood memories. I wanted to forget you, but every night, I dreamed of laying my head on your chest. I missed both your smile and perfume. Please forgive me."

"Karabo, we talked about it. I regret the day I left you, your sisters, and your father." She remained silent for a second before adding, "Tell me. Why did you have to leave on your wedding day? What did Sugira do to you? I'm listening. Talk to me like a daughter to mother."

"Sugira did nothing wrong," I replied. "I cheated on his love."

"Okay, I understand. Calm down. Go and drink a cup of milk. We will talk about it later."

"Hmm? Milk?"

"Yes, I am a mother, and your neck tells me more than

you could say. You will tell me who is responsible for your pregnancy."

"It's... Mama... you know..."

"Please, let's talk about it later. Take the time to breathe. Let me bring you some milk."

She went to the kitchen.

After drinking milk, I don't know if it was because I hadn't eaten anything since morning, nausea came back, and I hurried to the restroom to vomit. Nothing came out of my throat. I went back to the living room.

"Yes, Mama, I'm pregnant. I did the pregnancy test the day before I was to wed Sugira."

"It's from who?"

"Shema."

"You saddened Sugira's heart. He told his parents not to come for the traditional wedding because you had left with a guy named Shema. Gatarina called me to warn me Shema was a drug addict. I didn't tell her I had met the Shema she was talking about. I was worried about you. I prayed every day for you to come back to me. I was insulted. I was called names. All because of you..."

"Oh, Mama, forgive me. Who insulted you? Why?"

"Don't worry. I was chastised for my sin. It's a cross I have to carry. These are some of the consequences of the eleven years you were alone without your mother to guide you and show you the right path. Although I don't approve of what you did, you must keep in mind you are my daughter. I will always share your joy, your pain, and your shame, if necessary."

"Mama, I love Shema. But I can't live with him. I will never get married."

"If you love Shema, why did you accept Sugira's proposal?"

"I did everything for you, Mama. I had to choose between you and Shema. It was a challenging puzzle for me. But now everything is settled. I have Shema in my belly and Mama by my side. You will take care of this child the same way you took care of Shema in the hospital."

"Where is Shema?" Mama asked.

"He left. He went to Europe. He won't come back. Our love is impossible."

I told Mama more about the extent of Shema's hatred against Hutus and how he had assaulted me the day he had learned that I had lied to him about my Hutu mother. I added that I was still afraid that, even though Shema loved me, he regretted the fact I had Hutu blood in me and tried to persuade himself I was not of mixed ethnicity, but rather a Tutsi 100 percent.

"Don't worry. Time shall teach him nobility has nothing to do with ethnicity. Karabo, we must make an appointment with a gynecologist. You will also go to apologize to your uncle Kamanzi."

"Yes, I must see a gynecologist. About Uncle Kamanzi, I wanted to meet him with Kamana's family, you, and some of my friends. I wanted to talk to you all at the same time."

"How?"

"We can invite them all for next Saturday. Those who won't come will lose the right to ask me questions later."

"What are you talking about?" Mama asked, with a reproving voice. "Stop it. Do you think you can summon your uncle to listen to what you have to say to him?"

I argued that if Uncle Kamanzi couldn't come to my mother's place, he had no right to question what I did. Mama maintained her disagreement and demanded that I go talk to Uncle Kamanzi.

All afternoon, Mama gave me some health tips for pregnancy. She told me about eating habits that I had to develop and that I needed to rest as much as possible. She would stop, tingle the tss, and say, "This isn't how I had dreamed. I was looking forward to your wedding, and when you would get pregnant, you would call me to accompany you to the hospital, but your husband would also be there to massage your legs."

"I'm sorry, Mama."

"My darling, the important thing now is that I am about to become a grandmother. I thank the Lord. It is a great blessing to see Kalisa's first grandson. Your father must be in seventh heaven."

"Is he?" I asked. "Maybe he is mad at me for the fact that I'm pregnant out of wedlock."

"Yes, it hurts every parent's heart, especially in our culture; a girl must keep her virginity until marriage. But now that he is in heaven, I am sure he looks at us with eyes full of forgiveness and mercy."

After sharing dinner with Mama, I walked to the bedroom. Before closing my eyes, I turned on my laptop to check my emails. Shema had not replied. *Perhaps he did not arrive safely in France*, I wondered. *Or he just ignored my email.*

The next morning, Mama accompanied me to the gynecologist.

The doctor performed an ultrasound, and said, "You're six weeks. Can you see the baby's heartbeat? It will be more visible after eight weeks."

I noticed a ticking not so evident on the screen, then asked, "Is it a boy or a girl?"

Mama and the doctor both laughed.

"It's too early to tell," replied the doctor.

He gave me tips on how to behave and the kind of food to eat. Mama gave me the look of Didn't I tell you? The doctor gave me a paper to take to the laboratory for further routine tests. After taking blood and urine samples, they told me to come back for results in three days.

At the gates of the hospital, Mama said, "Now, take the bus to Kiyovu. Go talk to your uncle Kamanzi. Go ask for forgiveness. He is like your father. He will understand."

"Do you want to go with me?" I asked.

"No, it's better you go alone."

Mama took a bus to Biryogo, and I jumped in the one to Kiyovu.

My aunt and uncle were still at work when I arrived. In the meantime, I entered the guest room and lay down on the bed.

At 6:00, I heard their voices. I gave them a few minutes to finish their conversation, change their clothes, and return to the living room. At the right moment, I left the room.

"You? What are you doing here?" Uncle Kamanzi asked. "Please get out of my house. Get out."

His words hit the bottom of my sadness basket and made me explode in anger.

"Don't worry," I replied. "I'm getting out, and for good. But before I do, give me a minute to say a word: Forgive me."

"I don't want to listen to your stupidities anymore. You made me lose all my dignity. Yes, you are an adult, as you always reminded me. Get out of here. I'm done with my job as a parent."

"Okay, if you don't want to listen to me, I have no reason to insist. Good-bye." I headed for the door.

"Karabo, come back here," shouted Birungi. She turned to her husband and said, "Please, listen at least to what she has to say."

I returned and resumed my seat on the chair at the coffee table.

"I'm sorry for having asked you to support me for a wedding I was not ready for. All I want is your forgiveness."

"I'll never forgive you," said Uncle Kamanzi. "Why didn't you tell me before you ran away? Where had your mother hidden you?"

"Mama has nothing to do with what happened. Her sin is the same as yours."

"How? Am I the one who advised you to marry a Hutu family before you finally realized it was a bad decision? Or, maybe your mother has found you another Hutu?"

I looked at Uncle with so much anger but interspersed with pity. I could not understand him anymore.

"If I had not chosen a Hutu, who else would I have picked? The Tutsi I loved, you had thrown him out to die of sorrow in this wicked world. He recollected his ordeal began the day the Hutu militants killed his family. And you know who paid the price? Me. He hit me. He vomited on me all his fury against the world and his bitterness against the Hutus."

"Are you talking about Shema? What do I have to do with his failures? Am I a drug seller?"

"Yes. I am talking about Shema, whose family was exterminated by Hutu militants. Shema, who had run to you, longing for love from a Tutsi whom he could trust. What did you do to him? Instead of giving him shelter in your house and in your heart, you sent him back to face the world alone with his grief. Would you have done the same to your son, no matter what sin he could have committed? Wasn't Shema a Tutsi? Did he deserve to be treated like a garbage bag by those he called his?"

"Karabo, stop, shut up," said Birungi. "You never talk to your uncle like that."

"Birungi, let her show her bad manners," said Uncle. "What did you expect from her?"

"Uncle, I don't mean to disrespect you. I just wanted to express the truth I have kept for many years."

"I thought I'd raised you to be a smart girl," said Uncle. "Tell me how, in all of Rwanda, the only Tutsi you could find is that drug addict you call Shema or marry one of the Hutus who killed your father. Is that what you want to tell me?"

"Yes, I searched in Rwanda, and none could marry me. Some are Hutus whom you despise because of what their relatives did to our Tutsi families. Others are Tutsis who don't want to associate with me, a Tutsi but born of a Hutu mother."

He made a derisive smile before saying, "You chose a Hutu, and you asked us to support you. Why didn't you marry him?"

"Sugira is a very noble person. Like me, he also carries the burden of ethnicity. He isn't just a Hutu as you call him. He has both Hutu and Tutsi heritage. And even if he was a Hutu, I have so much respect for his family. They have proven to me that nobility has nothing to do with ethnicity. They were by my side when I needed a chest to lean on and someone to wipe my tears. You rejected Devota, a Tutsi survivor; they bathed her, fed her, and laid her to rest when she waved goodbye to this world. I wish I could pay them back that, but my heart chose Shema, another soul that longed for love."

"Karabo, I don't like how you are talking to me. Why didn't you marry that drug addict you were madly in love with?"

"In the same way, your heart wounds prevented you from feeling Shema's pain, his sorrow also prevented him from noticing tears on my cheeks."

"So, everything was my fault? Is that what you are trying to say?"

"No, Uncle. I mean, even though I loved Shema so much, he was too sad to decipher my own pain. Shema, like you, keeps a very bitter heart and condemns Hutus for the misfortunes he has endured in his life. He loved me but did not accept me for who I am. You, too, love me, that, I never doubt. But your resentment towards Hutus prevented you from realizing the pain I was caused by the Rwanda's tragedy. How many times have you reminded me I have Hutu blood? Do you think it's by scorning Mama that you wipe the tears that have run down my cheeks since Papa and my sisters were killed?"

Instead of responding, Uncle stood up and went out.

"Karabo, why did you say all that?" asked Birungi.

"I had to tell him the truth."

"No, that's not how you should talk to your uncle. You had come to ask for forgiveness, but all you did was condemn him."

"No, I didn't want to blame him. I wanted him to realize that what happened is one of the consequences of what we went through. We have all suffered."

"Yes, you're right. Tell me, please, don't lie to me. Are you pregnant?"

"Yes. It's Shema's."

"How?"

I told her everything that had happened between Shema and me, and how I had tried in vain to forget Shema and get married to Sugira, who shared the same burden of being of mixed ethnicity.

"I was wrong," I said. "I couldn't force love. It's Shema that I am in love with. He loves me too, but we can't get married surrounded by the Tutsis and Hutus of Rwanda."

"I'll talk to Kamanzi," Birungi said. "He loves you so much. He sees you as his own daughter. As you told him, we all have unhealed wounds. Sometimes he feels heartache for everything his family went through, and it blinds him. I, too, can confess to you that you have opened my heart's eyes. I'm sorry for everything you've gone through."

I said good-bye to Birungi and got out of their house.

As usual, Mama was sitting on the couch in the living room. I said hello, hurrying to my room. She reminded me a pregnant woman should never skip a meal. She had prepared fish and spinach soup for me. I returned to sit at the table to drip the soup before eating *Imvange* as the main dish.

"How did it go at Kamanzi's?" she asked.

"Not good," I replied.

"Have you managed to apologize?"

"Yes."

"And? Has he forgiven you?"

"No."

I told her all about my conversation with Uncle Kamanzi and Birungi. She said Birungi was right, and that I should never speak impolitely to my uncle.

"Mama, I don't want to talk about Uncle Kamanzi. He has his problems to resolve."

"We all have problems, and none is perfect. But as I always tell you, Kamanzi deserves your respect. He took the place of your father to raise you when you were alone in this country."

"Indeed, that's the reason why I don't want to talk about him. I thank him for having given me shelter, clothes, and food. But if he had given me his chest to shed my tears on, maybe I wouldn't have fallen into Shema's chest."

"Karabo, don't blame your uncle for all that. We all have our share of responsibility. There is no saint among the residents of this world." She remained silent for a second before adding, "I have spoken to Gatarina on the phone."

"What has she said?" I asked.

"She is still saddened by what happened. She will come here on Saturday."

"No, Mama, I won't be able to face the eyes of Sugira's mother. If there is one person for whom I have a lot of respect, it's Gatarina. She is such a gracious and generous person. She trusted me. She believed in me. I betrayed her love. Will Sugira come with her?"

"No. Sugira is in Europe."

"In Europe? Where exactly? What is he doing in Europe?"

"He's in France, pursuing postgraduate studies. His mother has told me that after the disappointment, Sugira asked to leave the country. He was dispirited."

"I bet he meets Shema in Paris."

"France is a vast country," argued Mama. "They can't meet."

"I hope."

We kissed good night.

The next morning I woke up to my usual breakfast of fruit and milk. I went to work, after almost two months of leave. Everyone at work was watching me, but nobody dared to ask me a single question. I only told the director that the wedding did not take place and that I was pregnant, but I did not give her any other details.

On Saturday, I was in my room when Mama called me to greet Sugira's mother. I was in a long jumper over a long, fluffy skirt. I joined them in the living room. With a shock in her eyes, Gatarina accepted my handshake. I sat on the chair, picking at my nails.

"I...I wanted to apologize," I said, interrupting their conversation about rain and seasons.

"Apologize for what?" Gatarina asked.

That simple question was tough for me to answer. *How can I describe how much I disappointed the family that had offered me love when I needed it the most?*

"For having left the day I was supposed to wed Sugira."

"Is that a sin?" Gatarina asked. "Or maybe the sin is what made you leave. Why did you do that to him?"

Gatarina's eyes were making my heart sick.

"Please forgive me. You were a good mother to me when Mama was away from me. You wiped my tears. I had found the warmth of a family in your home. I will never forgive myself for having betrayed that love."

"If I had been a good mother, my son wouldn't have been abandoned by his fiancée on his wedding day."

"No. Mother, everything was my fault. I betrayed Sugira's love and nobility." I burst into tears before adding, "I don't want to talk about philosophies of love, which have no meaning. I love and respect Sugira. But my love for him couldn't reach the level of madness we needed to live under the same roof and in the same room."

"Karabo, stop talking nonsense," shouted Gatarina. "Why did you lie to Sugira you loved him? Why did you make him fall in love with you? You broke his heart. Sugira was about to commit suicide. What did you do to my son?" Gatarina turned her eyes to Mama. "Musanabera, speak to your daughter."

Mama kept silent.

"Mother, please, forgive me. You were always there when I didn't have anyone else to talk to. Sugira was my best friend, a brother I had never had. He fell in love with me. I longed for love, and I had found it from the best, but my heart didn't pay back to him the same love. I am sorry."

Before she responded, I knelt down in front of her.

She asked me to get up, and said, "You don't need to do that. You should know you disappointed us all. But it's over now. Nothing can be done."

I got up and went back to my room to shed tears on my red pillow. After about an hour, Mama called me to say good-bye to Sugira's mother. The eyes of both had turned red.

Sugira's mother invited me for a hug, and said, "Your mother has told me everything. We aren't happy about what you did. But, as your mothers, we understand you. You should never hide anything from your mothers. If you had told me about everything you were going through, I could have given you some advice."

After Gatarina left, I asked Mama what they had discussed. She said they had talked mother to mother.

Days, weeks, and months passed. I kept sending emails to Shema, but he did not reply to any. At five months of pregnancy, I went back to the gynecologist. He did an ultrasound.

"Do you see that little organ?" asked the doctor.

"Which one?"

"That is the genital organ of your child. It's a boy."

My heart jumped with joy. I imagined a dark-skinned baby with a chocolate gum. I had a name in mind, Davis Shema Kalisa.

From the hospital, I took money out of the nearby ATM and went to town to shop for the baby at Mother's Smile.

At home, I turned on my laptop and wrote another email to Shema: "God gave me another Shema. Your Shema, our

Shema. Thank you for having left me a part of you. The Shema I carry in my belly will always remind me of the one I carry in my heart. His name is Davis Shema Kalisa. If you prefer other names, you will have to organize a naming ceremony on the eighth day. Good-bye. I love you. Karabo."

I turned off the computer. That was my fifth email to Shema.

While I was sorting the clothes I had bought for the baby, my phone rang. The call was from Uncle Kamanzi.

"Karabo, how are you?" he said.

"I'm okay, thank you."

"Tell your mother I am coming to pay you a visit tonight."

Uncle Kamanzi had never paid a visit to Mama since she returned to Rwanda. I ran to the living room to announce Uncle's visit.

"The Virgin Mary has answered my prayers again," Mama said.

"How? Have you been praying for Uncle Kamanzi's visit?"

"Not only that. This is just the beginning. I prayed to God to give me a chance to play my role as a good wife to your father and daughter-in-law for his family. Kalisa isn't happy that my relationship with his family is not the best."

Mama prepared what I knew to be Papa's favorite food, green banana, chicken, green vegetables, and peanut sauce. She decorated the whole house with flowers. I could watch her and laugh. Did she think Uncle Kamanzi would replace Papa? She could never dare to make his bed but considered him her husband.

At 6 p.m., Uncle Kamanzi's car honked. Mama asked me to get the gates. The people of Biryogo were in the street gossiping about the tall, giant soldier with scary stars on his shoulders. I opened the door, eyes down. Uncle Kamanzi invited me for a hug.

"Don't you know you should be the first to greet me?"

"How?"

"You must say *Amashyo*, and I would respond *Amashongore*."

"Hmm? I thought it was the elder who said *Amashyo*."

"Yes, normally, the elder is the first to greet the younger. But when it comes to a man and a woman, it's the woman who always says *Amashyo* to the man, regardless of age differences."

"*Amashyo*," I said.

"*Amashongore*," he replied.

His face was both delighted and distressed as he scrutinized the design and décor of our house.

"Musanabera, what did you do? I can't believe my eyes."

"Thank you. Shall you greet me?" Mama said, inviting Uncle in her arms. "*Amashyo*."

"*Amashongore*," he replied. "The last time I was here, there was no house. It smelled of death. I could only hear the voices of the ghosts of Kalisa and his children begging Hutus not to kill them. But now, it smells of Kalisa's presence."

"Thank you," said Mama. "What would you like to drink?"

"Whatever is available."

"We have everything. Would you like some beer?"

"Yes, please, give me a cool Primus."

Mama brought the beer and served Uncle. She sat on the couch. They talked about the rain and the seasons. After a few minutes, Mama pretended to adjust her African loincloth and put her hands in her hair to put it back in order.

"Karabo told me she came to talk to you a few months ago."

"Yes, she did. I was so upset with her. But, as her parents, we have no other choice. If we can't forgive her, who else shall?" Uncle Kamanzi turned to me and said, "Karabo, my daughter, you must keep in mind that I love you. I heard what you told me last time. How is the baby?"

"The baby? He is fine."

Is my pregnancy visible despite the long jumper? I mused. *How did he know I was pregnant?*

"Birungi told me everything. As your parent, I can only rejoice that I am going to have a grandson. And Shema? Where is he?"

I told Uncle Kamanzi that Shema had left the country and that he might not return to Rwanda.

"Don't worry, you are with your family. You won't lack anything. When the right time comes, you will find another fiancé who deserves the precious lady you are." He turned his eyes to Mama and added, "Your mother is a brave and noble woman. She will give you advice."

I could not believe my ears and my eyes. *What has happened to Uncle Kamanzi? Who the angel has appeared in his dreams to change his heart?* I wondered as I fled to my room to give my mother and my paternal uncle time to talk in privacy. They had a lot to discern.

Their conversation took about an hour, after which Mama called for dinner with Uncle. After dinner, Uncle Kamanzi said good-bye.

"Mama, tell me everything. What have you talked about?"

"We've had a sincere and honest conversation."

"Tell me more."

"Why do you want to know the secrets between a

husband and his wife?" Mama asked with a big smile on her face.

I insisted, and Mama gave me a glimpse of what they had talked about. They had talked about Papa and his marriage with Mama. They had talked about their families, the Hutu family of Mama, and the Tutsi family of Papa. They had talked about the history of Rwanda, the genocide against the Tutsi, and, more importantly, the consequences to our family.

"Kamanzi has apologized to me if that's what you wanted to know," Mama said, giving me another smile. "He has told me how his heart was pained by all that his family went through, the murder of his father in 1963, the misery they lived as refugees in Uganda, and the death of Kalisa and many members of their families, killed by Hutu militants during the 1994 genocide."

"What does that have to do with his apology to you?" I asked.

"His grief prevented him from recognizing that I also suffered from losing my husband and children during the genocide against the Tutsi."

"That's not enough. I am not enchanted."

"Why?" Mama asked.

"Uncle Kamanzi should understand that nobility and greatness have nothing to do with ethnicity. He shouldn't put you in the same hamper with those who killed his family members."

"Yes," responded Mama. "He has said he realized that not all Hutus were bad people and that some Hutus also suffered the consequences of the genocide against the Tutsi. He has added that he sympathizes with me for what I experienced in Rwanda and in the refugee camps in Congo and Malawi."

Nineteen

The kicks of the baby growing inside my belly confirmed he was as active as his father.

On May 20, 2010, I felt tired, dizzy, and nauseous. My breathing became difficult, and my vision was blurred. With my hands on my stomach, I sat on the bed. I tried to shout for Mama, but my voice failed. I got up to find her in the living room, and when I opened the door, I fell. Mama called the ambulance from the Kigali General Hospital. In a few minutes, they were there. They took me to the hospital. In the ambulance, paramedics put something on my nose to give me more oxygen. They asked Mama if I had ever complained about unstable blood pressure. Mama said no. I was afraid of what was happening to me.

At the hospital, they took me to the intensive care unit.

"We'll do some tests," the doctor said to Mama.

"Doctor, tell me. What does she have? Please tell me."

"We don't know yet. But it's critical. The symptoms are very alarming."

They took blood samples, performed an ultrasound, and took me to the room near the theater room.

After a moment, the doctor called Mama, and said, "She

is suffering from a serious and deadly condition. Where is her husband?"

"Please, Doctor, tell me," Mama said. "What is she suffering from? I am her mother."

"She has an amniotic embolism. The liquid has entered the blood vessels. It can cause cardiac arrest and rapid respiratory failure. We should save the child or the mother. The chances of saving the lives of both are minimal."

Before Mama could say anything, I opened my mouth to speak, but my voice could not come out. I waved to the doctor, asking him to approach me. I said in a low voice, "Save the child."

He could not read my lips.

I grabbed the paper he had in his hands and wrote: "*Save my baby. Write to his father, Shema. His email: shema@ lovemates.fic.*"

The doctor took the paper and went to check if everything was ready in the operations room. I closed my eyes to pray to my Lord. Mama had already put a rosary on my neck. I touched the cross and asked the Virgin Mary to save my child.

➤

After a few minutes, something happened. I entered a dark tunnel. At the end of it, there was graceful daylight with blue and white colors. I saw Papa, Dudu, Fifi, Devota, Grandma, and so many of my family members who had died. *Maybe the doctor has done as I asked,* I thought. At the end of the tunnel, Dudu and Fifi gave me smiles. But Papa, Devota, and Grandma were not thrilled. They refused to greet me.

"What are you doing here?," Papa shouted. "Go back to the world of the living."

"No, Papa, I want to be with you," I replied.

"You can't stay here. So many people need you there."

"Papa, I finished my job. Mama is back in Rwanda. She reconciled with Uncle Kamanzi."

"Karabo, you have more work to do and more years to complete it. Follow me. I will show you."

He held my hands and took me to the top of a mountain, where the view was decorated with many hills.

"Look at this lady who is making fire with wooden sticks."

"Yes, I can see her," I replied.

"You have to wipe her tears. She is one of those you call Tutsis. Hutus killed all members of her family. But the food she is preparing is not for calming their spirits. It's for her husband, who is in prison. It was he who killed the poor lady's father with a machete."

"Why does she have to take food to the killer of her family, even if it's her husband?"

"She doesn't do it for him, but for her six children, who love the man they call Father. Let me show you other people."

He zoomed another hill before saying, "Do you see that young lady in a black skirt? Can you read the sadness of her face?"

"Yes. What happened to her?"

"She has never met her father all her life. She first heard about him when the man who was betrothed to her dumped her one day before the wedding."

"Why?" I asked.

"He canceled the wedding after learning that the father

of the girl he was about to marry was a genocide perpetrator. Her mother and father never lived together as husband and wife. The father never accepted her as his daughter. The mother of that young lady, her grandmother, and all members of her maternal family were killed by Hutu militants during the genocide against the Tutsi. She shares the shame of a father who has never recognized her as his daughter, while her heart is saddened by the assassination of her mother."

Papa zoomed another hill that was not far from Muhazi Lake.

"Look at that lady who is cultivating. The sadness is about to send her to death. She is one of those you call Hutus. Many members of her family participated in the genocide against the Tutsi. Those who aren't in prison have left the country. But that's not what breaks her heart the most."

"Maybe she's remorseful for what her family did," I said.

"She had married a Tutsi. Her husband and two sons were killed by her own father. The genocide against the Tutsi made her a widow. But her troubles are more than that. Three of her children survived the genocide, one son and two daughters. They hate their mother. They never talk to her. They live in Kigali and tell all those who don't know them well that their parents were killed during the genocide against the Tutsi. Whenever they come to Kayonza, their primary purpose is to insult their mother by blaming her for the actions of her Hutu family."

"Oh, that's very sad. It must be a great risk to marry someone who is not part of one's ethnic group."

"No. That's not true. Many others suffer, but not because they married outside their ethnic group."

He zoomed another hill, showed me Mount Huye, and

said, "Do you see that old lady with a bottle in her hands? That bottle is full of water; she calls holy water. She has no family members in this world. Her entire family, her husband, and all her seven children were killed during the genocide against the Tutsi. But what is sad is that those who should save her soul make her life more miserable. Some say she is crazy. Others say she is possessed. Even those who say that she does all that to attract sympathy and beg for free food. She thinks that everyone in the world is mean and wicked, which is why she spreads what she considers holy water." Papa placed his hand on my shoulder and said, "Karabo, that woman needs love."

"Oh my God, there are so many broken and wounded hearts in this country."

"Yes. You must go to help them. They need love and hugs."

He pointed to another hill, enlarged it, and said, "Look at that man in a wheelchair. He was wounded during the 1990-1994 war. He lost his manhood. The government has sent him to all the good hospitals in the world, but his condition is incurable. He lives in pain day and night and has no one to wipe his tears because all the members of his family were killed during the genocide against the Tutsi."

"Papa, what about Hutus, who did not marry Tutsis? Have they also gone through the ordeal?" I asked.

"Look at that old lady who is making fire. Her sons and her husband participated in the genocide against the Tutsi. During the genocide, whenever her husband returned from the killings, she warned him what he was doing was wrong, and the husband hit her, sometimes with a machete or a wooden stick. She suffers from injuries caused by her husband. Three of her sons are in jail, and others have fled the country. Many people don't know what her thoughts and feelings are. It's sad. I can hear what she says to herself, but I can't help. She still condemns what her family did, but no one believes her. Many people call her an old genocide perpetrator."

"I understand," I said. "But at least the Hutus are not dead. You can't compare her sadness to that of those whose families were exterminated during the genocide."

"Karabo, my daughter, the tragedy of Rwanda reached many Hutu families before, during, and after the genocide against the Tutsi. Think of Mugabo, your cousin, whose mother and sister were killed in Congo. What about those who died in Kibeho or in other parts of Rwanda?"

He pointed to a city, and when he zoomed in, I recognized the Kacyiru neighborhood.

"Look at that lady," he said. "She identifies herself as Hutu. Her husband was killed during the genocide against the Tutsi. He was neither Tutsi nor one of those Hutu politicians commemorated every April 13."

"Why was he killed?" I asked. "Maybe his face looked like those they identified as Tutsi."

"No, he did not look like the way Tutsis were described. He supported the struggle of Patriotic rebels. He said the Patriot rebels were not enemies of Rwanda, but Rwandans who wanted to come back home. He was very active in collecting our contributions to support the struggle. He was a good friend of mine. We sent him where we couldn't go because we believed he wouldn't be suspected. But it didn't last long before Hutu extremists suspected him. Even before April 1994, he was already on the list of those who were targeted. He was among the first victims of the genocide against the Tutsi. Hutu militants attacked his house on April 8, 1994. They shot at the whole family, but by God's goodness, his wife and their last two children survived. He was killed with his two daughters. What is sad today is that his children cry every time some Rwandans insult them, call them names such as *abaginga* or *Interahamwe*, and put them in the same basket with the genocide perpetrators who killed their father and sisters. They don't feel recognized among survivors of the genocide against the Tutsi."

"Oh, Papa, that's very sad."

"Karabo, I could show you many more people. But you must go back to Rwanda and save all those hearts. Just let me show you the last two."

He zoomed in on another part of the city, which looked like Kicukiro, then said, "Look at that old lady. She was a refugee in Uganda since 1963. All three of her sons lost their lives in the battlefield. Her situation is the same as that of the other lady. She returned from Burundi, where she had been a refugee since 1959. Likewise, the one who returned from Uganda, her two sons didn't survive the 1990–1994 war. Her eldest daughter died of AIDS in Rwanda in 1998. She believes that more attention was paid to survivors of genocide than to families who lost theirs during the four-year war. These families sometimes feel forgotten."

"Papa, I don't want to go back to Rwanda. I cannot live in that torn society where everyone cries day and night."

"Karabo, you have to go. I wish I could return, but the cord that connects me to life is already broken. You keep yours. You haven't yet crossed to the zone of death. Let me tell you one more thing before you leave. Take good care of your mother and heal all the wounds of her heart."

"Papa, wait, listen, I have a lot of questions... Papa..."

Something pushed me, and I lost sight of Papa, Fifi,

Dudu, Devota, Grandma, and others. I went back into total darkness. It did not look like a tunnel. It was merely a dark state where I could neither see nor hear anything. I had lost the sense of time and space until the noise caressed my eardrums. I opened my eyes. There were many silhouettes of people in white aprons.

"It's a miracle. Her mother's prayers brought her back."

"Karabo," shouted Mama. "Oh, the Virgin Mary of grace and mercy, thank you for having pleaded to Jesus to bring back my daughter in the same way he raised Lazarus."

"You should get out," said the doctor to the other people in the room. "When a person comes out of a coma, she feels exhausted. She needs to rest."

They went out as my eyes tried to close.

After a few hours, a nightmare or dream woke me up.

"My baby," I shouted. "Where is my baby? Who told you to let my child die? Let me die. Where is my baby?"

"Karabo, my love, our son is here. I'm sorry to have changed his name. His name is Rukundo Shema wa Karabo."

"Hmm? Shema… Am I dreaming?"

He put his hands on my cheeks and said, "My love, please forgive me. I beg you." He knelt in front of the bed and added, "Please, Karabo, give me the chance to raise this angel that God has sent to wipe away all our tears. I will climb mountains with you. I will walk valleys with you, and when we shall reach the crossroads, we will stop to welcome everybody with love, regardless of their names or the groups with which they identify. If you accept to be my wife, I will be your husband. God will bless us with sons and daughters who will make Rwanda, not just a land of honey and milk, but of love and life as well. Will you marry me?"

I pulled my hand from the bedsheets and gave Shema

my finger. He put on me a glittering gold ring he had brought from Paris. The voices in the room sang congratulations.

"Congratulations. May the Lord bless this couple."

"Sugira, you?"

"Karabo, my best friend. Never apologize for love. You know I love you, and I will always love you." Sugira turned his eyes to Shema and said, "Don't give me that look. I love her as my sister, my best friend. Congratulations to you both."

Sugira and Shema told me how they had met in France. Sugira had saved Shema when he was going to be assaulted in a cabaret owned by a Rwandan in Paris. At first, Sugira was surprised to see Shema in France when he thought he had flown with me. On the other hand, Shema wondered what Sugira was doing there. It was Sugira who informed Shema that there had been no wedding. Shema had read my emails a few days before he returned to Rwanda.

"I have the best man, Sugira. Are your bridal maids ready?"

"No, I won't be my rival's best man," Sugira said.

They exchanged laughter. I gazed at my two men, while my heart danced with love for them. On the other side of the room were Kamana and Gatarina—Sugira's parents—Mama, Uncle Kamanzi, and all the other people in my life, Mugabo, my cousin, Muhire, Devota's brother, and Karega, Muhire's friend.

→

Two months later, St. Michael's Cathedral celebrated my wedding with Shema, the only guy who knew how to excite my body. Beside him, there was Sugira, his best man, the friend who had lent me his ears when I needed it the most. Uncle Kamanzi led me down the aisle and handed me to the tall, handsome guy with a smile adorned with white teeth and a chocolate gum. He went to sit on a chair between Mama and his wife, Birungi.

In the night, Shema and I made love as if it were our first time. My body, my heart, and my brain, everything was his.

In the morning, I woke up to write the last chapter of this book. Shema brought me breakfast in the bedroom and had a glance at what I was writing. I told him about what I had seen during my near-death experience, and all the stories Papa had told me about. He listened, making copious tss sounds before saying, "Yesterday, they hid something from us. It's not over. We must pray that the fresh scars of Rwandans do not bleed again."

"Hmm? Shema, what are you saying? What did they hide from us?"

"Grenade attacks again. Two people have died in the city center."

"Again? Shema. I must tell you something. My uncles may be among those behind the attacks. They are now in the opposition. This time around, I am talking about both my Tutsi paternal uncle Rutayisire and my Hutu maternal uncle Gasana."

"I didn't know they are now members of the opposition groups. But, my dear, stop drawing conclusions. Nobody knows who is behind the grenade attacks. It might be some political games that you and I may not understand."

"How?" I asked.

"Karabo, in Europe, I met many Rwandans, Hutus, and Tutsis. Many people have been hurt by the Rwandan tragedy. I was wrong to think wickedness runs only in the veins of Hutus. Ethnicity has nothing to do with either nobleness or wickedness. If ten years ago, I had known what I know now, we would be parents to four children already."

"Hey, good that you changed. But who is throwing the grenades?"

"I don't know. In the same way, I don't know who killed Fred Rwigema, the Tutsi hero who kicked off the 1990 struggle. Neither do I know who shot down the plane of the former Hutu President Habyarimana in 1994. There are many things that we may never understand."

"Shema, you can't say that. Don't tell me you will now talk like those dissidents who accuse—"

"I haven't said anything. I don't know. Please have your breakfast and pray for Rwanda. Don't worry, if they throw the grenades in the air, I will swim with you in the lake's waters. If they throw them to the ground, I will fly with you in the air."

Author's letter to the Reader

Dear Reader,

Thanks for reading *Hearts Among Ourselves*.

Before I pressed the button to release the manuscript to the publisher, my heart crumbled, and my legs trembled. I wondered how my dear compatriots who suffer from the "them and us" syndrome would react to my debut novel.

I was scared that *Hearts Among Ourselves* could be accused of having not drawn some important details of the history of Rwanda before, during, and after the genocide against the Tutsi.

I was terrified that *Hearts Among Ourselves* could be accused of having ignored the stories of some Rwandans and what they endured before, during, and after the genocide against the Tutsi.

I was scared that *Hearts Among Ourselves* could be accused of having inked on the same pages the stories of those who stood on the right side of the tragedy and those who stood on the left side of the tragedy.

I was terrified that *Hearts Among Ourselves* could be accused of having not given credit to those who deserved it and having not blamed those who deserved to be condemned.

I was scared that *Hearts Among Ourselves* could be accused of having blamed those who deserved to be praised and wiped the tears of those who deserved to be cursed.

None of the above constituted the objectives of *Hearts Among Ourselves*.

When I began to write this debut novel, I aimed at a book that:

Focuses on the period after the genocide against the Tutsi with the objective to paint the fate of the survivors, the shame of the perpetrators, and, more importantly, the confusion of those who swung between the two.

Gives the characters, and the souls they represent, the freedom of thought, speech, and action, which was not culturally and politically common in Rwanda before and after the genocide.

Tells a story that demonstrates that nobleness and greatness have nothing to do with the so-called ethnicity.

Reflects the realities of the society we live in, where there are no 100 percent heroes or 100 percent villains. The world in which ordinary people live, tell lies, hate, love, and are sometimes confused by the intersection of love and hatred.

Binds the rather torn society with love, self-love, romantic love, motherly love, fatherly love, and love for the other.

However, as I followed the stories of the characters of *Hearts Among Ourselves*, it drew me back to the most important lesson that should be underlined from what happened in Rwanda:

Many of us have experienced the sorrow of losing loved ones to death. Some of us have gone through the terrible moments when our loved ones were murdered, and nothing and nobody can ever justify the killing of another human being. However, only a few of us know what it feels like when our loved ones are killed by those we considered to be our people, those we shared water and food with, those we called our neighbors, friends and/or family members.

Rwanda has experienced many types of crises and tragedies before, during, and after 1994. Still, none of those tragedies will ever be comparable to the genocide against the Tutsi, when babies, children, young and old women, and men were killed just because they were identified by society as Tutsis. One big difference between the genocide against the Tutsi and other tragedies Rwanda has known is that most killers, although supported and sponsored by the politicians and the soldiers, were ordinary individuals, known by names and faces in their communities, who hunted other ordinary community members to be tortured and slaughtered. Neighbors killed neighbors, spouses killed spouses, sons killed mothers, and uncles killed nephews. After the genocide, the same people had to live again together in the same communities and/or as members of the same families.

Hearts Among Ourselves reveals to readers that although the killings targeted Tutsis of all ages and both genders, it would be very wrong to put all Hutus in the same basket and call them all "perpetrators of the genocide." Another phenomenon that the world may never comprehend in time and space is how few Tutsis, including the leader of the *Interahamwe* (the lead militia group, mostly of Hutus), participated in the genocide against the Tutsi, and how some Hutus, labeled as moderate, were also killed during the genocide against the Tutsi. However, this should never give a platform to those—because of the "them and us" syndrome they suffer from—who fail to acknowledge that the main target group was Tutsis, including those who were still in the wombs of their mothers.

Hearts Among Ourselves reveals to readers that many hearts of Rwandans are wounded and that those they consider to be theirs continue to make their sores bleed once again and more.

Some Rwandans are blamed for having failed to forgive and forget as if it is that easy. They are accused of hatred against those they consider to have caused their wounds.

Some Rwandans have failed to pick up the pieces of their crushed lives, and their wounds are made fresh by those who point fingers to their miserable lives and blame them for having surrendered to depression, drug addiction, irresponsible sexual behaviors, alcoholism, or exaggerated spiritualism.

Some Rwandans are blamed for letting tears flow on their cheeks, despite the fact that they are considered to share the name of the perpetrators, even when they do not necessarily share their shame.

Some Rwandans are wounded by the fact that those they share Rwanda with are not ready to give them a platform to tell their stories and cry their sorrows, because, however overwhelming, those stories would put to light other dark sides of the Rwanda history and the realities that some people may love to sweep under the carpet in order to keep the momentum and move forward without necessarily knowing whether, where, and how the journey shall end.

Some Rwandans are scared by what the future holds in stock for their country. They want to shout and call all sons and daughters of Rwanda to gather on a mountaintop, sit on gacaca grass, and ask the prophets and philosophers of Rwanda if the cure of evil has been discovered and whether all Rwandans have taken their doses.

I recognize that *Hearts Among Ourselves* could neither tell the stories of all Rwandans, nor solve all the problems of its characters.

But, I am sure, as we take time to write more stories, we shall give more Rwandans the platform, maybe not to explore the debate about why it happened and who did it, but to express how it wounded their hearts and tore their dear Rwanda society.

From there, many Rwandans shall vow to listen to others, wipe their tears, and invite all sons and daughters of Rwanda to restore and rebuild their society. I am not only talking about buildings and roads, but more importantly, the foundations of who we are as organs of the entire humanity.

Once again, thank you.

A. Happy Umwagarwa

About the Author

A. Happy Umwagarwa is an author, novelist, storyteller, and poet from Rwanda.

In 1994, she survived the genocide against the Tutsi, which took the lives of her father and other members of her family. That experience left her with many puzzles on why people think, feel, and act the way they do.

Guided by the quote from Toni Morrison, "If there is a book that you want to read, but it hasn't been written yet, you must be the one to write it," Happy states that she writes for herself, her daughters, her compatriots, and the entire humanity. She hopes her books, stories, and poems shall promote a culture of peace and respect for diversity in her country and beyond.

Despite the thorns of life she had to step on, Happy graduated from the University of Greenwich, London, with a master's degree in management, and in addition to her writing endeavors, she works for an international organization as a Human Resources Professional.

Happy is married and a mother to two wonderful daughters she calls her little angels. In addition to writing, her passionate interests include singing and poetry performance as well.